Raves for the* Rivers of London *novels:

"This fast, engrossing novel is enjoyable, cheerful, and accessible to new readers." —*Publishers Weekly*

"Ben Aaronovitch has written a book that never left me disappointed in the choices he made as author, nor in the choices of his characters." —Fantasy Book Review

"Told in a narrative voice that seasons laconic humor with a dash of cynicism, the novel is fascinated with the geography and history of London. It is a rich formula with a bittersweet ending ..." —*The Daily Telegraph*

"The most entertaining book that I have read in such a long time.... It's very funny, it's very clever, it's very nicely written.... It's such a treat." —Nancy Pearl

"Aaronovitch makes the story sing, building momentum until the ending is literally breathless." —SF Revu

"The prose is witty, the plot clever, and the characters incredibly likeable." —*Time Out*

"This book is, at its heart, a police procedural with an overlay of urban fantasy elements. The voice is persuasive and funny as all get-out, and the reader is engaged with the narrative from the very first page. Aaronovitch has written a diverse cast of characters who all feel like real people with their own specific motivations. This book is simply wonderful." —*Romantic Times* (top pick)

BEN AARONOVITCH

BROKEN HOMES

A RIVERS OF LONDON NOVEL

DAW BOOKS, INC.

DONALD A. WOLLHEIM, FOUNDER

375 Hudson Street, New York, NY 10014

ELIZABETH R. WOLLHEIM
SHEILA E. GILBERT
PUBLISHERS

www.dawbooks.com

First Printing, February 2014

4   5   6   7   8   9

DAW TRADEMARK REGISTERED
U.S. PAT. AND TM. OFF. AND FOREIGN COUNTRIES
—MARCA REGISTRADA
HECHO EN U.S.A.

PRINTED IN THE U.S.A.

This book is dedicated to all the people who get up and do something about it, whatever "it" is and however small the thing it is they do.

The problem of the house is a problem of the epoch. The equilibrium of society today depends upon it. Architecture has for its first duty, in this period of renewal, that of bringing about a revision of values, a revision of the constituent elements of the house. We must create the mass production spirit.

—*Charles-Édouard Jeanneret (Le Corbusier)*

1

Perfectly Human Monsters

AT TWENTY-THREE MINUTES past eleven Robert Weil drove his 53 registered Volvo V70 across the bridge that links Pease Pottage, the improbably named English village, with Pease Pottage, the motorway service station. We know the exact time because the Highway Agency cameras picked him up at this point. Despite the rain and the poor visibility, image enhancement of key frames clearly show that Robert Weil was alone in the front of the car.

Driving with what looks like, in hindsight, suspiciously deliberate care Robert Weil turned left at the roundabout to join the loop of road that curves around the service station and heads for Crawley proper across the second bridge above the M23. There's a tricky intersection there where traffic coming off the motorway slip road crosses traffic coming across the bridge — it's controlled by traffic lights to prevent accidents. We don't know why Robert Weil ran those lights. Some believe that it was a cry for help, an unconscious desire to be caught. Others say that he was in a hurry to get home and took a calculated risk — which wouldn't explain the sedate thirty miles per hour he was going when he went through them. I think that he was concentrating so hard on keeping his speed legal and avoiding attention that he didn't even notice the lights—he had a lot on his mind.

We don't know what Allen Frust was thinking as he came up the motorway slip road, at right angles to Robert Weil, at an estimated fifty-three miles an hour in his five-year-old Vauxhall Corsa. The light was in his favor and so he continued bearing left and was halfway across the intersection when he hit Robert Weil's Volvo in the side just ahead of the front passenger door. Sussex Police's Forensic Collision Investigation Team determined later that neither vehicle slowed or took evasive action prior to the crash, leading them to conclude that in the dark and rainy conditions neither driver was consciously aware of the other.

The impact drove the Volvo onto the grassy verge and into the crash barrier where it stopped almost immediately. The Vauxhall, traveling at nearly twice the speed, spun several times in the wet conditions before rolling over and tumbling to crash into the line of trees further along. It was determined that while Allen Frust's life was saved in the first instance by his seatbelt and airbag, the belt unfortunately failed as the car tumbled and he was thrown against the roof, breaking his neck.

The first police officer in attendance was PC Maureen Slatt based at the nearby Northgate Police Station in Crawley. She'd been on a solo patrol less than a kilometer to the north and, despite the worsening weather conditions, arrived on the scene in less than two minutes.

Nothing kills and injures more police than attending a traffic accident on a fast road, so the first thing she did was park her Incident Response Vehicle in the "fend-off position" at the intersection with its lightbar, headlamps and hazard lights all switched on. Then, with that meager protection from insane nighttime drivers in place, she ventured first to the Volvo to find Robert Weil groggy but responsive and then to the Vauxhall to find Allen Frust limp and seriously dead. After a quick sweep of her torch to ensure no passengers had been thrown clear into the bushes along the verge, she went back to Robert Weil to see if she could help. It was at this point that PC Slatt, and I bet she got stick for that name, proved that she was a proper copper and not just a uniform hanger with good driving skills.

The Volvo V70 is a large estate car and upon impact its rear door had sprung open. Traffic cop lore is full of gruesome tales of unsecured family pets, grannies and even children being flung around the back of cars, so PC Slatt figured she should check.

She immediately recognized the smears of blood on the side panels, fresh enough to still glisten in the light of her torch. It wasn't much blood but it was enough to make her concerned—she searched thoroughly, but there was nobody in the back of the car or in a surrounding ten-meter area.

By the time she'd finished searching, the traffic cops had rolled up in their BMW 520 estates stuffed full of barriers, warning lights and enough reflective signs to set up a second runway at Gatwick. They quickly isolated the lane and got the traffic safely moving again. An ambulance arrived soon after and, as the paramedics fussed over Robert Weil, PC Slatt raided his glove box for his registration papers. Before the ambulance could leave, Slatt climbed in the back and asked Robert Weil whether anyone else had been in the car with him.

"He was absolutely terrified," she told detectives later. "Not only was he petrified by the question, but he was even more scared by the fact that I was police."

It's a police mantra that all members of the public are

guilty of something, but some members of the public are more guilty than others. When the ambulance left for the slog up the M23 to the casualty unit at Redhill, PC Slatt was following close behind. While she drove she was on her radio recommending to the duty inspector at Force Command and Control that CID have a look. Nothing ever gets done quickly at two o'clock in the morning, so it was dawn by the time the DC from the nearby Crawley nick deemed it worth calling in his DI. They stamped their feet, cursed the early morning commuters who honked and grumbled at the delay and decided that it was worth making this somebody else's problem. It went to the joint Sussex and Surrey Police Major Crime Team because that's what they were there for.

It takes more than a bit of a mystery to prize a senior DCI out of his nice warm bed so when Douglas Manderly, designated Senior Investigating Officer, arrived at his office he already had a couple of luckless DCs out at the scene, a DC heading for the West Surrey Hospital to relieve PC Slatt and his office manager had powered up the HOLMES suite and assigned the operation a name—"Sallic."

Little did Douglas Manderly suspect that as soon as Robert Weil's name was entered into HOLMES it would trigger a flash I'd inveigled out of a civilian tech in technical support, which sent an e-mail to my computer. My computer then texted my phone which went "ping" just as me and Toby were out for a walk in Russell Square.

I say a walk, but actually the pair of us had sloped off through the thin winter drizzle to the café in the park where I had coffee and Toby had cake. I checked the details as best I could on my phone, but it's not secure enough for the sensitive stuff so we squelched back to the Folly. To save time we went round the back door, through the rear courtyard and up the exterior spiral stairs to the loft conversion above the garage. There I keep the computers, the plasma TV, the sound system and all the other accoutrements of twenty-first-century life that, for one reason or another, I daren't keep inside the Folly proper.

I'd got my cousin Obe in after Christmas to fix a master power switch by the door. It cuts off the mains to everything electrical in the loft except the lights — very ecologically friendly, but that's not why I installed it. The truth is that when you do magic any microprocessor in the immediate vicinity gets slagged and, since these days just about everything with an on-switch has a microprocessor, that can get expensive really quick. Now, a bit of experimentation on my part revealed that the aforesaid microchips have to be powered up to fail — hence the off switch. I made sure Obe chose an old-fashioned toggle switch that was stiff enough to deter any casual use. When I reached out to flip it that morning I found it was already on. Now, I knew it wasn't me because just over a year of having my shit blown up by magic has made me very particular about these things. And it wasn't Lesley because she was currently in hospital having yet another operation on her face. I knew Nightingale occasionally sneaks up for illicit rugby, so it might have been him.

As soon as I was inside, with Toby shaking his wet fur and getting under foot, I fired up my Dell that is tasked as our AWARE terminal, fielded an e-mail reminder that I was due to take my Officer Safety refresher in two weeks and rechecked the alert which referred me to Operation Sallic on HOLMES — which wouldn't give me access. I considered logging in using Nightingale's warrant card, which seems to have access to everything, but the powers that be had been getting twitchy over unauthorized access to databases recently. So I asked myself what would Lesley say in this circumstance, which was, *Call the incident room, duh!*

So I did and after ten minutes on the phone talking to the MCT office manager I rushed off to tell Nightingale all about it—but I made a point of switching off the master switch as I went out.

An hour later we were heading south in the Jag.

Nightingale let me drive, which was good, though he still won't let me solo in the Jag until I've done the Met's advanced driving course. I've got my name down but the trouble is that just about every officer in the Met wants to take that course and priority goes to the boy- and girl-racers who drive the response cars for the borough commands. I had a tentative spot open in June. Until then I had to be content with being supervised as I opened up the inline-six engine and did a restrained seventy-six mph down the M23. She did it without any appreciable effort, which is not bad for a car that's almost as old as my mother.

"He was on the list that Tyburn gave us," I told Nightingale once we'd mercifully escaped the terrifying traffic singularity that is Croydon.

"Why haven't we spoken to him before now?" asked Nightingale.

We'd been tracking former members of an Oxford University dining club called the Little Crocodiles ever since we'd discovered that a former wizard named Geoffrey Wheatcroft had, against custom and practice, been teaching them magic. He'd been doing this since the early fifties so, as you can imagine, there were a lot of names to cover. Tyburn—that's Lady Ty to you, peasant—genius loci of one of the lost tributaries of the Thames and Oxford graduate herself had spotted some members of this clique during her time there. She claimed, and I believed her, to be able to literally smell a magical practitioner. So we gave her list priority.

And our Volvo driver was on it.

"Robert Weil," I said. "With a W. We were working through the list alphabetically."

"Just goes to show that there's such a thing as being too methodical," said Nightingale. "I presume you have been pillaging the computer records—what have you found out?"

Actually the office manager I'd talked to had e-mailed me the results of their inquiries, but I wasn't going to tell Nightingale that.

"He's forty-two years old, born in Tunbridge Wells, dad was a barrister, mum stayed at home. Educated privately at Beachwood Sacred Heart—" I said.

"Day boy or boarder?" asked Nightingale.

I've picked up a smattering of posh since working with Nightingale, so at least I understood the question.

"The school's in Tunbridge Wells, so I'd guess a day boy," I said. "Unless his parents were really keen to have him out of the house."

"And thence presumably to Oxford," said Nightingale.

"Where he studied biology—" I started.

"Read," said Nightingale. "You read subjects at university."

"Where he read biology, graduating with a second," I said. "So not the brightest banana in the bunch."

"Biology," said Nightingale. "Are you thinking what I'm thinking?"

I was thinking of the Faceless Man's chimeras, the manufactured cat-girls and tiger-boys that had issued from what we'd taken to calling The Strip Club of Doctor Moreau. That and the Pale Lady who'd done away with people by biting their dicks off with her vagina dentata.

And the other things in the club that Nightingale had deemed too horrible for me to see.

"I really hope not," I said, but I knew I really *was* thinking what he was thinking.

"And after he graduated?" asked Nightingale.

He'd gone to work for ICI for ten years before moving into the burgeoning field of environmental impact assessments. Worked for the British Airport Authority as an environmental control officer until he was sold, along with the rest of Gatwick Airport, in 2009.

"Made redundant last year," I said. "He was management so he got a good package and he's currently listed as being a consultant."

The Incident Room had been established at Sussex House on the outskirts of Brighton in what looked like a 1930s light-engineering plant converted into offices. At some point in the last thirty years the site had sprouted warehousing, a Matalan and an ASDA the size of a nuclear-powered aircraft carrier. It was the sort of out-of-town development that causes sober environmentally minded men and women to foam at the mouth with outrage and bite the rim of their Prius's steering wheel but I couldn't help thinking from a copper's point of view it would be bloody convenient for shopping after work. In fact, given that the Brighton Detention Centre was stuck just behind it, it was convenient for the suspects as well. And there was a Big-Box Self-Storage next door which would be handy if the cells ever got overcrowded.

DCI Douglas Manderly was a copper in the modern mold, understated tailored pinstripe suit, brown hair cut short, blue eyes, an up-to-date mobile in his pocket. Sober, works late, drinks lager in halves and knows how to change a nappy. He'd be looking to make Detective Superintendent soon-ish but only for the extra pay and pension. Good at his job, I guessed, but probably not at ease with things that fall outside his comfort zone.

He was going to love us.

He met us in his office to establish his authority but stood and shook our hands in turn to evoke the correct collegial atmosphere. We sat in the offered seats and accepted the offered coffee and did about a minute and a half of the niceties before he asked us straight out what our interest was.

We did not tell him we were witch hunting, as that sort of things tends to cause alarm.

"Robert Weil is possibly connected with another inquiry," said Nightingale. "A series of murders that took place over the summer."

"Would this be the Jason Dunlop case?" he asked.

Better than just good at his job, I thought.

"Yes," said Nightingale. "But not directly related."

Manderly looked disappointed. People have got the wrong idea about police territoriality—a full-scale murder inquiry is going to set you back a quarter of a million quid minimum. If Manderly could dump it on the Met then it would be our budget and our problem, not to mention it would improve his crime counting at the end of the year. He certainly didn't want to assign one of his precious DCs to escort us around, but he wasn't particularly pleased when Nightingale asked for PC Maureen Slatt.

"That's a matter for her line manager," said Manderly.

Then he asked whether, given our interest, he should be looking for anything in particular.

"You could inform us if you discover anything out of the ordinary," said Nightingale.

"Does that include a body?" he asked.

Technically, you don't have to have a corpse to convict for murder but detectives always feel better when they've found your actual victim—they're superstitious like that. Plus nobody wants to think they might be blowing a quarter of a million only to have the victim turn out to be living in Aberdeen with an insurance salesman called Dougal.

"Are we sure there was a body in the Volvo?" I asked.

"We're still waiting on DNA but the lab has confirmed that the blood is human," said Manderly. "And that it came from a body in the early stages of rigor mortis."

"So not a kidnapping then," said Nightingale.

"No," said Manderly.

"Where is Mr. Weil now?" asked Nightingale.

Manderly narrowed his eyes. "He's on his way here," he said. "But unless you have something substantial to add to his interview I'd rather you left it to us."

Now that it was clear that we weren't going to relieve him of this troublesome case he wasn't going to let us near the prime suspect until he had that case tied up in a neat bow.

"I'd like to talk to Constable Slatt first," said Nightingale. "I assume that Weil's home has been searched already?"

"We have a team there," said Manderly. "Is there anything specific you're looking for?"

"Books," said Nightingale. "And possibly other paraphernalia."

"Paraphernalia," said Manderly.

"I shall know it when I see it," said Nightingale.

The principal difference between town and country policing, as far as I could tell, was one of distance. It was thirty kilometers back up the A23 to Crawley where Robert Weil lived, which was further than I drove in a working week in London. Mind you, without London to get in the way we made it in less than half an hour. On the way we passed the spot where the accident had taken place. I asked Nightingale if he wanted to stop, but since Weil's Volvo had already been towed we pressed on to Crawley.

In the 1950s and '60s the powers that be made a concerted effort to rid London of its working class. The city was rapidly losing its industry and the large numbers of servants who were needed for the Edwardian household were being superseded by the technological wonders of the age of white goods. London just didn't need that many poor people any more. Crawley, which up until then had been a small medieval market town, had sixty thousand residents dumped on it. I say dumped but in fact they went into thousands of sturdy three-bedroom semis which my mum and dad would have loved to have lived in, if only they could have brought London's jazz scene with them, and Peckham market, and the Sierra Leonean expatriate population, or at least the half my mum was currently still talking to.

Crawley had managed to avoid the blight of out-of-town shopping centers by the simple expedient of dumping one in the middle of the town. Beyond this were the council offices, the college and the police station, all clustered together as neatly as something from a game of SimCity.

We found PC Slatt in the canteen, which was as reassuringly unimaginative as its London counterparts. She was a short, red-headed woman who filled out her stab vest like a three-bedroom semi and had clever gray eyes. She said she'd already been briefed by her inspector. I don't know what she'd been told, but she stared at Nightingale as if she expected him to grow an extra head.

Nightingale dispatched me to the counter, and when I got back with the tea and biscuits PC Slatt was describing her actions at the crash site. Spend any time around traffic accidents and you have no trouble recognizing blood when you see it.

"It glistens when you shine the torch on it, don't it?" she said. "I thought there might have been another casualty in the car."

It's quite common for people who've been involved in car crashes to escape from their vehicles and wander away in a random direction even with severe injuries. "Only I couldn't find a blood trail and the driver denied there was anyone else in the vehicle."

"When you first looked in the back of the vehicle did you notice anything odd?" asked Nightingale.

"Odd?" she asked.

"Did you feel anything unusual when you looked inside?" asked Nightingale.

"Unusual?" asked Slatt.

"Weird," I said. "Spooky." Magic, particularly strong magic, can leave a sort of echo behind it. It works best with stone, less well on concrete and metal and even worse with organic materials—but strangely well with some varieties of plastic. It's easy to spot the echo if you know what you're looking for, or if the source is very strong. It's where ghosts come from, by the way. And it's a bugger to explain to witnesses.

Slatt leaned back in her chair—away from us. Nightingale gave me a hard look.

"It was raining," said Slatt finally.

"How did he strike you?" asked Nightingale. "The driver?"

"At first, like every car crash victim I've ever met," she said. "Dazed, unfocused, you know how it is—they either babble or go catatonic. He was a babbler."

"Did he babble about anything in particular?" asked Nightingale.

"I think he said something about the dogs barking but he was mumbling as well as babbling."

Slatt finished her meal, Nightingale finished his tea and I finished my notes.

I drove as PC Slatt directed me past the train station, over the tracks and through, as far as I could tell, the Victorian bit of Crawley. Certainly Robert Weil's house was a stumpy detached brick Victorian villa with squared-off bay windows, a steep roof and terra-cotta finials. The surrounding houses were all Edwardian or even later so I guessed that the villa had once stood proudly in its own grounds. You could see the remnant in the big back garden that was currently the focus of a cadaver dog team—on loan from International Rescue, I learnt later.

PC Slatt knew the PC on door duty, who signed us in without comment. The house was big enough that its owners hadn't felt the need to knock down all the intervening walls and had, recently I thought, restored the decorative molding. The dining room had been abandoned and overrun by their children, aged seven and nine according to my notes, and was treacherous with toys, broken xylophones and DVDs that had come adrift from their cases. The kids were staying with friends but the wife remained. Her name was Lynda, with a Y, with faded blonde hair and a thin mouth. She sat on the sitting-room sofa and glared at us while we searched her house—the locals were looking for bodies, we were looking for books. Nightingale took the study. I did the bedrooms.

I did the kids' rooms first, just on the off chance that something interesting was hidden among the Lego Star Wars stickers, the Highway Rat and some slightly sticky coloring-in books. The eldest already had a laptop of his own in his room although, judging from its age, it looked like a hand-me-down. Some kids have all the luck.

The parents' bedroom had a fusty unaired smell and not much in the way of interest to me. Real practitioners never leave their *important* books lying around, but you pick up pointers. The key is unlikely juxtapositions. Lots of people read books about the occult, but if you find them alongside books by or about Isaac Newton, especially the long boring ones, then hackles are raised, flags hoisted and, more importantly, notes made in my notebook.

All I found in the bedroom was a dog-eared copy of the *Discovery of Witches* under the bed along with *Life of Pi* and *The God of Small Things*.

"He hasn't done anything," said a voice behind me.

I stood up and turned to find Lynda Weil standing in the doorway.

"I don't know what you think he did," she said. "But he didn't do it. Why can't you tell me what he's supposed to have done?"

It's good policing, when you're engaged in other tasks, to avoid interacting with witnesses or suspects and especially with those individuals that might straddle both categories. Besides—I didn't know what her husband had done, either.

"I'm sorry, ma'am," I said. "We'll be finished as soon as we can."

We were finished even sooner because a minute later Nightingale called me downstairs and told me that the Major Crimes Team had found a body.

They'd done it with a wicked bit of policing too. I was seriously impressed. The MCT had CCTV footage of Robert Weil heading out through the Pease Pottage roundabout and off down the ominous sounding Forest

Road—so called because it ran along the central axis of St. Leonard's Forest, a patchwork of woods that covered the ridge of high ground that ran from Pease Pottage to Horsham.

Prime body dumping country, according to PC Slatt, easily accessible via footpaths and forest tracks and not covered by speed cameras. Wherever he'd gone, Robert Weil hadn't returned to Pease Pottage for over five hours so he could easily have been anywhere in the forest. But they'd caught a break because Lynda Weil had phoned her husband at nine forty-five, presumably to ask him where the hell he was, and that allowed the Sussex Police to triangulate the position of his phone to a cell just short of the village of Colgate. After that, it was just a matter of checking the appropriate stretch of the road until they spotted something—in this case tire tracks from a Volvo V70.

The gray overcast was darkening to countryside black when we arrived at the murder site. There wasn't a proper turn off, so I had to park the Jag further up the road and walk back.

PC Slatt explained that the landlord had only recently blocked off the entrance to an access route through the forest here.

"Weil probably remembered the turn off from a walk in the area," she said. "He hadn't planned on it not existing any more."

Important safety tip for serial killers—always scout out your dumping locations before use. We had to clamber over an artificial hillock made of sticky yellow mud and discarded tree limbs, because the marginally visible path was still being checked forensically.

"He had to drag the body," said PC Slatt. "It left a trail."

"He doesn't sound very prepared," I said. The rain was making silver streaks in the beam of my torch as I shone it back to guide Nightingale over.

"Perhaps it was his first kill," he said.

"God, I hope so," said PC Slatt.

The path beyond was muddy but I walked with the confidence of a man who made sure he packed a pair of DM boots in his overnight bag. Town or country, it doesn't matter, you don't want to be wearing your best shoes at a crime scene. Unless you're Nightingale, who seemed to have an unlimited supply of quality hand-made footwear that were cleaned and polished by someone else. I suspected it was probably Molly—but it might have been gnomes for all I knew, or some other unspecified household spirit.

On either side of the path were stands of slender trees with pale trunks that Nightingale identified as silver birch. The gloomy stand of dark pointy trees ahead were apparently Douglas firs interspersed with the occasional larch. Nightingale was aghast at my lack of arboreal knowledge.

"I don't understand how you can know five types of brick bond," he said, "but you can't identify the most common of trees."

Actually, I knew about twenty-three types of brick bond if you counted Tudor and the other early modern styles, but I kept that to myself.

Somebody sensible had strung reflective tape from tree to tree to mark our path downhill to where I could hear the rumble of a portable generator and see blue-white camera flashes, yellow high-viz jackets and the ghostly figures of people in disposable paper suits.

Back in the dim and distant past, your victim was bagged, tagged and whipped away to the mortuary as soon as the initial photographs were taken. These days the forensic pathologists stick a tent over the body and settle in for the long haul. Luckily, back in civilization it doesn't take that much longer. But out in the country there's all sorts of exciting insects and spores feasting on the corpse. These, so we're told, reveal ever so much information about time of death and the state the body was in when it hit the ground. Getting it all catalogued can take a day and a half and they'd only just started when we arrived. You could tell that the forensic pathologist wasn't happy to have yet another random set of police officers interfering with her nice scientific investigation. Even if we were good boys and wore our noddy suits, with the hoods up and masks on.

Neither was DCI Manderly, who'd got there before us. Still he must have reckoned the sooner we were started the sooner we'd be gone, because he immediately beckoned us over and introduced us to the pathologist.

I've been racking up some corpse time since I joined the Folly. And after the hurled baby and the Hari Krishna with the exploded head, I'd thought myself toughened up. But, as I've heard experienced officers say, you never get tough enough. This body was female, nude and caked in mud. The pathologist explained that she'd been buried in a shallow grave.

"Only twelve centimeters deep," she said. "The foxes would have had her up in no time."

There was no sign of staging. So Robert Weil, if it had been him, had just dumped her in the hole and covered her over. In the harsh artificial light she looked as gray and colorless as the holocaust pictures I remember from school. I couldn't see much beyond the fact that she was white, female, not a teenager and not old enough to have loose skin.

"Despite the sloppy burial," said the pathologist,

"there's evidence of forensic countermeasures, the fingers have all been removed at the second knuckle, and of course there's the face . . ."

Or lack thereof. From the chin up there was nothing but a pulped red mass flecked with white bone. Nightingale crouched down and briefly got his own face close enough to kiss where her lips had been. I looked away.

"Nothing," Nightingale said to me as he straightened up. "And it wasn't *dissimulo* either."

I took a deep breath. So, not the spell that had destroyed Lesley's face.

"What do you think caused that?" Nightingale asked the pathologist.

The pathologist pointed to where the top of the scalp was traced with tiny red furrows. "I've never seen it in the flesh, so to speak, but I suspect a shotgun blast to the face at close range."

The words "Perhaps somebody thought she was a zombie" tried to clamber out of my throat with such force that I had to slap my hand over my mask to stop them escaping.

Nightingale and the pathologist both gave me curious looks before turning back to the corpse. I ran out of the tent with my hand still over my mouth and didn't stop until I cleared the inner forensic perimeter where I could lean against the tree and take my mask off. I ignored the pitying looks I got from some of the older police outside—I'd rather they thought I was being sick than that I was trying to stop myself from giggling.

PC Slatt wandered over and handed me a bottle of water.

"You wanted a body," she said as I rinsed my mouth out. "Is this your case?"

"No, I don't think this is us," I said. "Thank god."

* * *

Neither did Nightingale, so we drove back to London as soon as we'd stripped off our suits and thanked DCI Manderly for his cooperation—Nightingale drove.

"There were no *vestigia* and it certainly looked like a shotgun wound to me," he said. "But I'm minded to ask Dr. Walid if he might like to come down and have a look for himself. Just to be on the safe side."

The steady rain had slacked off as we drove north and I could see the lights of London reflected off the clouds just beyond the North Downs.

"Just an ordinary serial killer then," I said.

"You're jumping to conclusions," said Nightingale. "There's only the one victim."

"That we know of," I said. "Anyway, still a bit of a waste of time for us."

"We had to be sure," said Nightingale. "And it does you good to get out into the countryside."

"Oh yeah," I said. "Nothing like a day trip to a crime scene. This can't be the first time you've investigated a serial killer."

"If that's what he is," said Nightingale.

"If he is then he can't have been your first," I said.

"Unfortunately true," said Nightingale. "Although I've never been the one in charge."

"Were any of the famous ones supernatural?" I asked, thinking it would explain a great deal.

"Had they been supernatural," said Nightingale, "we'd have ensured that they were not famous."

"What about Jack the Ripper?" I asked.

"No," said Nightingale. "And believe me there would have been relief if he had turned out to be a demon or some such. I knew a wizard who'd assisted the police investigation and he said that they'd all have slept far sounder knowing it wasn't a man doing such terrible things."

"Peter Sutcliffe?"

"I interviewed him myself," said Nightingale. "Nothing. And he certainly wasn't a practitioner or under the influence of a malicious spirit." He held up a hand to stop me asking my next question. "Nor was Dennis Nilsen, as far as I could tell, or Fred West or Michael Lupo or any of the parade of dreadful individuals I've had to vet in the last fifty years. Perfectly human monsters every one of them."

2

The Sons of Weyland

IF HE WAS our perfectly human monster, then Robert Weil was keeping schtum about it. I kept track of the interview transcripts via HOLMES and in the first round of interviews it's about what you'd expect. He denies having a body in the back of his car, claims that he went out for a drive and a walk, doesn't know how the blood got there, certainly has no knowledge of dead women with their faces shot off. As it becomes clear that the forensic evidence is overwhelming, what with blood on his clothes and mud under his fingernails, he stops answering questions. Once he was formally charged and remanded in custody he ceased talking to anyone—even his brief who then recommended that he be psychologically evaluated. Even just skimming the actions list I could feel the MCT's frustration as they settled into a long hard slog, grinding down every lead into fine powder and then sifting it for clues. The victim stayed stubbornly unidentified and the autopsy revealed nothing more than to confirm that she was white, female, mid-thirties and hadn't eaten for at least forty-eight hours before her death. Cause of death was most likely a shotgun blast to the face at a range close enough to leave powder burns. Dr. Walid, gastroenterology's answer to Cat Stevens and, as far as we knew, the only practicing crypto-pathologist in the world, popped in on his way home with his own autopsy report.

So we had afternoon tea and pathology, sitting in the stuffed leather armchairs downstairs in the atrium. The Folly had last been refurbished in the 1930s when the British establishment firmly believed that central heating was the work, if not of the devil per se, then definitely evil foreigners bent on weakening the hardy British spirit. Bizarrely, despite its size and the glass dome, the atrium was often warmer than the small dining room or either of the libraries.

"As you can see," said Dr. Walid laying out pictures of thin slices of brain on the table, "there are no signs of hyperthaumaturgical degradation." The slices had been stained a variety of lurid colors to improve the contrast, but Dr. Walid complained that they remained stubbornly normal—I took his word for it.

"Nor was there any sign of chimeric modification to any of the tissue samples," he said and sipped his coffee. "But I have sent off a couple of them to be sequenced."

Nightingale nodded politely, but I knew for a fact that he only had the vaguest idea of what DNA was, since he was old enough to have been Crick and Watson's father.

"I think we may as well consider this case closed," he said. "At any rate, from our perspective."

"I'd like to keep monitoring it," I said. "At least until we have an ID for the victim."

Nightingale drummed the table with his fingertips. "Are you sure you have the time for that?" he asked.

"Sussex and Surrey MCT will produce a weekly summary while the case is ongoing," I said. "It'll take me ten minutes."

"I don't think he takes me as seriously as he should," Nightingale told Dr. Walid. "He still slopes off to conduct illicit experiments whenever he thinks I'm not looking." He looked at me. "What is your latest interest?"

"I've been looking at how long various materials retain *vestigia*," I said.

"How do you measure the intensity of the *vestigia*?" asked Dr. Walid.

"He uses the dog," said Nightingale.

"I put Toby in a box along with the material and then I measure the loudness and frequency of his barking," I said. "It's no different from using a sniffer dog."

"How can you be sure of consistency of results?" asked Dr. Walid.

"I ran a series of control experiments to eliminate variables," I said. Toby on his own in a box at nine a.m. and then at hourly intervals for the volume baseline. And then Toby in a box with various guaranteed inert materials for a baseline on that. The third day Toby hid under the table in Molly's kitchen and had to be lured out with sausages.

Dr. Walid leaned forward as I talked—he at least appreciated a bit of empiricism. I explained that I'd exposed each material sample to identical amounts of magic, by conjuring a werelight—the simplest and most controllable spell I knew—and then put it in the box with Toby to see what happened.

"Were there any significant findings?" he asked.

"Toby's not very discriminating, so we're talking a wide margin for error," I said. "But it was about what I expected. And in line with my reading. Stone retains *vestigia* the best, followed by concrete. The metals were all too similar to differentiate. Wood was next and the worst was flesh." In the form of a leg of pork which Toby subsequently ate before I could stop him.

"The only surprise," I said, "were some of the plastics, which scored almost as high on the yap-o-meter as stone."

"Plastic?" asked Nightingale. "That's most unexpected. I'd always assumed that it was natural things that retained the uncanny."

"Can you e-mail me the results?" asked Dr. Walid.

"Sure."

"Have you considered testing other dogs?" asked Dr. Walid. "Perhaps different breeds would have different sensitivities."

"Abdul, please," said Nightingale. "Don't give him any ideas."

"He is making progress in the art," said Dr. Walid.

"Barely," said Nightingale. "And I believe he's replicating work that's already been done."

"By who?" I asked.

Nightingale sipped his tea and smiled.

"I'll make a bargain with you, Peter," he said. "If you make better progress in your formal studies I shall tell you where to find the notes of the last brain-box who filled the lab with . . . Actually it was mostly rats, but I seem to remember a couple of dogs in his menagerie."

"How much better progress?" I asked.

"Better than you're doing now," he said.

"I wouldn't mind seeing that data," said Dr. Walid.

"Then you should encourage Peter to study harder," said Nightingale.

"He's an evil man," I said.

"And cunning," said Dr. Walid.

Nightingale eyed us placidly over the rim of his tea cup.

"Evil and cunning," I said.

The next morning I drove up to Hendon for part one of mandatory Officer Safety Training. You're pretty much expected to do one of these courses every six months until Chief Inspector rank, but I doubt we'll ever see Nightingale do one. We had a fun lecture on Excited Delirium, or what to do with people who are stoned out of their box. And then role-playing in the gym where we practiced how to handle suspects without having them fall down the stairs. A couple of the officers had been at Hendon with me and Lesley, and we stuck together at lunch. They asked after Lesley and I gave them the official version, that she was physically assaulted during the riots in Covent Garden and that her attacker subsequently committed suicide before I could arrest him.

In the afternoon we took it in turns to hide offensive weapons about our person while our colleagues searched us, a contest I won coming and going because I know how to hide a razor blade in the waist band of my jeans and I'm not afraid to go all the way up a suspect's inner leg. Doing all the physical stuff left me weirdly energized, so when one of the other officers suggested we go clubbing I tagged along. We ended up in a UV saturated cattle shed in Romford where I may, or may not, have got off with the goddess of the River Rom. Not in a serious way, you understand, just a bit of clinch and some tongue. Which is what happens when you overdo the WKD. I woke up the next morning in one of the chairs in the atrium with surprisingly little hangover and Molly looming over me. She looked disapproving. I would have preferred a hangover.

My trusty Ford Asbo was parked safely in the garage, so after a breakfast and a bucket bath I departed for Hendon once more. As I climbed into the driver's seat a powerful *vestigium* rushed over me. I tasted vodka, smelled machine oil and felt the slip slide of lip balm. There was shouting and screams of excitement and illegal acceleration that pushed you back into your seat while your engine growled like something big and endangered.

There was an open lipstick on the dashboard—shocking pink.

I didn't know about Goddess of the River Rom, but I'd definitely brushed up against something supernatural. Maybe it hadn't been the vodka after all.

That's it, I thought. No more clubbing without a chaperone for you.

I revved up the Asbo, but despite the tweaking I'd given the engine it did not cry like a panther.

It did get me all the way back up to Hendon on time for the start of day two, which was officer equipment safety. The morning lecture was on stop and search with reference to spotting suspicious behavior. The lecturer who gloried in the full name of Douglas Douglas illustrated the weird stiffening of the limbs exhibited by shoplifters known as "the robot," or the exaggerated mime-like behavior adopted by the truly guilty when they unexpectedly encounter the police. "You can't go wrong," he said, "by searching anyone who engages you in conversation." On the basis that nobody willingly engages the police in conversation unless they're trying to deflect attention from something. But he did warn us to make an exception for tourists, because London needed the foreign currency.

After that we were back in the gym being reminded how to use our handcuffs properly. We use the ones with a solid middle which you can grab hold of and twist to put pressure on your suspect's arms, and ensure what our instructor called compliance and cooperation. In the afternoon one of the instructors donned a padded suit and adopted a mad aspect and challenged us to subdue him with our extendable batons. This bit used to be called the "nutter" training but now it's officially called "the person with differences."

It's useful stuff. You never know when you're going to have to ensure compliance and cooperation from people with differences, in a state of excited delirium or not.

When we'd finished I was invited out again but I declined and drove slowly and carefully home instead.

Lesley got out of hospital and turned up unexpectedly while I was trying to perfect a forma called aqua which, for those of you who didn't have a classical education, is a base forma for manipulating water. It used to form the empedoclean along with lux, aer and terra—two of which went out of fashion when the four-element theory of matter failed to survive the age of Enlightenment.

It's a lot like *lux* in that you shape the *forma* in your mind, open your palm and, hopefully, find yourself with a globe of water the size of a ping-pong ball. Nightingale claimed not to know where the water came from, but I assumed it was drawn out of the surrounding air. It was that or it was being sucked out of a parallel dimension, or hyperspace or something even weirder. I hoped it wasn't hyperspace because I wasn't ready for the implications of that.

In my case, so far, I'd managed a small cloud, a frozen rain drop and a puddle. And that was after it had taken me four weeks to get anything at all. Nightingale was supervising me in the teaching lab on the first floor when the vapor haze above my palm shrank down to a wobbly globe. The trouble with this stage of mastering a *forma* is that it's almost impossible to tell why what you're currently doing is working better than what you were doing two seconds ago. That's why you end up doing a lot of practice and why it isn't easy maintaining a new *forma*— particularly when someone decides to start singing the chorus of "Rehab" outside the door—loudly and a quarter tone flat.

The globe exploded like a water balloon, splattering me, the bench and the surrounding floor. Nightingale, who had become wise to my peculiar aptitude with exploding *formae* had been standing well back and wearing a raincoat.

I glared at Lesley, who struck a pose in the doorway.

"Got my voice back," she said. "Sort of." She'd stopped wearing the mask inside the Folly and, while her face was still ruined, at least I could tell when she was smiling.

"No," I said. "You always sang flat."

Nightingale waved Lesley over.

"Good," he said. "I'm glad you're here. I've got a demonstration and I've been waiting until I could show both of you at the same time."

"Can I dump my stuff first?" asked Lesley.

"Of course," said Nightingale. "While you do that, Peter here can clean up the lab."

"It's a good thing it was water," said Lesley. "Even Peter can't explode water."

"Let's not tempt fate," said Nightingale.

We reconvened half an hour later and Nightingale led us to one of the unused labs down the hall. He pulled off dust sheets to reveal scarred work benches, lathes and vises. I recognized it as a Design and Technology workshop, like the one I'd used at school, only stuck in a time warp back in the days of steam power and child labor. He pulled off a last sheet, under which was a black iron anvil of the sort I've only ever seen falling onto the heads of cartoon characters.

"Are you thinking what I'm thinking, Lesley?" I asked.

"I think so, Peter," she said. "But how are we going to get the pony up here?"

"Shoeing a horse is a very useful skill," said Nightingale. "And when I was a boy there used to be a smithy downstairs in the yard. This, however, is where we turn boys into men." He paused to look at Lesley. "And I suppose young women into women."

"Are we forging the one ring?" I asked.

Nightingale held up a walking stick. "Do you recognize this?" he asked.

I did. It was a silver-topped gentleman's cane, the head a bit tarnished looking.

"It's your cane," I said.

"And what else?" asked Nightingale.

"It's your wizard's staff," said Lesley.

"Well done," said Nightingale.

"The cadwallopper," I said, and when Lesley raised what was left of her eyebrow I added, "A stick for walloping cads."

"And the source of a wizard's power," said Nightingale.

Using magic has a very specific limitation. If you overdo it your brain turns into Swiss cheese. Hyperthaumaturgical degradation, Dr. Walid calls it, and he has some brains in a drawer which he whips out at the slightest excuse to show young apprentices. The rule of thumb with brain injuries is that by the time you feel anything, the damage is already done. So a practitioner of the arts tends to err on the side of caution. This can cause tension when, for the sake of argument, two Tiger tanks emerge suddenly from the treeline on a rainy night in 1945. In order to be the hero of *Boy's Own Weekly* and still have an intact brain, a sensible wizard carries a staff in which he has personally imbued a great deal of power.

Don't ask me what kind of power that is, because the only thing I've got that can detect it is Toby the Dog. I'd love to stick some high *vestigia* material into a mass spectrometer, but first I'd have to get myself a mass spectrometer and then I'd have to learn enough physics to interpret the bloody results.

Nightingale took his walking stick over to one of the workbenches, unscrewed the top and clamped the stick part in a vise. Then, taking a hammer and chisel, he cracked it along its length to reveal a dull gun-metal blue core the thickness of a pencil.

"This is the heart of the staff," he said and fished a magnifying glass out of a nearby drawer. "Have a closer look."

We took it in turns. The surface of the core had faint but distinct ripples of shade that appeared to spiral up its length.

"What's it made of?" asked Lesley as she looked.

"Steel," said Nightingale.

"Folded steel," I said. "Like a samurai sword."

"It's called pattern welding," said Nightingale. "Different steel alloys, forge-welded in a deliberate pattern. Done correctly it creates a matrix that retains magic so that a master can draw upon it later."

With a great saving on wear and tear of the brain, I thought.

"How do you get the magic in?" asked Lesley.

"While you're forging it," said Nightingale and mimed using a hammer. "You use a third-order spell to raise the forge temperature and another to keep it hot while you hammer the work."

"What about the magic?" I asked.

"It derives, or so I was taught, from the spells you use during the forging," he said.

Lesley rubbed her face. "How long will that take?" she asked.

"This staff will take upward of three months." He saw our expressions. "Working say an hour or two a day. One has to avoid overdoing the magic otherwise the purpose of the staff becomes moot."

"And we're going to make a staff each?" she asked.

"Eventually, yes," said Nightingale. "But first you're going to watch and learn."

Faintly we heard the phone ringing in the distance and all turned to the doorway and waited for Molly to appear. When she did she inclined her head at Nightingale indicating that the call was for him.

We followed at a discreet distance in the hope of overhearing the conversation.

"I knew I should have paid more attention in D&T," said Lesley.

We were already on the landing when Nightingale called us down. We found him standing with the phone in his hand, a look of total amazement on his face.

"We have a report of a rogue magician," he said.

Me and the rogue magician stared at each other in mutual incomprehension. He was wondering why the hell there was a police officer sitting by his bed and I was wondering where the hell this guy had come from.

His name was George Nolfi and he was an ordinary-looking white man in his late sixties—sixty-seven according to my notes. His hair was thinning but still mostly brown, he had blue eyes and a face that had obviously gone for a gaunt old age rather than jowls. His hands were bandaged from the wrist down so that only the tips of his fingers showed—occasionally he held them up and examined them with a look of utter surprise on his face. My notes said that he'd suffered second-degree burns to his hands during the "incident," but that nobody else had been injured although several young children had been treated for shock.

"Why don't you tell me what happened?" I said.

"You won't believe me," he said.

"You made a ball of fire appear out of thin air," I said. "See, I believe you—this sort of thing happens all the time."

He stared at me stupidly. We get this a lot even from people with some experience of the supernatural—bugger that—we get this from people who *are* supernatural.

He was from Wimbledon and was a retired chartered surveyor. He wasn't on our list of Little Crocodiles. In fact he'd been educated at Leeds University, and the Nolfi name was not listed among the rolls of Nightingale's old school or the Folly. And yet he'd conjured a fireball in the living room of his daughter's house—it had all been captured on camcorder.

"Have you ever done it before?" I asked.

"Yes," he said. "But not since I was a boy."

I made a note. Nightingale and Lesley were even then going through his house looking for books on magic, *vestigium* hotspots, *lacuna*, household gods and malign spirits. Nightingale had made my job clear; first establish what Mr. Nolfi had done, then why he had done it and, finally, how had he known how to do it.

"It was Gabriella's birthday party," he said. "She's my granddaughter. Delightful child but, being six, a bit of a handful. Have you got any children?"

"Not yet," I said.

"En masse a room full of six-year-old girls can be a daunting prospect, so I may have fortified myself with a tad more sherry than I meant to," he said. "There was a problem with the cake."

Even worse, the lights had already been switched off in anticipation of its entrance and candles lit, accompanied by a chorus of "Happy Birthday to You (Squashed Tomatoes and Stew)."

And so Mr. Nolfi, granddad, was instructed to keep the children entertained while the problem was sorted out.

"And I remembered this trick that I used to do when I was a boy," he said. "It seemed like a good idea at the time. I got their attention, not an easy thing, mind you, rolled up my sleeves and said the magic word."

"What was the magic word?" I asked.

"*Lux!*" he said. "It's Latin for light."

But of course I knew that already. It's also the first *forma* that a classically trained apprentice wizard learns. I asked Mr. Nolfi what he'd expected to happen.

"I used to be able to make a fairy light," he said. "It used to keep my sister amused."

A bit of prodding revealed that he only knew the one spell and that he'd stopped performing it once he was sent off to school.

"Mine was a Catholic school," he said. "They took a dim view of dabbling in the occult—or even just dabbling, to be honest. The headmaster believed that if you're going to do something you should do it all the way."

He gave me details of the school, but warned me that it had closed due to a scandal in the late 1960s. "Headmaster had his hand in the till," he said.

"So who did you learn this magic trick from?" I asked.

"From my mother of course," said Mr. Nolfi.

"From his mother," said Nightingale.

"So he says," I said.

We were in the so-called private dining room where we were all eating— to be honest we weren't sure what it was, Molly was experimenting again. Shanks of lamb, according to Lesley, casseroled with something fishy, possibly anchovies, possibly sardines and two scoops of mashed—I said swede but Nightingale insisted at least one of them was parsnip.

"I'm not sure we should eat stuff when we don't know what it is," said Lesley.

"I'm not the one who bought her the Jamie Oliver book for Christmas," I said.

"No," said Lesley. "You're the one who wanted to get her Heston Blumenthal."

Nightingale, trained—as he pointed out—from an early age to eat what was put in front of him, tucked in with enthusiasm. Given that Molly was hovering in the doorway, me and Lesley had little choice but to follow suit.

It tasted remarkably like lamb in sardine sauce, I thought.

After a sufficient wait to ensure that we hadn't been poisoned, we continued our discussion about Mr. Nolfi.

"It strikes me as rather unlikely," said Nightingale. "Or at least it's not something I've come across before."

"We didn't find anything at his home," said Lesley.

"There must have been female practitioners even in your day," I said.

"There were some Hedge Witches," said Nightingale. "Especially out in the countryside, there always are. But there was nobody with formal training that I knew of."

"Hogwarts was all male," I said.

"Peter," said Nightingale. "If you'd like to spend the next three days cleaning the lab then by all means keep referring to my old school as Hogwarts."

"Casterbrook," I said.

"That's better," said Nightingale and polished off the last of his swede—if it was swede.

"But it was boys only," I said.

"Indubitably," said Nightingale. "I'm sure I would have noticed otherwise."

"And these boys came from the old wizarding families?"

"You have such a delightfully quaint notion of how things were," said Nightingale. "There were a number of families who generally sent one or more of their sons to the school. That's all."

Traditionally, the landed gentry had kept the first son at home to inherit the estate, the second went for a soldier, the third to the clergy or the law. I asked Nightingale where the profession of magic stood in that list.

"The Folly was never that popular among the aristocracy," said Nightingale. "We were all much more proudly bourgeoisie than that. It would be best to think of us as professionals—like doctors or lawyers. It was common for a son to follow in his father's footsteps."

"But not his daughter?"

Nightingale shrugged. "It was a different age," he said.

"Was your father a wizard?" I asked.

"Good Lord no," said Nightingale. "It was my Uncle Stanley who carried on the tradition in that generation— it was he who suggested that I attend Casterbrook."

"He didn't have sons of his own?" I asked.

"He never married," said Nightingale. "I had four brothers and two sisters so I believe my father felt he could spare me. Mama always said I was a curious child, asking far too many questions at the most inopportune times. I'm sure they were relieved to have someone else take up the responsibility of answering them."

He caught me and Lesley exchanging looks.

"I'm amazed you find this at all interesting," he said.

"You've never talked about your family before," I said.

"I'm sure I must have," he said.

"Nope," said Lesley.

"Oh," said Nightingale and promptly changed the

subject. "Tomorrow I want the pair of you to practice on the range in the morning," he said. "Then it's Latin in the afternoon."

"Shoot me now," I said.

"Isn't there some police work we should be doing?" asked Lesley.

Pudding arrived, a jam suet pudding, red and steaming. Molly put it down in front of us with way more confidence than she'd offered up the lamb shanks.

"Did everyone make their own staff?" asked Lesley.

"Everyone who?" asked Nightingale.

"In the old days," she said and gestured around the dining room. "Everyone who was a member of this place?"

"No," said Nightingale. "In the first instance, very few of us needed one for everyday use. So to speak. And in the second, the making of them became something of a specialty. A group of wizards in Manchester, of all places, who styled themselves the Sons of Weyland would construct them to order. Luckily for you, I considered myself a modern day renaissance man—ready to turn my hand to every art and science."

Nightingale had gone to Manchester, where he had learnt the weird of the Sons of Weyland, or at least those bits of the weird that were appropriate to a gentleman. When I asked what had happened to the people who trained him, Nightingale's face clouded and I knew the answer. Ettersberg. Everyone, the cream of British wizardry, had gone to Ettersberg. And only a few had come back.

"Did Geoffrey Wheatcroft learn the weird way of the Weylands?" asked Lesley.

Nightingale gave her a thoughtful look. "What are you thinking?" he asked.

"I'm thinking sir," she said, "that if Geoffrey Wheatcroft didn't learn how to make a staff then he can't have passed that knowledge on to the Little Crocodiles or the Faceless Man."

"We know his protégés could make demon-traps," I said. "And worse."

"Lesley's right," said Nightingale. "Anyone can make a demon-trap, providing he's a vile specimen of the first water. But there were secrets involved in the shaping of a staff—ones I seriously doubt that old Geoffrey ever learnt. I'm not sure how that helps us."

I did. "It means we've got something the Faceless Man's going to really want for himself," I said.

"In other words, sir," said Lesley, "bait."

3

The One Under

JUST BEFORE CHRISTMAS I'd assisted with a murder that took place on Baker Street Underground station. It was during that investigation that I made the acquaintance of one Sergeant Jaget Kumar, urban explorer, expert pot-holer and the British Transport Police's answer to Mulder and Scully. Together we helped catch the murderer, discovered an entire underground civilization, albeit a small one, and, unfortunately, destroyed one of the platforms at Oxford Circus. During that mess I ended up buried underground for a half a day, where I had a waking dream that still keeps me from sleeping. But that, as they say, is a whole different counseling session.

Despite the fact that services had returned to normal by the end of January, I was not really Mr. Popular with Transport for London, who run the Underground and the BTP who have to police it. Which might be why, when Jaget said that he had some information for me, we didn't meet in the BTP Headquarters at Camden Town but in a café just down the road.

We sat down for coffee and Jaget unshipped his Samsung and pulled up some files.

"We had this one-under at Paddington last week," he said. "And he came up on your list." The Folly maintains a list of potentially interesting people, the dwindling number of surviving practitioners from World War Two, suspected Little Crocodiles and people that consort with fairies, which raises a flag should anyone run an Integrated Intelligence Platform check on them.

Jaget turned the tablet to show me a picture of a middle-aged white man with thinning fair hair and thin bloodless lips. Judging by his pallor and glassy stare the picture was post-mortem—the kind you did to show to relatives and potential witnesses without scaring the shit out of them. That made sense since *one-under* was tube slang for when a member of the public throws themselves under a train. Two hundred and forty tons of locomotive can mess up your whole day.

"Richard Lewis," said Jaget. "Aged forty-six."

I looked him up in my little black book—I had all the potential Little Crocodiles listed by date of birth. Jaget smiled when he saw it.

"Good to see you embracing the potential of modern technology," he said, but I ignored him. Richard Lewis had indeed been at Oxford between 1985 and 1987, but wasn't on the main list of confirmed Little Crocodiles— he was on a secondary list made up of those who had been personally tutored by Geoffrey Wheatcroft, former official wizard and the man stupid enough to start teaching magic unofficially. Nightingale doesn't swear very often, but when he talks about Geoffrey Wheatcroft you can tell he really fucking wants to.

"Is it just the fact that he's on the list?" I asked.

"There was something off about the suicide," he said.

"He was pushed?"

"See for yourself," said Jaget and cued up the CCTV footage on his tablet. Because London's tube stations are the target for everything from casual public urination to mass murder the CCTV coverage is literally wall to wall.

"Here he comes," said Jaget.

Jaget had obviously spent some time editing the footage together because it told the story with quite a bit of unnecessary flair. You could have put it to music, something grim and German maybe, and sold it to an art gallery.

"How bored were you when you did this?" I asked.

"We don't all have careers full of mystery and magic," said Jaget. "See, he rides the escalator all the way up but, before he reaches the ticket barrier, he turns round and heads back down again."

I watched as Richard Lewis shuffled patiently along a corridor with the rest of the crowd, down a flight of stairs and onto the platform. He wormed his way forward until he was standing on the yellow line that marked the edge. There he waited, staring straight ahead, for the next train. When it arrived Richard Lewis turned his head to watch its approach and then, at what Jaget said was precisely the right moment, jumped in front of it.

I presumed there was more footage of the collision but luckily Jaget hadn't felt it necessary to inflict it on me.

"Where did he travel from?" I asked.

"London Bridge," said Jaget. "He worked for Southwark Council."

"Why would he travel from one station to another before topping himself?" I asked.

"Oh, that's not unusual," said Jaget. "We had one woman who paused to finish her crisps before she stepped off and one guy at South Ken who wouldn't go while there were any kids that might see him." Jaget described how the man, dressed respectably in a pinstripe suit and holding an umbrella, had grown visibly more agitated with each missed opportunity. Finally when he had the platform to himself, you could see him on the CCTV straightening his cuffs and adjusting his tie.

"As if he wanted to make a good impression when he got there," said Jaget.

Wherever "there" might be.

Then when the next train was a minute out, an entire school party, fresh from the museums, descended on the platform. Kids and harassed teachers from one end to the other.

"You should have seen his face," said Jaget. "He was so frustrated."

"Did he manage it eventually?" I asked.

"Nah," said Jaget. "By that time somebody in the station control room had noticed and ran down to intervene." And less than six hours later the man in the pinstripe suit was detained, sectioned and whisked off to a psychiatric unit for a quick chat with the duty psychologist.

"I wonder if he tried again?"

"Just as long as he didn't do it on our time," said Jaget.

"So what makes our Mr. Lewis suspicious?"

"It's where he jumped from," said Jaget. One-underers tended to be quite predictable when it came to choosing their jumping-off point into oblivion.

"If they're just making a cry for help," he said, "then they go from the far end of the platform—so that the train has almost stopped before it gets there. If they're serious, then they go to the other end where the driver has no chance to react and the train's going full speed. Shit, if you do it there you don't even have to jump—just lean out and the train will take your head right off."

"And if they jump from the middle?"

"Then they're not sure," said Jaget. "It's a graduated thing, a bit of doubt and they go one way, if they're pretty sure they go the other."

"Mr. Lewis went from the middle," I said. "Meaning he was in two minds."

"Mr. Lewis," said Jaget winding the footage to just before the jump, "went from just in front of the passenger entrance. If a train had come immediately, I'd understand. But he had to wait. It's like his position on the platform was irrelevant."

I shrugged. "So?"

"Your position is never irrelevant," said Jaget. "It's the last thing you're ever going to do—look at him. He just glances once at the train to get the timing right and bang! He's gone. Look at the confidence in that jump, nothing hesitant at all."

"I bow to your superior knowledge of train suicides," I said. "What exactly is it you think might have happened?"

Jaget contemplated his coffee for a moment and then asked, "Is it possible to make people do things against their will?"

"You mean like hypnotism?"

"More than hypnotism," he said. "Like instant brainwashing."

I thought of the first time I'd met the Faceless Man and the casual way he'd ordered me to jump off a roof. I'd have done it, too, if I hadn't built up a resistance to that sort of thing.

"It's called a glamour," I said.

Jaget stared at me for a bit—I don't think he'd expected me to say yes.

"Can *you* do it?" he asked.

"Do me a favor," I said. I'd asked Nightingale about

glamour and he'd told me that even the easiest type was a seventh-order spell and the results were not what you'd call reliable. "Especially when you consider that it's hardly a chore to defend against," he'd said.

"What about your boss?"

"He says he learnt the theory but he's never actually done it," I said. "I got the impression he didn't think it was a gentlemanly thing to do."

"Do you know how it works?"

"You activate the *forma* and then you tell the target what to do," I said. "Dr. Walid thinks it alters your brain chemistry, making you unusually suggestible, but that's just a theory."

Not least because me and Dr. Walid's putative experimental protocol, zap some volunteers and check their blood chemistry before and after, was at the far end of a long list of other things we wanted to test. And that's assuming we could get Nightingale and the Medical Research Council to approve.

"You think our Mr. Lewis was compelled into suicide?" I asked. "Based on what? Where he jumped from?"

"Not just that," said Jaget and cued up another mpeg on his tablet. "Watch this."

This one was stitched together from close-ups of Richard Lewis's head and shoulders as he rode the escalator up to the concourse. The resolution on CCTV cameras has been rapidly improving and the London Underground, a terrorism target since before the term was invented, has some of the best kit available. But the image still suffered from the grain and sudden lighting changes that hinted at some cheap and cheerful enhancement.

"What am I looking for?" I asked.

"Watch his face," said Jaget. So I did.

It was your bog-standard commuter's face, tired, resigned, with occasional flickers as he spotted something, or someone, that caught his eye. He checked his watch at least twice while riding the escalator—anxious to catch the early train to Swindon.

"He lives on the outskirts," said Jaget and we shared a moment of mutual incomprehension at the inexplicable life choices of commuters.

The image was good enough to capture the moment of anticipation as he stepped off the escalator at the top and the scan for the least crowded ticket gate. He checked his watch once again and set off purposefully for his chosen exit. Then he stopped and hesitated for a moment before turning on his heel. Heading for the down escalator and his date with the business end of a Mark II 1972 rolling stock.

It looked like he'd just remembered that he'd forgotten something.

"It's too quick," said Jaget. "You forget something, you stop, you think 'Oh god I have to go all the way back down the escalator, do I really need whatever it is that badly?' And *then* you turn."

He was right. Richard Lewis stopped and turned as smartly as if he was on a parade ground and had been given a command. As he rode back down his expression was abstracted and intent—as if he was thinking about something important.

"I don't know if it's a glamour," I said. "But it's definitely something. I think I need a second opinion."

But I was already thinking it was the Faceless Man.

"Tricky," said Nightingale after I'd lured him into the tech cave and shown him the footage. "It's a very limited technique and an Underground station at rush hour is hardly an ideal environment in which to practice it. Do you have any film that shows a wide view of the booking hall?"

It took me a couple of minutes to dig out the files Jaget had sent me, not least because of his eccentric file labeling scheme. Nightingale made an impressed murmur at the ease and speed at which the "film" could be manipulated. "Or is it called tape?" he asked.

I didn't tell him that *it* was all stored as binary information on rapidly spinning shiny discs, partly because I'd have to look up the details myself, but mostly because by the time he'd understood the technology it would have been replaced by something else.

He spent about an hour shuttling back and forth through the footage of the booking hall to see if he could spot a practitioner among the crowds of passengers. Nightingale's level of concentration can be frightening, but even he couldn't isolate anyone suspicious.

"He might have been walking two steps behind him," said Nightingale. "It's not as if we know what he looks like."

Lesley, when we briefed her later, wanted to know why we were assuming it was the Faceless Man at all. "It could have been one of Peter's watery girlfriends," she said. "Or something else equally weird that we haven't encountered yet."

I pointed out that Richard Lewis had been on the list of potential Little Crocodiles, which she agreed was a possible lead and should be checked.

"You need to get over to his house and have a sniff around," she said. "If you find something, then we'll know it will be worth looking into the suicide."

"Want to come with?" I asked but Lesley said that while the prospect of a day trip to Swindon was an attractive one, it was a pleasure she'd have to forgo.

"I've got to finish the report on Nolfi the magnificent," she said. There would be two reports, one for the Folly files and a sanitized version for the wider Met. Lesley was particularly good at coming up with the latter.

"I'm going to blame it on his attempt to do the lighter fluid trick but with brandy," she said. "That way his official statement—that he was doing a magic trick that went wrong—will match the evidence."

It went without saying that we weren't going to charge him. Instead he was going to get what we like to call "the safety lecture" from Dr. Walid. Half an hour with the good doctor and his brain sections was enough to put anyone off magic for life.

So it was that I climbed into the Asbo on my tod and headed up the M4 for the wilds of the Thames Valley.

It rained most of the way and the radio threatened floods.

Richard Lewis had lived in a Grade II listed thatched cottage with its own private approach lane and what looked like, through the rain, its own orchard. It was the sort of madly picturesque place that gets bought by people with rural fantasies and a shed full of cash. Looking at it, I really wished I'd had time to go over Mr. Lewis's finances—because there was no way he could afford a place like this on what he earned from Southwark Council. I wondered if he'd had his hand out under the table. Maybe he'd got greedy and asked for a bit extra from the wrong person.

Or his registered civil partner, a Mr. Phillip Orante, could have been rich.

I parked outside next to a Sloane green Range Rover, less than a year old and never been driven off road judging by its wheel arches, and crunched up the wet gravel drive to the front door. Although it was early afternoon, the low cloud and the drizzle meant it was gloomy enough for the inhabitants to need to put the downstairs lights on. Seeing that someone was at home was a relief, since I'd decided not to call ahead.

You don't call ahead if you can avoid it, on account of it always being better to arrive on someone's doorstep as a horrid surprise. Things generally go smoother if the people you're talking to don't have a chance to rehearse their alibis, think about what they're going to say, hide evidence, bury body parts—that sort of thing.

The oak front door had an authentic bell pull with what sounded like a cow-bell attached to the other end. The thatch overhanging the porch tried to drip water down my back so I stepped away while I waited. The grounds around the house—they were too large for me to call it a garden—were damp and quiet in the soft rain. Somewhere around the corner I could smell a wet rose bush.

The door was opened by a middle-aged woman with a round brown face with black eyes and short dark hair—Filipino if I had to guess. She wore a white plastic apron over a blue polyester tunic and a pair of yellow washing-up gloves. She didn't seem thrilled to see me.

"Can I help you?" She had an accent I didn't recognize.

I identified myself and asked to speak to Mr. Orante.

"Is this about poor Richard?" she asked.

I said it was, and she told me Phillip's heart was broken.

"Such a shame," she said and invited me in and told me to wait in the living room while she went to fetch Orante.

The interior of the cottage was disappointingly furnished in bog standard designer bland—cream-colored sofas, steel tube occasional furniture and the walls painted in estate-agent-friendly shades of tinted white. Only the pictures on the walls, black and white photographic prints for the most part, had any character. I was examining a vérité portrait of a couple of New Orleans jazzmen when the woman in the apron returned with Phillip Orante.

He was a short, slight man in his late thirties. Despite the thinner face, his features were similar enough to the older woman's to mark her as a relative. His mother, I thought, or at the very least an older sister or aunt. She seemed a bit young to be his mother.

The beauty of being the police, though, is you can satisfy your curiosity without worrying about being socially awkward.

"Are you a relative?" I asked.

"Phillip is my son," she said. "My eldest."

"She came over to, ah, help out, you know," said Phillip. "After."

He motioned for me to sit down, I automatically waited until he'd chosen the sofa before perching on an occasional chair—the better to maintain my height advantage. We worked our way through the normal conversational openings—I was sorry for his loss and he was sorry I was sorry and would I like some coffee.

You always take the coffee from bereaved relatives, just as you always start with the rote expression of condolences. The banality of the exchange is what helps calm the witness down. People who've had their lives disrupted are looking for order and predictability—even if it's just in the little things. That's when being PC Plod is at its most useful—look stolid, talk slowly and, ninety percent of the time they'll tell you everything you want to know.

Phillip had an accent which I thought was Canadian but which turned out, when I asked, to be Californian. San Franciscan to be precise. His mum was Filipino but had moved to California in her twenties and had met

Phillip's dad, whose parents had been Filipino but had himself been born in Seattle, while both were visiting relatives in Caloocan. So we did a bit of bonding over a discussion of the joys of growing up with the extended diaspora family and mothers who unreasonably felt that a young man's priorities should be schoolwork, household chores and family commitments. Time enough for a social life once you've finished university, got married and provided grandchildren. The obvious contradiction never seems to bother them.

"We were working on the grandchildren," said Phillip.

Adoption or surrogacy, I wondered? It didn't seem the time to ask.

His mum brought us coffee on an enamelled tray with kittens painted on it. I waited until she'd bustled back out before asking how he'd come to move to the UK and meet Richard Lewis.

"I was a dot.com millionaire," he said simply. "Co-founder of a company that you've never heard of, which was bought out by a bigger company that I signed a non-disclosure agreement with. They gave me a huge share option which I cashed in just before the market went south."

He gave me a thin smile. Obviously this was his standard spiel with its appropriate pauses for rueful laughs and self-deprecating chuckles—only this was the first time he'd told it with his partner dead.

"I always worry when there's too much of a good thing," he said.

Having made his millions he headed to London, for the culture, the nightlife and most of all because, as far as he knew, none of his immediate relatives lived there.

"I love my family," he said, glancing after his mother. "But you know how it is."

He'd met Richard Lewis at the Royal Opera House

during a performance of Verdi's *Un Ballo in Maschera*. He'd gone on impulse and had been in the standing-room-only section when a well-dressed stranger had turned to him and said, "God this is a bloody awful performance."

"He said that he could think of at least five things that he'd rather be doing," said Phillip. "I asked him what was on the top of the list and he said, 'Well, a stiff drink would be a good start, don't you think?' So off we went for a drink and that was it, cupid's arrow right between the eyes."

But it hadn't quite been love at first sight. Phillip hadn't flown across the pond with a large fortune just to fall for the first half-decent proposition. "He worked at it," said Phillip. "He was methodical and patient and—" Phillip looked away and stared at a blank piece of wall for a moment before taking a breath. "Really fucking funny."

Three months later they were married, or more precisely they entered into a Civil Partnership, with due ceremony, celebration and a suitable pre-nup.

"That was Richard's idea," said Phillip.

I judged that this was about as good a time as any to wheel out the questionnaire. It had been drawn up by Dr. Walid and Nightingale to uncover evidence of real magical practice—as opposed to an interest in the occult, ghost stories, fantasy novels and that old time religion. Dr. Walid had thrown in some questions from established psychometric and sociological surveys to make it sound kosher. I called it the Voight-Kampff test even though only Dr. Walid got the joke—and he had to look it up on Wikipedia.

"It's to provide background about these . . . tragic incidents," I said. "To see what can be done to prevent them in the future."

Up till now I'd mostly given the spiel to potential Little Crocodiles who I was pretending to interview on a totally random basis. Watching Phillip's face, I decided we were going to have to dream up a whole new strategy for dealing with bereaved relatives. Either that or Dr. Walid could come and administer his own bloody tests.

Phillip nodded as if this was all perfectly reasonable — perhaps he was just pleased we were taking an interest.

The test started with a couple of psychological questions as warm up, and I almost skipped number five, "Did the subject indicate dissatisfaction with any aspect of his life?" But Dr. Walid had stressed consistency in application.

"I didn't think so," said Phillip. "Not until I saw the tape of the accident."

"They let you see it?" I asked.

"Oh, I insisted," said Phillip. "I thought there was no way that Richard would kill himself. What reason would he have? But it's hard to argue with the evidence of your eyes."

I moved onto the "spiritual" questions which revealed that Richard had almost been an Anglican in the same way that Phillip had almost been a Catholic. Phillip told me proudly that his mum had ceased to be a practicing Catholic the day after he came out.

"She says she will go back to the Church the day it apologizes," he said.

Lewis hadn't had any interest in the occult beyond that needed to appreciate Wagner or the *Magic Flute* and he didn't own any books about magic, or many books at all.

"He gave away most of his old books when we moved here," said Phillip. "And he said his Kindle was much handier for the commute to London. Now I resent all the hours he spent on that train. But he loved his home here and he wouldn't give up his job."

Not that Phillip could understand why. "I know he didn't get anything in the way of job satisfaction," he said. Phillip could have certainly used him in his own company, which arranged finance for high-tech start-ups. "He hated working in London, said he hated the city and I begged him to quit for like five years, but he wouldn't."

"Did he say why?" I asked.

"No," said Phillip. "He always changed the subject."

Up till then I'd been doodling, but now I started taking notes. Keeping a secret always makes the police suspicious. And while we're willing to believe in the possibility of a totally innocent explanation, we never think that's the way to bet.

I asked whether there was any aspect of Richard's work as a town planner that he'd talked about more than others, but Phillip hadn't noticed. Nor had Richard complained about incidents of corruption or coming under any pressure to influence a planning decision one way or the other.

"And whatever it was keeping him there," said Phillip, "he was obviously over it, because he told me that he was quitting." He looked away from me and fumbled for his tea cup to cover his tears.

The mother bustled back in, saw the tears and gave me a poisonous look. I worked my way quickly through the last of the questionnaire, offered my condolences once more, and left.

Something fishy and possibly supernatural had happened to Richard Lewis but since he obviously wasn't a practitioner I couldn't think what his connection with the excitingly terminal world of modern magic might be. When I got back to the Folly I wrote it up and filed the requisite two reports. The thinking in police work with this sort of non-lead is that either some other completely different line of inquiry will prove unexpectedly connected or you will never find out what the fuck was going on.

My gut instinct was that we were never going to find out why Richard Lewis threw himself under a train — which just goes to show why you should never trust your gut.

4

Complex and Unspecific Matters

AFTER CAR-RELATED INCIDENTS, burglary and theft are the most common crimes which MOPs, that's members of the public to you, are subject to. It's also the one they moan about the most, mainly because they know that the clear-up rate for burglary is low.

"I don't know why you bother writing this down," they say as they exaggerate the value of their goods for insurance purposes. "It's not like you're going to catch them, is it?" To which we have no answer—because they're right. We're not going to catch them for that particular burglary, but we often catch them later and then get some of your stuff back—the stuff that's now been replaced by better stuff from the insurance. Most of the recovered goods are junk but some of it attracts the eagle eye of the Arts and Antiques Squad who grab it, photograph it and put it on a database called, with the Met's unerring ear for a euphonious acronym, LSAD—the London Stolen Art Directory.

They keep saying that they're going to make it searchable by the public but I wouldn't hold my breath. It *is* possible for it to be searched by a police officer, if he can persuade his line manager to push for his OCU to be granted access via their terminals. Not an easy thing to do, when the line manager in question is hazy on the concept of databases, Internet searches and indeed the very notion of a "line manager." I'd gained access just after the New Year and now made checking new arrivals part of my morning routine. "Anything to avoid real work," was Lesley's verdict and Nightingale gave me the same long-suffering look he gives me when I accidentally blow up fire extinguishers, fall asleep while he's talking, or fail to conjugate my Latin verbs.

So you can imagine how pleased I was when one cold dark morning, a fortnight after my visit to Swindon, I spotted my first find. I always start with the rare books and I almost missed it because it was in German; *Über die Grundlagen, die der Praxis der Magie zugrunde liegen* but fortunately it had been translated as *About the Basics that the Practice of Magic Reference Lies* probably by Google Translate. There was a picture of the frontispiece listing the author as Reinhard Maller, published in 1799 in Weimar. I checked for Maller in the mundane library's card index but found nothing.

I made a note of the case number, printed the description and showed it to Nightingale later that morning during practice. He translated the title as *On the Fundamentals that Underlie the Practice of Magic*.

"Show off," I said.

"I think you had better secure this," he said. "And see if you can track down where it came from."

"Is it something to do with Ettersberg?" I asked.

"Good Lord, no," he said. "Not everything German relates back to the Nazis."

"Is it a translation of the Principia Artis Magicae?" I asked.

"I can't tell without having a look."

"I'll get onto Arts and Antiques," I said.

"Later," said Nightingale. "After practice."

Arts and Antiques, definitely not known by the rest of the Met as the Arts and Crafts squad, occasionally recover an item so valuable that even the evidence storage locker in the middle of New Scotland Yard isn't secure enough. For those items they rent space at the auction house Christie's where they laugh at cat burglars, tweak the nose of international art thieves and have some of the most serious, and rumored to be illegal, security measures in the world. That's why the following morning I found myself down on King Street in St. James's where even a miserable icy rain couldn't wash away the smell of money.

Nor could a stick of incendiary bombs, back in April 1941, when it destroyed everything except the façade of number 8 King Street, the London home of Christie's since 1823. They rebuilt in the 1950s, which was why the foyer was disappointingly shapeless and low ceilinged, albeit in an expensive air-conditioned and marble-floored way.

The Folly doesn't generate the gigabytes of paperwork that the rest of the Met does but what we do produce tends to be a bit too esoteric to be outsourced to an IT company in Inverness. Instead, we have one elderly guy in a basement in Oxford, although admittedly the basement's under the Bodleian library and the guy is a Doctor of Philosophy and a Fellow of the Royal Society.

I found Professor Harold Postmartin D.Phil. F.R.S. B.Mon hunched over the book in a viewing room upstairs. Designed, I learnt later, to be deliberately neutral and not distract from whatever it was you were supposed to be viewing, the room was all beige carpet, white walls and aluminum and black canvas faux Bauhaus chairs. Postmartin was examining his prize on an unornamented lectern. He was wearing white gloves and using a plastic spatula to turn the pages.

"Peter," he said when I entered. "You have surpassed yourself this time. Truly surpassed yourself."

"Is it kosher?" I asked.

"I should say so," said Postmartin. "A proper German grimoire. I haven't seen one of these since 1991."

"I thought it might be a copy of the Principia."

Postmartin glanced at me over the top of his reading glasses and grinned. "It's certainly based on Newtonian principles but I think it's more than a copy. My German is somewhat rusty but I believe I'm right in saying that it looks like it came out of the *Weiße Bibliothek* in Cologne."

My German's worse than my Latin, but even I thought I could translate that.

"White Library?" I asked.

"Also known as the *Bibliotheca Alba* and the center of German magical practice until 1798 when the French, who owned that bit of Germany at the time, shut down the university."

"The French didn't like magic, then?"

"Hardly," said Postmartin. "They shut down all the universities. It was one of the unfortunate side effects of the French Revolution."

Details of what happened to the contents of the library next were sketchy but, according to Postmartin's records, the entire *Weiße Bibliothek* had been smuggled out of Cologne to Weimar.

"Where, buoyed no doubt by the rising tide of German nationalism," said Postmartin, "it became the *Deutsche Akademie der Höhere Einsichten zu Weimar* or the *Weimarer Akademie der Höhere Einsichten* for short."

"Because that is much shorter," I said.

"The Weimar Academy of Higher Insights," said Postmartin.

"Higher insights?" I asked.

"*Höhere Einsichten* can translate as either that or 'higher understanding,'" said Postmartin. "As both in fact. German really is a splendid language for discussing the esoteric."

It wasn't quite the German version of the Folly. "Far more rigorous, much less smug," said Postmartin who believed that the *Akademie* had probably been in advance of the Folly for much of the nineteenth century.

"Although one likes to think it was neck and neck by the 1920s," said Postmartin. In the 1930s it was swallowed up by Himmler's *Ahnenerbe*, an organization dedicated to providing both an intellectual framework for Nazism and Indiana Jones with an endless supply of disposable bad guys.

And round we come to Ettersberg once more, I thought. And whatever it was Nightingale and his doomed chums had been doing there in 1945.

I asked whether the Germans had a modern equivalent of the Folly.

"There's a branch of the *Bundeskriminalamt*—that's the Federal Police Force—based in Meckenheim called the *Abteilung KDA* which stands for *Komplexe und Diffuse Angelegenheiten* which translates as the Department for Complex and Unspecific Matters."

Leaving aside the wonderful name, the Federal Government maintained a most un-German vagueness about what the department's responsibilities are. "A stance uncannily similar to that taken by their counterparts in Whitehall with regards to the Folly," said Postmartin. "That in itself is quite distinctive, really."

"I supposed it never occurred to you to just phone them up and ask," I said.

"That's an operational matter, so nothing to do with me I'm afraid," said Postmartin. "And besides we didn't think it was necessary."

It had been an article of faith among the post-war survivors of British wizardry that the magic was going out of the world. You don't need to establish bilateral links with sister organizations if your raison d'être was melting away like the arctic icepack.

"And besides, Peter," said Postmartin, "if this book did come from the White Library then there's a good chance the Germans may want it back and I for one have no intention of letting it out of my grasp." He laid his white gloved hand gently on the cover as emphasis. "However did Arts and Antiques come by it in the first place?"

"It was handed in by a reputable bookseller," I said.

"How reputable?"

"Obviously," I said, "reputable enough. Colin and Leech in Cecil Court."

"The thief must have been blissfully unaware of what he had," said Postmartin. "That's like trying to *flog*," he rolled the word around, obviously enjoying the sound of it, "a Picasso down the Portobello. How did they wrest the book from him?"

I told him that I didn't know the details and that I was following that up as soon we were finished.

"Why hasn't that been done already?" asked Postmartin. "Leaving aside its more esoteric qualities, this is still a very valuable item. Surely an investigation has already begun?"

"The book hasn't been reported stolen," I said. "As far as Arts and Antiques are concerned, there's no crime to investigate." And what with the Met currently being seriously mullered by spending cuts, nobody was in a hurry to find an excuse for more work.

"Curious," said Postmartin. "Perhaps the owner doesn't realize it's been stolen."

"Perhaps the owner is the guy who tried to sell it," I said. "He might want it back."

Postmartin gave me a horrified look. "Impossible," he said. "I have a security van coming to whisk this book and myself away to Oxford and safety. Besides, if he is the owner, he doesn't deserve what he's got. To each according to his abilities and all that."

"You've hired a security van?"

"For this?" said Postmartin, looking fondly at the book. "Of course. I even considered coming out with my revolver." He checked to make sure I was suitably horrified. "Don't worry. I was a crack shot in my day."

"What day was that?"

"Korea," he said. "National Service. I still have my service revolver."

"I thought the army had switched to the Browning by then," I said. Clearing out the Folly's arsenal the year before had been an education in twentieth-century anti-personnel weapons and just how many decades you could leave them to rust before they became dangerously unstable.

Postmartin shook his head. "My trusty Enfield Type Two."

"You didn't, though? Bring it."

"Not in the end. I couldn't find my spare ammo."

"Good."

"I searched high and low."

"That's a relief."

"I think I must have left it in the shed somewhere," said Postmartin.

Charing Cross Road was once the bookselling heart of London and disreputable enough to avoid the multinational chains in their unceasing quest to turn every street of every city into a clone of every other. Cecil Court was a pedestrianized alleyway that linked Charing Cross to St. Martin's Lane where, if you ignored the upmarket burger restaurant at one end and the Mexican franchise at the other, you could still see what it might have been like. Although, according to my old man, it's a lot cleaner than it once was.

Amidst the specialist bookshops and galleries was Colin and Leech, established 1897, current proprietor Gavin Headley. He turned out to be a short burly white man with the sort of smug Mediterranean tan that comes from having a second home somewhere sunny and sufficient Mediterranean genes to stop your skin going orange. The inside of the shop was warm enough to grow pomegranates, and smelled of new books.

"We specialize in signed first editions," said Headley and explained that authors were persuaded to "sign and line" their freshly published books—"They write a line from their book at the top of the title page," he said— and his customers would then buy these and lay them down like a fine wine.

The shop was tall, narrow and lined with modern hardbacks on expensively varnished hardwood shelves.

"As an investment?" I asked. It seemed a bit dodgy to me.

Headley found that funny. "You're not going to get rich investing in new hardbacks," he said. "Your kids maybe, but not you."

"How do you make your money?"

"We're a bookshop," said Headley, shrugging. "We sell books."

Postmartin had been right. The thief would have to have been unbelievably stupid to try and sell a properly valuable antique on Cecil Court, particularly in Colin and Leech. Headley hadn't been impressed.

"He had it wrapped up in a bin-bag for one thing," he said. "As soon as he unwrapped it, I thought 'fuck me.' I mean, I may only be at the contemporary end of the market but I know the real thing when it's plonked down in front of me. 'Do you think it's valuable?' he asks. Is it valuable? How could he be kosher and not know? Okay, I suppose he could have found it in his granddad's attic but is that likely when it was in such good nick?"

I agreed that this was a low probability scenario and asked how he'd managed to separate the book from the gentleman in question.

"Told him I wanted to keep it overnight, didn't I? So that I could get someone in to make an accurate valuation."

"And he fell for that?"

Headley shrugged. "I offered him a receipt and asked for his contact details but he told me he'd just remembered that he was parked on a double yellow and he'd be right back."

And off he went, leaving the book behind.

"I reckon he must have realized he'd fucked up," said Headley. "And panicked."

I asked if he could give me a description.

"I can do better than that," he said and held up a USB. "I saved the footage."

The problem with the so-called bloody surveillance state is that it's hard work trying to track someone's movements using CCTV—especially if they're on foot. Part of the problem is that the cameras all belong to different people for different reasons. Westminster Council has a network for traffic violations, the Oxford Street Trading Association has a huge network aimed at shoplifters and pickpockets, individual shops have their own systems, as do pubs, clubs and buses. When you walk around London it is important to remember that Big Brother may be watching you, or he could be having a piss, or reading the paper or helping redirect traffic around a car accident or maybe he's just forgotten to turn the bloody thing on.

In a proper major investigation team there's a DC or DS whose job it is to arrive at the crime scene, locate all the potential cameras, gather up all the footage and then scan through however many thousands of hours there is, looking for anything relevant. He or she has a team of as many as six detectives to help with the job—muggins of course had himself, Toby and the dogged determination to see justice done.

The book had been turned over to Arts and Antiques in late January and most private premises keep less than forty-eight hours' worth of footage but I managed to scrape some up from the traffic camera and a pub which had recently installed their system and hadn't yet figured out how to delete the old stuff. In the old days, when a gigabyte was a lot of memory, I would have been lumbered with a big bag full of VHS tapes but now it all ended up fitting on the USB that Headley had provided.

Counting a stop for refs at Gaby's, salt beef and pickle, it took me a good three hours and I didn't get back to the Folly until late afternoon. I wanted to head straight for the tech cave to check the footage but Nightingale insisted that both me and Lesley practice knocking a tennis ball back and forth across the atrium using only *impello*. Nightingale claimed it had been a popular rainy day sport back when he was at school and called it Indoor Tennis. Me and Lesley, much to his annoyance, called it Pocket Quidditch.

The rules were simple and about what you'd expect

from a bunch of adolescents in an aggressively all-male environment. The players stood at either end of the atrium and had to stay within a two-meter-wide chalk circle drawn on the floor. The referee, in this case Nightingale, introduced a tennis ball at the mid-point of the pitch and the players attempted to use *impello* and any other related spells to propel the ball at their opponent. Points were scored for strikes to the body between neck and waist and lost for losing control of the ball in your half of the court. As soon as he got wind of the sport, Dr. Walid had insisted that we wear cricket helmets and face guards when we played.

Nightingale grumbled that in his day they would never have dreamed of wearing protection—not even in the sixth form when they'd played with cricket balls— and besides it reduced the player's incentive to maintain good form and not be struck in the first place. Lesley, who never liked wearing a helmet, objected right up to the point where she found she could get an amusing *boing* sound by bouncing the ball off mine. I'd have been more irritated except, 1) helmet, 2) Lesley would pass up easy body shots to go for my head, which made it easier to win.

Back in the day at Casterbrook the boys had placed bets on the game. They had wagered fag-days, fagging being when a younger boy acted as a servant for an older one, which tells you just about everything you need to know about posh schools. Me and Lesley, both being aspirational working class, staked rounds at the pub instead. The fact that I had a seven month head start as an apprentice on Lesley probably being the only reason she ever had to pay for her own drinks.

In the end it was a draw with one body strike to me, one *boing* to Lesley and a disqualified point caused by Toby jumping up and catching the ball in midair. We broke for what me and Lesley called dinner, Nightingale called supper and Molly, we'd begun to suspect, thought of as field trials for her culinary experimentation.

"This potato tastes a bit different," said Lesley poking at the neat conical pile of mash that balanced one side of the plate against what Nightingale had identified as seared tuna steak.

"That's because it's yam," said Nightingale — surprising me. It's not like yam is big on the traditional English menu. Although if it had been, they probably *would* have mashed it and then covered it in onion gravy. My mum boils it like cassava, slices it up with butter and a soup spicy enough to cauterize the end of your tongue.

I looked over at Molly, who watched over us as we ate, and she lifted her chin and met my gaze.

"It's very nice," I said.

We heard a distant ringing noise that confused everyone until we recognized the Folly's front door bell. We all exchanged looks until it was established that since I wasn't intrinsically supernatural, a chief inspector or required to put on a mask before meeting the public I was nominated door opener in chief.

It turned out to be a cycle courier who handed over a package in exchange for my signature. It was an A4 envelope stiffened with cardboard and addressed to Thomas Nightingale Esq.

Nightingale used a serrated steak knife to open the envelope at the wrong end, the better, he explained, to avoid unpleasant surprises and extracted a sheet of expensive paper. He showed it to me and Lesley — it was handwritten and in Latin. Nightingale translated.

"'The Lord and Lady of the River do give you notice that they will be holding their Spring Court together at the Garden of Bernadette of Spain,'" he paused and re-

read the last bit. " 'Bernie Spain's Garden and that you are hereby charged as if by ancient custom to secure and police the fair against all enemies.' And it's sealed with the Hanged Man of Tyburn and the Waterwheel of Oxley plus signatures."

He showed us the seals.

"Somebody's been watching way too much *Game of Thrones*," said Lesley. "And what is the Spring Court?"

Nightingale explained that it had once been traditional for the Old Man of the Thames to hold a Spring Court upriver, usually near Lechlade, where his subjects could come and pay their respects. It generally occurred at or around the spring equinox but there hadn't been a formal court since the Old Man abandoned the tideway in the 1850s.

"Nor, if I remember history correctly, did the Folly play a role," said Nightingale. "Except to send an envoy and our respects."

"I notice it says 'as if by ancient custom,'" I said.

"Yes," said Nightingale. "I imagine both Tyburn and Oxley enjoyed the ambiguity of that statement."

"Perhaps they're not taking it very seriously," I said.

"If only that were true," said Nightingale.

After supper I headed for the tech cave for a beer and to see what I could find on cable. I thought Lesley might join me, but she said she was knackered and going to bed. I pulled a Red Stripe from the fridge and futilely flicked through the channels for five minutes before deciding I might as well process that afternoon's CCTV footage.

I started with the stuff from the shop. Judging from the angle, the camera was mounted above the counter looking down the long narrow shop to the front door. I cued up and ran it from the moment our man stepped inside, clutching his black bag of swag, and briskly approached the counter.

He was white, pale faced, thin nosed, in his mid-forties I guessed, dark hair going gray, bags under dark blue eyes. He was dressed in a tan zip-up jacket over a light-colored shirt and khaki chinos.

I watched the transaction going the way Headley had described, and the moment when the thief realized he'd made a mistake was well obvious. He glanced involuntarily up at the CCTV camera, realized what he'd done and was out the door less than a minute later.

Thirty-six seconds precisely in fact—by the time-code in the corner of the screen.

The CCTV from the shop was the latest kit. I rolled it back and got a capture of his face when he looked at the camera. It blew up nicely just using Paint Shop Pro—I printed a couple of copies for use later. Despite the poor angle I was pretty sure that the book thief turned right when he exited the shop—going toward St. Martin's Lane—but just to be on the safe side I checked the footage I had from the Barclays' branch on Charing Cross Road. Banks in central London have top of the line CCTV and one of the branch's fifteen cameras just clipped the entrance to Cecil Court. I scanned twenty minutes either side of the time of his departure and confirmed that he definitely hadn't come out onto Charing Cross Road.

There had been a couple of good camera positions in Cecil Court itself, but the footage hadn't been kept. So the best I had for the St. Martin's Lane side was from the Angel and Crown who hadn't figured how to delete yet—thank god. Still, it was a low-spec system that recorded ten frames a second, and had more ghosting than a camera operating in daylight should have. Despite that, he was easy to spot, tan zip-up jumper and khaki slacks, emerging onto St. Martin's Lane, turning left and climbing into an off-white Mondeo estate—Mark 2 from what I could see.

This got my hopes up. If it was his own car, then it was just a simple matter of getting another IIP check which would include the DVLA database and I'd have his name, DOB and the registered address courtesy of the National Insurance Database. Proving that Big Brother does have his uses after all.

Shit—I couldn't see the index. Even when it pulled out, the Mondeo was at too oblique an angle, and the image too low quality for me to identify the number plate. I ran it back and forth a couple of times but it didn't get any clearer. I was going to have to persuade Westminster Council to release some of their traffic cam footage and see if I could pick up the Mondeo when it turned into Charing Cross Road.

And I wasn't going to get that this side of six o'clock, because another problem with the so-called surveillance state is that it mostly works office hours.

I had another Red Stripe and went to bed.

After breakfast and Toby walking duty it was back to the tech cave and my continuing search for a clear shot of the book thief's car number plate. I was just about to take a deep breath and start wading through the swampy hinterland of Westminster Council's bureaucratic interface when it suddenly occurred to me to that I'd overlooked an easier option. Pulling up the footage from St. Martin's Lane, I clicked it back to watch the Mondeo being parked in the first place. My book thief wasn't a brilliant parker and the second time he adjusted his angle I got a good view of his plate.

One IIP query later and I had his name—Patrick Mulkern. His face matched the CCTV and his police record matched the profile of a professional safe-cracker. A good and careful one too, judging by the lack of convictions in the later half his career. Tons of interest, as in "person of interest" and a few arrests, but no convictions.

According to the appended intelligence notes Mulkern was a specialist hired by individuals or crews to crack any troublesome safes they might come across in the course their work. He even had a legitimate locksmith business, Bromley address I noted, which made doing him for "going equipped" a bit tricky since he used the same tools for both jobs. The notes also suggested that he'd recently "retired" from safecracking if not from the locksmithing.

His last known home address matched both the one on his driving license and his registered business address—I decided to give him a tug.

5

The Locksmith

IT WAS RAINING again and it took me about as long to drive across the river and down to the London Borough of Bromley as it had taken me to drive to Brighton the month before. A big chunk of the time was spent negotiating the Elephant and Castle traffic system and crawling down the Old Kent Road.

Once you're south of Grove Park the Victorian bones of the city dwindle and you find yourself in the low-rise mock-Tudor land of London's last big suburban expansion. Places like Bromley are not what people like me and my dad think of as London but the outer boroughs are like in-laws—like it or not, you're stuck with them.

Patrick Mulkern's address was a weird mutant hybrid that looked like the developer had got bored of building mock-Tudor semis and had rammed two together to create a mini-terrace of four houses. Like most of the homes on the street, its generous front garden had been paved over to provide more parking space and an increased flood risk.

An off-white Ford Mondeo was parked outside, glistening in the rain, I checked the index—it matched the ones from the CCTV. Not only was it a Mark 2 but it had the wimpy 1.6 Zetec engine as well. Whatever the wages of crime were Mulkern certainly wasn't spending it on his wheels.

I sat outside with the engine off for five minutes and watched the house. It was a gloomy day but there were no lights visible through the windows and nobody twitched the net curtains to check me out. I stepped out of the car and walked as fast as I could into the porch shelter. At some point the house had acquired a thick coating of a vicious flint pebble dash that almost had the skin off my palm when I rested my hand on it.

I rang the doorbell and waited.

Through the frosted panes either side of the door I could see a spray of rectangular white and brown smudges on the hallway floor—neglected post. Two, maybe three days' worth judging by the amount. I rang and kept my finger on the bell way beyond polite but still nothing.

I considered going back to my car and waiting. I had my *Georgics* by Virgil to plow through and a restocked stake-out bag that I was fairly certain didn't contain any of Molly's scary culinary surprises, but as I turned away my fingertips brushed the lock and I felt something.

Nightingale once described *vestigia* to me as being like the afterimage left on your eyes in the wake of a bright light. What I got off the lock was like the aftermath of a photoflash. And embedded in it, something hard and sharp and dangerous like the strop of a razor on a whetstone.

Nightingale, by virtue of his vast experience, claims to be able to identify the caster of an individual spell by their *signare*—that's signature in proper English. I'd thought he was having me on, but just recently I'd started to think I could sense his. And the *signare* off the door zapped me back to a Soho roof top and a fucker with a posh accent, no face and a keen non-academic interest in criminal sociopathy.

I checked the living-room windows—nobody was there. Ghostly, through the net curtains, the looming furniture was old-fashioned but neatly kept and the TV looked twenty years old.

What with the book not being actually reported stolen, I wasn't going to get a search warrant. If I broke in I'd have to rely on good old Section 17(1)(e) of the Police And Criminal Evidence Act (1984) which clearly states that an officer may enter a premises in order to save "life and limb" which doesn't even really require you to hear anything suspicious. This is because not even the most hardened member of Liberty wants the police to be dithering around outside their door while they're being strangled inside.

And if I broke in and the Faceless Man was still in there?

I'm not as practiced as Nightingale, but I was almost totally sure that the *vestigia* on the lock had been laid down more than twenty-four hours earlier and that the Faceless Man was long gone.

Almost totally sure.

I'd only survived our last encounter because he'd underestimated me and the cavalry had turned up in the nick of time. I didn't think he would underestimate me again and the cavalry was currently the other side of the river.

Not that a Sprinter van full of TSG would make much difference. Nightingale had been certain that only he could take the Faceless Man in a fair fight. "Not that I have any intention of offering him such a thing," Nightingale had said.

But I couldn't wheel out Nightingale every time I wanted to enter a suspect house, otherwise what was the point of me? And I couldn't hang around outside until one of the neighbors got suspicious enough to dial 999.

So I decided to make a forced entry. But just to be on the safe side I'd phone Lesley to let her know where I was and what I was doing.

This is what we in the job call "making a risk assessment."

Her phone went straight to voicemail so I left a message. Then I turned off my phone, checked no one was watching, and blew the Chubb out of the door with a fireball. Nightingale's got a spell that pops out a lock much neater, but I have to go with what I've got.

I waited for a moment in the doorway—listening.

Ahead of me stairs went up, to the right open doors led to the living room, another door at the rear of the house and beyond the bead curtain at the far end, I assumed, the kitchen.

"Police," I shouted. "Is anyone in the house?"

I waited again. When you go in mob-handed you go in fast to overwhelm any resistance before it can get started. When you go in alone, you go slowly with one eye on your line of retreat.

Another *vestigium*—a burned meat, rusty barbecue smell overlaid with another whetstone scrape of the blade and a flash of heat.

Much as I wanted to, I couldn't hang about in the doorway all day. I darted across the hall and checked that the living room was clear. Then, going as quietly as I could, I slipped back out and into the back room.

What had obviously once been a dining room had been transformed into a de facto workroom. There was an antique drop-leaf table that had been colonized by a key-cutting machine and boxes of blanks and French windows that looked out over a patio and sodden strip of lawn. An old-fashioned mahogany sideboard with a framed imitation Stubbs hung above it—horses in a brittle eighteenth-century landscape.

The room had the scent of metal dust but I couldn't tell if that was *vestigia* or the aftermath of key-cutting. The silent hallway behind me was making me nervous so I moved on quickly to the kitchen.

Clean, old-fashioned, a couple of mugs and a single blue china plate on the yellow plastic drying rack.

The burned-meat smell was less evident here and when I checked the cupboards and the upright fridge they were well stocked but nothing had spoiled.

I was getting a feel for the house. A single man rattling around in a family-sized home—his parents'? Or was there an estranged wife and kids? My mum, had this been her house, would have filled it with relatives or rented out the rooms or probably both.

I went back out into the hall and stood at the bottom of the stairs.

The rusty barbecue smell was stronger and I realized that it wasn't a *vestigium* at all—it was a real smell.

"Mr. Mulkern," I called because at some distant point in the future a defense barrister might ask me if I had. "This is the police. Do you need assistance?"

God, I hoped he was out visiting his sick mother or down the shops or getting a curry.

At the top of the stairs I could see the top of a half-open door that, barring a radical departure from typical design, would lead to the bathroom.

I put my foot on the stairs and flicked out my extendable baton to its full length. It's not that I don't trust my abilities, particularly with *impello*, but nothing says *long arm of the law* like a spring-loaded baton.

I went up the stairs slowly and as I did the smell got worse, the coppery overtones mingling with something like burned liver. I had a horrible feeling I knew what the smell was.

I was halfway up the flight when I saw him, lying on his back inside the bathroom. His feet were pointed at me, black leather shoes, good quality but worn at the heels. They were turned outward at the ankle in a way that's very hard to maintain unless you're a professional dancer.

As I climbed the final stairs I saw that he was staring straight up. What bare skin showed on his face, neck and hands was a horrible pinkish brown like well cooked pork. His mouth was wide open and stained a sooty black and his eyes were a nasty boiled white. Even this close up, though, the stench remained just bearable—he must have been dead for a while. Days, maybe. I didn't try to check his pulse.

A well trained copper is required to do two things when he finds a body, call it in and secure the scene.

I did both of those while standing outside in the rain.

Murder is a big deal in the Met. Which means that murder investigations are really fucking expensive, so you don't want to be launching into one and then find that the victim was merely pissed out of their box and having a lie down. That actually happened once, although truth be told the guy was in a coma from alcohol poisoning—but it wasn't a murder, that's my point. To prevent the Murder Investigation Teams' senior officers being dragged away from their all-important paperwork, London is patrolled by HAT cars, Homicide Assessment Teams, ready to swoop down to make sure that any dead people are worth the time and money.

They must have been close because the team pulled up less than five minutes later—in, of all things, a brick red Skoda that must have been painful to sit in the back of.

The DI in charge of the car was a rotund Sikh with a Brummie accent and a neat beard that was going prematurely gray. He went upstairs but came down less than five minutes later.

"They don't get much deader than that," he said and sent the DCs away to tape off the scene and prep for house to house. Then he spent a long time on his phone, reporting back I guessed, before beckoning me over.

"Are you really with SCD 9?" he asked.

"Yeah," I said. "But we're supposed to be called the SAU now—Special Assessment Unit."

"Since when?" asked the DI.

"Since November," I said.

"But you're still the occult division, though?"

"That's us," I said although "occult division" was a new one on me.

The DI relayed this down his phone, listened, gave me a funny look and then hung up.

"You're to stay here," he said. "My governor wants a word with you."

So I waited in the porch and wrote up my notes. I have two sets, the ones that go in my Moleskine and the slightly edited ones that go into my official Met issue book. This is very bad procedure, but sanctioned because there are some things the Met doesn't want to know about officially. In case it might upset them.

DCI Maureen Duffy, as I learned she was called, pulled up in a Mercedes E-class soft top convertible which seemed a bit male menopause for the slender white woman in the black gabardine trench coat who got out. She had a pale narrow face, a long nose and what I thought was a Glasgow accent but learned later was from Fife. She spotted me in the doorway but before I could speak she held up her hand to silence me.

"In a minute," she said and went inside.

While I waited to become a priority I called Lesley for the second time and got her voicemail again. I didn't bother calling Nightingale on the mobile I'd got him for Christmas because he only turns it on when he wants to call someone—the new technology being strictly there for his convenience, not anybody else's.

Forensics had now arrived and the house to house team were already knocking on doors by the time I was summoned back upstairs.

DCI Duffy met me at the top of the stairs, high enough up to view the body but far enough down not to get in the way of a couple of forensic types in blue paper suits who were working the scene.

"Do you know what killed him?" she asked.

"No, ma'am," I said.

"But in your opinion the cause of death is something 'unusual'?"

I looked at Patrick Mulkern's boiled lobster face, considered saying something flippant, but decided against it.

"Yes, ma'am," I said. "Definitely unusual."

Duffy nodded. I'd obviously passed the all-important keeping your gob shut test.

"I've heard you have a specialist pathologist for these cases," she said.

"Yes, ma'am," I said.

"You'd better let him know we have work for him then," she said. "And I'd like your boss to be there as well."

"He's a bit busy."

"Don't take this the wrong way, Peter, but I'm not interesting in talking to the monkey—just the organ grinder."

But I did take it the wrong way, although I was careful not to show it.

"Can I have a look through his stuff downstairs?" I asked.

Duffy gave me a hard look. "Why?"

"Just to see if there's anything . . . odd," I said and Duffy frowned. "My governor will want it done before he gets here."

"Is that so?"

"Yes, ma'am," I said.

"Fine," she said. "But you keep your hands to yourself and anything you find comes to me first."

"Yes, ma'am," I said meekly and headed downstairs to call Dr. Walid who unlike some others I could mention picked up his phone on the first ring. He was suitably pleased to have a new body to examine and promised to be down as soon as he could. I left another message on Lesley's voicemail, stuck my hands in my pockets and got down to work.

My dad reckons he can tell one trumpeter from another after listening to three notes and I'm not talking about just differentiating your Dizzy Gillespie from your Louis Armstrong. He can tell early Freddie Hubbard from late Clifford Brown. And that ain't easy, I can tell you. My dad can do this not just because he's spent years listening to these guys solo, but because he makes it his business to know the difference.

Most people don't see half of what's in front of them. Your visual cortex does a shit load of imaging processing before the signal even gets to your brain, whose priorities are still checking the ancestral savannah for dangerous predators, edible berries and climbable trees. That's why a sudden cat in the night can make you jump and some people, when distracted, can walk right out in front of a bus. Your brain just isn't interested in those large moving chunks of metal or the static heaps of brightly colored stuff that piles up in drifts around us. Never mind all that, says your brain, it's those silent fur-covered merchants of death you've got to watch out for.

If you really want to see what's staring you in the face, if you want to be any kind of half-decent police officer, then you've got to make it your business to look at things properly. That's the only way you're going to spot it—the clue that's going to generate the next lead. Especially when you have no idea what the clue is going to be.

I figured that whatever it was this time, it was probably going to be located in the makeshift workshop stroke dining room. Still, I checked the front room and the kitchen first because there's nothing worse than finding out later that you walked right past a major lead. Or, and I'd only been on the job a week when it happened, a suspect.

Lesley got him—in case you're wondering.

Whatever else the lately dead Patrick Mulkern had been, he wasn't a slob. Both the kitchen and living room were tidy and had been cleaned to an adequate, if non-professional, standard. This meant that when I donned my gloves and pulled the sofa away from the wall I found an assortment of pens, bits of paper, fluff, a boiled sweet and thirty-six pence in change.

It was one of the bits of paper, but I didn't realize the significance of it until later.

The back room was the only part of the house that had any books, two stand-alone 1970s MFI bookshelves stuffed with what looked like technical manuals and trade magazines with names like the *Independent Locksmith Journal* and *The Locksmith*. Since joining the Folly I've had to study a lot of suspect bookshelves and the trick is not to glance. You methodically work your way along each shelf starting with the top one and working your way down. This netted two issues of *Loaded* magazine from 2010, an Argos Christmas catalogue, a paper-back copy of Tintin's *Destination Moon*, a folder full of invoices that dated back to the 1990s and a National Trust booklet on the wonders of West Hill House in Highgate. I left the booklet half off the shelf so it was easy to find again and popped back into the living room to check one of the scraps of paper again.

It was still there, an old-fashioned ADMIT ONE paper ticket of the kind that gets torn off the end of a roll by, say, volunteer guides at one of the smaller National Trust properties. A property like West Hill House in Highgate. I made notes but left the ticket where I found it. The Met gets pretty fundamentalist about chain of evidence in murder cases—not only does it help prevent any anomalies that might be exploited by a defense barrister, but it also removes any temptation to "improve" the case by the investigating officers. Or at least makes it much harder than it used to be.

I took the time to check the sideboards in the work room and, with permission from DCI Duffy, checked the upstairs rooms—just in case Peter Mulkern had been an enthusiastic visitor of National Trust homes and had a pile of guidebooks stashed by his bed. Nothing. Although I did note a copy of *Cloud Atlas* on the bedside table.

Once I was satisfied I wasn't going to make a fool of myself, I persuaded one of Duffy's mob to run an IIP search looking for crimes at National Trust properties in London. The response was pretty instantaneous—a break in at West Hill House Highgate—unusual because the custodians didn't know what was stolen. I was just noting down the crime number when Nightingale tooled up in the Jag. I went out to meet him and as we walked back to the house I filled him in as to how I got here.

He paused to examine the burned hole in the front door.

"Is this your handiwork, Peter?" he asked.

"Yes sir," I said.

"Well at least you didn't set the door on fire this time," he said. But his smile faded as he stepped into the hall. He sniffed and I saw a flicker of memory on his face — quickly repressed.

"I know that smell," he said and went up the stairs.

Negotiating the interface between the Folly and the rest of the police is always tricky, especially when it's the murder squad. You don't get to be a senior investigating officer unless you have a degree in skepticism, an MA in distrust and your CV lists suspicious bastard under your hobbies. Nightingale says that in the good old days, which for him is before the war, the Folly got immediate and unquestioning cooperation. No doubt with plenty of forelock tugging and doffing of trilby hats. Even post war he said there just weren't that many cases and the senior detectives back then were still much more relaxed about paperwork, procedures or, for that matter, evidence. But in modern times, where an SIO is expected to match up specific villains to specific crimes and faces an exterior case evaluation if they don't, you have to use a certain amount of tact and charm. A detective chief inspector is, by definition, more charming than a constable. Which is why Nightingale went up the stairs to talk to Duffy. He wasn't gone that long — I think it's the posh accent that does it.

I asked him if it was definitely one of ours.

"I've never seen anything quite like it," said Nightingale. "Judging from the smell I'd say he was cooked."

"Could you do that? I mean, do you know how?"

Nightingale glanced back up the stairs. "I could set you on fire," he said. "But in that case his clothes would have burned as well."

"Was it magic?"

"We won't know until Dr. Walid has had a chance to examine him," said Nightingale. "I didn't sense any *vestigia* on the body."

"How else could it have happened?" I asked.

Nightingale gave me a grim smile. "Peter," he said. "You of all people should know that it's dangerous to reason ahead of your evidence. You say you sensed a *vestigium* at the door?"

I described what I'd felt—the cutthroat razor terror of it.

"And you're sure you recognized it?"

"You're the expert," I said. "You tell me. Is that likely?"

"It's possible," said Nightingale. "I wouldn't have been able to tell at your stage of apprenticeship. But I was only twelve at the time and easily distracted."

"Easily distracted by what?"

"Peter!"

"Sorry," I said and told him about the break in at West Hill House in Highgate.

"A somewhat slender thread," said Nightingale.

"Yes," I said. "But what if I was to tell you that West Hill House was the home of Erik Stromberg the famous architect and German expatriate."

Nightingale's eyes narrowed. "You think the book might have belonged to Stromberg?"

"He got out before Hitler came to power," I said. "What if he brought some secrets with him? What if he was a member of the Weimar Academy?"

"London was full of expatriates in the run up to the war," said Nightingale. "German or otherwise. You'd be surprised how few of them turned out to be practitioners."

"That book had to come from somewhere," I said.

"True," said Nightingale. "But Whitehall had a bee in

its bonnet about German infiltration and hence much of our manpower was devoted to spotting them and rounding them up."

"They were interned?"

"They were given a choice," said Nightingale with a shrug. "They could join the war effort or be shipped over to Canada for the duration. A surprising number of them stayed. Most of the Jews and the Gypsies, of course."

"But you might have missed some?"

"It's possible—if they kept quiet."

"Perhaps that's where Mr. Nolfi's mother learnt her party tricks," I said. "She might have been an expatriate. I didn't think of asking in the hospital." Tracking down the exploding granddad's antecedents was yet another thing that was still sitting in the low priority things-to-be-done pile. It might have to be moved up.

"Indeed," said Nightingale. "I'd like you to have a look at the house."

"Today?"

"If possible," said Nightingale which meant, yes absolutely today. "I'll liaise with the Detective Chief Inspector and Dr. Walid, when he arrives. Once you've done that you and Lesley can join us for the post-mortem—which I suspect will be instructive."

"Oh joy," I said.

6

The International Style

I FELT A bit weird on my way north and had to pull over on the Old Kent Road and take a breather.

I sat in the car for a while listening to the rain dinging off the roof of the Asbo and glaring at the red metal doors of the fire station.

When you're a young copper, the old sweats like to scare you with the horrors of the Job. Eviscerated motorists, bloated floaters and little old ladies who had ended their days as a protein supplement for their house cats were common themes—and so was the smell of burned human flesh.

"You never get the stink out of your nostrils," the old sweats would say and then, without fail, go on to tell you that it was worse when you hadn't had your dinner. "Because then your mouth starts watering and then you remember what it is exactly that you're smelling."

As it happens I *was* feeling a bit hungry and the memory of the smell was definitely taking the edge off my appetite. Still, I don't work well on an empty stomach so I bailed at the Bricklayers Arms and found a place that sold industrial strength vegetable samosas—the kind that are spicy enough to anesthetize your sinuses—and had a couple of those. While I ate, I looked up the National Trust on my phone and spent a fun ten minutes bouncing around their switchboard—they wanted to be helpful but nobody was sure what do with a call from a random police officer. I told them I'd be up at West Hill House within the hour and left them to sort it out. When in doubt, make it somebody else's problem.

Mouth full of the last of my samosa, I pulled out into the wet traffic. As I stopped and started my way through the Elephant and Castle I realized that I was actually right next to one of Erik Stromberg's masterpieces—the Skygarden estate. A concrete spike which had dominated the area until they'd built the Strata building next door. They'd been going to tear Skygarden down in the 1980s , but it had been inexplicably listed. I'd read somewhere that Southwark Council were trying to get the decision reversed so they could finally blow the fucker up.

Skygarden had been famous for its resident pirate radio station, for being a no-go area where police only ever ventured mob-handed and qualifying as a top spot to commit suicide. It was the original sink estate back in the days before the media started slapping that label on any area with less than two artisanal cheese shops. There were all sorts of rumors about the architect—including one that he'd been driven mad by the guilt for what he'd created and thrown himself off the top. It was all bollocks, of course. Erik Stromberg had lived in luxury in a custom-built villa in the International Style at the top of Highgate Hill until the day he popped his clogs.

And at least, according to Google Earth, a kilometer from the nearest high-rise flats.

I went up the steep slope of Highgate West Hill with the houses peeking out from driveways and gated avenues and adding about a quarter of a million quid with every twenty meters of altitude. I turned right onto the summit of Highgate Hill, where most of the buildings dated back to the time when Highgate Village was a rural community that overlooked the stink and noise of London from a safe distance.

There was a terribly discreet National Trust logo marking the entrance to a drive and an open space beyond marked STRICTLY NO PARKING where I dumped the Asbo. I clambered out and got my first look at the house that Stromberg built.

It rose above the Georgian cottages like the flying bridge of the *SS Corbusier* and no doubt in bright Mediterranean sunlight the white stucco would have gleamed but in the cold rain it just looked dirty and gray. There were streaks of green discoloration fringing the top story—which is what you get when you do away with such bourgeois affectations as gargoyles, decorative cornices and overhanging eaves.

Like a good devotee of the International Style, Stromberg had probably wanted to raise the whole house on pillars, the better for us to appreciate its cubist simplicity. But land has never been that cheap in London, so he'd settled for lifting just the front third. The sheltered space was too shallow to make a useful garage and made me think of a bus shelter, but from the signs attached to the walls it was obvious the National Trust found it useful as a staging area for visiting parties.

Above the entrance was the compulsory Crittal-strip window so long and narrow that I almost expected a red light to start scanning from side to side while making a whumm, whumm noise.

I was met at the front door by a thin-faced white woman with short gray hair and half-moon glasses. She was dressed in shades of mauve in the tweedy hippy style adopted by many who sailed through the 1970s counter-culture on the back of an expensive education and a family place in the country. She hesitated when she saw me.

"PC Grant?" she asked.

I identified myself and showed her my warrant card—I find it reassures some people.

She smiled with relief and shook my hand.

"Margaret Shapiro," she said. "I'm the property manager for West Hill House. I understand that you're interested in our break-in."

I told her that I thought it might be connected to a related case.

"We recovered a book we think may have been stolen from this property," I said. "I understand your records of what were stolen are incomplete."

"Incomplete?" said Shapiro. "That's one way of putting it. You'd better come up and have a look."

She led me through the front door into a hallway with white plaster walls and a blond-wood floor. There were two doors to the left and right, both oddly smaller than standard—as if they'd shrunk in the wash.

"Servants' rooms," said Shapiro. "And what was supposed to be the main kitchen."

But post World War Two full employment had put an end to the service culture, and the Stromberg family then had to make do with a woman who came in and "did" for them three times a week. The servants' quarters were turned into flats and Mrs. Stromberg was forced to cook for herself.

Access to the main house was by a beautiful iron spiral staircase with mahogany steps.

"It is a bit narrow, isn't it?" said Shapiro who'd obviously led a tour or two in her time. "Stromberg found that in order to get much of his wife's furniture into the house he had to devise an ingenious pulley system on the first floor to hoist it up."

I certainly wouldn't want to maneuver a wardrobe up those stairs—not even flat packed.

Upstairs it was remarkably like stepping into a council flat, only bigger and more expensively furnished. The same low ceilings and rooms that were strangely proportioned—a dining room that was long and well lit but so narrow that there was barely enough room to put the uncomfortable looking Marcel Breuer chairs around the dining table, the tiny afterthought of a kitchen and the narrow beige colored hallways. Stromberg's office, I noticed, was a much better proportioned room. It had been preserved, Ms. Shapiro told me, just as Stromberg had left it the morning in 1981 when he went into hospital for a routine operation and never came back.

"Bowel cancer," she said. "Then complications, then pneumonia."

The wall behind the large teak desk was lined with plain metal bracket and pine bookshelves. On it were racked box files labeled RIBA, photograph albums bound in leatherette, stacked copies of *The Architectural Review* and a surprising number of what looked like textbooks on material science. Big fat A4 sized books with blue and purple covers and academic logos on their cracked spines. I pointed them out to Ms. Shapiro.

"He was known for his innovative use of materials," she said.

His enamelled steel and oak drawing table had sleek 1950s lines and was positioned to catch the light from the south-facing window. A picture on the wall above it caught my eye, a water color and pencil sketch of a nude black woman. The woman was depicted bent over, hands on knees, her heavy breasts hanging pendulously between her arms. The face was rough, outsized eyes and blubbery lips, and turned so she looked out of the picture. I thought it was a bit crude and sketchy to have pride of place opposite the desk.

"That's an original by Le Corbusier," said Mrs. Shapiro. "Of Josephine Baker—the famous dancer."

It didn't look much like Josephine Baker to me, not with those outsized cartoon lips, flat nose and elongated head. Well, it was a quick sketch and perhaps old Corbusier had been too busy staring at her breasts. The feet were nicely done though—properly proportioned and detailed—maybe he just hadn't been very good at faces.

"Is it valuable?" I asked.

"Worth about three thousand pounds," she said.

Next to the Josephine Baker was a picture I recognized, a framed architectural sketch of Bruno Taut's glass pavilion. Like all the other architects of his generation, Taut believed that you could morally uplift the masses through architecture. But unlike most of his contemporaries he didn't want to do that by sticking them in concrete blocks. Taut's big thing was glass, which he believed had spiritual qualities. He wanted to build *Stadtkronen*, literally "city crowns," secular cathedrals that would draw the spiritual energy of the city upward. His glass pavilion at the Cologne Exhibition in 1914 was an elongated dome constructed from glass panels with a step fountain inside—the Gherkin at St. Mary Axe is a scaled-up version, but stuffed with lots of offices. As a piece of architecture, it was as pretty and non-functional as an art nouveau bicycle and an odd picture for a committed brutalist like Stromberg to have on his wall.

"That's by Bruno Taut," said Ms. Shapiro. "A contemporary of Stromberg, bit of a rebel by all accounts. Can you tell which famous London building it influenced?"

"Is it valuable as well?" I asked.

"Definitely," she said, obviously disappointed that I didn't want to play. "Most of the works in here are original if minor pieces by some pretty famous names. The insurance estimate for the art alone is upward of two million pounds. Hence the expensive security system."

Even more expensive after the break-in, I thought. And yet none of the art was stolen. "If nothing was stolen," I asked, "how did you know there was a break-in?"

"Because we found a hole," she said with a note of triumph.

I actually knew all about the hole from the report, but it's always good to get a potential witness warmed up on something you can verify. That way you can tell how bad a liar they are. It's nothing personal, you understand— just good police work.

Ms. Shapiro gracefully dipped down and pulled back an ugly black and white striped rug to reveal where a neat rectangular section of the parquet floor had been recently replaced with a plain hardwood sheet. She hooked a finger through a ring handle at one end and lifted the board away to reveal the safe.

Custom built, possibly by Chubb in the 1950s, although the National Trust hadn't been able to verify the manufacturer yet.

"Which makes it an interesting item in its own right," said Ms. Shapiro. "We're thinking we may leave it uncovered so the public can see it."

Mulkern had left no tool marks on the casing so it either hadn't been locked—a possibility—or he'd cracked it the old-fashioned way.

"Do you reckon it was part of the original build?" I asked. The safe was shallow enough to fit into the concrete floor without protruding through the ceiling below but was definitely deep enough to hold *Die Praxis der Magie* plus a number of other books—maybe three or four more.

Ms. Shapiro shook her head. "That's an excellent question to which I wish I knew the answer."

I lowered myself onto the floor and stuck my face in the safe. It smelled of clean metal and what might have been old paper—there were no *vestigia* that I could detect. Nightingale had advised that the grimoire wouldn't have left a trace—"Books of magic," he'd said, "are not necessarily magical books." Still, I'd been hoping for a touch of the razor that I'd started associating with the Faceless Man.

But there was nothing. Mulkern, assuming it was him who broke into the villa, had either been working alone, or with hypothetical persons unknown who hadn't used magic. Apart from the barbecue down in Bromley we didn't have anything to link the Faceless Man to *Die Praxis der Magie* or the burglary. That's the trouble with evidence—either you've got it or you ain't.

In the report it mentioned the insurance company had found evidence that the door on the roof had been forced at some point in the recent past. I asked Ms. Shapiro about the lock and if she'd show me up to have a look.

"We don't know when that happened for sure," she said as she led me back to the spiral stairs. "Frankly, the insurance company were just trying to impress us with how keen they were."

"Did they put your premiums up?"

"What do you think?" she asked.

There was a poster-sized photograph of the Sky-garden Tower hanging on the second floor landing. It had been taken at night with the base lit by colored floodlights and the windows ablaze. I asked whether Stromberg had hung it there himself.

"No," said Ms. Shapiro. "But he regarded Skygarden as his best work, so we thought it would be appropriate to mark that. It was taken in 1969 just before the first tenants moved in."

Which explained why it didn't look like a sink estate—it looked like the future.

The one advantage of a flat roof is that you can walk around on it—structurally speaking it's just about the only advantage. Or, if you're a mad modernist architect, you can have a roof garden, far above all that messy natural dirt, where your plants can be contained in neat square tubs with sharp corners and nobody can steal your garden furniture.

The spiral staircase wound up to a glass-fronted stair enclosure. The insurance company report had stated that there were indications the door might have been forced from outside.

"Stromberg always left the key in the lock," said Ms. Shapiro. "So did we, but when the assessor tried to remove it from the lock they found it was stuck."

The key had partially fused with the lock mechanism. But whether that was due to external tampering or just old age, they couldn't determine.

"You changed the lock?" I asked.

"Of course not," she said. "We had it refurbished."

So it was worth a try, I thought, and bent down as if I was examining it.

I felt it for certain, although it was as faint a *vestigium* as I've ever sensed—the Faceless Man had used magic on the lock. But when exactly? And why? I asked if I could step outside.

"Help yourself," she said with a broad smile.

I found out why when I stepped out onto the roof garden and saw the view. It was stupendous. The sky was still gray overhead, but to the southwest a gap in the clouds framed the sun over the horizon so that sunlight lit the city below me.

Highgate Hill stands 130 meters above the London floodplain. Immediately below me the mansions of the Holy Lodge Estate, built to house the respectable spinsters left surplus by the First World War, marched down the south slope of the Hill. Beyond was the gray-green swamp of North London, scored by railway tracks which converged on the redbrick and iron piles of King's Cross and St. Pancras, and beyond them Holborn, the City, St. Paul's and the Shard—a sliver of silver and gold in the dying light of the sun.

A severely plain white enamelled garden table stood by the parapet and around it some equally severe folding chairs. I could imagine Herr Stromberg sitting up here drinking coffee, enjoying the view and thinking himself King of the City.

"It's a pity we can't keep the telescope up here any more," said Ms. Shapiro.

"Telescope?"

She showed me a photograph in the glossy guide to the villa, a color snap of Stromberg, a tall thin man in a loosely hanging red shirt and tan slacks, sitting just as I had imagined him. Only, as well as coffee, he had a brass-bound telescope mounted on a tripod at a convenient height for seated viewing.

"The assessor practically had a fit in front of me when I told him we normally left it out on fine days," said Ms. Shapiro. "We ended up taking it down and lending it to the Science Museum."

"I wonder what he was looking at?" I tapped the photo of Stromberg in the brochure.

"We wondered the exact the same thing," she said. "So, if you'd like to take a seat ..."

I sat in the folding chair and, having forgotten it had been raining earlier, I got a wet bum. Ms. Shapiro had me shift a little to the left, explaining that they'd used a number of photographs as a reference.

"He always pointed it roughly southeast," she said. "Toward Southwark or perhaps Biggin Hill beyond that. We certainly don't have any record of him using it to look at the stars."

"I wonder if you could do me an enormous favor?" I asked.

"If I can," said Ms. Shapiro.

"Have you got a list of all Stromberg's books?" I asked. "The ones he owned."

"I believe we compiled one just last month," she said. "For the insurance."

I figured they'd have had to.

"Could you run off a hardcopy for me?" I said. "I'd ask you to e-mail it to me, but this way I won't have to go back to the station first." I got up and gently hustled her toward the stairway.

"I don't see why not," she said. "Though I do wonder what you might need it for."

"I'd like to cross check it against a couple of Interpol lists," I lied. "See if there's any pattern."

As we reached the stairway I pretended to remember something and told Ms. Shapiro that I wanted to have a quick look around the roof perimeter.

"Possible point of access," I said.

Ms. Shapiro offered to wait but I told her that I would only take a couple of minutes and that I'd meet her downstairs in the office. She seemed reluctant to leave me on my own and I was grinding my teeth and trying not to push her down the stairs when she suddenly agreed and went.

I dashed back, sat back down on the wet seat, looked back out over London and took a deep breath.

You do magic by learning *formae* which are like shapes in your mind that have an effect on the physical universe. As you learn each one you associate it with a word, in Latin because that's what a scientific gentleman of Sir Isaac Newton's time would write his shit down in. You make it so that the word and the *forma* become one in your mind. The first one you learn is *Lux* which makes light. The second I learnt was *impello* which pushes things about. You make a spell—I still smile every time I say that word—by stringing the *formae* together in a sequence. A spell with one *forma* is a first-order spell, with two *formae* a second-order spell, with three a third-order spell—you get the idea. It's actually way more complicated than that, what with *formae inflectentes* and *adjectivia* and the dreaded *turpis vox*, but trust me, you don't want to get into that right now.

In January, Nightingale had taught me my first fourth-order spell, one created by Isaac Newton himself. He told me that he was only doing it because he'd already been forced to teach me an old-fashioned shield spell and two of the *formae* were the same. Now I ran through the components a few times and checked to make sure that Ms. Shapiro was safely gone before casting.

In the old days I expect it was all right to chant in Latin and wave your hands about but your modern, up-to-date, image-conscious magical practitioner likes to be a little bit more discreet. These days we mutter them under our breath which makes us look like nutters instead. Lesley wears a Bluetooth earpiece and pretends to be talking Italian, but Nightingale doesn't approve—it's a generational thing.

Newton's spell used the *aer forma* to grab hold of the air in front of your face and then craft it into two lenses that act like a telescope. The great man called it *telescopium*, which tells you everything you need to know about his approach to branding. Beyond the usual drawbacks—i.e., the risk of having your brain turn into a diseased cauliflower—if the lenses are the wrong shape you get a face full of rainbows. And if you're stupid enough to look at the sun you can make yourself permanently blind.

This may explain why Newton went on to invent the reflecting telescope for all his routine stargazing needs.

London jumped toward me, King's Cross, the green rectangle of Lincoln's Inn, the river and, beyond the river, the studied dullness of the King's Reach Tower and, beyond that, right in the center of my field of view— the grim brutalist finger of Skygarden Tower.

Had Stromberg been a practitioner as well as an architect? He'd called Skygarden Tower his greatest work . . .

Clouds covered the setting sun and the city dimmed to a dirty gray.

"When there's something weird in your neighborhood . . ." I said out loud.

When you get yourself killed in suspicious circumstances the law requires that a Home-Office-appointed pathologist cut you open and have a good rummage round inside to determine what did you in. It's the pathologist who decides where the post-mortem takes place and since DCI Duffy had foolishly agreed to have Dr. Walid do the job, she couldn't complain that he'd dragged her all the way across the river to Westminster Mortuary on Horseferry Road. But Duffy's loss was mine and Lesley's gain, as this was the famous Iain West Memorial Forensic Suite which boasted state of the art facilities, including a remote viewing suite. Here your sensible junior officers could drink coffee and watch the procedure via CCTV, while their elders and betters got up close and personal with the corpse. Also, unless said junior officers were stupid enough to flip the switch on their end of the intercom, their seniors couldn't hear them.

"Why the fuck would he do that?" asked Lesley once I'd told her my suspicion that Erik Stromberg had combined magic and architecture.

I told her that architects in those days truly believed they could make people better through architecture.

"Make people better what?"

"Better people," I said. "Better citizens."

"They didn't do a very good job did they?" said Lesley who, like me, had lived in her fair share of council housing growing up.

On the TV screen DCI Duffy, in green apron, face mask and eye protectors leaned over the body of Patrick Mulkern to look more closely at whatever grisly detail Dr. Walid thought was important.

"Burned from the inside out," said Duffy. Her voice sounded strangely nasal due, Lesley reckoned, to the sensible application of Vicks VapoRub underneath the nostrils. She turned to look off-screen. "Could you do that?"

Nightingale stepped into view of the camera.

"I can't answer that until we know what exactly was done," he sounded like he was avoiding breathing through his nose altogether. "But probably not."

"But you don't think it was natural?" asked Duffy.

"Duh," said Lesley.

We heard Dr. Walid say that he seriously doubted that it was natural. Duffy nodded. She seemed to accept things more easily from a fellow Scot than from Nightingale, so he was sensibly letting Dr. Walid do most of the talking.

"Keep an eye on the door," said Lesley and slipped her mask off.

There were fresh suture marks on her neck where they'd worked on her throat and the skin around them looked inflamed. She fetched out a small tub of ointment from her shoulder bag and started spreading it over her neck and jaw.

Her face was still a shock. I'd managed to teach myself not to flinch, but I was scared that I was never going to get used to it.

"Patrick Mulkern steals a magic book from the house of noted mad architect Erik Stromberg whose greatest work was Skygarden Towers in Southwark," I said. "In that very borough's planning department worked Richard Lewis. Have you watched Jaget's edited highlights yet?"

"He has way too much time on his hands," she said and rubbed cream into the twisted pink stub that was all that was left of her nose.

"So our planner, who suddenly jumps in front of a train for no reason, turns out to be on the Little Crocodile list," I said. "And then Patrick Mulkern turns up magically barbecued."

"You don't know it was magic," said Lesley and replaced her mask.

"Do me a favor," I said. "Magical, brutal and a really unpleasant way to die—that's the Faceless Man. It's practically his signature tune."

"It's not subtle," said Lesley. "Now that he knows we're after him, you'd think he'd be a bit more subtle."

"He built himself a man-tiger," I said. "How subtle do you think he is? Maybe he's not as smart as you reckon."

"That," said Lesley, "or he doesn't really rate us a threat."

"That's a mistake," I said. "Isn't it?"

Lesley glanced back at the screen where Dr. Walid was extracting a long blackened bone from Patrick Mulkern's thigh.

"You can see from the charring," he said, "that the bone itself seems to have caught fire."

"Oh yeah," said Lesley looking back at me. "He's making a big mistake."

7

Imperial Yellow

THERE'S A MANUAL the size of an old-fashioned telephone book about policing large public events, but Nightingale told me to put it away. He said that given the special nature of the participants, the fewer actual police on the ground the better.

"You don't need to concern yourself with breaches of the peace inside the bounds of the Court," said Nightingale.

"You don't think there's going to be any trouble, then?"

"Think of it as being like a football match," he said. "We only need to be concerned with the crowd, not the players. What happens on the pitch is not our concern." Which just went to show how long it was since Nightingale had policed a football match.

He did let me arrange for the TSG to be deployed in the area on standby even if he did balk at the chunk it took out of our operational budget.

"Why is it necessary to have three whole vans' worth?" he asked.

I explained that the TSG always deploys as a full serial and that's three carriers' worth. Anyway, that's the thing about the Territorial Support Group, you only really need them when the wheels come off. Which means you're going to want them in quantity or not at all—*and* you won't want to be waiting around for them to arrive, neither.

The TSG would need to be parked up nearby, as would a maddeningly vague number of trucks, caravans and, I suspected, funfair rides—preferably as far from the TSG as possible. Parking on the South Bank is a tangle of jurisdictions involving everyone from the Coin Street Community Builders to the GLA and the Borough of Southwark. Organizing it would be a bloody nightmare that I wouldn't dump on my worst enemy so, in the best traditions of policing, we passed the problem over to the Goddess of the River Tyburn.

She wasn't best pleased, but what could she say? As self-appointed fixer-in-chief for her mum, she had to prove her superiority.

"Leave it with me, Peter," she said when I called her. "And just let me say how much I'm looking forward to hearing your father's band."

"We knew you wouldn't mind," said my mum once I'd phoned her and waited the requisite hour and a half for her to finish chatting to whoever it was in Sierra Leone she was currently still talking to—and call me back. "And it was beaucoup money,"

What could I say? Of course it's beaucoup money. It's being paid for by the God and Goddess of the River Thames, no relation, who peddled influence and soft power the same way they breathed in and out and, presumably, regulated the waters of the river. And there was a good chance that they were just using Dad to get some traction on me.

"Fine," I said. "Just don't let Abigail know where you're going."

"Why do you not want Abigail to come?" asked my mum in a tone of voice I remembered from such conversations as *But I thought you didn't like that jacket* and *Well, I've paid the shipping costs already.* "I thought she was in your police club?"

I added *Warn Abigail to behave* to my to-do list. It was a long list.

One person I didn't have to worry about was Molly— who refused to leave the Folly.

"Why don't you join us?" Nightingale had asked her while she was busy brushing lint off the shoulders of his suit. "It would do you good to get out."

Molly froze and then skipped backward as if to make sure she was safely out of his grasp.

"You would be perfectly safe there," he said. "The Rivers have declared their *pax deorum* and no power on earth would be foolish enough to challenge them when they are all arrayed in their majesty on the banks of the Thames."

Molly hesitated then shook her head emphatically before vanishing off toward the back stairs. She stayed in hiding until after we'd left for the South Bank and we had to make our own coffee that morning.

"What's she so afraid of?" asked Lesley.

"I wish I knew," said Nightingale.

In 1666, following an unfortunate workplace accident, the city of London burned down. In the immediate aftermath John Evelyn, Christopher Wren and all the rest of the King's Men descended with cries of glee upon the ruined city. They had such high hopes, such plans to sweep away the twisted donkey tracks that constituted London's streets and replace them with boulevards and road grids as formal and as controlled as the garden of a country estate. The city would be made a fit place for the gentlemen of the enlightenment, those tradesmen they required to sustain them, and the servants needed to minister to them. Everybody else was expected to wander off and do whatever it is unwanted poor people were expected to do in the seventeenth century—die presumably.

But, alas, it was not to be. Because, before the ashes were cool, the inhabitants of the city moved back in and staked out the outlines of their old properties. London became a shadow city marked out in string, shanties and improvised fences. The buildings may have burned down, but the people had survived and they weren't going to give up their rights without a fight. Or at the very least a hefty wodge of cash. Since Charles II, despite being the king of bling, was famously short of readies and already had a war going with the Dutch, London got rebuilt with its donkey tracks intact. And Wren had to be content with the odd church dotted around the place.

In the 1970s a group of developers had similar grandiose plans for the strip of the South Bank between the London Studios and the Oxo Tower. Although, unlike Wren and his merry band of wig-wearing social improvers, their plans were ambitious only in monetary terms. Architecturally, the best they could come up with was a couple of glass boxes plonked down among windy concrete squares. It was indistinguishable from hundreds of similar schemes that had been inflicted on the inhabitants of London since the end of the war. But this time the locals weren't having it, and you really haven't seen aggro until you piss off a working-class community in south London. They fought the plans for years until finally they wore down the developers through a combination of organized protest, savvy media skills and cockney rhyming slang. Thus was born the Coin Street Community Builders whose unofficial motto was *Build-*

ing houses that people might actually want to live in. It was revolutionary stuff.

Another radical notion was the idea that people who lived near the river might actually want to walk along the riverbank. So they threw in a rectangular park that ran from Stanford Street down to the Thames Path. It was in this park, named after local activist Bernie Spain, that the God and Goddess of the River Thames planned to hold their Spring Court.

"But why there?" asked Lesley.

Nightingale, even after an afternoon in the library, couldn't answer that.

We'd recruited some PCSOs from the local Safer Neighborhood Team and they were already closing off Upper Ground Street when we arrived late in the morning. It had been bucketing down the day before. But that had let up overnight, to give way to one of the luminous pearl-colored days which would be almost pretty, if the persistent drizzle wasn't leaking down the back of your collar. We'd considered wearing uniform but Lesley said, what with her mask and everything, she'd look like a plastic cop monster from *Doctor Who*. I managed to restrain myself from telling her their real name.

As the highest ranking non-plastic policeman, Nightingale went off to marshal the PCSOs and their handlers while me and Lesley dealt with the stallholders who were beginning to arrive along Upper Ground. Next to the park was Gabriel's Wharf, a sort of permanent retail fair with cafés, pizzerias and a couple of upmarket restaurants. Lesley handled that side while I made sure that the booths were being set up in the correctly allocated spaces—ticking them off on my slightly damp clipboard as I went.

I'd just worked my way down to the Thames Path when I spotted a white skinhead approaching with a heavy duty power tool slung over his shoulder. I walked briskly to intercept him but found, as I got closer, that it was only Uncle Bailiff—Mama Thames's odd job man, carrying an angle grinder.

"Wotcha," he said. He was stocky, middle aged, but as a solid as a block of stone. He wore a spider web tattoo on his neck and had, according to rumor, arrived at Mama Thames's house to collect an outstanding bank debt and never left. Lesley had gone so far as to run a missing persons check. But whoever he was before he was Mama Thames's, she could never discover.

"All right," I said and nodded at the angle grinder. "What's that for?"

"Access, isn't it?" he said. "For the grand debarkation."

Poking out into the river at that point was a wooden pier, a remnant of the time when this part of the South Bank still boasted warehouses and industry. It was solidly built so that even my size elevens didn't rattle the boards as I followed Uncle Bailiff along it toward the end. The tide was out and I glanced over the railing at the glistening mud. The year before I'd pulled myself ashore not fifty meters downstream. I noticed that a metal railing had been retrofitted onto the pier, presumably to stop tourists and small children from taking a dive. I also noticed that there were no gaps to allow passengers to board, or climb off, a boat.

"Hey," I said to Uncle Bailiff. "What do you mean 'access'?"

"Don't worry," he said, stooping to pull the start cord—the angle grinder growled into life. "It's only a little adjustment."

By late afternoon the tide turned. And with it came a river mist that rolled in from the east. The stalls were all in place, but still had their tarpaulins down while their owners stood around chatting and sharing roll-ups, or at least things I decided to classify as roll-ups for the duration. That's your famous "operational discretion" at work. The Showmen had arrived while Uncle Bailiff was *adjusting* the pier. The park wasn't suitable for a full funfair, so this was a just token presence—a single antique steam-powered carousel and the kind of booth that invites you to lose money three hoops at a time. These too were quiet and shuttered, their owners drinking coffee from cardboard cups, chatting and texting.

Lesley and me met with Nightingale by the stall we'd set up at the point where Upper Ground Street bisected the park, to serve as a command post and lost children collection spot. We even had a blue and white placard with the Metropolitan Police crest and *Working Together for a Safer London* printed underneath. Nearby I spotted some familiar faces setting up their instruments in the jazz tent. It was going to be a popular venue, I thought, if the weather didn't let us down. The drummer looked up and waved me over, he was a short Scottish stereotype called James Lochrane.

"Peter," he said and gripped my hand. "Your dad's waiting in the BFI café with your mum."

I shook hands with Max Harwood, the bassist, and Daniel Hossack who played guitar, the three of them plus my dad constituting the Lord Grant's Irregulars. My dad was making his glorious third, or was it fourth, attempt at a career as a jazzman. Daniel introduced me to a thin jittery young white guy in an expensive coat—Jon something I missed—whose day job was in publicity. I wondered if he was the band's latest attempt to recruit a brass section until James mouthed the word "boyfriend" behind Daniel's back and all was clear.

"Where's Abigail?" I asked.

"Behind you," said Abigail.

Through a series of irritating mistakes, mostly mine, I'd been forced to invent a junior cadet branch of the Folly, consisting only of one Abigail Kamara, in an effort to keep her out of trouble. Nightingale had been way more sanguine about the whole thing than I was expecting, which only served to make me suspicious. Given his attitude, I led Abigail over to our little police stall and made her his problem.

She was a skinny mixed-race kid who had a fine range of suspicious looks, one of which she was happy to turn on Nightingale.

"Are you going to do some magic?" she asked.

"That, young lady," he said, "depends entirely on how you deport yourself in the coming hours."

Abigail gave him the look, but only for a moment—just enough to make sure he knew that she wasn't intimidated.

"Fair enough," she said.

Through the mist the sun was a wavering disc kissing the shadowy arches of Waterloo Bridge. I noticed that a fair number of civilians, mostly tourists and workers from the nearby offices, were wandering among the darkened stalls. All part of our contingency planning, and not yet arriving in the quantities I was expecting. Lesley noted that many of them were staying in the area of Gabriel's Wharf where the cafés and shops were still open.

As the sun vanished, the mist grew thicker and I started to wonder when the showmen were going to turn on their lights.

"Do you think this is natural?" Lesley asked Nightingale.

"I doubt that." Nightingale checked his watch. "Both sunset and high tide are due at around six thirty—I expect our principals to arrive then."

So we sent Abigail off to get coffee and settled in to wait.

We heard them before we saw them. And we felt them before we heard them—as an anticipation, like waking up on your birthday, the smell of bacon sandwiches, breakfast coffee and that initial glorious deep-lunged drag on the first cigarette of the day—the last of these being how I knew this wasn't truly my feelings, but something external.

And then a real sound floated out of the dark. Big heavy marine diesels throttled up suddenly as the blunt prows of two large river cruisers emerged from the mist, one on either side of the pier. They touched the embankment simultaneously and stopped. Behind them the superstructures were darker shadows in the murk.

Then the God and Goddess of the River Thames made their presence known.

The force of them rolled in like a wave and a confusion of images and smells. Coal smoke and brick dust, cardamom and ginger, damp straw and warm hops, pub piano, wet cotton and sloe gin, tonic water and rose petals, sweat and blood. The waiting onlookers went down on their knees around us, the showmen slowly with respect, the tourists with looks of utter surprise. Even Abigail went down until she realized that Nightingale, Lesley and me were still standing. I watched her face set into an expression that is discussed in hushed tones wherever teachers and social workers gather together, and she struggled back to her feet. She glared at me as if it was my fault.

The diesel engines stopped and there was silence— not even Abigail spoke. No wonder the showmen were kneeling in respect. PT Barnum would have banged his head twice on the ground in admiration.

Lady Ty emerged from the mist first. By her side was a wiry man with a thin face and a shock of brown hair — Oxley, the Old Man of the River's cunning right hand.

They stopped at the point where the pier met the embankment and Oxley threw back his head and shouted something that sounded like Welsh but was probably much, much older.

"The Queen and King of the River stand at your gates," bellowed Lady Ty in her best *Dragon's Den* minion-cowing voice.

Oxley shouted, or chanted, it's hard to tell with these Celtic languages, another phrase and again Lady Ty translated.

"The Queen and King of the River stand at your gates — come forward to receive them."

I felt a warmth on the back of my neck like an unexpected sunbeam and turned to see a young girl of no more than nine, in an antique silk jacket of brilliant yellow — Imperial Yellow she proudly told me later, and genuine Chinese silk — hair twisted up into a fountain of silver and gold thread over a round brown face with a big mouth set in a Cheshire Cat grin.

She came skipping down the central path, bringing with her the warmth of the sun. The yellow silk glowed, driving back the mist and with her came the smell of salt and the crash of gunpowder and the crack of canvas under strain.

"Who's that?" whispered Lesley.

"Neckinger," said Nightingale.

And I thought of myself studying my *formae* and my Latin and Blackstone's guide to procedure ... and all the time there were powers like this young girl among us who could bring spring into the world just by her presence.

On the other hand, the effect was diluted a little bit by

the fact that I noticed she was wearing black cotton leggings and a pair of Kicker boots.

She danced up to Oxley and Lady Ty, spread her arms, and bowed deeply from the waist. Then she bobbed back up and fidgeted impatiently from foot to foot just like a normal child starring in her first nativity play.

"We welcome the King and Queen of the River," she declaimed, stepped between the two adults and, seizing their hands, pulled them onto the embankment. Even Lady Ty, who'd been going for po-faced dignity, had to smile.

"Peter, Lesley," whispered Nightingale urgently. "Check the perimeter. And take Abigail with you."

Nightingale had insisted on this perimeter sweep at the planning stage, but I found I was reluctant to miss the actual debarkation. Given that your actual gods were going to walk among us, it seemed disrespectful not to stay and pay our respects. And maybe do a bit of cheering and, you know, possibly a little bit of a genuflect, just to show willing . . .

"Perimeter sweep," said Nightingale in his best command voice. "All three of you, now!"

"I wanted to watch the show," hissed Abigail as we dragged her away, but there was a hint of fear behind her usual belligerence. I set a brisk pace toward the Oxo Tower on the basis that Nightingale was obviously worried, and anything that worried Nightingale wasn't something you wanted worrying you.

We'd gone about ten meters when there was a great roar behind us, like what you get when the home side scores in injury time and the fans all know that it's all over now. Light exploded through the mist at our backs and, although we probably shouldn't have, we all turned round to watch.

It looked like a late rock show or early Spielberg—

fingers of golden light spilling through the trees and the gaps between the stalls. A wash of exultation, another roar from the crowd and a crashing disappointment that we hadn't been there to see it. It was impossible to separate what was real from what was glamour. I heard a trumpet fanfare that would have reduced my dad to tears, and then saw white flashes and heard the whoosh-crack of antique flashbulbs. The crowd roared one last time and I could see from the shifting position of the lights that the procession had left the embankment and was heading into the park.

The gold gradually seeped out of the lights over the stalls until they were bog standard tungsten area lamps. Out to our left a diesel coughed into life, a woman laughed and a propane stove ignited. If I listened carefully I could once again hear the comforting thrum of traffic on the Blackfriars Road.

Lesley gave a little bark of a laugh.

"I'll never call anyone else emotionally manipulative again," she said. "That was world class."

"Ha," said Abigail. "That was nothing. You should meet my brother."

"Every time I think I know what I'm dealing with ..." I said.

"More fool you," said Lesley. "Come on, this perimeter's not going to check itself."

Since we were out there anyway, we took a couple of minutes to check that our three Sprinter vans' worth of up-for-anything riot gear and tasers on standby TSG officers were fed and watered. Because the only thing worse than putting up with a bored and testy bunch of TSG is finding they're all out looking for food when the wheels come off.

Stamford Street, which marked the southern end of our area of operations, was strangely hushed with the traffic closed down. The trucks of the stallholders and showmen were washed-out shapes in the mist. We checked that the PCSOs on road detail had had a smooth shift change and that the skipper in charge was happy.

"Easiest overtime I've ever had," said one of the PCSOs. He seemed strangely serene, in a way that I found vaguely disturbing.

The mist was noticeably thicker on the other side of the red brick wall that marked the end of the park. Looking through the entrance I could just make out a swirl of color that might have been the merry-go-round, and hear the muffled mechanical cheer of its organ.

I was just about to ask Lesley whether she thought we should go back in, when a white European family, obviously tourists by their matching blue Swiss Air backpacks, strolled past us and, before we could stop them, vanished inside the park.

"Shit," said Lesley in surprise. "We'd better get back in there before something weird happens to them."

"Might be a little bit too late for that," I said, but we followed them in all the same.

8

The Pissing Contest

BERNIE SPAIN PARK was neatly bisected by Upper Ground Road. South of this line the showmen had placed their carousel. The mist was thick enough that you practically had to be riding on the thing to make out the expressions on the faces of the horses. But the colored lights pulsed and illuminated the faces of the kids who waited their turn. I made a point of watching the ride for at least ten minutes, just to make sure nobody was aging backward.

Nearby was a stall where I bought a toffee apple for Abigail in the hope it might glue her teeth together for a while, and we worked our way through the narrow shadowy gaps between the stalls until we'd reached the jazz tent and the Metropolitan Police stall where Nightingale was waiting.

"So, what was all that?" asked Lesley.

"That was the joint Court of the Thames in session for the first time since 1857," said Nightingale. "I fear they may have got a touch carried away in their enthusiasm."

I looked over at the northern half of the park where

the court was arrayed. In the mist it was just shadows and lights and looked exactly the same as the southern end. But I could feel it calling to me. A nagging little temptation, like a bad habit on a long dull day. I looked back at Lesley, who winked when she saw me looking.

"We could rope ourselves together like mountaineers," she said.

The operational plan was that one of us would remain with Abigail at the police stall while the other two proceeded about the fair and, by dint of being clothed in the awesome majesty of the law, head off any high spirits before they got out of hand.

Me and Lesley decided to start with the jazz tent on the basis that, being jazzmen, the Irregulars might have some beer. And I had this theory that alcohol, being a depressant, might counteract all the glamour that was washing around us. And even if it didn't, it could still get you drunk. Lesley was skeptical, but seemed open to some practical experimentation in that area. When we ducked into the tent we found that it was already half full of punters and totally full of my mother.

In honor of the fact that my dad was playing she was wearing her upmarket beatnik outfit, all skinny jeans, black roll-neck jumper and silver bling—all now back in fashion among the cognoscenti, much like my dear old dad. No beret, I noticed. Some things that happened in the sixties stay in the sixties—even if in my mum's case most of them happened in the late seventies. When she saw me she bustled over and, after hugging me, greeted Lesley and asked how she was.

"Much better," said Lesley.

Mum gave a dubious look and turned to me for confirmation.

"*How e day do?*" she asked in Krio.

"*E betta small small,*" I told her.

Mum nodded and looked around. "*You girlfriend day cam?*" she asked.

It took me a moment to realize who she was talking about. Girlfriend? I'd never actually got that far with Beverley Brook before she'd moved upstream as part of a hostage swap. That had been my idea as part of, if I say so myself, a very clever way to stop the two halves of the River Thames going to war with each other. Beverley, for a lot of good reasons, had been an obvious choice for the swap although Lesley said it was down to my unconscious desire to head off a meaningful relationship before it could get started. Lesley says she could write a book about my relationship issues, only it would be long, dull and pretty similar to all the other books on the market.

"She's not my girlfriend," I said, but my mum ignored me.

"*Dis nah fambul business?*" she asked.

"Sort of the family business," I said.

"*Dem people den very strange and differend,*" she said. Lesley snorted.

"I've noticed that," I said.

"*But this one notto witch?*" asked my mum, who incidentally had attacked my last girlfriend for being same. "*E get fine training.*"

"How's Dad?" I asked. Always a reliable way to sidetrack my mum.

"*He day do fine. Den day ya he do a lot of wok.*"

So the Irregulars had told me, lots of gigs and rumors of an exclusive vinyl-only release carefully designed to appeal to fans of "proper" jazz—whatever that was these days.

She glanced back at where my dad, properly turned out in pressed chinos and a green v-neck cashmere jumper over a white cotton shirt with button-down collar, was having a technical discussion with the rest of the band. Lots of hand gestures as he indicated where he wanted the solos to come in during the set because, as my dad always says, while improvisation and spontaneity may be the hallmarks of great jazz, the hallmark of being a great player is ensuring the rest of the band is spontaneously improvising the way you want them to.

"*Are wan talk to you in private,*" said my mum.

"Now?"

"Now now."

I waved off Lesley and followed Mum out into the mist.

"*Are know you papa sabie play the piano,*" she said. "*But e good more with dee trumpet. En dee trumpet nah e make am famous.*"

Despite Mum's best efforts, heroin had done for my dad's teeth and so he "lost his lip," his embouchure if you're going to be posh about it, and unless you're Chet Baker that's pretty much all she wrote for a man with a horn.

"*If e bin day play the trumpet e bin for sell more records,*" said my mum in a wheedling tone of voice that suggested something expensive was about to happen to me.

"How much are you looking for?" I asked, because my mum will circle around a request like this for half an hour if you let her.

"*I don see one dentist way go fix you papa een teeth den,*" she said. "Four thousand pond."

"I haven't got that," I said.

"*Ah feel say you bin day save you money,*" said Mum.

I had been but I'd blown it all on an artic full of booze to propitiate a certain Goddess of the River Thames—one who even at that moment was holding court less than ten meters from where we were standing. Mum frowned at me.

"*Watin you spend you money par?*" she asked.

"You know, Mum," I said. "Wine, women and song."

She looked like she wanted to ask me exactly which women and what songs, but while I was never going to be too big to beat, I was no longer living at home so I couldn't be worn down.

"Well we go raise some of de money by selling de records but you go get for fend some of de money too," she said.

I almost asked whether she'd tried Kickstarter but knowing mum she probably would have. Instead, I made the usual squirmy excuses and promises of the fully grown man faced with his mum's uncanny ability to knock ten years off his age at will.

"I'll see what I can do," I said and we returned to the tent to find that Lesley had indeed acquired a pint of beer, in a straight glass no less, and was cheerfully drinking it with the straw she carries for just such emergencies.

"Where'd you get that?" I asked.

Lesley gave me a sly look. "I seem to remember you lecturing me about the scientific method," she said. "And for this experiment to be valid one of us has to stay off the booze—as a control. Right?"

I nodded sagely. "You're right," I said. "We need a control."

"Seriously?" she asked.

"Otherwise, how do you know the variable you've changed is the one having the effect?" I said.

Lesley retrieved another pint from the top of one of the amps behind her. "So you don't get this?"

"No, no," I said. "In fact you should drink both of them because we're going to need your blood alcohol levels to be sufficiently elevated if we're going to get a measurable result."

Lesley stared at me. Her mask is a horrible shade of off-pink that can be barely called skin toned even by white people's standards and it pretty much conceals Lesley's expressions. But I'd learnt to read the shape of her eyes and the way her jaw moves under the hypo-allergenic plastic. For just a moment she'd totally bought it. Then she relaxed and passed me the pint.

"Funny," she said.

"I thought so," I said.

"Drink your bloody pint."

So I did, and had a chat with my dad although this close to a gig he never takes in anything you say. But he seemed pretty pleased to see me, and asked if I was going to watch the set.

"As much as I can," I said.

Beer finished, we left the tent. It was beginning to get crowded as what I took to be more tourists and curious locals wandered in. A couple of years patrolling the West End and Soho and you get used to crowds, but the mist muted the voices and made it seem unnaturally quiet. A quiet crowd is a bit of a worry to a copper, since a noisy crowd is one that's telegraphing what it's going to do next. A quiet crowd means that people are watching and thinking. And that's always dangerous, on the off chance that what they're thinking is, *I wonder what would happen if I lobbed this half brick at that particularly handsome young police officer over there.*

"We might want to break that up," said Lesley nodding at the police booth.

There Abigail had been cornered by a slim white guy dressed in a red hunting jacket, camouflage trousers and Dr. Marten boots. He was looming over her in the classic school disco manner and while she had her arms folded and her face turned away from his, Abigail's expression was tolerant and craftily self-contained. She saw me coming before he did, and her smile became ever so smug.

"Oi you," I said. "Sling your hook."

The man spun around fast enough to make me take an automatic step back and check my stance. He was small, barely ten centimeters taller than Abigail but definitely at least ten years older. His face was triangular underneath a brush of rust-colored hair, his eyes hazel flecked with gold, and when he smiled his teeth were white and sharp.

"Oh, you startled me, Officer," he said in the kind of posh voice posh people use when they're doing an impression of someone with a posh voice. "Is there something wrong?"

Underneath the open jacket he was wearing a white T-shirt with what looked like a medieval woodcut of a man being torn apart by hounds. Printed above the picture, in a modern font, were the words *But they hardly suffer at all*. I seriously doubted his name was going to be something like Mr. Badger.

"Yes," I said. "It's called the Sexual Offenses Act 2003. Which in this case would mean life imprisonment for you, but only if her father didn't catch up with you first."

"I assure you, Officer," said the man. "My intentions were entirely honorable."

"Parked around the corner I've got a van full of very bored officers," I said. "Who, having spent most of their career in the morally ambiguous world of modern policing, would probably just love to be introduced to something as clear cut and despicable as an old-fashioned nonce."

"You wound me, Officer," said the man, but I noticed he was unconsciously backing away from Abigail and the booth.

"Nothing that wouldn't see me exonerated by the Department of Professional Standards," I said.

"Okay," said the man uncertainly. "Nice meeting you, Abigail, Officers." He turned and scampered off.

"What's so funny?" I asked Lesley, who was trying not to giggle.

"Peter," she said. "When you threaten people it's usually more effective if they don't have to spend five minutes working out what you just said first."

Abigail folded her arms and gave me a bad look.

"Hey," she said. "I was having a conversation there."

"Is that what it was?" said Lesley.

"You can talk to that one in five years," I said.

"If you still want to," said Lesley.

Abigail was about to answer back when a voice called Lesley's name. She had just enough time to turn in the right direction when a young woman with a mane of dreads came barreling out of the mist and threw her arms around Lesley. I recognized her—it was Beverley Brook.

She pushed Lesley to arm's length and stared at her—mask and all.

"They said you were walking about," she said. "But they didn't say you were fit. I was worried about you, but I was stuck upriver with the shire folk and the students." Lesley was too stunned to speak, which was something to see.

Beverley glanced over at me. Her eyes were as black as I remembered and shaped like those of a cat. Her nose was sleek and flat, her mouth wide, her lips full and her skin, despite the winter, smooth, flawless and dark.

"Hi, Peter," she said and turned back to Lesley.

Peter Grant at the South Bank, I thought. *His eyes wide, his testicles on fire.*

Beverley leaned in and, much to Lesley's discomfort, sniffed Lesley's neck.

"It's true," said Beverley. "You've fallen into bad ways

like Mister Never Texts over there." She glared at me. "Not one in nine months, no phone calls, not even an e-mail." I knew better than to make excuses. "There are some people living by the river who are still waiting on their insurance because of you, and I ain't joking about that." She turned back to Lesley. "You two had better make sure you pop in and pay your respects to Mum and the Old Man before they start to think you're taking them for granted."

A small figure in an Imperial Yellow silk jacket bounced into our midst like a little sun grenade.

"Bev Bev Bev," shouted the girl. "You've got to come with me—you promised."

"Wait, Nicky," said Beverley. "I'm talking here."

Nicky shortened from Neckinger, I guessed, another lost river which ran across the top part of Southwark. The girl, temporarily thwarted, turned to me and gave me a big radiant smile.

"Wizards." She pointed and laughed as if this was hilarious.

A deep voice that I recognized called Nicky's name.

"Uh oh," she said and pulled a face at me.

Oberon strode out of the mist toward us. A tall man with a square handsome face, he wore an archaic military coat that had once been dyed red but had now faded to a muddy brown, black combat trousers and boots. At his waist he wore what looked to me like a genuine antique British Army sword, and not the ceremonial type either, one hand resting easily on the pommel to keep it from tangling with his coat. He nodded politely to me and Lesley.

"Constables," he said. "I trust all is as it should be."

"Insofar as it can be," I said, but despite the temptation I didn't add forsooth.

He held out his hand to Nicky, who sighed theatrically before skipping over to seize it.

"You're going to come see me," she said to me, even as Oberon towed her away. "Make sure you bring presents."

"Is that her dad?" asked Lesley.

Beverley shook her head. "Oberon is Effra's man, but they've both been roped into babysitting Nicky. Speaking of which, I have to go. But we need a girls' night out. So text me, right?"

I coughed and asked Beverley if I could have a word later.

She gave me a sly smile. "Sure," she said. "Later."

Lesley punched me in the upper arm.

"Let's go see her mum," she said. "While your brain is still engaged."

It comes as a surprise to many that the rivers of London have their goddesses. Even people who have been officially raised to believe in such things as river spirits, and that's about a third of the world's population by the way, have trouble with the idea that the Thames might have a deity. The Niger, definitely. The Amazon, of course. The Mississippi, certainly. But the Thames?

Actually there are two of them. The Old Man of the River is the eldest by a couple of millennia, possibly a Romano-Brit called Tiberius Claudius Verica who ruled the Thames from source to estuary until 1858, when the mere fact that the city had reduced the river to an open sewer caused him to move upstream in a huff. So London did without his help until the late fifties when a heartbroken trainee nurse from Nigeria threw herself off London Bridge and found the position of goddess open. Well, that's the way she tells it anyway.

The Old Man feels that as the original his dominion, however titular, should be recognized. And she in turn says that since he couldn't be bothered to step up for the

Festival of Britain, let alone the Blitz, he can't just arrive and demand to sit at the head of the table. It's the sort of exciting intergenerational and ethnic conflict that makes life in the big city worth living. The fact that we're the police and it's our job to interpose our precious bodily selves between such potential conflicts explains why me and Lesley made a point of being polite and respectful when dealing with them.

So we marched up to where they sat, resplendent in their Sunday best. Father Thames in a black pinstripe double-breasted suit, a paisley waistcoat and a matching porkpie hat that did its best to keep his tangle of white hair under control. In honor of the occasion he was clean shaven, which served to emphasize his thin lips, beaky nose and bleak gray eyes.

Next to his dull self, Mama Thames blazed in a blouse and lapa of gold, silver and black. Her face was as smooth and dark as her daughter Beverley's but rounder, although the eyes had the same upward tilt. Her hair had been braided into an elaborate birdcage shot through with gold thread in a style that must have kept her cronies busy for hours, if not days.

Following Nightingale's instructions we made sure that we slipped in and out as unobtrusively as possible, receiving the equivalent of, *And how long have you been a police officer? Jolly good.* Lady Ty standing at her mother's right shoulder gave me a dangerously cheerful little smile which left the spot between my shoulder blades itching as I walked away.

Then it was back to the jazz tent for Dad's set where we found Nightingale discussing the evolution of Ted Heath's big band from the Geraldo orchestra with a guy who said he'd driven down from Nottingham especially for the gig. I stayed long enough to make sure my dad registered my presence and then headed back out. After all, we couldn't have the entire forces of law and order stuck in one place—who knew what someone might get up to while we were all grooving on a spring evening? As I reached Abigail standing disconsolately beneath the *Working Together for a Safer London* banner, I heard Lord Grant's Irregulars start into my dad's eccentric arrangement of "Misty." I said she could have a look around the fair as long as she didn't talk to any strange people.

"Okay," she said.

"Or strange things," I said.

"Whatever," she said and skipped off.

"Or strange things that are also people," I called after her.

Neither category seemed interested in stopping at the police stall for a chat, although a couple of Brazilian students wanted to know what the fair was in aid of.

"It's a celebration of the spring equinox," I said.

They looked around at the bare mist-shrouded trees and shuddered before they were sucked toward the jazz tent by the music. They passed Lesley coming the other way and stared curiously at her mask, only realising what they were doing when Lesley stopped and asked them if they needed something. They shook their heads and scuttled off.

Lesley was carrying another pint of beer which she presented to me when she reached the stall.

"Compliments of Oberon," she said. "He says you're going to need it before the day is done."

"Did he say why?" I asked.

Lesley said no, but I drank the beer anyway. It was proper beer, I noticed, not your fizzy lager from a cask—probably off one of the stalls, I thought.

I heard Abigail laughing somewhere out in the mist—it's a very distinctive laugh. I wondered if I should go get her.

"Hello, gorgeous," said a voice behind us.

"Hi Zach," said Lesley. "I thought you were persona non grata."

"I was," said Zach. He was a skinny white boy with damp brown hair and a big mouth in a thin face. He was dressed in genuinely un-prewashed faded jeans and a gray hoodie that was going at the elbows. He bowed theatrically.

"But this is the Spring Court," he said. "The seasons have turned and cruel winter has passed. Lambs are gambolling, birds build their nests and the hardy bankers get their bonus. It is a time of forgiveness and second chances."

"Yeah," said Lesley and fished a tenner out of her jacket and waved it at Zach. "Go get us some dinner then."

Zach swiped the tenner out of her hand.

"Your sternest command," he said and legged it.

"He really does have no self-respect," I said.

"None whatsoever," said Lesley.

While we were waiting, I suggested I do a perimeter check.

"That way you can round up Abigail while you're at it," she said.

My dad had started in on what had recently become his signature piece, an arrangement of the "Love Theme from Spartacus." The rest of the band faded down to almost nothing while my dad did his best Bill Evans impression—except hopefully without the untreated hepatitis. His piano followed me into the mist, fading in and out behind the hawkers and the mechanical organ on the carousel. It was frustrating in the way my dad's music always frustrates me—going off the melody just when I was enjoying it and going to places that I couldn't follow.

I found Abigail standing in front of a tall thin stall shaped like an outsized Punch and Judy booth. The edges of the proscenium arch were decorated with carved owls, quarter moons and occult symbols and it must have been very fine once. Now the gold and blue paint was chipped and the yellow curtain that hid the interior was washed thin and dingy. A carved sign at the top of the arch proclaimed, *Artemis Vance: Purveyor of Genuine Charms, Cantrips, Fairy Lures and Spells*. Pinned just below were the words, written in sharpie on an index card, *No Refunds!*

"Lend us a fiver," said Abigail.

I was curious enough about the booth to hand over the money.

Abigail knocked on the side of the stall which shuddered alarmingly. The curtain flew open to reveal a hook-nosed young man whose hair was silver white and stuck out at all angles like punk candyfloss. He was wearing a maroon velvet jacket with a tall collar over a ruffed lilac shirt.

He peered suspiciously at me and then even more suspiciously at Abigail—at least he had his priorities right.

"What do you want?" he asked.

"I want to buy a fairy lure," she said.

"Sorry," said the man. "We don't do fairy lures any more."

"Why not?" asked Abigail tilting her head to one side.

"Because fairy hunting has been deemed unlawful under the ECHR," he said. "No fairy hunting, no fairy lures. Mind you, technically, I could sell you a fairy lure providing you didn't actually use it to lure fairies. That's if I could still make them."

"Why can't you make them?"

"Because you have to use real fairy," said the man. "Otherwise it won't work."

"But if I'm not going to use it to hunt fairies, why can't you make one without any fairy in it?" asked Abigail. "A fake fairy lure."

"Don't be absurd, young lady," said the man. "Only a mountebank would think to purvey a fairy lure that failed in its most requisite aspect. Even to suggest such a thing stretches absurdity to the point of effrontery."

"How about a spell then?" I asked.

"Alas," said the man. "I would not presume to disgrace myself by offering the pathetic outpourings of my own craft to one such as you, a gentleman if I am not mistaken, and I never am, already schooled in the high and puissant arts of the Newtonian practitioner."

"What about me then?" asked Abigail.

"Underage," said the man.

"What about a cantrip?" asked Abigail.

"Alas, cantrip is merely a synonym for spell, and thus my previous answer must suffice," said the man, and glanced up at his sign. "Its inclusion is merely there to facilitate a more attractive rhythm to our advertisement and thus engage the jaded attentions of the common ruck."

"Do you actually sell anything at all?" asked Abigail.

"I can do you a charm," he said.

"Can I have a charm against geography teachers?"

"Alas, my child," said the man. "As your large and terrifying brother can no doubt explain to you, one does not choose a charm—rather the charm chooses you. It is all part of the great and wearisome cosmic cycle of the universe."

"All right," said Abigail. "What charm can I have?"

"I'll have a rummage," said the man and ducked down out of sight.

Me and Abigail exchanged looks. I was about to suggest we go, but before I could open my mouth the man popped up and dangled a small pendant for our inspection. A little yellow semi-precious stone, rough cut and mounted in a silver basket with a leather matinée length cord. Abigail eyed it dubiously.

"What's it a charm for?" she asked.

The man thought about this for moment.

"It's your basic all-enveloping protection charm," he said, his hands describing a cupped circle in the air. "For protection against . . ."

"Envelopes?" asked Abigail.

"The uncanny," he said and then in a serious tone. "The mysterious and the sinister."

"How much then?" asked Abigail.

"Fiver."

"Done," she said and handed over the money. When she reached for the charm I took it first. I closed it in my fist and concentrated, but could sense nothing. The stone felt chilly and inert against my skin. It seemed harmless, so I handed it over.

Abigail gave me questioning look as she slipped the charm over her head. There followed a brief undignified struggle as it caught in the huge puffball afro she wore at the back of her head before she could tuck it under her jumper. Then I waited while she pulled off her scrunchies, yanked her hair back into place and re-secured it with a couple of practiced twists.

"You'd better get back to our stall," I said.

Abigail nodded and trotted away.

"And you owe me a fiver," I called after her.

I glanced back at the man in the booth who gave me a benign little nod.

I strolled up the line of stalls and turned right where a booth was selling traditional cheeses, beers and rat traps. Once I was out of sight I paused, counted to sixty and then quickly retraced my steps around the corner until I could see where the Artemis Vance stall had been.

It was still there and the man was still visible, elbows resting on his counter and looking right at me. He waved. I didn't wave back. I decided that it probably wasn't a mysterious magic booth after all and set off on the rest of my perimeter check.

Beverley was waiting for me opposite the entrance to Gabriel's Wharf, propping up the garden wall of the imitation Regency terrace that had proved, surprisingly, to be the locals' preferred style of house. She wore a black corduroy jacket over a denim halter that left a bare strip of skin above her red, waist-high skinny jeans. Mist had beaded her locks and the shoulders of her jacket and I wondered how long she'd been standing there.

"You wanted a word," she said as I approached.

She smelled of cocoa butter and rainwater, of snogging on the sofa with *News at Ten* on mute and Tracy Chapman singing "Fast Car" on your parents' stereo. Paint-smelling DIY Sundays and sun warmed car seats, of pound parties with the furniture piled up in the bedrooms and wardrobe speakers wedged into the living room thudding in your chest cavity while somebody's mother holds court in the kitchen dispensing rum and Coke. I wanted to snake my arm around her waist and feel the warm skin under my fingers so badly that it was like a memory of something I'd already done. My arm twitched.

I took a deep breath. "I need to ask you something important."

"Yes?"

"While you were upriver . . ." I said.

"So far away," she said, her hand toying with the lapel of my jacket. "A whole hour by car—forty minutes by train. From Paddington. They leave every fifteen minutes."

"While you were away," I said, "Ash got himself stabbed with an iron railing."

"You should have heard the screams at our end," she said.

"Yeah, but I got him into the river and he was healed," I said. "How did that work?"

Beverley bit her lip. The sound of my dad's eccentric arrangement of "The Way You Look Tonight" wound its way through the mist and around us.

"Is this what you wanted to ask me about?" asked Beverley.

"I was thinking of Lesley's face," I said. "Whether we could do the same thing."

Beverley stared at me in what looked like amazement and then said she didn't know.

"It worked for Ash," I said.

"But the Thames is his river," she said.

"I thought that bit was your mum's."

"Yeah," said Beverley. "But it's also his dad's."

"It can't be both at once," I said.

"Yeah, it can, Peter," she said crossly. "Things can be two things at once, in fact things can be three things at once. We're not like you. The world works differently for us. I'm sorry about Lesley's face, but you go ducking her in the river and all she's going to get is blood poisoning." She took a step back. "And you shouldn't care whether she has a face or not," she said.

"She cares," I said. "Wouldn't you?"

"I can't help you, Peter," she said. "I would if I could—honest."

My backup phone, the one I don't mind risking around potential magic, sounded a message alert.

"I've got to get back," I said. "You coming?"

Beverley stared at me as if I was mad.

"Nah," she said. "I'm going to go flood Rotherhithe or something."

"See you later," I said.

"Sure," she said. Then she turned and walked away. She didn't look back.

I know what you're thinking. But hindsight is a wonderful thing, it was only a little flood and the property damage was a couple of million quid tops. And besides, the insurance companies covered most of it.

I arrived back at the jazz tent just in time to say goodbye to my parents, who were heading home now the set was finished, and Abigail who was getting a lift back with them.

There was a perceptible change after they left. And not just because the sound system near the Thames path that had been silent in deference to my dad turned on its speakers with a sound like an Airbus A380 clearing its throat. The tourist families with kids were draining away and gaps between the stalls were suddenly full of young men and women, drinking from cans and plastic glasses or openly passing joints back and forth. Me and Lesley knew this crowd of old, or at least the West End Saturday Night version of it. It was our cue to slip back to the Asbo and don the stab resistant and high-visibility raiment of the modern constable. Not to mention the knightly accoutrements of extendable baton, pepper spray and speedy cuffs. I clipped on my airwave and checked to make sure that the ruinously expensive second shift of TSG were awake and on call.

When the sound system kicked in, it was strictly BBC 1Xtra playlist. Rough enough for the upriver crowd with enough proper beats to stop the Londoners from getting restless. Lesley liked it and I could cope, but the couple of times we ran into Nightingale we could see he was suffering. We took turns to hit the improvised dancefloor at the river end of the park, although the thermal properties of the Metvest means it's not your ideal club wear.

At one point I found myself alone by the river watching a three-quarter moon grazing the roof of Charing Cross station. There was traffic humming through the mist, the sky was clear enough that you could almost see a star and I thought I might have heard a scream of outrage coming from the direction of London Bridge. It was long, low and thin and yet shot through with a kind of mad glee, and I might have recognized it. But you know what I reckon? I think I imagined the whole thing.

The pissing contest took place at three or four in the morning. I'd lost track when even the supernatural among us were beginning to wilt. The first I knew of it was when Oberon grabbed my arm and started dragging me to the east side of the park.

"It's a contest," he said when I asked what was going on. "And we need you to step up and represent."

"Represent what?" I asked.

"The honor of the capital," he said.

"Let Lady Ty do that," I said. "She's keen enough."

"Not for this, she's not," said Oberon.

We picked up a cheering section which included Olympia and Chelsea, goddesses of Counter's Creek and the Westbourne and winners of the London-wide heats of *I'm A Posh Teenager . . . Get Me an Entitlement* five years running.

"Do it for London," called Chelsea.

"Aim straight," called Olympia.

"What the fuck are we supposed to be doing?" I asked Oberon again.

He told me, and I said he had to be fucking kidding.

So we lined up with me and Oxley in the middle, Father Thames on our right with Ash and a couple of followers beyond him. Beside me on my left was Oberon, Uncle Bailiff and some guys I didn't recognize.

The women—thank god the girls were all tucked up

asleep—lined up three or four meters behind us—thus saving our blushes.

"All right boys, unsheathe your weapons," called Oxley and there was the sound of zips and unzipping and cursing as some fumbled with buttons. "On my mark. Wait for it. Wait for it!" called Oxley to groans and catcalls.

"Loose," shouted Oxley and we did.

I ain't going to say where I came in the pack except to mention that it was embarrassing. But I obviously hadn't had the chance to put away the pints like some of my competitors. Thankfully most of it was beer because a wall of steam arose in front of us and could have been a lot ranker than it was. It came down to Oxley, Oberon and the Old Man himself. The two younger men ran out at the same time with yells and groans.

Father Thames, as casual as a gentleman in a pub urinal, glanced left and right down the line to ensure he had our full attention before cutting himself off in midstream and calmly buttoning himself up.

"Well, what did you expect, boys?" he said into the silence. "I am the master of the source, after all."

I woke up in the backseat of the Asbo and, despite that, I felt surprisingly good. Fucking wonderful in fact. I got out of the car and stepped into warm early morning sunlight. Immediately suspicious, I powered up my mobile and used to it to check the date—it showed what I expected—I hadn't spent fifty years in enchanted faerie revelry. But in my line of work you can't be too careful.

Still, the faerie fair had vanished with the morning sun, leaving behind drifts of rubbish and muddy rectangular footprints pressed into the lawns. Just like a big dirty river that had burst its banks and left its mark on the dry land. It was in a state, but fortunately I'm a man who has a mum who knows a woman who runs a company that specializes in cleaning up after rock festivals. The woman who ran it said that if you've ever done cleanup at Glastonbury then nothing short of high-grade nuclear waste will ever scare you again.

Her people arrived and parked in the areas recently vacated by the TSG. Most of them were young Somalis, Central Africans, Albanians and Romanians with a smattering of Poles, Turks and Kurds. They were dressed in boiler suits, steel toecapped boots and carried shovels and rakes and implements of destruction.

Lesley looked cheerfully oblivious, curled up in the front seat, so I left her to it and went in search of coffee and bacon sandwiches. When I got back she was up and waving at me from the eastern edge of the park where we'd held the pissing contest.

"What the fuck happened here?" she asked.

In front of where the Old Man of the River had stood flowers had bloomed. Nightingale named them when he rolled up to join us, Wild Angelica, Red Clover, Yellow Melilot, Wild Mignonette, Garlic Mustard, Scabious, blue spherical Devil's-bit and tall stands of Red Valerian. He seemed delighted and said he would return to pick a bouquet for Molly.

"But first we need to deal with those railings," he said.

Despite the sunshine the wind coming up the river from the east was brisk. Uncle Bailiff had at least left the cut sections of the handrails in a neat stack and secured them with plastic ties. Me and Nightingale each took an end of the first section and lifted it into the gap. Nightingale put his hand around the join and spoke quite a long spell, fifth or sixth order I guessed. I felt a vibration like a tubular bell being struck neatly with a hammer and a tingle in my hands where I held my end of the rail and then a warmth.

"I haven't done this in a long time," he said.

"Is this part of the weird way of the Weylands?" I asked. It wasn't exactly fashioning a wizard's staff, but it was the same line of work. The metal was getting warmer and I was just wishing that I had a pair of proper workman's gloves when Nightingale released his end. I slid my grip over so that he could take hold of my end and watched closely as he repeated the spell. *Lux* was in there but also *formae* and modifiers that I didn't recognize.

"Which reminds me," said Nightingale. "We must continue with our own blacksmithing." He released his grip, leaving an orange glow in the rough shape of his fingers on the metal which faded to leave no sign of a join.

"Do we have time?" I asked as we moved on to the next railing. "What with the Mulkern case and the Faceless Man?"

"I've spent too long in the land of the lotus-eaters," he said. "It won't profit me to find that faceless bastard." The railing shone white under his hands then faded. "Not if you and Lesley aren't ready to take up your duties."

A gust of wind chilled me as I realized that Nightingale was planning against the possibility that he wouldn't survive that encounter.

"And the exercise will do me good," he said.

When we were finished we walked up to join Lesley, who was packing up our stall. The last, I noted, to be taken down.

"Notice anything odd?" she said.

I looked around. The cleaners had nearly finished and clear plastic bin bags stuffed with rubbish awaited collection along the paths. A man was walking his dog and a couple of curious teenagers in hoodies were watching us in the hope that we did something interesting enough to post on YouTube.

"Not really," I said.

Lesley tapped me on the shoulder and pointed up at our official Metropolitan Police crest with the reassuring slogan in script. Only someone had altered it while we slept. Someone with some proper skills, because if I hadn't known it had changed I would have assumed it had always read—**Metropolitan Police:** *Working Together For A Stranger London.*

9

The Night Witch

ONLY LONDON DIDN'T get any stranger. It stayed resolutely normal for the next week or so—at least on the surface.

Operation Tinker, the investigation into the murder of Patrick Mulkern, was headed by Bromley Murder Investigation Team under DCI Duffy, although Nightingale made a point of attending every morning briefing in case something magical came up. My presence, or Lesley's, was apparently not required.

"You have a relationship with the Belgravia team," Nightingale had said as explanation. "And Westminster has a tradition of dealing with unusual cases that Bromley does not share. Inspector Duffy wants someone senior enough to shoulder the blame should things go seriously awry."

Still, there's never any shortage of work for idle police hands, especially ones that double up as apprentices, so me and Lesley got on with our paperwork, chasing the paper trail made by our suspected Little Crocodiles and doing the preliminary reading for the detective exams we hoped we'd be taking by the end of the year. At least,

I was hoping to take them by the end of the year. Lesley's current status of being on semi-permanent medical leave was causing her grief.

Professor Postmartin wrote me a letter in which he thanked me for the list of books at Stromberg's Highgate villa and said that he was appending a list of texts in English, German and Latin that were associated with the 1920s. I dutifully passed this on to Bromley MIT to add to their inquiry database with flags to contact me if anything turned up.

Despite the best efforts of the Spring Court it snowed that weekend, although it didn't settle inside London's urban heat island. It certainly didn't deter Abigail, who arrived on Sunday morning for what Lesley insisted on calling *Junior Apprentice*. Then, as I did each week, I attempted to find new ways to keep Abigail occupied and out of trouble. Often this involved us following up things she'd put down in her notebook, working our way through the ghost-spotting books, playing what Nightingale called the Game of Jewels or, if we were really desperate, teaching her some Latin. The high point was usually tea downstairs in the atrium, especially since Molly had reached the cake section in the Jamie Oliver book.

"What is Oberon?" she asked that Sunday.

"I don't know," I said and looked at Nightingale.

"Some variety of fae I presume," he said stirring his tea.

"Yeah," said Abigail. "But fae just means different, don't it?"

Nightingale nodded.

"Is he king of the fairies?" she asked.

"Royalty among the fae is a strictly protean concept," said Nightingale. "Why do you ask?"

"There was this Asian kid that got lost and Oberon

got into an argument with Effra about who got to keep him," she said and showed me his picture on the phone.

He was a very handsome brown-skinned child with black ringlets and mahogany eyes. The kind of boy who was going to be mistaken for a girl until his teens and would leave a trail of broken hearts behind him thereafter.

"What do you mean Effra wanted to keep him?" asked Lesley suspiciously.

She never had so sweet a changeling, I thought. We'd done *A Midsummer's Night's Dream* at school when I was twelve—I was third magic tree on the left. I'd wanted to play Bottom, but then so did everyone else.

"Don't worry," said Abigail. "I got his name out of him and then got Reynard to sniff out his parents."

"Who's Raymond?" I asked.

"Reynard," said Abigail. "Just this guy. You know . . ."

"No, we don't know," I said.

"You met him," she said. "You know—earlier."

"You mean the fox?" said Lesley. "The one that was trying to chat you up?"

"Hold on," I said. "Is that the same fox that talked to you at Christmas?"

"Not unless he's shed a lot of fur," said Abigail, "started walking upright, oh and let's see, put on about fifty kilograms . . . Unless you think that's possible."

I wasn't sure what to say. There were reports of were-creatures and shape changers in the Folly's library, but nothing after the nineteenth century. Nightingale had taught me to be cautious of the early sources. "A great deal of it is accurate," he'd said. "And a great deal is less so. Unfortunately it can be difficult to determine which is which."

"Unlikely," Nightingale told Abigail. "But I have to

say that recently I have lost my faith in the word impossible."

But "impossible" still seemed to apply to catching a break in any of our cases. Nightingale returned from the Monday morning briefing and reported that the mood was not optimistic.

"At this rate," said Lesley, "no one's going to want to work with us. We're clear-up rate poison."

Nightingale—who came from an era when clear-up rates were something applied to char ladies—decided, as he had threatened in the aftermath of the Spring Court, to teach us some magical blacksmithing. So we trooped into the classroom with a forge—Nightingale insisted that we call it the smithy—and donned our heavy leather aprons and protective goggles.

The forge itself looked bolted together out of random sheets of blackened steel. There was an extractor hood surmounted by what appeared to be a lawnmower engine and a shelf filled with coke at groin level which was fed by what looked to me to be a suspiciously jury-rigged gas line.

"The Sons of Weyland maintain," said Nightingale as he turned the gas on, "that the smiths were the first true practitioners of magic." He lit the forge with a practiced flick of his finger and a *lux* spell.

For the hardy men of the North, the alchemists and the astrologers that preceded the Newtonian revolution were a bunch of conmen and grifters. "As above, so below," was so much bollocks. Not that Nightingale used the word bollocks. Craft, dedication, hard work and hitting bits of metal very hard with a hammer—that was the true path to wisdom.

"And it is true," said Nightingale. "That you can always tell where a smithy stood by the *vestigium* it leaves behind."

"What about hospitals?" asked Lesley. "You get tons of *vestigia* off old hospitals."

"But not the new ones," said Nightingale. "Have you noticed that?"

I hadn't, until he pointed it out.

"Sudden death seems to imbue a locality with a degree of power," he said. "People don't die in hospitals in the quantity they once did." He paused and frowned. "Or perhaps the technology mutes the effect. In either case, it is of a quite different quality from the *sensus illic* of a smithy."

"You don't get much around graveyards," I said.

"The magic is released upon the point of death," said Nightingale. "Despite the attachment spirits have for their bodies, I was taught that little magic stays with those earthly remains."

"What about massacre sites?" I asked. "You know, like when they get the victims to dig a pit and then—"

"Extremely magical and extremely unpleasant," said Nightingale. "I suggest you try to avoid such sites if you wish to sleep soundly again. Although I imagine becoming inured would be worse."

He pulled out a steel rod, ten centimeters long, from a box on a nearby work surface.

"This will be our raw material," he said. "One rod of sprung steel, six of mild."

But first they needed cleaning with wire wool, which can be a surprisingly painful experience if you're not careful. By the time we'd finished, the forge was good and hot—two thousand degrees Fahrenheit according to Nightingale, which was just over a grand in real temperature.

"You need to learn to read the color of the flame," he said.

He bundled the seven rods together with wire and pushed one end into the glowing center of the forge.

"Now, this is where you need to watch carefully," he said, and stretched his hand over the forge. He said the spell quietly and I caught that weird echo you get when someone does some serious magic in your presence. Heat bloomed off the forge, real heat not *vestigia,* that crisped the hairs on my forearm and made me and Lesley step smartly backward. Nightingale pulled back his hand equally sharply and, using a pair of tongs, rotated the bundle of rods a couple of times before withdrawing them from the forge.

For a moment the heated end shone like a magnesium flare and I added an arc welding mask to my list of things to acquire before the next lesson. The light faded to merely bright as Nightingale swung around and placed the bundle on the anvil.

"What now?" asked Lesley.

"Now?" said Nightingale. "Now, we hit it with a hammer."

At breakfast the next morning Lesley pitched her plan for using the weird way of the Sons of Weyland and the staffs they made to lure out the Faceless Man.

"Because he's bound to want to know how it's done," she said.

Nightingale finished a mouthful of scrambled egg before speaking.

"I understand the principle," he said. "I'm just not sure of the practicalities."

"Such as?" asked Lesley.

"Where do we cast our lure?"

"I thought we'd start at the Goblin Fair," she said. Nightingale nodded.

"We should be looking to maintain a presence at the

fairs anyway," I said. "We need to get that whole community used to seeing us out and about."

"The community?" asked Nightingale.

"The," I groped for a word, but I couldn't find any other term that fit, "magical community. We need to open up channels of communication." It was your basic *policing by consent,* currently referred to as *stakeholder engagement,* and we'd done at least one lecture on it at Hendon—although judging by Lesley's amused snort I might have been the only one who stayed awake.

She exchanged looks with Nightingale, who shrugged.

"Perhaps we could do with a bit of dredging in that direction," he said. But before I could ask what *that* meant, he asked Lesley for specifics.

"We go in as if we're looking to scoop up any staffs floating around on the open market," she said, and explained that having established our interest we'd then imply that we were looking for the materials to construct new ones. "We want to make," she tilted her head at me, "*the community* link our presence with the staffs. That might be enough to draw the Faceless Man out—although I think it might be a bit of a long-term strategy."

Nightingale sipped his coffee and gave it some thought.

"It's worth a try," he said. "And who knows? We might recover some genuine staffs into the bargain. Do we know when the next fair is?"

"We know a man who does," I said.

"I presume that would be our Mr. Zach Palmer?" asked Nightingale.

"Well if you want to know where the goblins are . . ." said Lesley.

The Goblin Fair was, as far as we could tell, a combination mobile social club, shabeen and car boot sale for London's supernatural community. I'd actually gone digging in the mundane library and found references to a *Goblin Fayre* and to a hidden market that was *tucked into great St. Bartholomew's feast as a flea hides upon a dog*. The earliest reference was recorded in 1534, which meant that the institution predated Isaac Newton and the establishment of the Folly.

Nightingale had said that there'd always been a supernatural demi-monde at the fringes of the great horse fairs and the traditional markets, but he'd never had anything to do with them.

"Not my department," he'd said.

Not that the Folly had departments, you understand, it being the child of an era when a gentleman might serve his country in any number of ways regardless of previous experience, probity or talent. And if at the same time he might accrue some influence, some status and a huge estate in Warwickshire—then so much the better. Still, Nightingale had worked abroad at the behest of the Foreign and Colonial Offices while others had worked with the Home Office, offering assistance to the police and other civil authorities. Some had done what I considered scientific research, and others still had researched by studying the classics or collecting folklore. Many just used the Folly as their London club while in town from their parsonages, estates or university positions— "Hedge Wizards," Nightingale called them.

At least a couple of those had probably taken an interest in the goblin fairs and had perhaps written a useful tome on the subject. It was just possible that one day I might stumble upon it in the library or an Oxfam in Twickenham—you never know.

Still, as Lesley said, why do it the hard way when we could just call Zach.

According to Zach, the next fair was due the day after and was in north London. Athlone Street, off Grafton

Road, Kentish Town—my manor, as it happens. One of my first girlfriends used to live up the other end, so I'd walked down it enough times.

"Did you get any?" asked Lesley as we parked the Asbo. We were suffering a standard gray London drizzle, the sort that makes it clear that it can keep it up all day if needs be.

"I was twelve," I said.

"I bet you were precocious, though," said Lesley. "She was older, wasn't she?"

"Why'd you say that?" I asked. It was true. Her name had been Catherine and she'd been a year above me in school.

"It was your big brown eyes wasn't it?"

I didn't know what to say. When I was twelve, introspection was not my most prominent characteristic.

"We were in the swimming club together," I said.

The address was a strange Victorian wedge of a building that backed into a railway viaduct. The ground floor was given over to a print shop, and according to Lesley's intelligence there should be a sign advertising this. This intelligence came from Zach Palmer, who was half human and half—we weren't really sure what, including the possibility that the other half might be human as well. But anyway he was hooked into what Nightingale insisted on calling the demi-monde.

Speaking of which ...

"You know the Fleet runs under here," I said.

Lesley groaned. "Do you think she's in there?"

"Believe it," I said.

"At least it will be out of the rain," she said.

There was a sign—a sad bit of damp cardboard cut into the shape of an arrow with the word "VENUS" handwritten and pointing to a side door. Lesley knocked.

"What's the password?" shouted someone from inside.

"It's a slippery slope," I shouted back.

"What?" shouted the voice.

"It's a slippery slope," I shouted louder.

"What kind of slope?" shouted the voice.

"A fucking slippery one," yelled Lesley. "Now open the bloody door before we kick it down."

The door opened to reveal a tiny hallway and a flight of stairs leading upward. Peering cautiously around the door was a small white boy of about ten, wearing a black and white bobble hat, fingerless gloves and an adult-sized lime colored lambswool cardigan that was draped over him like a rain cape.

"You're the Isaacs," he said. "What you doing here?"

"Why aren't you in school?" asked Lesley.

"I'm home tutored," he said.

"Really," said Lesley. "What are you learning at the moment?"

"Never talk to the filth," he said.

I told him that we didn't want him to talk to us.

"On the contrary," said Lesley. "We just want to get out of the rain."

"Nothing's stopping you," said the boy.

We stepped inside, but before we could troop up the stairs the boy tapped Lesley on the arm.

"Miss," he said. "You can't—"

"I know," she said and took off her mask.

"Oh," said the boy staring up at her. "You're that one."

"Yes I am," she said and then waited until we were safely up the stairs to whisper, "That one what?"

I said that I hadn't got the faintest idea.

At the top of the drab staircase was a windowless hallway lit by a forty watt bulb in a red Chinese paper lamp shade that managed to make it seem even darker. We had a choice of going up another flight of stairs or out through a door, but before we could even express our indecision the door slammed open and we were confronted by a young white woman in a pink tracksuit with an Adidas logo on it. I recognized her as one of the waitresses from the Goblin Fair we'd visited back in December.

"What can I do you for?" she asked.

"We're here to buy some stuff," said Lesley.

"Yeah? What kind of stuff?"

"Stuff from the far off land of mind-your-own-business," said Lesley.

"Scrap metal," I said. "Stuff that's a little bit—you know." I wiggled my fingers.

Lesley gave me a theatrical glare. "Have you quite finished broadcasting our business to all and sundry?" she asked.

The girl gave me a sympathetic look. "Upstairs," she said. "You want to talk to the gentry."

"Thanks," I said and wondered who the hell the gentry were, and if they were like the Quiet People or the Pale Lady. What was it with this general lack of personal pronouns? I remembered that I'd heard Nightingale referred to as "The Nightingale" and realized that I'd only assumed that was his actual name.

I followed Lesley, who was having trouble stopping herself from laughing, up the narrow staircase.

"The far off land of mind-your-own-business?" I whispered.

"I didn't want to seem too obvious," she whispered back.

"No, that wasn't obvious at all," I said.

We were two thirds of the way up the stairs when the door at the top opened and a woman stepped out onto the landing. She was white, middle-aged, with dirty blonde hair cut into a neat business-like bob. She wore an expensive charcoal gray skirt suit of conservative cut and carried a slim burgundy attaché case. Her eyes were a faded blue.

Recognizing faces is a key cop skill, and although she was looking younger and happier than we'd last seen her I remembered her immediately—Varenka Debroslova, probably an alias—former live-in nurse to one Albert Woodville-Gentle, a.k.a. the Faceless Man version one.

She recognized us at the same time—well, Lesley's very distinctive—and took an automatic step back. Lesley didn't hesitate. She lunged up the last couple of steps and I followed her.

The normal thing to do in Varenka's situation would be to bolt back up and out the door. But instead she lifted her attaché case in both hands and shoved it into Lesley's face. As Lesley recoiled backward into me, Varenka practically launched herself headfirst down the stairs toward us. Lesley was knocked back toward me and I had no choice but to catch her and try and twist us both out of the way as Varenka landed on us. She'd obviously planned to surf down the stairs on top of us, but I wasn't playing that game. I ducked down over Lesley and let the other woman roll across my back toward a hard landing.

Or that was the plan, anyway. Unfortunately, the staircase was too narrow and too steep, so we all bumped down it together. Stairs are a killer and we all might have ended up with sundry cracked ribs and broken legs except we were jammed in so tight we went down in slow motion. Even so, my shoulder slammed into a riser hard enough to make my teeth click, somebody's knee slammed into my back and I definitely smacked my head on the rough plasterboard wall at one point.

Lesley yelled in fury as we tumbled out onto the landing. In a fight, if you want to be the last man standing it's important to be the first guy back on your feet. So I levered myself off Varenka's back and tried to grab her arm. But she had other ideas. She sprang to her feet and used my own grip on her arm to pull me off balance and slam me against the wall. It would have gone much harder on me if Lesley hadn't grabbed a handful of expensive suit jacket and climbed up Varenka's back.

"Oi," yelled the girl in the pink tracksuit. "None of that. It's Pax bloody Domus here." I noticed that she was putting the stress on the wrong syllable. It's pax-blud-eee DO-mus, I thought, and I might have gone on to mention this except that Varenka put an elbow in my stomach that left me disinclined to discuss the finer points of Latin pronunciation.

I got my leg out of the way of a kick that would have broken my knee, and felt like it broke my thigh bone instead, and realized that Varenka had not said a single word since she'd met us on the stairs. There was something terrifying about the ferocity and silence with which she fought. I understood suddenly that this was a woman who had done real fighting, against people who'd been trying to kill her. We were just trying to restrain her, but she was trying to maim us—if we didn't shut her down quick she was going to cut us to pieces.

Varenka whipped round and sent Lesley staggering across the hallway and into the girl in the pink tracksuit who went down swearing. Then Varenka spun to face me but with Lesley clear that was my chance to summon up the *impello-palma* combination that I feel is my own personal contribution to specialist law enforcement.

Varenka reacted even before I'd finished the spell, and flung up her arm to protect her face as it slammed into her like a body block from an invisible riot shield. She rocked back on her heels and I realized the implications of her early reaction just in time to feel her building a counter spell. In the confines of the landing there wasn't anywhere to go but back up the stairs, so I faked toward the landing door and then lunged up the steps.

I felt the bite of cold metal and caught the smell of alcohol and wet dog. Something went past me with the instant violence of an articulated lorry slipstreaming a layby, wood splintered, somebody screamed and a billow of choking white plaster dust filled the landing. A meter-wide section of the doorjamb and the wall beside it had smashed open. Through the hole I could see chairs and tables and startled pale faces.

"That's it," screamed the girl. "You three are barred!"

But it was just us up there, Varenka having scarpered.

"Watch it," I yelled as Lesley cautiously peered down the staircase toward the exit. "She's a practitioner."

"No shit," said Lesley and vanished down the stairs

I followed her down using both hands for balance as I took the stairs three at time. When I reached the bottom there was no sign of the boy who'd let us in and I hoped he'd been smart enough to do a runner.

Lesley was too good a copper just to bang through the door. She paused to check that Varenka wasn't waiting in ambush before slipping out. She veered left as she went, so I veered right. Varenka was the other side of Grafton Road yanking open the driver's side door of a silver Audi. When she saw us, she gave an exasperated snarl and flung out her arm in my direction. I did a dive behind the nearest car and slapped the pavement just in time for something to smash into the side of the vehicle with a noise of breaking glass. The car alarm went off, but behind the endless electronic hooting I heard the Audi pulling away. I thumbed the jury-rigged battery switch on my mobile and risked a glance over the bonnet just in time to be able to read the index on the back of the Audi as it accelerated south down Grafton Road.

The other side of the car I'd been sheltering behind, a red VW Golf, had been smashed in and was white with what looked like frost. I resisted the urge to touch it, just in case. I looked over and found that Lesley was unhurt and walking to join me.

My phone jingled to let me know it was finally ready. I rang Metcall, gave my rank and name and asked to speak to the supervisor for EK, meaning Camden. While I waited to be put through I wrote the index number on my arm with the biro Lesley handed me. When the supervisor came on I asked for an urgent circulation on a vehicle and gave them the index.

"If seen it must not be stopped without Falcon assistance, repeat Falcon assistance," I said. Falcon was our brand new call sign and I said it twice because it doesn't get used much and I didn't want some poor sod in an IRV coming to grief tackling somebody as obviously dangerous as Varenka. I invoked Nightingale's authority to back it up, since a chief inspector goes a long way to smoothing out any bureaucratic lumps and bumps. I looked over to confirm that Lesley had Nightingale on her phone and she nodded when she saw me and signaled "ten minutes." Once I was sure Metcall was going to put out the action report, I hung up and trotted over to the Asbo to grab our airwave sets.

"You know, if you'd grabbed your airwave first you could have circulated the report on the local channel," said Lesley when I handed over her set. "Just saying."

I noticed that my hand was trembling, not shaking you understand, but definitely a reaction. Lesley glanced at my hand and then gave me a wry look. We both looked back at the red VW Golf. The driver's side door had been stoved in as if hit by a girder end on. Slashes of silver metal showed through where the paint had been stripped away.

"You wouldn't want to be standing in front of that, would you?" said Lesley.

Members of the public were beginning to arrive in numbers and Lesley stepped forward to shoo them back. There were a couple of gasps and one half shriek from the crowd.

What now? I thought and looked around to see if there was a new threat or a body or something equally unpleasant. I wondered about the boy at the door again, but saw that he was back at his post. I checked back with the crowd to see what they were staring at, and realized that it was Lesley.

She'd come out of the fair without her mask. She looked at me and I could tell from her expression that she'd only just realized it too. A couple of white teen-aged girls had their phones up and had them pointed at Lesley. A third girl was too transfixed by the sight to do more than clap her hand over her mouth.

"Shit," said Lesley softly. "I must have left it inside."

"Oi." I turned to the gathering crowd. "Back you go. You've all watched enough telly to know we need to keep the area clear."

Behind me Lesley walked briskly back toward the Goblin Fair.

"Back up," I shouted. "Nothing to see here."

10

Game Relish

VARENKA ABANDONED THE Audi five minutes' drive away on the Chalk Farm Road and presumably ducked straight into Camden Lock where she
could lose herself among the crowds and leave the area
on no less than five modes of transport, including canal
boat. We could have pulled all the surrounding CCTV
but we didn't have the manpower, budget or stamina to
wade through that much tape. Besides, as Lesley pointed
out, this was Camden Lock where she could have bought
a complete change of clothes, had her hair dyed, sipped
a fresh latte and acquired a nice handcrafted henna tattoo before leaving.

That didn't stop Nightingale screeching to a halt outside in true Sweeney style and striding into the Market,
kicking down doors and putting the frighteners on the
locals with some pithy Latin tags. At least, I'd like to think
that's what he did. But I wasn't there because me and
Lesley were under strict instructions to secure the crime
scene around the Goblin Fair, and see if we couldn't dig
up any witnesses. Only everyone including the boy from

the door and the girl in the pink track suit had vanished—all except Zachary Palmer.

"They all went out the emergency exit," said Zach.

I'd found him on the roof sitting at a round café table covered in a red-and-white checked tablecloth and laid out for dinner for two. A fluted glass vase with a single yellow rose sat in the center and a champagne bottle in a frosted brass ice-bucket sat on a separate stand at his elbow.

The roof was triangular in shape and littered with scraps of plastic, abandoned white polystyrene cups rolling around in the breeze and free copies of the *Metro*. They'd taken all their stock with them, so it couldn't have been that much of a panic.

"You know," said Zach, "until you came along I used to be the local loose cannon. Now people have started warning me about the dangers of associating with *you*."

A London Overground train growled past us. The tracks were less than a meter from the edge of the roof and the carriage windows were level with our kneecaps.

I gestured at the waiting champagne.

"We didn't interrupt your dinner, did we?"

"Nah," said Zach and tapped his foot against a wicker hamper with F&M stencilled on its side. "I'm just waiting for your colleague. It was part of the deal."

I went downstairs to where Lesley was searching the room at the bottom of the landing—the one Varenka had blown a hole in. It was full of overstuffed furniture, chintz and white plaster dust. I contacted Nightingale on the airwave to see if we were needed, but he said no.

"She's long gone," he said. "I'm going to arrange for her car to be towed away and then I'll be with you in an hour. Any luck your end?"

I told him that nobody was left except Zach.

"At least getting him to talk shouldn't be that hard," said Nightingale and signed off.

"Isn't that Peter O'Toole?" asked Lesley who was pointing to a row of framed photographs on the wall. It looked like a publicity still from *Lawrence of Arabia* and had been signed. The other photographs were also vintage actors in black and white portraits, most of whom I recognized in the it's-that-guy way you do with people who were famous before you were born.

"If you've got time for refs," I said, "then your boy Zach is upstairs and waiting."

"I did promise," said Lesley.

"Save some for me," I called after her as she went up the stairs and then wondered what exactly it was you got in a Fortnum and Mason hamper—beyond "posh stuff," that is.

She was still up there when Nightingale arrived so I left them to it and met him down by the VW Golf. He was sitting comfortably on his heels, staring at the stoved in side panels and stroking his chin.

"It was covered in frost," I said when I joined him. "Immediately after. Like it had been frozen."

"This is a worrying development," he said.

I tapped the mangled metal. "I thought so," I said. "Especially at the time. Any idea who trained her?"

"Not our man in the mask, that's for certain." He nodded at the car. "Not with that spell."

Lesley emerged from the house and joined us—her own mask back on. Nightingale straightened when he saw her.

"Did Mr. Palmer have anything useful to say?" he asked.

"Not noticeably," said Lesley. "He did tell me that he's only seen Varenka at the fair recently and that she just seemed to be there for the same reasons as everyone else—a bit of shopping, the odd glass and gossip."

"Did she gossip with anyone in particular?"

"Not that he noticed," she said.

"I assume you asked him to keep an eye out," said Nightingale.

"Yep," she said, and held up a large jar with an old-fashioned orange label. "And this is for you."

Nightingale took the jar, read the label and smiled.

"Game relish," he said. "Excellent—we'll have to see what Molly can do to this."

The jar vanished into his coat pocket and his face became grim.

"When she cast the spell did you get a sense of her *signare*?"

"Weirdly yeah," I said. "Bread, grain, something yeasty."

"Hungry dog," said Lesley.

"Dog or wolf?" asked Nightingale.

Lesley shrugged. "To be honest I don't think I'd know the difference."

"*Nochnye Koldunyi*," said Nightingale. "A Night Witch."

"Is that like a person or another thing?" asked Lesley. "Like Peter's Pale Lady?"

"A type of Russian practitioner," said Nightingale. "Recruited during the war, the training had a very narrow scope. It was concentrated almost entirely on combat. We heard rumors that there were whole regiments of women trained in this manner. Hence the nickname."

"Sounds like a good idea to me," I said.

"We tried something very similar ourselves in 1939," said Nightingale. "Unfortunately it didn't turn out well, and the whole project had to be abandoned."

"Why?" asked Lesley.

"Half of everything I try and teach you is to stop you from killing yourselves," said Nightingale. "Skimp on that aspect of the training and many more of your apprentices will die. We felt that the casualty rate with the New Training was too high—I suspect the Russians were willing to make greater sacrifices. Our war was pretty desperate but theirs was a war of annihilation—victory or death was not an empty slogan."

"Hold on," said Lesley. "That was seventy years ago—she'd be an old woman." She paused and narrowed her eyes at Nightingale. "Unless she's doing the backward aging thing, like you."

"Or she might have been trained by her mother," I said. "Or perhaps the Russians still have a military magic program."

"Maybe she's an unauthorized agent," said Lesley. "Maybe we should tell the Russians."

"Well, prior to that," said Nightingale, "we'd have to determine which Russians to tell. We'd better consult with the Professor about that."

"If we can pry him away from his new German grimoire," I said.

"Nonetheless," said Nightingale. "Regardless of her provenance, the fact is we now have two confirmed fully trained practitioners at large in London. You two are going to have to be even more careful when operating without me. In fact, I don't want either of you operating alone or without letting me know where you are—you can consider that an order."

"We should start routinely carrying tasers," said Lesley. "That would be our best bet—zap them before they know we're there. I'd like see someone concentrate on a *forma* with fifty thousand volts running through them."

"No warning," I said. "I like it."

Lesley glared at me and I realized she was serious.

Nightingale nodded. "I'll have to clear it with the

Commissioner first. And I'll need you both to demonstrate to me that you'll hit the target you're aiming at."

"In the meantime?" I asked.

"In the meantime, let's see if we can't bowl over Varenka before she has a chance to go to ground," said Nightingale.

Criminals, even professional ones, are not spies. They might be cautious but they don't practice what professional agents call "tradecraft," especially when they're off the clock. Case in point, Varenka's Audi which was registered to one Varvara Tamonina aged sixty-two—that got a snort of derision from Lesley—but the picture matched the face we'd seen briefly trying to kill us that morning. The license gave us an address in Wimbledon but when Nightingale and Lesley went knocking with a warrant there was no sign that Varenka, or Varvara Tamonina, had lived there in years. Then they started a bit of door to door on her neighbors, because you never know what you might find.

Meanwhile I got stuck compiling the intelligence report, which consisted of me wading through a ton of IIP responses and seeing if Ms. Varvara Tamonina's vehicle had popped up in relation to another inquiry. This led me to DAFT, Southwark's Drugs and Firearm Team and winner of the mostly badly thought out acronym award three years running, who'd spotted the car while running surveillance on a drug network in Elephant and Castle. I checked with them to see if they'd followed up and found that the inquiry had wound down shortly afterward.

"The principal suspect dropped dead," said a helpful DC.

"Suspiciously?"

"Nope," said the DC. "Died of a heart attack."

Aged twenty-six, most likely a congenital heart defect that had gone undetected until one day he went face down in his breakfast cereal.

"Couldn't've happened to a nicer guy," said the DC.

His name had been Richard Dewsbury and he'd been heavily involved in the drug trade around Elephant and Castle since his fifteenth birthday. Suspected of running most of it for at least five years before keeling over at his mum's kitchen table.

"And guess where his mum's kitchen table was?" I asked.

"Skygarden," said Lesley.

I was briefing Nightingale and Lesley over coffee in the atrium—still pretty much the warmest bit of the Folly. It had actually snowed a couple of days after the Spring Court and, despite one sunny day, the weather had stayed unseasonably cold.

"The very same," I said.

Lesley had taken off her mask and I saw that patches of skin on her face were so white with cold as to be almost blue. Dr. Walid had warned that the reduced circulation in the damaged skin around her mouth and cheeks could make them susceptible to chilblains and/or tissue necrosis—which is exactly as horrible as it sounds.

"If we combine that with the architect and the unfortunate planner, it would seem that all roads lead to Elephant and Castle," said Nightingale.

"Circumstantially," said Lesley.

Molly glided over with a folded towel resting on a tray and offered it to Lesley. The towel was sky blue, fluffy and steaming gently. Lesley thanked Molly, tested the temperature with the back of her hand and then draped it over her face with a contented sigh.

Molly looked at Nightingale and tilted her head.

"That will be all," he said. "Thank you."

Molly drifted away silently toward the back stairs.

"God, that feels good," said Lesley, her voice muffled under the thickness of the towel.

"Circumstantial but enough that I believe we should take a closer look," said Nightingale, getting back to Elephant and Castle.

"We could talk to the local Safer Neighborhood team," I said.

Lesley mumbled something under the towel.

"What?" I asked.

She lifted the towel off her mouth long enough to say, "That's the East Walworth team. They work out of Walworth nick."

"Peter can go down and see them tomorrow," said Nightingale. "Lesley, you can stay in the warm and check whether our Russian friend has emerged onto the radar anywhere else. Meanwhile I'll see if any of my contacts at the Foreign Office are still alive."

There was a skittering sound from the back stairs and then Toby burst into the atrium and scampered toward us, his claws clicking on the marble floor. When he reached our table he snuffled around our chairs before stopping beside Lesley's and barking twice. Then he sat on his haunches and looked up expectantly. When she offered him a biscuit, he ignored it and instead swung his snout until it pointed at where she'd put the discarded the face towel.

"Do you want this?" asked Lesley and dangled the towel in front of him.

Toby barked once, seized the towel in his jaws and scampered off with his stubby little tail wagging. We all watched him go.

"Do you think Molly trained him to . . .?" I asked.

"I'm not sure that's an alliance we want to encourage," said Nightingale.

"We should get Dr. Walid to look at Richard Dewsbury's PM report," I said, suddenly remembering my visit to DAFT. "Just in case it was something other than a heart attack."

"Aren't heart attacks a bit subtle for the Faceless Man?" said Lesley.

"There's merit in having two forms of attack," said Nightingale. "If you're principally known for setting your enemies on fire you could well avoid suspicion by poisoning one instead."

"And if Varenka—"

"Varvara," said Lesley.

"And if Varvara Sidorovna Tamonina," I said slowly, "did the deed, then maybe heart attacks are her specialty. How hard would it be to give someone a heart attack?"

"With magic?" asked Nightingale.

"Yes."

"Not hard as such," he said. "But complex and laborious. I think I'd have to be in the same room as my target to do it as well. Much better to poison them or to use a glamour to make them poison themselves."

"What makes it so complicated?" asked Lesley suddenly leaning forward—eyes fixed on Nightingale.

"The human body resists magic," he said. "Particularly if you try to make gross physical changes."

Lesley unconsciously lifted a hand to her face.

"Stopping somebody's heart with magic is a fifth- or sixth-order spell, depending on how one attempts it, and even then the results would be less certain than setting the victim's bones on fire."

I thought of the braised corpse of Patrick Mulkern and really wished Nightingale had used another example.

"Abdul has a theory about why," said Nightingale. "You can ask him next time you see him."

Lesley lowered her hand from her face and nodded slowly.

"I think I might just do that," she said.

"Richard Dewsbury," said Sergeant Daverc. "He was one in a million—thank god."

Sergeant William Daverc was in his early fifties and had a proper London accent to go with his proper Huguenot name which was properly pronounced D'Averc. He'd been patrolling Southwark since his probation thirty years ago and was a famous pioneer of community policing from back in the days when it was just called "policing."

"Ricky when he was younger," said Daverc who'd met me in his team's office at Walworth nick. "Mister Dewsbury as soon as he was middle management—didn't have a 'street' name and that should have been a giveaway right from the start."

"Violent?" I asked.

"Not particularly," said Daverc. "Single minded. He was a tower boy, you understand."

Meaning born and raised in the central tower of Skygarden, not the surrounding blocks. Local folklore said that people from the tower never did anything by half, never settled for mediocrity or middle management—not even in the drug trade. The tower had produced a footballer, two pop stars, a stand up comedian, a high court judge, a semi-finalist on *Britain's Got Talent* and the most ruthlessly efficient drug baron in south London.

"When he popped his clogs you could hear the dealers giving a sigh of relief from Rotherhithe to Wimbledon," said Daverc. "Without him it was the usual story—his organization fell apart, turf wars—the usual aggro. But your lot don't care about drugs. Do you?"

I told him that we had reason to believe that there

might be activities going on inside the tower that could lead to breaches of the peace of a more esoteric nature.

"Like what?" asked Daverc, who'd spent too long as an operational copper to be fobbed off with generalities. I tried honesty.

"We have no fucking idea," I said. "We have a break-in and murder related to the original architect, we have an apparent suicide of a Southwark planning officer who was, in part, responsible for the estate and we have this link to Richard Dewsbury, local resident and pharmaceutical entrepreneur. We were sort of hoping you'd have something."

"Like what?"

"Anything strange," I said.

"The tower's always been strange," he said. "Even more so now they've closed down the surrounding blocks."

"I heard about that," I said. "Are they knocking it down or not?"

"I've given up trying to work out what the council's doing at Skygarden," said Daverc. "I know they want to flatten it and turn it over to the developers in return for some new build—they had all the plans on show and we was even doing our preliminary impact studies and then it all seemed to fizzle out."

"Have you got any contacts in the tower?" I asked.

"I go up there regular," he said. "I have my community liaisons who bend my ear about kids nicking stuff and people weeing in the lifts." He paused and narrowed his eyes. "If you want to know what's going on in the tower, guy like you, your best bet would be to move in yourself."

"I don't know," I said. "I've heard flats aren't that easy to get."

"I've got access to one," said Daverc. "I set it up for

DAFT so they could get someone on the inside—they were going to share their intelligence with me—only Richard Dewsbury keels over and DAFT lost interest. Say the word and I can get you in there in less than twenty-four hours." He paused to give me another shrewd look.

"If you're interested."

There's two approaches to dealing with large bureaucracies. Well, technically there's three but the last one is only available to officers of ACPO rank and people who went to the right school. On the one hand you can phone ahead, explain that you're the police, give a quick and largely inaccurate summary of your investigation and make an appointment to see the relevant supervisor stroke line manager. Or, if you're in a hurry, you can flash your warrant card at the security guards, fast talk your way past the reception and see how far up the hierarchy some classic cockney bullshit will take you.

In this case it took me through the fiercely rectangular and marble-lined atrium at Southwark Town Hall via Grace on the front desk—it turned out that, while we weren't related to each other, we definitely had family in the same part of Freetown—into the lifts and before anyone could say "Hey you, what are you doing here?" into the work area of one Louise Talacre who was employed in the same office as the late Richard Lewis.

She was a ridiculously cheerful young woman with Italian looks and a Midlands accent who was happy to help the police in any way she could—you'd be surprised how many people are.

She was familiar with the Skygarden redevelopment and knew that Richard had been particularly involved in trying to get the estate unlisted.

"He said it shouldn't even have been listed in the first

place," she said but someone—Louise always thought Richard might know who, although he never said—had swung a Grade II so that it wouldn't be pulled down in the late 80s. The council had to spend millions on refurbishment and remedial repairs and resented every penny.

"They put in a concierge system and everything," said Louise in a horrified tone. "But you still hear stories about what went on in that tower."

"Really?" I asked.

"I heard there was a bunch of New Age druids squatting in one of the blocks and worshipping the trees," she said.

Druids, I thought. I asked for that one.

"But he never got the tower unlisted, though?"

"He wasn't happy about that," she said. "But he didn't seem happy about anything toward the end. I told your lot that the first time they came round." That would have been the BTP investigation. Jaget's people. "Not that I thought he would ... you know ..."

Now Lesley may contend that I am, occasionally, lacking in the police work department but even I can spot a lead when a witness waves it in front of my face.

"Did he seem like he was under pressure?" I asked.

"Well, we're all under pressure aren't we," said Louise. "What with the cuts and everything."

I explained that I meant outside pressure—say from unscrupulous developers and the like.

"Don't be silly," she said. "They never bother with the likes of us. They always go for the CEOs or the councilors." She pulled a face. "We never get no baksheesh. Still, you know, now you mention it, there ... no, that sounds stupid."

"What does?"

"About a year ago when we thought the tower was

going to be delisted or unlisted or whatever they call it," said Louise. "He came in all happy and smiling and of course I asked him what he was so happy about and he said that he was soon going out of this dreadful city for good. And then when they announced that it was going to stay listed he looked like he was going to burst into tears. I say that, but it might have been hay fever—he was never what you'd call demonstrative. He said that he couldn't leave until the tower came down."

"I want you to think very carefully," I said. "What were his exact words?"

"Wait a minute," Louise held her fingers by her temples and wiggled them. "He said, 'He won't let me go until the tower comes down.'"

"Did he say who 'he' was?"

"Might not have been 'he,'" said Louise. "It might have been 'they.'"

"I see," I said.

"I'd have asked him, you know, but he wasn't exactly sociable," said Louise. "I didn't even know he was married, a mail order bride I heard—from Thailand or somewhere like that."

Okay, so dying to be helpful. But not actually particularly helpful except to point the finger at Skygarden again. Something that I reported back at the Folly during the daily seven thirty briefing session, otherwise known as the evening meal. Nightingale, running on some internal calendar of Mayan complexity, had declared that evening a full dress dinner. So me and Lesley donned our best approximation while Nightingale slummed it in an exquisite navy-blue evening jacket and his blood-red regimental tie.

Molly always wore her most Edwardian servant's outfit for these occasions and swept around the dining room so silently that even Nightingale was unnerved when she materialized suddenly at his elbow with the next dish.

Fortunately the next dish was spinach tortellini with ricotta, herbs and parmesan, indicating that Molly had reached the pasta section of *The Naked Chef* and, judging by the absence of those esoteric animal offcuts that get the traditionalist all excited, was getting better at interpreting modern recipe books. Lesley and Nightingale were considering slipping in a Nigella, but I've got to say I was beginning to miss the suet puddings.

"I thought Sergeant D'Averc's notion had some merit," said Nightingale. "Even if we were only there for a short time it would give us easier access to the whole building."

I paused with a forkful of green pasta halfway to my mouth.

"Us sir?" I asked.

"If the tower is indeed the fulcrum of this case," said Nightingale, "it must follow that the Faceless Man will be taking an equal interest. Now that we know he's working with a trained Night Witch it would be extremely unwise if we didn't operate as a mutually supporting unit."

I unpacked that to mean—*I need to be close enough to intervene before you get yourselves killed.*

Me and Lesley exchanged glances.

"You don't think I'm capable of blending in?" he asked.

"Molly's getting very handy with the parmesan," said Lesley politely.

"Yes, you may be right," said Nightingale, considering. "However, I plan to position myself nearby in the event that you need reinforcing."

Lesley glanced down to where Toby, having established that this was to be a largely sausage-free supper, had curled up and gone to sleep.

"Are we going to take the dog?" she asked.

"Of course," I said. "Combination excuse to go out walking at odd hours and magic detector."

Lesley nodded and then looked back at Nightingale.

"How will you know if we need reinforcing?" she asked.

"I think you'll find I am perfectly capable of using a radio," said Nightingale. "And if that fails, I'm sure Peter here can be relied on to blow something up."

11

A Machine For Living In

W E WENT IN early like a dawn raid, on the theory
that if we were already in place when the locals
woke up they'd just accept us the way badgers accept a
naturalist's low-light camera in their sett. The other reason we went in early was because we were borrowing a
van from one of my relatives and he needed it back first
thing. We couldn't hire a removal van as we didn't have
enough stuff to make that credible, and we had more stuff
than we could carry ourselves since otherwise we would
look like squatters or, worse, undercover police officers.

Not that we really were undercover police officers, because UC operations are subject to strict guidelines and
operational oversight by senior officers. What we were
doing was in fact an extremely subtle form of community
policing. So subtle that, if we were lucky, the community
could carry on, blissfully unaware that they were being
policed at all. Just to be on the safe side, Lesley wore her
other mask. The one which was colored olive tan instead
of surgical pink, which she claimed was strictly for when
she was off duty. She let Toby sit in her lap.

You didn't get a good view of Skygarden when you arrived by road. Stromberg had surrounded the central tower with five long thin blocks, each nine storys high, a very conventional design that, one architectural critic complained, *obscured the exuberance of Stromberg's central conceit*. These were built in a conventionally slipshod manner which certainly obscured the exuberance of most of the people that lived there, who also comprised the bulk of the population of the estate. Arriving from the Elephant and Castle side you emerged from under the railway bridge to get a quick glimpse of the tower before turning into the estate and dropping down past the, by then, sealed-off garage areas of the blocks and into a narrow culvert sunk six meters below ground level. It was just wide enough for a VW Beetle and a Mini to pass each other and the pavements were only a little bit wider than curbs, pedestrian traffic having theoretically been channelled onto the walkway that was suspended overhead. During the 1981 riots the residents had built a barricade across the culvert and waited with petrol bombs and stones, but the police declined to turn up—I don't blame them. Back then the Skygarden had been as close to being a real no-go estate as ever existed in the fevered mind of a journalist but Sergeant Daverc said its glory days were long past, and you were as safe there now as you would be in Chipping Norton. Certainly it was home to fewer professional criminals.

The access road opened into a sunken tarmacked area that surrounded the base of the tower, the outer perimeter of which was lined with garage doors. The actual garages, built just slightly too small for modern-sized cars, were set into the soil of the surrounding landscaping. Above these doors was another meter and a half of concrete cladding topped by a chain-link fence beyond which I could just see, despite the fact that I was effectively standing at the bottom of a wide hole, tufts of grass and the tops of distant trees. I was willing to bet big money that the fence hadn't been in the original plans and wondered how many kids had injured themselves jumping down from the park before the council put it in.

We'd asked Frank Caffrey to drive the van for us, since out of his London Fire Brigade kit he looked the part of White Van Man. It was a character he certainly grew into when he elected to stay in the cab and read the *Sun* while me and Lesley unloaded our stuff.

Like his hero Corbusier, and many of his contemporaries, Stromberg had had a strange phobia about ground-floor flats. In Skygarden the lower ground floor was strictly for loading and unloading and what is always referred to on blueprints as "plant." The "ground floor," where the elevated walkways converged, was for pedestrian entry, community areas and storage. Thus ensuring that no matter how far down the block the council parked your granny, she was still going to get some much needed exercise when the lifts stopped working.

After we'd got the sofa bed out the back of the van and were taking a breather, I glanced up and saw a white kid in a navy-blue hoody staring down at us from the nearest walkway. I know trouble when it's below the age of criminal responsibility, and while my first instinct was to arrest his parents on general principles, I gave him a cheery wave instead. He gave me a blankly suspicious look before whipping his head out of sight.

"The natives know we're here," I said.

The doors to the atrium were constructed from heavy metal and wire mesh reinforced glass. We used one of our heavier boxes to jam them open while we hefted the sofa bed toward the lift.

"You all right in there, Frank?" called Lesley as she strained to lift her end.

Back in the van, Frank gave her a cheery thumbs-up.

The atrium had a concrete floor and what looked like recently repainted plaster-covered breezeblock walls. Stair access was to the left, doors leading to "plant" to the right and a pair of reassuringly familiar dimpled graffiti-resistant lift doors to our front. I pressed the call button. There was a red square of plastic inset into the wall above the door which remained resolutely dark.

"Shouldn't we at least get the rest of the stuff into here?" asked Lesley.

"I want to check the state of the lift first," I said.

I put my ear to the cold metal of the door and listened—there were some comforting rumbles and clanks from above. I stood back and the doors opened.

It was urine and graffiti free, which is always a good sign in a lift, but it was small—an expression of the architect's faith that the proletariat were unencumbered by such bourgeois affectations as solidly built furniture. Me and Lesley had to wrestle the sofa bed into an awkward diagonal to get inside. Leaving the rest of our stuff in Frank's care, we ascended to our new home.

The flats in the tower came in two basic varieties, two bedroom and four bedroom. The four-bedroom flats were on two floors linked by an internal staircase and the two-bedroom flats were stacked one on top of the other with an external staircase leading up to the top flat. Thus the lifts only went to every other floor and Stromberg had cunningly managed to combine some of the disadvantages of a terraced street with all the disadvantages of a tower block.

When we reached the twenty-first floor we managed to extricate the sofa bed with just a bit of scuffing to the armrests and only minor damage to the lift doors.

For some reason, Stromberg had designed a hexagonal central shaft that ran up the middle of the tower so that for the first few years you could lean over and stare all the way down to the basement level. Since it didn't function as a light-well and it was ten times wider than needed for the building's tuned mass damper, it was a bizarre bit of architectural whimsy even for the late 1960s. The tenants soon put it to good use as a combination waste disposal area and emergency urinal and after two suicides and a notorious murder case, the council installed heavy duty wire mesh to seal it off from the walkways.

Our flat, of course, was right on the other side of the shaft. As we lugged our increasingly heavy sofa bed around the walkway, I noticed that half the flats on our floor had been sealed shut with steel security doors. COUNTY GARD was neatly stenciled at eye height and attached below that a legal warning to all squatters that it was a crime punishable by six months in prison or a £5,000 fine.

"Or both," said Lesley with satisfaction.

The front door for our new flat was a plain modern design lacking those traditional panels of frosted glass that allowed light in and your more entrepreneurial neighbors a chance to determine whether the place was occupied or not—just in case you had some big ticket items lying around unwanted.

Inside, the flat had been painted mostly white with a hint of apple and recently enough for the walls to be clean—although we did leave a graze at waist level in the hallway as we squeezed the sofa bed in. We plonked it down in what I assumed was the living room, and sat down to recover.

I've got to say that Stromberg was consistent in his architectural principles. The hallways were narrow, the rooms were too long and the ceilings were low. It also had sliding patio doors out onto a huge balcony—the size of a small urban garden. You could have added an extra bedroom to the flat and still had enough balcony left over to feed pigeons, hang washing and dump all the stuff you couldn't be bothered to wrestle down the stairs.

"Right," said Lesley. "We'd better get back downstairs before Frank drives off in search of a fry-up."

Fortunately he was still there when we reached him, trapped in his cab by a formidable white woman who was bending his ear. Dressed in an M&S blouse and Peacock budget slacks, she was the type of large white woman who's been apprenticing for the role of saucy granny since late adolescence. By the looks of it, this one was going to graduate in the top two percentile.

She said her name was Betsy.

"You just moving in?" she asked and seemed delighted to hear that we were. She introduced the junior Hoodie I'd spotted earlier as her son Sasha and sent him off to fetch Kevin—her eldest, and a bit more useful in the hefting of heavy objects department.

"What happened to your face?" asked the woman. "If you don't mind me asking? Well, of course you mind. But I'm nosy, me. Was it an acid attack? Only I heard they had a couple of those down Bromley but that was an honor thing. You know, like an honor killing only with acid. Are you a Muslim? You don't look like Muslims, but then what does a Muslim look like?"

"Chip pan," said Lesley quickly. "Accident with a chip pan."

The woman gave me such an unfriendly look that I took a step back.

"It wasn't him who did it was it?" she asked. "Only we don't stand for that kind of stuff round here."

Lesley assured Betsy that it had been an industrial accident rather than domestic violence, but I was still pleased when Kevin arrived and I could retreat into what had suddenly been designated as "men's work."

Kevin himself was a big man with sandy hair and layers of muscle under rolls of fat. He lifted his end of Lesley's bed with ease while Sasha carried one of the smaller boxes.

"What do you do, then?" asked Kevin.

"Anything I can get," I said.

Kevin nodded sagely. He was an old hand at cramming stuff into the lift, so we only had to make two journeys. It was a neighborly gesture that either demonstrated that the spirit of community was not dead or allowed Kevin to suss out whether we had anything worth nicking. Or possibly both.

Lesley returned the favor by running an IIP check on the whole family as soon as our front door was safely closed. While she did that, I put Toby's lead on and headed out to the shops.

Of the three elevated walkways leading from the Ground Floor, two went to the Old Kent Road and Heygate Street respectively, piercing the blocks in front of them exactly the same way the monorails do in old-fashioned depictions of the future. Both of these had been sealed off at the block end by Southwark Council to restrict access and prevent vandalism. The last remaining walkway was the one built on pillars over the access road and gave out in the gap between two blocks at the corner of Elephant Road. I'd wondered about the culvert. But as I walked away from the tower I realized, looking around, that I couldn't see any roads or signs of vehicles at all. Stromberg, I decided, had he been given the budget, would have gone the whole hog and buried the road underground. When I reached the ramp at the far end I turned to look back and saw that the blocks acted as gigantic garden walls cupping a green bowl in which grew some of the biggest plane trees I've ever seen, thirty meters tall some of them, high enough to overhang the walkway and, sheltered as they were, they were nonetheless in full spring leaf. And rearing out of the center was the dusty brown crenellated spike of Skygarden Tower.

"Fuck me," I said to Toby. "We're living in Isengard."

It started raining as soon as I was off the estate. But one good thing about Skygarden was that it was handy for the shops. On the way back I let Toby off his lead but, far from rushing off to explore, he stuck close to my heel and seemed grateful to reach the lifts.

As I juggled my shopping bags looking for my keys, I noticed a nervous white woman eyeing me from the flat to our right. She was small, thin, with long lank brown hair and dressed in a faded red sweatshirt and faded jeans that were probably much tighter before she lost weight. I recognized the mixture of hope and trepidation on her face and realized that she was our resident fallen princess.

Every estate has at least one of these per block. Middle- or upper-middle-class girls who've managed to overcome the advantages of their birth and end up in council housing with a child or an addiction or both. They're easy to spot because they have a constant air of bewilderment, as if they can't understand why the universe has stopped tilting in their favor. They don't get much in the way of sympathy on an estate—I'm sure I don't have to explain why.

"Hello," I said.

"Hi," she said. "Have you just moved in?"

She advanced along the walkway until she was halfway toward me and then hesitated. Her feet were bare and she placed them like a ballerina.

"Just this morning," I said. "Got any tips?"

"Not really," she said and advanced again.

I put my bags down and stuck my hand out. "My

name's Peter Grant," I said using my full name in the hope that she'd reciprocate. She gave me a limp handshake.

"Emma Wall," she said—it's so much easier to run someone through the system if you have their full name.

Close up she smelled of cigarette smoke and twitched like a junkie, but if I had to guess I'd have said she was in recovery. Not that you can really tell—I should know.

"How long have you lived here?" I asked.

"Why do you ask?"

"Just looking for a native guide," I said.

Emma bit her lip and then, after a long pause, gave a false little chuckle.

"Sure," she said. "Would you—"

I never found out what I might have done, because the door opened and Lesley stuck her face out.

"Hello," she said cheerily. "Any chance of the shopping arriving?"

I sighed and picked up the bags and told Emma I'd see her later.

"Sure," she said and fled back to her flat.

"Who was that?" asked Lesley as I unpacked the groceries in the kitchen. By the style and level of wear on the kitchen fittings I could narrow the date the work was done to the early 2000s. The top edges were dented and discolored and when I opened the wall-mounted cupboard, the doors were wonky. The styles may change but it's always laminated chipboard underneath.

I gave her Emma's full name and flat number so she could run a check later, which reminded me to ask whether anything had popped on Betsy and her family.

"Public order offenses," she said. "Threatening behavior, assault, GBH, drunk and disorderly."

"Kevin?"

"Betsy," she said. "Or rather Elizabeth Tankridge née

Tuttle, most of it steadily accumulated over the last twenty years or so except for the threatening behavior which was last week."

"One to ask Sergeant Daverc about," I said.

"Son Kevin on the other hand has never been charged with anything, although his name comes up in relation to thirty-six separate investigations mostly burglaries and receiving. Why did you get so much Weetabix?"

"It was a BOGOF," I said.

The flap on the letterbox rattled and we both leaned out of the kitchen door to see why. It rattled again and it was impossible to tell whether someone was trying to push something through, or use it as a substitute door knocker.

I walked quietly over to the door and when I was sure that Lesley had taken a secure place in the living room doorway, out of the line of sight, I turned the Chubb handle and pulled it open.

A man was stooped over in front of our letterbox, caught in the act of either snooping or pushing a leaflet through.

"Hello," I said. "Can I help you?"

The man stayed bent over but turned his head so he could see me out of the corner of his eye.

"As it happens," he said and held out a hand. "If you would?"

I took his hand, his skin was soft, wrinkled but his grip was very firm. He took a deep breath and then letting me take some of his weight levered himself painfully upright. He was a white man of medium height with a blunt honest face that would have been his fortune had he been selling second-hand cars. His hair was white but thick, long and pulled back into a pony tail.

"Oh, the back of the working man," he said, and shook the hand he was already holding. "Jake Phillips, local activist, busybody and thorn in the side of late stage capitalism."

"Peter Grant," I said. "Recent arrival, slacker and man of very little fame."

Jake Phillips thrust a leaflet into my hand. "Well, I'm offering a once in a month-time opportunity to attend a Skygarden TRA meeting. Everyone welcome."

"I'll see you there," I said.

This caused Jake to pause.

"Really?" he asked.

"Yeah—why not?"

"Oh," he said. "Okay. I'm the chair, by the way."

Of course you are, I thought.

We exchanged good-byes a couple more times before Jake moved off toward the stairwell—I closed the door.

"Man of very little fame?" asked Lesley.

"First thing that came into my head," I said.

We returned to the kitchen where we found that Toby was still sitting and staring intently into the shopping bags. I pulled out a tin and showed it to him.

"Look," I said. "Meaty chunks."

Toby barked.

"We did bring a tin opener, didn't we?" asked Lesley.

Well, the exercise probably did me and Toby good. And, like I said, the shops were nice and close.

Everyone who ever grew up on an estate and had parents who cared enough to give them a birthday party knew about the community room. A room set aside for whatever it was that idealistic young architects thought the working class might need it for—workers' soviets is my guess. What they actually get used for is Tenant and Resident Association meetings, keep fit for the over fifties and birthday parties. Generally they're large, low-ceilinged rooms set on the ground floor with, if you're lucky, a kitchen area and toilets attached. They're usually as charmless and as welcoming as a Job Centre, but I have some good memories of the one at my parents' estate. Particularly my thirteenth birthday when I managed my first proper snog with Samantha Peel who was a year above me and strangely keen. Who knows where it might have gone if my mum hadn't descended like the wrath of god and broken it up. Not long after her throw down with my most recent girlfriend, my mum pointedly informed me that Samantha was now a qualified dental nurse, married with two kids and living in a terrace in Palmers Green. I'm not sure what she expected me to do with that information.

The Skygarden TRA meeting was about as exciting as you'd imagine, although much better attended than I expected. At least twenty to thirty people sat on the formed plastic chairs in a big ragged circle. Betsy and Kevin were there, which surprised me, and Jake Phillips was chair, which didn't. He was a good chair too, working briskly through the agenda. We were introduced as new tenants and were welcomed and stared at curiously—especially Lesley. A nervous Somali man reported that Southwark Housing Services had promised faithfully that the lift repair contractors would look at the broken lift in the next week. There were groans and catcalls from the audience.

"Remember it's important to log all these problems," said Jake. "That way you can give them chapter and verse when they try to stall you."

A few people nodded—this was obviously familiar advice. There were some reports on rubbish collection but nothing on the central issue of preserving the tower itself. Me and Lesley listened intently and made notes of names and faces, the better to have them sent for re-education later. During the planning phase of this operation, or more precisely what we discussed after dinner at the Folly, we had considered the possibility that the Faceless Man might have his own agents planted in the tower.

"It's not like me and Lesley are inconspicuous," I'd said.

Nightingale had winced, as he always does, at my incorrect use of the accusative pronoun but I think I'm beginning to wear him down.

"We're not really the ones hiding anything," Lesley had said. "If they spot us and react, then we have a better chance of spotting them back. If they don't panic they're still going to have to alter their plans on the fly, and that'll also make them easier to spot. Meanwhile, we'll be poking around in their business and they won't be able to do anything about it."

I couldn't help thinking of Patrick Mulkern cooking from the inside as his bones caught fire.

"And if they come after us?" I'd asked.

"Then Frank and I will deal with them," Nightingale had said.

If the Faceless Man *did* have people in place, then I figured they'd have to attend the TRA meetings in case the residents threatened to accidentally disrupt their plans. But they wouldn't want to be obvious. So I concentrated my attention on people who'd managed to stay awake during the meeting but hadn't made a contribution themselves.

I mentally earmarked several candidates, but top of my list were a pale young man with a floppy haircut who looked like an off-duty Goth and a second white guy, middle-aged with short brown hair, who wore a tweed jacket with leather trim and looked like he collected stamps or built cathedrals out of matchsticks. I thought it unlikely that the off-duty Goth would attend without an ulterior motive, and that the stamp collector would sit through the meeting without giving his opinion.

The last item on the agenda was a resolution to see if we, that's the TRA, could drum up some media interest in the fact that the Council was paying County Gard more to secure the empty flats than it would cost to refurbish them for new tenants.

This was carried unanimously and the meeting broke up.

Because we only had the one bit of comfy furniture, we both ended up on the sofa drinking Special Brew and watching TV. Well, I say TV. Actually it was our laptop propped up on a kitchen chair playing the BBC iPlayer, and it worked pretty well apart from the frequent stops for buffering caused by the fact that we were pirating WiFi from someone who'd failed to stick a password on their router and the signal was weak.

"I may be from a small town," said Lesley. "But didn't that seem just a little bit too sociable for the inner city?"

I knew most of the people on my estate. Although, that said, mine was a bit smaller than the Skygarden proper.

"This is not a normal estate," I said. "The council probably offered to rehouse anyone who wanted to leave. These are the people that either liked it here or are too stubborn to change."

"In America I heard they come round with cake," said Lesley.

"I bet they don't in New York," I said.

A flurry of rain struck the window panes.

"What do you think Jake would say if he knew we were taking down names?"

"He'd love it," I said. "After all these years the secret police are finally taking an interest."

Toby, who seemed to have adapted rapidly to the idea that we weren't going home, jumped up into the gap between us and made himself comfortable.

"So what do we do tomorrow?" asked Lesley.

"Tomorrow," I said, scratching Toby's head, "we have a good sniff around."

12

Sky's Garden

I WOKE UP early to bright sunshine pouring through the patio doors. I made myself a cup of instant coffee and stepped out onto the balcony to drink it. Our floor was high enough to overlook the blocks and see all the way out across the gray-green smear of southeast London to the green belt beyond Croydon. The balcony really was ridiculously huge, with unnecessarily thick parapets that had mysterious trough-shaped depressions along their tops—built-in window boxes I decided in the end. I was high enough for the air to be as fresh as it can get in London, the traffic was a muted rumble in the distance and somewhere nearby a bird was singing.

Despite the sun, the wind was too chilly to stand out there in my underwear so I went back inside and wrestled myself in and out of the tiny shower retrofitted into the bathroom. I stuck my head round Lesley's door to ask if she wanted to go check out the garden with me, but she threw a pillow at my head.

I told Toby it was time for walkies but he was already waiting by the front door.

Landscaping is the great cardinal sin of modern architecture. It's not your garden, it's not a park—it's a formless patch of grass, shrubbery and the occasional tree that exists purely to stop the original developer's plans from looking like a howling concrete wilderness. It was also, in the case of Skygarden, strangely hard to access.

Me and Toby first went down to the lower ground floor, where we'd unpacked the van the day before, and did a full circuit of the base of the tower before we realized that there was no access from there. The whole circumference was lined with garages topped with a fence with not even a ladder to get you up to the greenery. Half the garages were sealed with more of the County Gard's shiny steel doors—Southwark Council's reluctance to reallocate locked garages to residents had been a major grievance at the TRA meeting.

I remembered the drive in through the culvert and figured you'd have to walk practically the entire distance back to the Walworth Road before you reached ground level. Rather than slog all the way there, me and Toby jogged up the first flight of stairs to the ground floor and checked the elevated walkways. A third of the way along the one leading to Heygate Road there was a ramp spiraled down into the green. I almost missed it because it was overshadowed by one of the big plane trees. You practically had to duck under a branch to walk down it.

Toby cautiously stayed close to my heel as we descended. There was a gravel path winding away through the hummocks and random slopes that landscape designers like to litter their designs with. The path was poorly maintained, the gravel scattered and wearing thin. A couple of times I had to step over places where giant roots had rumpled the path out of existence. The sun was well over the top of the housing blocks now, the light tinged with green and falling on secondary growths of tall skinny trees with silver bark and bushy things that I'm sure

Nightingale could have identified for me—at length—
had he been there.

But even I can recognize cherry blossom trees when
they are white and pink as candyfloss.

Unless they were peach blossom, of course.

The, probably, cherry trees lined one side of what had
obviously been a children's play area before the council
had removed all the play equipment—presumably to
stop children playing on it.

Toby growled and I stopped to see what he was looking at.

A white girl was watching us from across the defunct
playground. She was wearing an old-fashioned Mary
Quant dress in green and yellow and her blonde hair was
cut into a pixie bob under a battered straw sunhat. Her
face and limbs were long and thin and seemed oddly out
of proportion with her torso. She was standing in the
shade of one of the smaller plane trees, so still that I
wasn't sure she hadn't been standing there all the time
I'd been walking up and I just hadn't seen her.

I heard a child giggling from behind a nearby tree and
the girl gave me a smile that was like the sun coming out
from behind a cloud. Then she pivoted and skipped away
so fast that I could barely follow the movement. A moment later a small brown imp of a girl broke cover from
behind her tree and dashed after the older girl. This one
I recognized—it was Nicky, who I'd last seen wearing
Imperial Yellow at the Spring Court. Her river, the
Neckinger, practically ran right under the estate.

Toby gave chase, yapping continuously, his stubby tail
wagging as he vanished into the shade. I followed at my
own pace, letting the sound of Toby's barking lead me in
the right general direction. I'd gone ten meters or so
when Nicky jumped out from behind a tree and yelled,
"Boo."

I pretended to jump, which went down well—I've got a play center's worth of younger cousins, so I know how that game is played.

"Behind you," shouted Nicky.

I turned theatrically to find nothing behind me.

"There's nothing behind me," I said, which caused more laughter.

I turned back to Nicky and this time I did jump—well, more accurately, I flinched.

The girl in the green dress was standing right in front of me, her face centimeters from mine, her eyes were large and hazel with golden flecks around the iris. This close she smelled of rough bark and crushed leaves. I could also see that she was a grown woman, physically in her twenties, and that I'd been fooled by her body language into thinking her younger.

"Boo," she shouted and laughed when I started back.

"Old man," shouted Nicky.

I turned to look, and when I turned back the woman in a green dress was gone—and so was Nicky.

Toby came scampering toward me, stuck his nose into the grass in front of my feet and snuffled around. Obviously finding nothing, he looked up at me and gave me a frustrated yap.

I told him to be quiet—I could see someone else approaching. Jake Phillips, activist at large.

"I see you've discovered the true secret of Skygarden," he said and for a moment I thought he might be yet another supernatural something or other, but he went on to say that the trees were some of the finest examples of their kind of London.

"They're the real reason the council couldn't get the tower delisted," he said.

Behind him I saw two impish faces peering around a tree trunk and sniggering.

"But there's no one here," I said. "It wouldn't be like this if people were still living in the blocks."

"You reckon?"

"I know it," I said. "This would be dog shit central during the day and pusher park at night."

He squinted at me. "Are you working for the council?"

"Chance would be a fine thing," I said.

"Or the media, or County Gard?" he asked.

"Who's County Gard?" I asked, because the easiest way to deflect suspicion is to side track your questioner onto a subject that *they* love to talk about. Sure enough, Jake Phillips started in on a lengthy diatribe which I cut short because I couldn't keep track without taking notes—and that would have been suspicious.

"Look," I said. "I've got to finish walking the dog but I am interested in hearing more."

"Don't give me that," he said.

"No, seriously," I said. "I don't believe in backing away from a fight. Besides, I've only just got here and I can't be arsed to move again."

I may have come across as a little bit too keen, but characters like Jake Phillips have been fighting the long defeat too long to pass up any help they can get.

"I'll tell you what. Why don't you and your partner come around to my place for tea?" he said and gave me his flat number.

I said I would, and we parted company—Toby was nowhere to be seen.

I found Toby further along the vanishing path in a glade full of sunlight and shining dust motes. A wool blanket of scarlet and green had been spread upon the grass and upon it sprawled, in the approved French impressionist manner, Oberon, Effra and Beverley Brook. Disappointingly, however, Beverley was wearing all her clothes.

Toby was sitting up at the edge of the blanket and doing his best small dog on the edge of starvation impression while Effra teased him with an M&S party-sized sausage roll. When she saw me she smiled and flicked the roll at Toby, who caught it in midair.

Oberon gestured grandly at a space on the blanket and I joined them.

Effra offered me a glass of white wine. Her nails added at least two centimeters to the length of her fingers and were painted with intricate designs in black, gold and red. I accepted the wine, it was a bit early in the day for me but that's not why I hesitated before drinking.

"Take this as a gift freely given," said Effra. "Drink with no obligations."

I drank. But if it was a fine vintage, it was totally wasted on me.

"So what brings you south of the river?" asked Beverley. She was wearing a bright blue jumper with a loose enough neck to show the bare brown curve of her shoulder. "Business or pleasure?"

"Just work," I said.

"Is there anything we can help with?" asked Oberon.

I caught a flash of green and yellow in the corner of my eye. But by the time I'd turned my head all I saw was Nicky in laughing pursuit of the vanished young woman.

"You can tell me who that is," I said.

"You could call her Sky," said Effra, which caused Beverley to choke on her wine.

"No?" I asked Beverley.

"Sky for short," she said. "Maybe."

"And what is she?" I asked. "And don't give me any of that stuff about reductionism and the dangers of labeling things you don't understand. I get enough of that from Nightingale and Dr. Walid."

"I suppose you'd call her a dryad," said Effra and then looked at Oberon for confirmation. "Yes?"

"*Drys*, in all truth refers to the oak tree," said Oberon which caused Beverley to roll her eyes. "Tree nymph would be more accurate, although I doubt the ancients had the London Plane in mind when they named them."

"Didn't you do this at uni?" I asked Effra, who had a history of art degree.

"I avoided the Pre-Raphaelites," she said. "All those virgins in the water. It was too much like my home life."

"Can I talk to her?" I asked.

Effra frowned. "I think I'd have to ask why first."

So I told them that there had been suspicious activity around the tower recently and that we were just checking it. Lesley would have been pissed off, had she found out. She thinks that however polite we're being, the police should never concede anything to anyone short of a full public inquiry. And even then we should lie like fuck on general principles, Lesley being part of the "you can't handle the truth" school of policing.

I, being a sophisticated modern police officer—given the specialist field I was working in—preferred to actively promote police/magic community stakeholder engagement in order to facilitate intelligence gathering. Besides, I knew better than to mess Effra about.

Effra nodded and called Nicky's name in a tone of voice that actually caused me to flinch guiltily. Oberon noticed my reaction and raised his glass in salute.

Nicky rushed in from the trees and flung herself on my back, little arms half strangling me, her cheek pressed against mine—I could feel her grinning. Sky, the possibly tree-nymph, despite being the size of a fully grown adult, jumped on Oberon's back. He didn't even grunt under the impact—the flash git. Sky leaned over his head and grabbed a bottle of Highland Spring off the picnic blanket, but the cap defeated her. Effra took the bottle from her hand, twisted the top off and handed it back.

"Peter here would like to ask you a few questions," she said. "But you don't have to answer if you don't want to."

"Hello, Sky," I said.

"Lo," said Sky, fidgeting her Highland Spring bottle from side to side.

"Do you live down here all the time?"

"I've got a tree," she said proudly.

"That's nice," I said. "Do you live with your tree?"

Sky gave me a strange look, and then lowered her head to whisper something in Oberon's ear.

"No, he lives in a big house on the other side of the river," he said.

"It's the prettiest tree in the world," said Sky, answering my question.

"I'm sure it is," I said and Sky beamed at me. "All I want to know is if you've seen anything strange happening near the tower."

"The tower is pretty, too," said Sky. "It's full of lights and it makes music."

"What kind of music?"

Sky's face screwed up as she thought of it.

"Happy music," she said and pointed up. "At the top."

Skygarden had once been famous as the site of Sanction FM, a pirate radio station which I used to listen to in my teens, even though the signal tended to go in and out. At least two Sanction DJs had gone on to hit the mainstream big time—one now had a two-hour prime slot on Radio 1Xtra. But I didn't think Sky was listening in on her FM radio. I tried to get her to clarify the kind of music she'd heard, but what she described could have been a distant party or the wind blowing around the strange angles of the tower.

Sky fell off Oberon's shoulders and sprawled melodramatically on her back. I was losing the witness and, while I've never done the training, I know that interviews with children or witnesses with low mental ages can take days. Because once they've stopped talking to you, they've really stopped talking to you. I asked whether she'd seen anything happening at the bottom of the tower.

"Lorries," she said.

"You saw lorries?"

"Lots of lorries," she said and sighed.

"When did you see the lorries?"

"Days ago," she said.

"How many days ago?" I asked.

"It was cold," she said, which could have been any time in the last four months. "I'm going to go play now." Sky launched herself to her feet in one fluid motion, and was gone before I could open my mouth. Nicky whooped and, putting her knee between my shoulder blades, launched herself in pursuit.

"Any use?" asked Beverley.

"I don't know," I said and got to my feet. "I may have to talk to her again."

"One of us," Effra indicated herself and Oberon, "would need to be on hand."

"Really, why's that?"

"She shouldn't be questioned without a responsible adult present," said Effra.

"These plane trees were planted in the 1970s," I said. "She's older than I am."

"And in the spring she's not competent to be questioned," said Effra.

"Perhaps I should call social services," I said.

"Don't be ridiculous," said Effra. "Do you think she has a birth certificate?"

"You can't have it both ways, Effra," I said. "You can't

have protection from the law and then pretend it doesn't exist when it suits you."

"Technically, we can," said Effra. "Human rights are not contingent upon the behavior of the individual."

This is not an argument you want to use with the police, but before I could counter with the traditional rebuttal centering around the competing notions of citizenship—and the fact that I had a body in the morgue that had been set on fire from the inside, and would you like to talk about my right not to have my head bashed in by a psychotic Russian witch? And in any case I didn't see your family helping with the clean up the other day—Oberon spoke.

"It is the spirit of the law that you should follow," he said. "In this instance she has the mind of a child and what blackguard would take advantage of her innocence to advance his cause, however noble?"

I didn't really have a counter argument for that, although I'm fairly certain Lesley would have, so I climbed to my feet with as much dignity as I could muster. Beverley followed me up and said that I could make myself useful and walk her back to her car. As we walked toward the Walworth Road, Nicky and Sky took turns to sneak up behind us and make hilarious farting noises.

"Is Sky always this childish?" I asked.

"Nah," she said, "this is just spring. She goes clubbing in the summer and does evening classes in the autumn."

"And in the winter?"

"In the winter she curls up around a good book and dreams away the cold."

"Where does she do that, then?"

"There are some questions it's not polite to ask," she said. "And some questions you shouldn't ask unless you're sure you want the answer."

We reached her car, which turned out to be another

two-seater Mini Roadster a bit like the one that got torched at Covent Garden, only with a honking 2-liter diesel engine and painted fire-engine red.

"What's with you and the Minis?" I asked.

"The Thames Valley," she said as she climbed in. "It's not just cottages and universities you know. There's still a bit of industry left." Then she flicked her dreads over her shoulder and drove away.

When she was safely out of sight I called Lesley.

"I think it's time we checked the basement," I said. "Bring the bag with you."

Lesley met me and Toby in the lift foyer of the lower ground floor. I took a moment to tell her about Sky the wood nymph. She seemed to find Beverley's appearance amusing.

"And she just happened to be there, didn't she?" she said. "Total coincidence."

We had two gray metal doors to choose from, one on either side of the entrance.

"Which one?" asked Lesley and she dumped the black nylon carry bag at my feet.

"Either," I said. "It's a circular plan—we should be able to work our way round."

Lesley chose a door at random and used the skeleton key that Sergeant Daverc had provided to open it up. She quickly found the light switch and stepped inside, so I grabbed the bag and followed. After a moment's hesitation, Toby followed me.

Inside, the room smelled of breezeblocks and moist cement. A row of metal lockers lined the exterior and interior walls. A door at the far end was marked with a yellow "Danger Electricity" triangle. I figured the wet cement smell came from what looked like recent work on the floor, visible as a darker-colored strip running across the room. I opened the bag and me and Lesley took a couple of minutes to tool up.

"Feel anything?" asked Lesley as I slipped on my Metvest, the undercover beige version without pockets that theoretically fits under your jacket.

"Nothing," I said.

"Me neither," she said. "Do you think that's normal?"

"Too early to tell," I said.

Once we had our Metvests on under our jackets we turned off our main phones and fired up a pair of airwave handsets that, while actually more expensive than our phones, were provided out of the police budget and thus expendable. These went on our tactical belts on which we also hung extendable batons, cuffs and pepper spray—but alas no taser yet.

"They're probably waiting for one of us to get freeze dried," said Lesley, whose attitude toward taser deployment was that people with heart conditions, epilepsy and an aversion to electrocution should not embark upon breaches of the peace in the first place.

Once we were kitted up, all we were missing was a motion tracker—the kind that makes sinister pinging noises. Instead we had to make do with Toby. Given the electrocution warnings, I picked him up as Lesley used the skeleton key on the next door.

"I want a nice clean dispersal this time," I said, and in we went.

The trick to spotting *vestigia*, or any of the other weird sensory impressions you get hanging around magic or magical folks, is separating them from all the memories, daydreams and randomly misfiring neurones that are the background noise of your brain. You start by spotting things that couldn't possibly be related to your current situation—as when you think of a barking dog while examining a man with his head knocked off. Your teacher reinforces your perception by confirming when you're right. The more you practice, the better you get. And it's not long before you ask the question — is this what causes schizophrenia?

Well, if you're me you ask that question. It never seemed to have occurred to Nightingale at all.

When I raised it with Dr. Walid he said one test would be for me to take anti-psychotic drugs and see if the *vestigia* went away. I declined, but I'm not sure whether I was more worried that it might work than that it might not.

There's a sort of background level of *vestigia* which I've come to expect pretty much everywhere in London. It falls away noticeably in the countryside, but you can get some very strong hot spots and what Nightingale calls *lacunae* — the remnants of recent magic. Because where you find high levels of *vestigia*, you generally also find the weird shit that the Folly is supposed to deal with. So me and Lesley have got into the habit of checking any new scene before we do anything else. This procedure, were we more integrated into the Met proper, would be called an Initial *Vestigia* Assessment or IVA, pronounced *I-vah*, as in — *I knew that Gandalf was a villain as soon as I'd finished my IVA.*

As far as I can tell, *vestigia* build up over time. So modern buildings like Skygarden tend to exhibit low background levels.

The next room was the building's power incomer, its electrical substation, recently modernized judging by the clean and compact gray boxes that lined one wall. The lighting was good, all the better to see the many warning symbols — particularly the one which showed a body lying on the ground with a stylized lightning bolt in its chest.

"Danger of death," read Lesley.

"Moving on," I said.

The next door put us in what I recognized as the base of the northern fire exit, and unlike everything else in the estate it was well designed. Fleeing residents were neatly channelled off the bottom flight of stairs and out through a pair of double fire doors.

"What's that smell?" asked Lesley.

"Old urine," I said. "And bleach." Almost from day one people would have used the stairwell as a convenient spot for a crafty slash and every two to three years the council would have brought in high pressure hoses and scrubbed it down.

"Animals," said Lesley.

"I think the dogs did it outside," I said. "It's odd that the doors are securely closed."

"They're alarmed," said Lesley pointing to a set of sensors at the top of the doors.

"This block is on the council shit list," I said. "The response to repeated abuse would be to shut the alarms off permanently. The doors should be propped open with bricks and there should be needles and condoms all over the floor."

"Mysterious, yes," said Lesley and then nodded at Toby who was yawning. "Magical, no. Next door."

We found the stairs down in the next room. As far as I could tell, we'd been working our way around the circumference on the lower ground floor and were now opposite the main entrance foyer. The breezeblock walls were bare but there had been work done on the floor here too—a strip of freshly laid cement running from the interior wall to the outer. A new damp course? I wondered.

A wide staircase descended to a familiarly shiny door with a County Gard logo and not one but two serious-looking padlocks in addition to the door's own lock. All three were resistant to the skeleton key.

"That's a health and safety violation," I said. "We've got the same key as the Fire Brigade."

"What's behind the door, do you think?" asked Lesley.

"The base of the central shaft for one thing," I said. "I'd like to find out what the fuck Stromberg was thinking of when he built it."

"We could burn the locks off," said Lesley.

"Subtle. I like it."

"Nah, you're right," said Lesley. "We can get Frank to ask County Gard to provide keys."

Frank Caffrey, as an official fire investigator, could just demand access. After Southwark got pasted for the six fire deaths at Lakanal House neither they nor their contractors were going to mess with the Fire Brigade. I wished I'd thought of that.

"Let's finish the rest of this floor," said Lesley, and that's what we did. We worked our way through the southern emergency exit, as suspiciously unsoiled as the northern one, the water incomer and another room with lockers. Apart from the now familiar fresh cement on the floor they were resolutely uninteresting. Toby didn't so much as growl which was, if anything, said Lesley, a sign of even less than background magic.

Our IVA completed, we put our kit back in the bag and let ourselves out into the foyer.

"Well, that was rewarding," said Lesley as we rode up in the lift.

"I don't think this place was built for people," I said.

"You say that about all modern architecture," said Lesley. "You want us all to live in pyramids."

"Actually," I said, "did you know the Egyptians invented the terrace?"

"Really?"

"They did sleep on the roof in the summer though."

"That must have been nice," said Lesley.

"I think Stromberg built this place as a magical experiment," I said.

The lift door opened and we stepped out.

"Why do you think that?"

"How many estates do you know that have wood nymphs living in the middle?" I asked.

"I don't know, Peter," said Lesley with a sigh. "Maybe all of them do. Certainly everywhere we go we seem to be tripping over these supernatural buggers." She stopped suddenly outside our door and pointed at the door jamb—the slip of paper we'd agreed to leave wedged into it was missing. I unzipped the bag and extracted our batons and passed Lesley hers. They made comforting little *shink* sounds as we flicked them open.

Lesley turned the key in the lock as quietly as she could, and nodded down from three. On zero she flung the door open and charged in, I went in a meter behind to avoid the embarrassing police dog-pile effect you get if the officer in front trips over something—say a skateboard. It's hard to project the full majesty and authority of the law when Lesley is sitting on your back and calling you a muppet.

Lesley went into the kitchen and yelled, "In here!" And I piled in behind her.

"I surrender," said Zach around a mouthful of cereal. He was sitting at our tiny kitchen table with a packet of Weetabix, an open loaf of bread, a now almost empty liter bottle of milk and open jars of raspberry jam and honey in front of him—both with knives stuck in them.

"How did you get in?"

"I've got a way with locks," he said. "It's a family thing."

"This would be the thieving side of the family," said Lesley.

"There's another side to his family?" I asked.

"Hey, leave my family out of this," said Zach, fishing the last two Weetabix out of the packet and then reaching for the milk.

"Is there a reason you came round, or did you just run out of food?" I asked.

Lesley put the kettle on and snatched the milk from Zach before he could finish it.

"There's this pub up west that Lesley wanted to know about," said Zach. "I can get me and her in this afternoon."

I looked at Lesley, who shrugged.

"We never did get to lay out our bait for the Faceless Man," she said.

"What's so special about this pub?" I asked.

"Full of fairies," said Zach.

"I've got to come with you," I said.

"Better if you don't," said Zach as he spread honey on his cereal. "You're a little bit too closely associated with the Thames girls, if you know what I mean. Makes the gentry a tad nervous."

"Besides, if we go in as a pair we will look like Old Bill. If I go in with Zach it will look more natural," said Lesley.

"Just another victim of my legendary charm," said Zach.

"And if our Night Witch is in there getting a rum and black?" I asked. "What're you going to do then?"

"Trust me, bro, it's not that kind of place, is it?

"Isn't it?"

"They wouldn't let your boss through the door, and he's respected," said Zach. "It's all strictly fae plus one and no wizards."

"Except Lesley?"

"Lesley's the exception that proves the rule, ain't she?" said Zach and I couldn't argue with that.

"Are you going to clear it with Nightingale?" I asked her.

"Duh!" said Lesley and handed me a cup of instant.

"In that case, I'm going to take Mr. Phillips up on his invitation. I bet he keeps an eye on who comes and goes," I said. "And while you're out you can pick up some more Weetabix." I checked the kitchen. "And bread and cheese and—did you eat the dog food?"

"Of course not," said Zach. "I fed the dog."

I checked Toby's bowl and saw he was already working his way through a suitable pile.

"Although I'll put my hand up to having some of his biscuits," said Zach.

13

The Back of the Lorry

IN BERLIN, THE Weimar Republic a massive work-ers' estate did decree. And they handed out the job to, among others, Bruno Taut, who built his estate in the shape of an enormous horseshoe. Once Lesley and Zach had gone, I used our fluctuating WiFi to look it up on Google Earth. As I'd remembered it, Taut's *Hufeisen-siedlung* enclosed a park with a central pond. Stromberg had admired Taut enough to have his prints on the wall of his study and I knew enough about architects' egos to know that they don't stick potential rivals on their walls unless they really like them. Or perhaps there'd been a professional connection that went beyond architecture — could they have been colleagues? Members of the *Weimarer Akademie der Höheren Einsichten,* the German equivalent of the Folly? Could he have been Taut's protégé? When the Nazis had taken power, Taut had fled to Istanbul and Stromberg to London. Nightingale had told me that the German expat wizards had either enthusiastically joined the fight or had been shipped to Canada. Had Stromberg kept his skills secret to avoid the fight? Given the subsequent casualty rate, I can't say I blamed him.

Had the Skygarden Estate been built in emulation of the *Hufeisensiedlung* only with a tower at its center instead of a pond? And did it have some purpose beyond inefficiently housing large numbers of Londoners?

I really didn't think the Faceless Man would be taking this much interest unless it had.

The WiFi connection dropped off and, search as I might, nobody else was offering free connections to the good people of Elephant and Castle. There were plenty of Internet cafés in the immediate area, but I wasn't that keen on doing without my TV that evening. Or at least that was the story I was planning to stick to.

Betsy Tankridge lived four floors up from us in one of the four-bedroom flats. When I rang the doorbell it was opened by Sasha, who stared at me for a good fifteen seconds before asking what I wanted.

"Is your mum in?" I asked.

It seemed to take an inordinate amount of time for him to parse a simple question before he turned his back on me.

"Mum," he yelled as he walked away. "Someone at the door."

As he stomped up the internal stairs his mum peered around the kitchen door and gave me a big smile.

"Peter, come in," she said and bustled me into the living room before retreating back into the kitchen to rustle up tea and biscuits. I sat down in the sort of large leather sofa that my mum would have approved of, and checked the room. The sideboards I reckoned were genuine antique oak but the cupboards, complete with decorative plates, were the new Polish furniture—although the high-end stuff made from real wood cut from an identifiable tree. The top row of plates were from Royal

Weddings starting with Princess Anne and ending with Will and Kate. The shelf below was all Royal Jubilees starting with the Silver Jubilee in 1977. Old Liz II looking increasingly dyspeptic with every plate.

Mounted on the wall opposite the sofa was a 75 inch Samsung LED which neatly confirmed that I'd come to the right place.

There were at least half a dozen pictures of Kevin, twice as many of Sasha—although mostly from when he was younger and less sullen. There were older pictures of a pleasant looking white man with a square face and lank brown hair—including a couple of him in a wide-lapelled penguin suit and top hat getting married to a stunningly attractive Betsy. Mr. Tankridge I presumed.

Betsy came back and caught me looking, but instead of telling me about her husband she put her tea tray down on the coffee table and asked if I took sugar. She poured from a pot-bellied teapot hidden under an obviously hand-knitted tea cozy into two mismatched but clean mugs. She dropped in two sugar lumps from a red bowl with a green Easter egg frieze around its lip and handed me the mug.

"I've only just moved down here and—" I started.

"Oh, where were you from before?"

"Kentish Town."

"That's in Camden isn't it?" asked Betsy.

I said it was and this seemed to satisfy Betsy, who lifted her mug to her lips, took a big slurp and gave me a calculating look.

"So what can we do you for?" she asked.

"I don't know the area and I was just wondering if you could point me in the direction of a reliable second-hand shop," I said.

"What you looking for?" asked Betsy.

"Just a TV for now."

Betsy gave me a happy smile.

"Well, it just so happens that you've come to the right place."

"You're mad to be moving in now," said Kevin in the lift going down.

"Yeah?"

"Oh, yeah," he said. Because what with the council wanting everyone out it was only a matter of time before they started cutting off the electricity, or the water, or "forgetting" to send the dustbin men around. I asked him why he was still there.

"Can't leave Sasha and Mum on their own, can I?" he said. "Christ knows what would happen to them."

I thought it more likely that his dear old mum would happen to somebody else rather than the other way round. But I kept my mouth shut.

"What about your brother, is he keen to move out?"

"He lives in his own little world in his room, don't he? Hardly ever comes out of that room," said Kevin. "And he won't be here for much longer."

I had Sasha pegged at about fourteen, fifteen tops— so I asked where he was going.

"Oxford," said Kevin with obvious relish. "Cambridge, somewhere like that."

"Don't tell me," I said. "Computers?"

Kevin gave a little bark of laughter.

"Computers?" he said. "I wish. God that would have been so useful. Nah. I got him a computer, state of the art and he just uses it for his homework. Pure mathematics, that's what Sasha does, he's taking his A-level this year."

God, he was proud—I didn't blame him. I would have been too.

We came out at the garage level and Kevin led me to

one of his two official garages, both of which he used for storing just about anything other than a car.

"I'm doing up a nice semi in Thornton Heath ready for when they throw us out," he said. "Get away from this shit hole." He unlocked the padlock on his garage and threw it open to reveal stacks of boxes. "See anything you like?"

Most of the boxes were small-ticket consumer items but I found a compact flatscreen TV with built-in digital which Kevin let me have for a ton now and a ton by the end of the week—a saving on the retail of about fifty percent, not counting VAT. I didn't ask him where it all came from, because he would have just told me it was a mystery.

As Kevin locked up again, I noticed that there were signs that fresh tarmac had been laid down in the last couple of months. It looked like a narrow trench had been dug from the base of the tower to the garages and then filled in and resurfaced. In fact, it was trenches plural. And, although I couldn't be certain, I was pretty sure that they matched the lines of fresh cement I'd seen inside.

"What's all that about?" I asked Kevin.

"Don't know," said Kevin. "Something to do with electrics I think."

Afternoon tea was not a concept much practiced in my household. After school I had tended to get fed according to my mum's schedule, not mine, although my dad, if straight, could whip up a mean cheese on toast. In the Folly, tea was available on demand to all members named Thomas Nightingale—me and Lesley had to get our own. So without any clear guidance, I turned up at Jake Phillips' front door at seven minutes past five.

"Come in, come in," said Jake when he opened the door. "Lesley not with you?"

"She's out job hunting," I said.

"It kills me," said Jake. "To see young people like you thrown on the scrap heap."

Jake lived in a two-bedroom flat with the same layout as mine and Lesley's but it was obvious as soon as I walked in that he'd been there for decades, and that the only way Southwark Council were going to extract him was feet first.

The narrow hallway was lined with framed photographs while the far end was dominated by a faux movie poster for *Gone with the Wind* starring Ronald Reagan sweeping Margaret Thatcher off her feet while a mushroom cloud bloomed behind them. *She promised to follow him to the end of the world. He promised to organize it.*

"We can have tea, or would you prefer a beer?" asked Jake.

I took the beer which turned out to be something called Young's Special London Ale. We chinked bottles in the kitchen and walked through to the living room. Unlike everyone else I'd ever met, Jake still had thick shag pile carpet in his flat. To my professionally trained eye, professionally trained by my mother that is, it looked worn but scrupulously clean—here was a man who shampooed his carpet regular. A rare individual. Two of the walls were covered floor to ceiling with pine and steel bracket bookshelves and, despite being jammed solid, the books had spilled over onto an antique gateleg table and were piled on the side tables that stood beside a pair of venerable green leather armchairs which would have fitted right in at the Folly. A third wall was dominated by a huge reproduction of Picasso's *Guernica*—and in case you're wondering, we did it at school in year nine as part of an integrated project on the Spanish Civil War.

"Since it's a nice day," he said, "why don't we go out into the garden?"

So we took our beers out through the patio doors and into his garden. The first thing I noticed was the fricking palm tree growing in the far corner. Its trunk, at least three meters high, curved over the end of the balcony so that its fronds framed the view over the Elephant and Castle and the fraudulent wind turbines of the Strata building opposite. The trenches at the top of the walls were planted with pink and yellow flowers and a cascade of honeysuckle that fell down to the impossible lawn that covered the floor of the balcony.

I squatted down and dug my fingers into the grass and the soil underneath.

"Welcome to how Skygarden was supposed to be," said Jake. "What old Erik Stromberg really intended."

Two red, blue and white striped deckchairs were propped up by the patio doors. We unfolded them on the lawn and, after a couple of collapses, sat down.

"All the balconies were originally built with a foot of clearance, especially to lay down topsoil," said Jake. "They're waterproofed and designed to drain slowly— look," he pointed at the underneath of the balcony directly above us. "You can see the drainage channels." These were three raised ridges in the concrete that fanned out from where the main waste water drop pipe ran down the length of the tower, adjacent to the two-meter thick support column.

"The lawn I believe," I said. "But what about the trees?" I pointed my beer at the three meter palm and, in the other corner, what looked like some kind of ornamental fruit tree.

"There's an additional foot of depth of soil at the end so you can plant trees," said Jake. "Stromberg knew you'd need the trees as cover to protect the rest of the garden from the wind."

"But our balcony's just concrete," I said.

"Yeah, well, they lost their nerve," he said. "They" being the Greater London Council, London's city government as it was before getting abolished in the 1980s. "Some of the early tenants complained and they concreted over the lot."

"Except for yours?"

"No," he said "I had to dig mine up, bit by bit. Took me the best part of six years. Then I had to make sure the drainage system still worked, not to mention having to shift all the soil in."

"God," I said. "No wonder you don't want them to knock this place down."

"That and it's a waste," he said. "You see those blocks? The Council said they were going to provide Housing Association build for those tenants, but have they fuck. They all got told six months to find alternative flats in the system or they was out—so they took what they could get."

"Those blocks were rubbish, though," I said.

"They were as good as any system-built block in London," he said. "And it's not like they're going to replace them with country cottages, is it? The trouble with people is they've got a romantic view of the past."

I doubted that I did, but I was enjoying the garden and the beer and it's rude to stop people talking.

"I've lived here for over forty years but I can still remember what it was like before," said Jake and then proceeded to tell me in great detail, including with statistics, about the outside toilets, the damp, the overcrowding, the bomb sites and just how vile a sublet terraced can be when there's a lot of you sharing the same bathroom. Assuming there is a separate bathroom and not a bath in the kitchen that serves as a table when not in use.

Bath in the kitchen? I could hear my mother saying. *Luxury! In Sierra Leone we used to dream of a bath in the kitchen.* Only obviously not in a Yorkshire accent.

For Jake, the problem was not in the design but in the people.

"People were proud to get a flat," he said. "They appreciated having all the mod cons." This being the proper working class who did a day's work with their hands and scrubbed their front step. Who understood the importance of education.

"If you went into the library in them days it was full of men who'd just come off the morning shift," he said. "You could have heard a pin drop in there." And they were all diligently improving their minds and occasionally buying the *Daily Worker* on their way out.

"I used to sell half my copies outside the library," said Jake. "That's the kind of working man who used to be allocated a council flat. Back then it was a privilege, not a right." He finished his beer. "Not that decent housing shouldn't be a human right, you understand? But in those days people appreciated what they had."

And what they had were streets in the sky with indoor plumbing. High above the noise and smell of the traffic, where the elongated artist's impression of young white mothers with strollers waved to their friends from improbably clean concrete walkways under a sky of Battle of Britain blue.

"If we'd had the right political structures in place," said Jake, "proper local democracy, we could have kept the communities intact. Now everything's handled at arm's length through contractors and *agencies*." He practically spat the last word. "There used to be people you could hold to account. But now it's all call centers explaining that your job doesn't seem to be on the system. Nobody is accountable any more."

"Contractors like County Gard?" I said. Normally I'd have tried to avoid asking such a direct question in case it garnered suspicion, but I didn't think Jake would notice. He was one of those people who constantly seems to be having a conversation with someone other than the person he's actually talking to—presumably someone much more politically committed. And interested.

"Lackeys of the capitalist class," he said. "Although it has to be said they are full service lackeys, offering a comprehensive range of products and services designed to keep the working class in their place."

Because they didn't just secure the flats against squatters. They were also the debt collection agency responsible for collecting rent and poll tax arrears. "Although you only find that out if you're willing to spend some time in Companies House," he said. "There's a whole series of nested shell corporations it takes ages to work through."

"Suspicious," I said.

"Par for the course really," said Jake. "All part of the tax avoidance merry-go-round."

County Gard, along with the companies behind them, were desperate to get the development going. "There's no commercially owned land this close to the City that wouldn't be so expensive it would cut into their profits." So instead they looked to gull cheap land out of local councils desperate for cash.

"Why pay full whack when you can get it off the back of the lorry cheap?" said Jake. "Council land is essentially cheap land because the councils are desperate to increase their housing stock, but don't have the funds to do it. All these *developers* have to do is promise to have some so-called affordable housing and it's money in the bank."

"They must have been pissed off when this place stayed listed," I said.

"That was down to the trees, that was," said Jake. Because English Heritage, being a bastion of middle class privilege, were that much more concerned with rare trees than they were with common people.

"But they're just plane trees," I said.

Apparently not, because we got through another beer on the subject of the local arboreal diversity before I could make my excuses and leave. I did wonder whether this diversity had something to do with the presence of our favourite wood nymph. Or vice versa.

Once I got back to the flat I called the inside inquiry team at Bromley MIT and suggested they check to see whether the recently cooked-from-the-inside Patrick Mulkern had any connection to County Gard. It was a long shot, but the rule of a major investigation is always throw everything into the pot. You might not find that bit of okra tasty, but somewhere deep in the bowels of the investigation some DC on a mission might snap it up.

I remote-checked my messages at the tech cave and found that I had three. Two from my mum re: my dad's teeth and one from Professor Postmartin who, having trawled through the list of Stromberg's books provided by the National Trust, had found one that was of interest.

"It's called *Wege der industriellen Nutzung von Magie*," said Postmartin when I called him back. "I've already asked them to deliver it to the Folly."

"What does that translate as?"

"*Toward the Industrial Use of Magic*," said Postmartin.

"Have you read it?"

"Never heard of it before," said Postmartin. "But, by

a stroke of good fortune, we're listed as having a copy here." Here being the semi-secret stacks of the Bodleian Library. "I thought I might spend today and tomorrow reading it so I can give you a précis. Although I believe I can make a wild guess based on the title that it's a treatise on the industrial uses of magic."

"Impressive deduction," I said.

"Merely an outgrowth of my mad academic skills," said Postmartin.

"Indubitably," I said.

When Lesley hadn't returned by early evening I decided I might as well get some practice in. I figured that casting in the flat, with the consequent effect on the surrounding electronics, would be anti-social. So I went downstairs to what I now thought of as Sky's garden. That way it would be a combination practice, dog walk and wood nymph observation.

Having been lectured by Jake Phillips on the arboreal variety of the gardens I'm fairly certain that I correctly identified the shorter bushy rowan trees, including a couple of small ones that looked like they'd grown from seeds. And the crab-apples were easy to spot, with their purplish bark and hairy buds. I was also pleased to note that what I thought earlier were silver birches were really silver birches. Nightingale would have been proud of me.

I chose the dismantled children's playground, making sure I stood with my back to the cherry trees so I could keep an eye on the tower and avoid accidentally shredding the blossom.

When I first started my apprenticeship, practice was a slog. And, while my appreciation and skill have improved, running through your *formae* again and again as you strive to perfect them is never going to be a laugh a minute.

And you don't even get to do cool martial art stances while you do them. Although me and Dr. Walid have speculated that the *formae* somehow represented the interaction between our electrochemically powered nervous system and the magical—field? Subspace dimensional manifold? Banana flavored milkshake? —that creates observable effects in the material world. If that was the case, then surely it might be possible to generate the same effect through gesture, stance and movement. Certainly it seemed natural to enhance a spell-casting with gestures. Even Nightingale had his quirks—the little flick of his hand for *impello*, the admonitory finger wag for *aer* and the opening hand movement that accompanied the first spell I ever learnt—*lux*.

What frustrated me was the thought that with three thousand years of history someone in China, some monk in a monastery halfway up a mountain, must have developed a magic *kata*, a physical expression of *formae*. Or at least have got close enough to explain all those legendary swordsmen and their inexplicable desire to roost in the tops of bamboo trees.

Toby lay on his back in the grass while I worked my way through *lux*, *aer* and *aqua*, but stirred when I started adding my second-order effects with *impello*, *iactus*, *palma* and my personal favourite *scindere*. Then he jumped up and started chasing my little globes of water around the playground. He seemed to particularly enjoy the way they burst when he bit them.

Just as I'd expected she would, Sky appeared and chased after Toby and the water globes. I added a couple of low level werelights to follow them both—for fun and because it was good practice. When I paused for breath Sky rushed over and grabbed my hand.

"Follow me," she said.

"Where?" I asked.

She put her hands on her hips and pushed out her lip. "Just follow, okay?"

"Okay," I said and when she skipped off I followed. When we reached the edge of the playground she did a sharp turn and followed its perimeter. Once we'd completed a circuit and returned to where we'd started, she turned and gave me a cross look.

"You've got to do the dance," she said.

It's a sad fact of modern life that sooner or later you will end up on YouTube doing something stupid. The trick, according to my dad, is to make a fool of yourself to the best of your ability.

The sun dropped into the dark slot between the blocks and the garden was filled with a dusty orange light. Sky danced around the dismantled playground and me and Toby followed. He yapped at my heels as I tried to match her turns and stretches and suddenly I was feeling it—feeling that now familiar change in the phase state of existence, like a catch in the silence at the moment of creation.

And then she jumped and spun sideways, lifted whirling into the air like a leaf on the wind. Or like Zhang Ziyi in a flying rig. She touched down a few meters further away and, spinning, danced on. I caught up and matched her step for step, move for move and when she jumped again I followed.

And for a second I felt the wind lifting me and experienced a surge of joy at my escape from the constant pull of the earth, my freedom.

And then the ground smacked me in the gob.

I lay face down for a while, soil and grass mixing with blood in my mouth. Two meters away Sky had collapsed in a heap and was laughing hysterically, drumming her heels on the grass and pausing only to draw breath and point.

I spat the grass out of my mouth and sat up. I'd bitten my lip, not badly but just enough to draw blood.

"It's not that funny," I said but obviously Sky thought it was. Toby did a lap of honor around the playground, yapping occasionally.

The shadow of the blocks had stretched across the gardens, except for the strip of sunlight we were sitting in. I looked up and saw that the dirty brown concrete had been shaded russet by the sun, which reflected a brilliant orange off the windows. Now I knew what to look for, I could easily spot Jake Phillips' balcony with its palm and trails of honeysuckle and ivy.

I looked further up to the top of the tower, but at this angle I couldn't see anything on the roof proper.

I called Sky, who had at least stopped laughing by then, and she wriggled over on her belly until she was by my side. I noticed that if she was getting grass stains on her dress, they were blending imperceptibly into the fabric.

"Sky," I asked.

"What d'you want?"

"Is there still music coming from the top of the tower?"

Sky arched her back to stare up at the top of the tower, her face screwing up in concentration.

"Yep," she said and collapsed on her face.

I calmed my breathing and waited for Toby to shut up—then I listened carefully. There was traffic on the Walworth Road, and behind that the background thrum of the city. I think there might have been a snatch of conversation from somewhere halfway up the tower. But no music—at least nothing I could hear.

"Is it coming from the very top or from the floor below?" I asked.

Sky gave it some thought.

"Top," she shouted and pointed to the sky. "Top, top, top!"

"Would you like to come and have a look with me?" I asked as I stood up.

Sky shuddered. "Nope. It's cold—bedtime," she said, and I saw that the sun had set behind us and the shadow had crept all the way to the base of the tower. Sky followed me up and gave me a little wave.

"Bye bye," she said and walked away into the gloom.

I took Toby back to the flat where he stuck his face happily in a bowl full of biscuits while I asked myself— what could be going on at the top of the tower?

I still had the skeleton key in my pocket, so I put on a jumper and took the lift to the top floor and used it to access the stairs to the roof. While I was traveling up I composed a text explaining where I was going and sent it to Lesley and Nightingale. Your colleagues can't come and rescue you if they don't know where you are.

God, I'm seeing a lot of the city these days, I thought as I stepped out onto the roof. The sun was sinking into the folds of West London and I might have spent more time picking out landmarks if I hadn't been losing the light and not carrying a torch. The first thing that struck me was the strange hexagonal structure at the center which rose like a truncated gazebo roof and was surmounted by a concrete cylinder, three meters across and four tall.

It wasn't a water tank or pumping station, because Skygarden had four conventional tanks all mounted in an offset cruciform over four of the housing stacks. It couldn't be the housing for the lift machinery because it was mounted dead center right over the tower's hollow central shaft. The only thing I could think it might be was part of the building's tuned mass damper.

Beyond their limitations as social housing, tall buildings have another problem—which is that they sway in the wind. If the swaying motion amplifies it can quickly exceed the structural integrity of the building and, in a system-built structure, many of the inhabitants get to be the squishy filling in a concrete sandwich. Even the most idealistic architect tries to keep fatalities to a minimum and the standard answer is a tuned mass damper. This is essentially one or more compensating heavy weights which swing left when the building swings right, and vice versa, dampening the oscillation and thus avoiding embarrassing questions like "Where's the skyline gone?"

When I say heavy weights, I mean heavy. For a building the size and height of Skygarden, a couple of tons at least.

There was a single door set into the ridged concrete side of the mysterious cylinder. The door's surface was metal but old, pitted and rusted at the edges—definitely not the work of County Gard. Amazingly, with a bit of artistic jiggling, the skeleton key worked, which meant that the door dated back to the original build.

Inside, it was very dark but I am, if not exactly a master, then definitely an apprentice in the secret arts. And as such I laugh in the face of darkness.

Now, making a werelight was the very first spell I ever learnt and I've spent more than a year practicing it so I'm pretty confident with it. I can run you up a werelight in torrential rain or while reading the newspaper and the size and intensity of the light will be consistent every time.

So imagine my surprise when I flicked open my palm and got a werelight the size of a football and the color of a yellow party balloon. I closed down the spell and tried again, this time adding *impello* so I could move the light about. Nightingale says that spells become more stable with each increase in complexity, so I was hoping the second *forma* would calm things down.

It still came out so bright I expected lens flare, and as it rose up I suddenly understood why Bruno Taut's sketches had been on Stromberg's wall. Inside the concrete cylinder was a scaled-down version of Taut's glass pavilion, like a giant acorn made of interlocking panes of glass. In the brilliance of my werelight the panes reflected back in greens, blues, purples and indigos. I tried to imagine what it would be like without the concealing concrete cylinder. You'd barely see it from ground level. But from a distance, or if it were lit from within . . .

There was even a central plinth where, if it had been a lighthouse, the lamp would have stood. A meter across, it was raised to waist height and covered in a thick layer of dust. I wiped at it with my hand and got a static electric shock. Which was a surprise, because I could have sworn the surface was plastic. I used the sleeve of my jacket to clean the top. It was plastic, smooth black PVC with a pattern incised into the surface—a complicated series of interlocking circles and intersecting lines I didn't recognize from anything I'd read.

It *was* a lighthouse, I realized, or more precisely a *Stadtkrone*, a city crown. But it had always been assumed that the "spirit" of the city was a metaphorical concept at best and a bit of metaphysical bollocks at worst.

Is this what Erik Stromberg had been watching for with his telescope from his rooftop garden on Highgate Hill? Gazing over the city and waiting to see—what exactly? A magic lighthouse? The mystical energy of the metropolis?

I glanced up at my unnaturally bright werelight bobbing a meter above my head.

Magic, *vestigia* . . . Whatever it is that powers what we do.

Watching for a burst of magic like the burn-off at the top of a refinery flare tower?

Making Skygarden what? A magic refinery, a drilling rig, magic mine? And extracting the magic from where? The ground? The people? Sky's garden?

Now I knew what it was, I was sensing I could identify it as the greasy, static-charged sense of power in the air. If Toby had been in there with me he would have barked himself right off the yap scale.

Wege der industriellen Nutzung von Magie, I thought. *Toward the Industrial Use of Magic*—oh yeah.

Now I knew what the Faceless Man was interested in.

14

Something Missing

THERE HAVE BEEN developments. Please see me at your earliest convenience. Nightingale.

"Still hasn't really got the hang of texting yet, has he?" said Lesley.

She'd been in the kitchen making coffee when I woke up the next morning. I asked her what her evening had been like.

"We ended up at Shepherd Market," she said. "In one of those pubs that are tucked into a side street."

"Do you want to know why that is?"

Lesley handed me a coffee. "If I said 'no' would there be any chance you wouldn't tell me?"

"Yes. But then it would just niggle away at you until it became unbearable," I said.

"That's the way *you* are," she said. "I'm a little bit more focused on the practical things in life."

"Like fairies?"

"Do you want to know what happened or not?"

I tasted the coffee. It was vile. It always is when Lesley makes instant.

"Thanks," I said.

She sat down at the other end of the sofa-bed.

"It was an ordinary pub," she said. "A bit traditional looking, Australian barman, but no TV though and no music. There was a stage area, so maybe they prefer it live. But you can feel it, like at the Spring Court—that something."

There was a man there so beautiful that he would have stopped a hen party in its tracks, and a woman dressed in strips of fur.

"You don't know what it's like to take your mask off in front of people," she said. "And know they don't care." She must have caught something in my expression, because she hastily added, "People that aren't you and Nightingale. These people don't care, in fact they don't even notice—that includes Beverley you know. So whatever she sees in you, it ain't your face. Lucky escape for you there really—isn't it?"

"Funny," I said.

"So Zach introduces me to some suitably dodgy-looking geezers, who I shall write up when I get back to the Folly." She waved her hand vaguely in the direction of central London. "I did the spiel to them and they said they'd keep an eye out for the materials we wanted."

"Did they ask what you wanted it for?" I said.

"First lot didn't, but then this woman sidles over and says she couldn't help overhearing, blah blah blah. 'What on earth could you want all *that* for?' That's how she spoke. 'You *simply* must tell me what you're planning.'"

So Lesley refused to give any details, while dropping enough hints to make it clear that we were making our own staffs.

"Did you find out anything about her?"

"It's all in my notebook," said Lesley. "Said she was an artist. Made batik prints and flogged them up Camden Lock."

Where our Night Witch had gone to ground. Coincidence?

"After that we all got hammered. And me and Zach ..." She frowned. "And some friends, crashed out in a portacabin on the Crossrail site."

"How did you get in there?"

"Oh Zach's all over Crossrail now," she said. "What with him being semi-official liaison between the project and the Quiet People." Without whose tunneling expertise, I learned, Crossrail would have been behind schedule. "He must be making some serious money."

"Not enough to get his own place, though."

"I don't think he can, Peter," said Lesley. "I think he has something missing that means he literally can't settle down. If you put him in a mansion, with servants and a swimming pool, he still wouldn't be able to sleep there more than a couple of nights." She rubbed irritably at the ridge of skin that ran down between her eyes. "I think it's part of what makes Zach Zach. I think they're all like that you know? Not quite all there."

Which was when we received Nightingale's text.

He met us in a Colombian café tucked under one of the arches by the Elephant and Castle National Rail station. It had orange walls hung with bundles of wickerwork baskets and shelves crowded with mysterious bottles with red labels. Half the food counter was devoted to hard-to-get treats for the homesick expatriate — *La Gitana Tostados* and *Wafers Noel*. The menu was bilingual and I had the *arepa con carne asada* which was translated on the menu as corn bread with grilled beef. Lesley had a ham omelette on the basis that it was almost impossible to mess a ham omelette up.

Nightingale said the coffee was good, so I ordered a double espresso with a cappuccino chaser.

Nightingale put down his free copy of *Express News* as we joined him at his table.

"Dr. Walid has made a disturbing breakthrough in the Robert Weil case," he said. "He's discovered evidence of chimeric cells on the body of the woman Weil dumped."

"Shit," said Lesley. "So the Faceless Man was involved in that as well."

"A chimera of what crossed with what?" I asked. Because, having gone mano-a-mano-tiger with one of the Faceless Man's creations, I really wanted to know what it was going to be this time.

"Abdul said you would ask. But he didn't have enough of a sample to determine that," said Nightingale. Despite the shotgun to the victim's face, Dr. Walid had managed to extract tissue cells that had been driven into the eye sockets by the blast. It had taken this long to get them sequenced.

"It's not like Old Faceless to make a mistake like that," said Lesley. "He's always been very forensically aware."

"He's just another criminal, Lesley," said Nightingale. "His training makes him personally dangerous but it doesn't make him invincible. And he's not Professor Moriarty—he doesn't have a plan for every contingency. He made a mistake with Peter in Soho and almost got himself caught."

Coffee arrived and the espresso was excellent, like an aromatic electric fence.

"Robert Weil was clearly an associate of some kind," said Nightingale.

"Shouldn't we pass that on to Sussex Major Crimes?" I asked.

"They won't thank us," said Lesley. "They have their victim and they easily have enough to send Robert Weil up the steps for it. As far as they're concerned it's a result, and they're not going to be interested in widening it out."

"I'm going to call Sussex this morning and after that Bromley," said Nightingale. "As I believe you have both impressed upon me often enough that the currency of modern policing is information."

"Yeah," I said. "But we didn't think you were paying attention."

My corn bread arrived with a slab of grilled beef. I thought the corn bread was a bit dry, but according to Nightingale that was how corn bread was supposed to be. I slathered on enough chili sauce to moisten it up, which I gathered from the waitress's approving looks was exactly what I was supposed to do.

"Can you actually taste the meat?" asked Lesley, who was cutting her omelette into squares small enough to fit in the mouth hole of her mask.

"It's the combination," I said.

"One thing does puzzle me," said Nightingale. "Why would Stromberg build himself a *Stadtkrone* and then wrap it up in concrete?"

"I got that figured out," I said. I'd checked the enclosing cylinder before heading downstairs. "Everything in Skygarden is either constructed of formed concrete or breezeblocks." In the case of the formed concrete, with the ridges and irregularities of the mold left on the finished surface —the better to emphasize the basic honesty of the design and ensure that small children could pick up really painful grazes while playing in the corridors. "But the cylinder is constructed of vertical strips with a narrow rectangular cross section that have been cemented together."

Nightingale and Lesley gave me glazed looks.

"It's durable enough to survive the weather outside,"

I said. "But in the event of an overpressure event inside, I think it's designed to flower open like a Chocolate Orange."

Me and Lesley then had to explain Terry's Chocolate Orange to Nightingale.

"Not unlike a practitioner's hand opening to reveal a werelight," said Nightingale.

"Not unlike at all," I said. Yeah, exactly like that, I thought.

"And then what?" asked Lesley. "What did Stromberg expect to happen then?"

"Inspired by the light of reason," said Nightingale, "the good people of Southwark would march arm in arm into a utopian future."

"I think he needed to get out more," said Lesley.

Nightingale sipped his coffee, his brow furrowed.

"In view of his discovery," he said, "Peter will go back to the Folly and have a look at this German book in case it can shed some light on what Stromberg thought he was doing."

"My German's non-existent . . ." I began, but Nightingale held up his hand.

"What the pair of you have discovered makes me even more certain that the Faceless Man has a strong interest in this particular locale," he said. "If there's even a chance he, or our Russian friend, might turn up in person then this is an opportunity I can't pass over. If we can put just one of them out action we'll be cutting the threat in half."

"So you're leaving Lesley hanging out as bait?"

"I have much more faith in Lesley's sense of self-preservation than in yours," said Nightingale. "In any case, the Faceless Man has your measure as a practitioner, while Lesley will be an unknown. I'm counting on his caution."

I wasn't sure I found that particularly reassuring, but in the event of an attack I wasn't going to be as much use as Thomas "Oh sorry, was that your Tiger Tank?" Nightingale. So after we'd finished breakfast I hopped on a 168 bus back to Russell Square.

I went in the front and, as I'd expected, there was a courier-delivered parcel balanced on top of the pile of junk mail that constantly accumulated on the occasional table just inside the atrium. I looked around for Molly, who usually appeared to greet us when we arrived home—if only to ensure that we understood we lived here purely at her sufferance. I thought that the atrium seemed strangely quiet, which was funny when you consider the deathless hush that hung over the place when I'd first moved in.

She wasn't in the kitchen when I stepped in to raid the pantry. I made myself a cheese and pickle sandwich, tucked the parcel under my arm and headed out the back door for the coach house. When I climbed the spiral staircase to the first floor I found that the door was unlocked, so I wasn't totally shocked when I opened up and caught Molly in the tech cave, feather duster in hand—mid dust.

She paused and turned her head to look at me.

"Sorry," I said. "I didn't know you were in here."

She gave me a reproving look and, with a snap, the feather duster vanished up her right sleeve. I stepped aside politely as she swept past me and closed the door behind her when she'd gone.

The master off-switch was in the off position, but when I felt the side of the PC's tower it was still warm. I fired everything up and got the blue screen of Your Computer Failed To Shut Down Correctly, as if I needed more confirmation. I wondered what Molly had been doing—I doubted it was solitaire. While I waited for my

PC to reboot I unwrapped my parcel, two layers of bubble wrap and tissue paper no less and a note that very politely informed me that I would be held responsible for any damage.

It was easy to see how the book might have been overlooked. It was smaller than a mass market paperback, with a dull red hardback cover and high quality paper that was only now faintly browning with age. The ink quality was good, easy on the eye, and it would have been a pleasure to read if I only I read German.

What made it truly valuable to the investigation were the initials *E.S.* pencilled on a corner of the first page, and the fact Eric Stromberg had gone on to mark parts of the text that interested him. It was just as well Postmartin had his own copy, because he regarded people who annotate books the way my dad looked upon people who left their fingerprints on the playing surface of their vinyl. I did wear a pair of thin latex gloves in Postmartin's honor though—which, come to think of it, is the way Dad would like to see people handle records.

One of the pages had a piece of card, the lid of a cigarette packet judging by the smell, as a place marker. And underlined here twice in heavy pencil was:

So sei nun meine These, daß sich Magie, die einen begrenzten Raum ausfüllt, wie eine übersättigte Lösung verhält und daß jeder Eingriff, ob natürlichen oder artifiziellen Ursprungs, zum spontanen Auskristallisieren des magischen Effekts führen kann.

Which according to Google translated as: *So now is my thesis that magic that fills a confined space, such as a supersaturated solution behaves and that any interference, whether natural or artificial origin, can lead to the spontaneous Auskristalliseren of magical effect.*

I looked up *Auskristallisieren* in my dictionary and online without success, but I was willing to bet it meant "crystallize." Not long after that passage was another underlined section:

Daher sollte es durchaus möglich sein, das magische Potential in industriellem Maßstabe auskristallisieren zu lassen und zur späteren Verwendung aufzubewahren.

Which translated as: *Therefore, it should be quite possible to crystallize on an industrial scale the magical potential and save them for later use.*

I made a note of all the pages and passages underlined or otherwise marked, and e-mailed the details to Postmartin.

So Skygarden really was a magic drilling rig. But that still left the problem of where the magic was being drilled from. And it would really help if we had a working definition of what magic was. I went back to the book—after all, if you were going to industrialize it, you pretty much had to know how it worked.

I found a promising section on types of *vestigium*— Stromberg had thought so, too, judging from his notes in the margin. These broke it down into four main types, *Todesvestigium*, *Magievestigium*, *Naturvestigium* and *Vestigium menschlicher Aktivität*. I didn't even need the Internet for the first three, death, magic and nature. And the fourth translated as *human activity*. Stromberg had pencilled *nicht sinnvoll*, "not useful," by death and *unwahrscheinlich*, "unlikely," by natural so probably not an old hospital site or gallows. Stromberg had obviously got as frustrated as me because beside human activity he'd written *aber welche Art von Aktivität?* "But what kind of activity?" Underneath in what looked like it might be a different pencil, or just a blunter one—as if written later—were the words *Handwerk nicht Fließband!* "Craft not pipelined!"

So what had brought Stromberg to the Elephant and Castle?

After the City of London itself, Southwark was the oldest bit of London proper, dating all the way back to the first ad hoc settlement on the south end of London Bridge. It had also always been the place that London stuck the things it didn't want inside its walls, the tanneries, fullers, dyers and other industries that involved urine on an industrial scale. And, likewise, the other things that London needed but didn't want too close, the bath houses and stews, the theaters and the bear pits. Carved through stinking, drunken, declaiming streets were the two Roman roads that linked the great bridge with Canterbury and the south coast. Shakespeare got pissed on a regular basis in Southwark. So did Chaucer—or at least his fictional pilgrims did.

But where Skygarden was built? Marsh, then farmland and then housing. Not so much as a smithy or a lunatic asylum. Not even the whiff of a plague pit or a temple of Mithras.

I had two theories. Either Stromberg had discovered something in the locality—an ancient temple, a stone circle, site of a massacre or iron age industrial site—or he'd been planning to extract magical power out of the everyday lives of council flat tenants. No wonder he was waiting up on his roof with his telescope until the day he died.

I decided I'd exceeded any useful activity, *Handwerk* or *Fließband*, that I could achieve where I was, so I shut everything down in the tech cave, placed our new German acquisition in the safety of the non-magical library and headed out to catch the bus back across the river.

Molly watched me leave, no doubt impatient for me to be gone so she could get back to the computer. The keystroke tracker I'd activated would tell me what she was up to.

Lesley was waiting for me in the living room, sprawled

on the sofa bed and twirling her mask by one of its eye-holes as she watched *Dennis and Gnasher* on CBBC. Toby was sitting in front of the TV, head cocked to one side as if judging Gnasher's form as a freestyle event.

"I'm going to go see Zach," she said without preamble.

"What for?"

"Because you never get everything out of Zach on the first go," she said. "And if I have to stay in this flat all evening I will not be held responsible. Any joy with the Germans?"

I floated my drilling rig hypothesis, which she agreed was farfetched. "Unless watching telly counts as human activity. Speaking of which, I dropped in on our neighbor."

"Emma Wall?" I asked—the fallen princess?

"You know how some people work at being stupid?" she asked. "If you give them a clear, common sense choice they give it a lot of thought and then choose stupid."

"I think we did probation with a couple of those," I said.

"For some people stupid comes natural—Emma Wall is one of those," she said and standing started hunting out clothes from a suitcase.

"So, not a mole for the Faceless Man?"

"Not unless he's got really low recruitment standards."

"Bugger," I said. "The fucker is so slippery."

Lesley held her two masks either side of her face. "Which one do you think?" she asked. "Vile pink or tax envelope tan?"

"Vile pink," I said as she disappeared into the bedroom. "You really think Zach's got more to tell you?"

"More to tell me, yeah," she shouted from inside the bedroom. "Useful? I don't know."

Ten minutes later she was out the door in a pair of skinny jeans, a cream blouse and a leather jacket that I happened to know had been modified so she'd have somewhere to carry her baton and her cuffs.

"You never know when you might need them," she'd said to me pointedly when she showed me the pockets. "And it gives the jacket a better hang."

I texted Nightingale to let him know our change in disposition and then I picked up my Pliny, because nothing says stuck all alone in your flat like a Roman know-it-all.

It had started raining when I took Toby out for his combination dog walk and snooping session. We strolled about the dismantled playground but Sky didn't make an appearance among the dripping trees. As we squelched back along the elevated walkway I heard the grumbling of van-sized diesels—at least two by the sound of them. When I reached the tower I leaned over the parapet and peered through the gray falling rain. Half hidden behind the curve of the tower I saw two Transits, Mark 7s with the 2.2 diesel, backing up in front of one of the garages. One of the vans was in the white, yellow and blue County Gard livery but the other was plain dark blue with no markings. I could have used my magical abilities to get a closer look, but instead I used the zoom function on my phone. That way I could record them at the same time.

The vans blocked my view of the garage but it was pretty clear that they were transferring stuff from the vehicles. I thought of Kevin's cache of dodgy goods and wondered if this might be similar. Not everything had to do with the mystical forces of evil—totally ordinary crime could be going on at the same time.

Toby sneezed. The vans finished unloading and drove away and we went up to the flat to dry off. Toby got dinner and I got back to my Pliny.

I woke up to the sound of rain driving horizontally against the window panes and no sign of Lesley. Since I was awake I got up and spent the morning accidentally running into the off-duty Goth and the man in a tweed jacket that I'd pegged as possible inside men for the Faceless Man. Goth boy was simple enough—I just stepped into the lift and struck up a conversation. It's amazing how easy it is to get white boys to talk to you when you share a lift. By the time we hit the ground floor I knew his name, flat number and more of his life story than I really wanted; Lionel Roberts, a flat two floors down from us and a wannabe poet currently working as security in Hannibal House—the office block built on top of Elephant and Castle shopping center. Tweed jacket man had a ten-year-old daughter who Toby quickly had eating out of his hand, or more precisely vice versa. Her name was Anthonia Beswick and his name was Anthony and he was currently unemployed, but optimistic that the recession wouldn't last forever. He said it was wife's idea to name their daughter after him but I didn't believe him. Could have been worse, I decided. It could have been Nigella.

I called in an IIP check on both of them, but my instinct was that neither were minions of the Faceless Man. The rain eased off by noon, so I had lunch out at the shopping center and then stopped off in the garden to do some of the less obtrusive bits of my practice. I thought I heard giggling in the distance but there was no other sign of Sky.

Lesley had returned while I was out, with a metric ton of neglected paperwork which we dutifully worked our way through before flopping down on the sofa bed with a microwaved lasagne and a Red Stripe each.

"Why aren't you fucking Beverley?" she asked suddenly.

I spluttered around my Red Stripe.

"Why aren't you fucking Zach?" I asked, finally.

"Who says I'm not?"

"Are you?"

"Maybe," she said. "A bit."

"How can you be fucking him a bit?"

Lesley gave this point due consideration.

"Okay, maybe more than a bit," she said.

"Since when?" I asked.

"Why do you want to know?"

That was a good question and I didn't really have a good answer. Still, nobody's ever let that get in the way of a conversation.

"You brought it up," I said.

"Yeah, I asked you a question which you still haven't answered," she said.

"What makes you think that Beverley's interested?"

"You're going with that? Really?"

I got up and took the dirty plates back to the kitchen and fetched another beer. I didn't fancy sitting down again, so I leaned against the doorjamb.

"We could call Beverley and find out," said Lesley, "She'd be here fast enough—you can practically see Barnes from our balcony."

"I'm not in a hurry to rush into that one," I said.

Lesley rounded on me and pointed at her face, forcing me to look at the whole horrid mess of it. "This is what happens if you wait, Peter," she said. "Or some other fucked-up thing. You've got to get it while you can."

And I thought that I'd like to know what I was going to get. But I kept my mouth shut because I'd had another totally unrelated thought.

"Why don't we call Zach now," I said.

Lesley gave me an exasperated look.

"Why?" she asked.

"Because there's one place in this whole tower where we haven't looked yet," I said. "And that's downstairs in the basement."

"And Zach?"

"Good with locks. Remember?"

15

Landscaping

WHICH TURNED OUT to be an understatement.
"It's just a padlock," said Zach as he casually tossed it to me and then checked Lesley to make sure she'd been watching.

It had taken Zach less than thirty minutes to arrive at our front door, wearing a surprisingly clean red T-shirt with the Clash logo on the chest and trailing the smell of antiperspirant—applied, I reckoned, when he was on his way up in the lift. He held up a plastic Lidl bag containing a three-liter plastic bottle of Strongbow.

"Where's the party?" he asked.

"Downstairs," said Lesley.

I examined the padlock Zach threw me and found that it was unmarked. We could put it back in place on the way out, and no one would be any the wiser.

"Is this entirely legal?" asked Zach.

"Oh yeah," said Lesley. "That was a clear health and safety violation."

"That's all right then," said Zach standing back so that me and Lesley could access the door to the basement. "I wouldn't want to think that you two were leading me into anything illicit."

"We're the law," said Lesley. "Remember?"

"You're the Isaacs," said Zach. "And that ain't quite the same thing."

Without the padlock, the door to the basement opened easily and we went inside.

We found ourselves at the bottom of Skygarden's pointlessly wide central shaft. Two floors above us, wire mesh had been strung across the width of the shaft, presumably so people could work at the bottom without being hit by rubbish dropped from above. Over thirty years of careful housekeeping the mesh had acquired such a thick layer of old newspapers, burger boxes, empty drink cans and stuff I didn't want to identify, that it blocked much of the light coming from above.

"That's a fire hazard," said Zach.

Fortunately, enough of the strip lights mounted on the walls were still working for us to see what we were doing. I peered up through the accumulated rubbish to trace the descent of Stromberg's so-called tuned mass damper down the center of the shaft until it terminated in the basement where we stood. Close up I could see it was a cylinder thirty centimeters across and it terminated a meter above the ground.

"What's holding it up?" asked Zach.

"There's cross cables at every other floor," I said. "The ones without walkways. And it's attached at the top." To a PVC plinth with occult symbols, no less. And I realized that this was Stromberg's mine shaft or drill bit or whatever—crystallising the magic out of wherever it was coming from and connecting it to the *Stadtkrone*.

"That's got to be supporting some of the weight," said Lesley, pointing up.

A meter above our heads what looked like heating

ducts emerged from four of the walls and met in the middle in a boxy girdle mounted around the fake mass damper.

"Look how clean they are," I said. "They're practically brand new." I made a mental note about where the ducts would come out on the other side of the walls. I jogged back out the door and up the stairs to the Lower Ground Floor plant room and found the darkish strip which marked where the new cement had been laid.

Plastic, I was thinking . . . Certain plastics retain *vestigia*. Nightingale had been right. I was replicating work from the 1920s, only not by members of the Folly, and not by British researchers but Germans. Professor Postmartin had said they'd been more advanced than us prior to the 1930s — and that included the chemical industry. At school Mrs. Lemwick had been big on German industrial superiority when we did the origins of the First World War.

"What's he up to?" asked Zach, who had followed me up here with Lesley, and was now staring at me oddly.

"He's doing his Sherlock Holmes impression," said Lesley.

I went out through the main doors into the rain and found the point where a freshly resurfaced strip of the tarmac emerged from the wall and headed for the garages.

"My granddad said he was bonkers," said Zach.

"Sherlock Homes?" asked Lesley.

"Arthur Conan Doyle," said Zach.

The strip vanished under the door of a garage sealed with a County Gard steel plate and another shiny padlock.

"You want to get this?" I asked Zach.

Zach pulled a pick from his jeans pocket and went to work. "Started seeing fairies and ghosts and talking to dead people," he said, still going on about Conan Doyle as the padlock came apart in his hands.

"But there *are* fairies and ghosts," said Lesley. "I met them down the pub—you introduced me."

"Yeah, but he used to see them when they weren't there," said Zach. "Which is practically the definition of bonkers."

I bent down, grabbed the door handle and pulled the garage door up and over with a grinding screech. Rainwater splattered my face.

"Okay," said Lesley. "This is not really clearing anything up, is it?"

The garage was completely filled with stacks of what looked like metal trays, held in wooden frames. They were so tightly packed you couldn't even squeeze inside and I couldn't see whether whatever had been laid under the tarmac surfaced inside the garage or carried on.

When I leaned closer I got a flash of straight razor and snarling dog that made me take a step backward.

"You know what those remind me of?" I said.

"Yeah," said Lesley and we all took a step backward, except for Zach who took two.

"We'd better get Nightingale to look at this," I said and closed the garage door as gently as possible.

Lesley and Zach went back upstairs because one person standing around in the rain looks less suspicious than three, and popped back down with Toby. Because one man standing in the rain with a dog is practically invisible. Nightingale arrived ten minutes later and spent half an hour staring at the things in the garage.

"I've never seen anything remotely like this before," he said at last.

"Any idea what they're for?"

"I'd have said they were demon traps," said Nightingale. "But I have no sense of the malice one gets with a true demon trap. At least not in the concentration I would expect from this many weapons all in one place."

"Same technology, though?" I asked.

"Technology? Yes, I suppose it is a technology," said Nightingale. "It was probably too much to expect our opponent to respect the fine craft tradition embodied in British wizardry."

"Probably," I said and closed the garage door.

The rain and overcast meant the evening got dark early and the abandoned blocks that surrounded the tower loomed over the garden.

"This much is certain—having invested so much here they're unlikely to abandon it now," said Nightingale.

"County Gard keep turning up," I said. "It might be time to wind up here and go after them directly."

"Missing Molly already?" said Nightingale. "Let's give Bromley and Sussex another twenty-four hours to see if they find a connection, and decide then."

That agreed, me and Toby returned to our gardenless flat in the sky and found that Zach and Lesley had already gone to bed.

Fortunately, the internal speakers on the new TV were adequately loud.

I had the dream where I was lying in bed between Beverley Brook and Lesley May which I'd been having every two to three weeks for the last year or so —and trust me it is not as erotic as it sounds—even if Beverley is wearing a wet suit. I hadn't told anyone about the dream, not least because Lesley always appears with her beautiful face intact and that always seemed like a betrayal. The bed we're in changes from dream to dream. Sometimes it was my bed in the Folly, sometimes the double bed that had belonged to Lucy Springfield who had rich parents and a desperate need to parade me up and down in front of them at breakfast. Occasionally it was my old bed at my parents' flat—which was improbable since it barely fit me, let alone three fully grown adults. But mostly it was an improbably wide and soft hotel bed—the sort of bed that James Bond might share with two women. And he wouldn't let the fact that one of them was in uniform, including her Metvest, cuffs and pepper spray slow him down either. So in my dream they lay there looking beautiful in the way only someone you love can look while sleeping, and all I could think about was that it was all right for some, because they were getting a good night's sleep and I was lying between them and staring at the ceiling. Which, as I'm sure either of them would have hastened to point out, was stupid because of course I was asleep, having the dream.

But tonight someone started screaming outside the window.

I woke up standing in the middle of the living room, my hands clenched into fists. But the flat was silent.

If you're police you quickly learn to recognize a real scream when you hear it and this had been a real scream—only I couldn't tell whether it had been confined to my dream.

I pulled on my jeans and hopped out onto the balcony.

At first all I could hear was the city grumbling out beyond the empty blocks, but then I heard an engine noise much closer. Not a car, a small engine like that on a lawnmower or a power tool, and coming from the garden below.

Then I heard the scream for real. A woman. Pain, despair, fear.

Lesley sat bolt upright when I banged open the bedroom door. Zach lay sprawled next to her, naked, one leg hooked possessively around her thigh.

"There's an incident in the garden," I said. "Hurry."

I grabbed the go bag, flung open the front door and ran for the lift. Unless it's a fire, the lift is always going to beat twenty-one flights of stairs. I had my trainers on by the time the lift arrived and stuck my foot in the closing door as I wrangled my Metvest out of the bag—it felt clammy against the bare skin of my chest and back.

Lesley arrived wearing her mask, leggings and Zach's outsized red Clash T-shirt. She followed me into the lift and I withdrew my foot. The doors closed in Zach's face as he came running, half naked, to join us.

"I think he wants his T-shirt back," I said to Lesley as she struggled into her Metvest. I pulled out my airwave and keyed in Nightingale's number—he answered within ten seconds. I told him we were heading downstairs to investigate strange noises.

"How strange?" he asked.

"Machine tool noises, possible scream," I said.

"I'll move to the perimeter at Station Road and hold there," he said.

Given that Nightingale was heavy artillery, we didn't want him piling in if this turned out to be common or garden criminality. Come to think of it, I wasn't sure we should be piling in—at least not while kitted up and with *The Fuzz* written on our foreheads.

This is why proper undercover operations have rules and procedures for handling this kind of shit.

The lift was too old and vandalized to go "ding," so the doors merely opened on to the ground floor and me and Lesley dashed out, and then slowed to creep through the foyer doors and out onto the walkway.

We heard it as soon as we were in the open air, a power tool whine over to the right and men's voices below and to the left. Unmistakably the sound of two people who were having a knock-down, drag-out argument while trying desperately not to raise their voices.

Then I recognized the noise the power tool was making, the crunching yammer of a chainsaw cutting into wood. I felt a cold flush as I realized what was going on and what the likely consequences were.

"They're going after the trees," I hissed. "We have to stop them now."

"Peter, it's just trees," she whispered back. "They can plant new trees."

I didn't try to explain because there's no pithy way of explaining that you believe that Sky the wood nymph is likely to be symbiotically linked, certainly to her own particular tree but also I suspected, to all the trees in the garden. At least no way I could think of on the spur of the moment.

I keyed Nightingale, warned him they were going after the trees and, before Lesley could ask any questions, ran for the ramp down to the garden.

Lesley followed me.

I came off the ramp at a dead run and headed straight for the chainsaw noise. With only the walkway lights the garden was a confusion of shadows. But I'd walked Toby down there enough times to keep me from running into a tree.

Then a bright light blossomed overhead and I thought wildly that a police helicopter had stupidly turned its sun-gun on the wrong person, when I realized that the light was everywhere.

Ahead of me was a chunky white guy in jeans and a leather biker jacket who was using a chainsaw on one of the cherry trees by the dismantled playground. The vibration had dislodged the blossom which swirled like pink snow in the harsh white light.

"Oi," I yelled as I charged him. "Step away from the tree."

Startled he turned to face me and instinctively raised the chainsaw. I skidded to a halt and eyed the whirring chain warily. If you're an old school zombie or trapped in a lift, a chainsaw is a fearsome weapon. But outside, where there's room to maneuver, you end up being more worried about what the stupid gits might do to themselves with it than anything they might do to you.

"Police," I shouted. "Put the chainsaw down before you hurt yourself with it."

He paused and then took a hesitant step forward as if he was actually going to charge me with the thing, but then I think it dawned even on him how stupid that would be.

"Dave," called a voice some distance behind him. "We are leaving?"

Dave vacillated for a second then slowly shrugged out of the shoulder strap.

He's going to throw it at me, I thought, just as he threw it at me and ran.

I dodged right, stupidly because it barely traveled a meter and a half toward me, which gave Dave a lead as he hared off toward the New Kent Road. I went after him but he was utterly reckless and I was unlucky enough not to notice the felled silver birch lying across the path. Down I went, throwing up my arms to protect my face as I skidded across the grass. I rolled over, grabbed my airwave and told Nightingale that two, maybe more, suspects were on foot and heading for the New Kent Road.

"Roger," said Nightingale.

I got up to follow, but suddenly I heard Lesley call my name.

"Peter," she yelled. "Get the fuck over here."

The tone of her voice stopped me in my tracks—I'd only heard that tone twice before—when the Cooper-town child had fallen to her death in front of us and again in the minutes before she'd lost her face.

I shouted back and followed her voice to the base of a huge plane tree, starkly outlined by what I realized was a super werelight that Nightingale had fixed in the air above the garden.

Lesley was crouched over a figure stretched among the roots, I recognized the yellow and green dress and slim bare feet. It was Sky, her face pale, her eyes open, staring and unresponsive. I reached for her neck, but Lesley grabbed my hand.

"She's dead, Peter," she said and her voice was muf-fled and indistinct behind the roaring in my ears.

I tried to open my mouth to ask the right questions, but nothing happened. In my mind I saw myself standing up, stepping back from the body, making a preliminary visual sweep of the locus and then securing the scene while we waited for the Homicide Assessment Team to arrive. But all that happened was I felt my face bend out of shape.

It was established later that Sky's plane, like all the mature trees in the garden, had had a ten centimeter deep wedge cut out of its trunk all the way around in a ring. It's a common enough technique used by disgrun-tled landowners or exasperated neighbors to kill trees that they think are getting in their way.

I thought I was there for a long time, hunched over Sky's body, trying to breathe, trying to move while si-lence pounded in my head and Lesley gripped my hand and stopped me from doing anything stupid. Nightin-gale's magical star shell faded and the darkness closed around us.

But in the Job you don't get to be human—not when you're on the clock.

Nicky came through the dying trees, lit up like a triple-masted man-of-war on fire and screaming like a Stuka in its final dive. I lurched to my feet as the small figure in red-striped pirate pajamas barreled across the clearing and threw herself down by Sky's body.

"Sky!" screamed Nicky. "Wake up! Wake up!"

She reached out to touch her friend's face but stopped short.

"Sky," she said in a small voice. "Sky?"

I put my hand on her shoulder and found it was soaking wet. Nicky screamed again and the sound was like a solid force that drove me to my knees.

"Nicky, stop that," I said.

She turned to look at me, and her face was twisted out of shape by anger, grief and terrible betrayal. It was the face you see from war zones and crime scenes, from every solemn appeal for emergency aid—it was the shape my own face had made only moments before.

She drew in her breath and I felt the ground beneath my knees tremble and imagined the mains water pipes of Elephant and Castle groan and twist and shiver. Lesley felt it too—I saw her back away.

But then Oberon was there.

In the moments before he arrived I swear I heard horse's hooves—and then he was in the woods with us. Naked except for a pair of Calvin Klein boxer shorts and brandishing that damn infantry sword. Heat washed off him, and sweat and the smell of blood and the cut of the lash.

"Nicky," he said and his voice rolled out deep as a distant cannonade.

Nicky threw herself into his arms and he scooped her

up with his left hand. She put her arms around his neck and howled.

"Hush, child," said Oberon and the howling cut off.

Oberon glanced at me and Lesley, then at Sky and then quickly and efficiently he turned a full circle, checking the whole area around him. As he did, I saw a crisscross of scars across his naked back.

Satisfied that no threat was near, he lowered his sword and strode across the gap between us.

"Is it all the trees?" he asked.

"Yes," said Nightingale, striding out of the darkness and putting himself between Oberon and the corpse. "All of them ringed or felled."

"This was an egregious act," said Oberon, looking around the garden.

Nicky squirmed out of Oberon's grasp.

"I want them dead," she said. "Dead, dead, dead."

"No," said Nightingale.

"That's the law," shouted Nicky, her little hands clenched into fists, her head pushed forward. "Life for a life."

"We will find them and we shall bring them to justice," said Nightingale. "That is the agreement."

"I am party to no such contract," said Oberon.

"Then I beg your forbearance in this matter," said Nightingale.

"My forbearance," spat Oberon, "is a well your nation has drunk all but dry."

"There will be justice done in this matter," said Nightingale. "My oath as a soldier on it."

Oberon hesitated and Nicky, sensing the change, turned on him.

"No, no, no," she shouted and smacked him hard in the stomach with her little fists.

"Enough," said Oberon and took her hands gently

but firmly in his own. He looked back at Nightingale. "Your oath as a soldier?"

"Yes," said Nightingale.

Oberon nodded, then he stooped and hoisted Nicky into the crook of his arm. She wasn't that small a child, but it didn't seem to cost him anything at all.

"Nightingale," he said by way of farewell, and then he was gone.

We all waited a moment and then we all exhaled slowly—including Nightingale.

16

The Puppy Farm

THE FIRST THING Nightingale ordered us to do was strip off all our identifiably police gear, stick it back in the go bag and head back up to our flat. Local response units were on their way and he planned to drop Sky's murder in Bromley's lap. I doubted DCI Duffy was going to be happy about that, but it was standard procedure in Falcon-related—that is, Folly-related—incidents that the fewer different specialist units involved, the easier it was to pretend nothing unusual was happening.

Me and Lesley, dressed in civvies and with Zach in tow, caught the lift back down to the walkways and joined the other residents staring over the parapets and asking each other what was going on.

"Fucking vandals," said Kevin as he nervously watched a couple of IRVs, light bars spinning, pull into the garage circle just below. A bunch of uniforms got out, milled about a bit before realising that they couldn't reach the garden from there, got back into their cars and drove away.

"I don't think they're worried about your lock-ups," I told Kevin.

He eyed me suspiciously. "What makes you say that?" he asked.

I pointed to where a troop of figures in white paper suits threaded ghostly through the trees. "They don't get those out for a garage full of dubious merchandise," I said.

"Somebody's had it," said Kevin when he saw the suits, and relaxed.

We were joined by Kevin's mum, who'd taken time to put on a coat. "It's diabolical," she said. "There's been a girl murdered down there."

I tried to look suitably fascinated, but what I felt was queasy.

"Was it someone from the tower?" asked Kevin.

"Don't know," she said.

Away to the right of the walkway floodlights kicked in and I could make out the white plastic top of a forensic tent. A woman's voice filtered through the trees, loud, annoyed, barking out orders—DCI Duffy not being happy, I suspected.

Kevin tapped me on the shoulder and nodded over at where Lesley was standing with Zach. "I thought that was your bird," he said.

"Nah," I said. "We're just friends."

On the border between Barking and East Ham, the North Circular meets the A113 among a confused tangle of retail parks, sewage plants and scrubby wasteland. According to witnesses, a scruffy old model Ford Transit, indistinguishable from a million other white vans just like it, pulled over suddenly onto the grass verge and bundled a body out the back. I recognized the body as soon as I saw him, lit by the crime scene lights inside the forensic tent. It was chainsaw guy.

It was midmorning and the traffic would have been

thundering past if it hadn't been squeezed down to one lane by the Traffic officers. Probably slowed even more by drivers trying to get a good look at the crime scene. A forensic pathologist had already arrived, but nobody so far had taken official control of the scene. All the MITs were scrambling to avoid taking on what looked like a seriously dodgy Falcon case, especially Bromley who were making it really clear that they didn't want it either. Which was why I'd been rousted out of my sofa bed after non-sleeping for three hours and dispatched to identify the victim. Bromley were not going to be happy with me for roping them into this—it would probably be wise to avoid southeast London for a bit.

"I can live without Bromley," I said out loud.

"Did you say something, Peter?" asked Dr. Walid, who was kneeling by the body and shining a light down its mouth.

"Just mumbling," I said.

Chainsaw guy was lying on his back, still in his biker jacket which was unzipped and splayed open to reveal a gray, white and black checked shirt soaked around the neck with what Dr. Walid assured me was water. I asked Dr. Walid whether he had any idea of the cause of death.

"I'm fairly certain he drowned."

"So this is the dump site," I said.

"No," said Dr. Walid. "I think he drowned right here."

"On dry land?"

"His lungs seemed to have filled up with fluid—can't be certain it's water until I've done tests—and he drowned."

"From the inside out?"

"That's my hypothesis," said Dr. Walid.

Probably better if I just avoided south London entirely for a year or two, I thought.

"Are you doing the post-mortem on Sky?" I asked.

"Later today," he said. "It should be very interesting—would you like to attend?"

I shivered. "No thanks," I said. "I'll give it a miss."

Outside the tent, the sun was bright and the air smelled of petrol. I walked up the scrubby grass slope to where Traffic had established a safe parking zone for emergency vehicles. Lesley was there, fast asleep in the passenger seat of the Asbo. I left her to it while I called Nightingale and confirmed the identification—he could pass on the bad news to DCI Duffy. He suggested we wait where we were in case they could get a lead on the van, so I climbed into the driver's seat and tried to get comfortable. Lesley opened her eyes and took off her mask to rub her face.

"Well?" she asked.

"Chainsaw guy," I said and explained Dr. Walid's theory.

"That was murder," said Lesley. "By your little friend."

"You can't prove that," I said.

"Oh, wake up, Peter," she said. "He drowned by the side of the road. You heard her say it—'one for one' she said and Oberon didn't have an answer to that. 'One for one.'" She pointed down the slope at the forensic tent. "That's one right there."

"Okay, you want to go back and arrest her?" I asked. "She's what—nine years old?"

"Is she?" said Lesley. "I don't know what she is. I know one thing—the law doesn't seem to apply to her, or to her mum or to any of these fucking people." Lesley closed her eyes and sighed. "And if it doesn't apply to them, then why does it apply to us?"

"Because we're the police," I said.

"Is Nightingale police?" she asked. "Because he's not beyond the occasional human rights violation when it suits him."

"Oh well, that separates him from the herd, don't it?"

"It's not like we'll ever prove it's her," said Lesley.

"It could have been the Faceless Man," I said. "He's got a thing for weird deaths."

"Why would the Faceless Man kill chainsaw boy?" asked Lesley.

"Why did he kill Patrick Mulkern?"

"Patrick Mulkern fucked up," said Lesley. "He got greedy and tried to sell a book he wasn't supposed to. Setting his bones on fire was a deliberate statement. Fuck with me and really horrible things will happen to you, like the guys who had their dicks bitten off and the amputated head of Larry the Lark."

"That was Faceless Man senior," I said.

"Yeah, but the principle's the same," said Lesley. "And when he just wants someone out of the way he does it very quietly like with Richard Lewis. If Jaget hadn't spotted it, then it would have been just another 'person under a train' wouldn't it? Or he uses a proxy like Robert Weil to apply a shotgun to the face."

"I don't think he's the killer," I said. "I think he was brought in to dispose of the body."

"Can you prove that?"

"Nope."

There was a bottle of Evian on the backseat. I tried it, but it was warm.

"Give me some of that," said Lesley and I handed it over.

"You know we've left Zach alone in our flat," I said. "What do you think the chances are of there being anything left inside when we get back?"

"It's not our flat," said Lesley after she'd finished the last of the water.

"It's my telly," I said. "I paid two hundred quid for it."

"That just makes you a handler of stolen goods," said Lesley.

"Not me, guv," I said. "I thought that TV was totally kosher. I genuinely believed that it fell off the back of a lorry."

"He's not going to nick from us," said Lesley. "Besides, I told him to look after Toby. Reinforced our cover."

It was a good plan. If any of our neighbors suspected we were old Bill, spending five minutes with Zach would disabuse them of that notion.

"Do you still have that app that finds coffee shops?" I asked.

"Don't need it," she said. "There's a retail park on the other side of the junction."

I was just going to suggest that we head over there when one of the Traffic police knocked on our window.

"Got something for you," he said and handed me a number on a scrap of paper. It was the index of the white van. The witnesses to the body dumping had given Traffic a time frame and so it was just a matter of checking the automatic cameras until something popped up. I thanked him and called in IIP on the index. While we waited for that to come back, we headed to the retail park and spent half an hour in a Sainsbury's the size of an aircraft assembly plant stuffing the go bag with water, snacks and sandwiches.

Then we sat in the Asbo with bucket-sized cardboard cups of coffee, just about drinkable if you put enough sugar in, and went through the results of the IIP as it relayed to us down the phone.

Our white van was owned by a limited company with a trading address in what looked like, on Google Maps, a farm in the middle of nowhere. It had been reported stolen by its owners at nine fifteen that morning, but their statement suggested that it might have been missing for two days or more.

"Convenient," said Lesley.

Clever criminals steal their getaway cars before doing a big job, but it's a bugger if you're just popping into town for something small, say for a bit of criminal damage, so you might use your own or a mate's. The problem there is if things get a bit out of hand and your mate, say hypothetically, starts mysteriously drowning to death in the back and you have to dump him at a road junction. Then you might need to create a bit of plausible deniability. Not with us, you understand, because we're naturally suspicious bastards, but with magistrates, juries and other innocents. So you report it stolen and, if you're sensible, you torch it in some remote location.

Obviously sometimes, just for the novelty value, the vehicle really is stolen.

We agreed it might be worth checking out the farm in Essex so we called Nightingale to let him know. He told us to be careful.

"Yes, Dad," said Lesley but only after Nightingale had hung up.

So, with my trusty native guide by my side, I started up the Asbo and set course for the dark heart of Essex,

We got off the M11 at junction 7 and sat behind a caravan for about half an hour, which gave us plenty of time to weigh up the alternative joys of fresh farm produce and/or cheap warehousing space. It was enough to push even me into taking a risky overtaking opportunity that caused Lesley to clutch the handhold and swear under her breath.

"What do you expect to find?" asked Lesley once her grip had unclenched.

"Don't know," I said. "But Nightingale is right, the Faceless Man's just a criminal. He makes mistakes. We only need to keep chipping away at this network he's built. Sooner or later we're going to find a crack we can exploit and then, crash, we can bring the whole thing down."

"Or some farmer's had his van stolen," said Lesley.

"Or that."

What I hate most about the country is that it's so hard to tell what anything is before you get there. Dutifully following the satnav we headed down a series of narrowing country lanes until we suddenly came to a halt in front of a metal five-bar gate. Beyond that was a muddy yard surrounded on three sides by an old brick barn, a building that looked like a warehouse that had been re-dressed for a post-apocalyptic dystopia and what appeared to be a pebble-dashed council bungalow uprooted from some northern housing estate by a tornado to come crashing down in the wilds of Essex. For all I knew, it could have been anything from a pig farm to a really down at heel outdoors activity center.

"You're rural," I said to Lesley. "Do we park here and go in, or do we open the gate and drive in?"

"Park here," she said. "That way no one can escape while they think we're not looking."

"The farmer's not going to like it if he comes tooling up in a tractor and he can't get in," I said.

"He'll get over it," she said. "Farmers are always pissed off about something."

I looked at the farmyard. I was still wearing my DM 1461 shoes which were not my best, but not what I wanted to get agricultural waste products on, either. But sometimes successful policing involves making a sacrifice.

We climbed out of the Asbo into the hot sunlight. The

air had that dried shit smell that I've been reliably informed indicates either muck spreading or a music festival. But not at this farm, I decided. Even I could see that there didn't seem to be enough actual livestock aftermath in the yard.

"He could be a cereal farmer," said Lesley when I pointed this out.

The dilapidated gray concrete barn was open to the elements at both ends. An ancient Land Rover was parked half inside, its bonnet propped open to reveal a rusted engine. Behind it there were strange concrete troughs and the spiky torture-chamber shapes of agricultural equipment. Beyond that, a rectangle of pale blue sky. The brick barn was older, sturdier and better maintained, its main front door firmly closed and padlocked.

The bungalow was blind, with grimy net curtains. Set down by its tornado at an off angle to the yard, it was also backward, with what was obviously the back door facing us—although Lesley said this was standard for farms. "Nobody uses the front door except to hang out washing," she said.

I tapped on the back door and then the kitchen window.

"Hello," I called. "It's the police, is anyone home?"

Somewhere in the distance I thought I might have heard a dog barking.

There were two rutted tracks in the gray dust leading left and right out of the yard. We took the right one because it looked like it curled around the side of the bungalow. It did, and Lesley had been right about the washing. A rough square lawn was fenced in by knee-high metal railings and sported a rotary clothesline and a scattering of sun-faded plastic toys. A rusty green metal swing stood in another corner and would no doubt have squeaked mournfully in the wind had the seat not been missing. Probably removed by someone who got fed up with it squeaking mournfully. What was unmistakably the front door of the house was painted a mottled blue and was wedged shut when I gave it an experimental shove.

"Could they be out in the fields?" I asked.

"There'd still be a car in the yard," said Lesley. "Although the farmer might be working and the wife in town."

"If there is a wife," I said.

"No sign of the Transit van," she said. "Want to break in?"

She didn't sound enthusiastic. Farmers meant shotguns, legal and illegal, and a loose interpretation of the common law when it came to self-defense.

There were what might have been fresh tire marks leading away further up the track. I stared in that direction and thought I could see what looked like a roofline poking up from behind a rise in the ground.

"Let's check up here first," I said.

We headed up the track until we topped the rise and found ourselves looking down at a pair of wooden storage sheds new enough for the pine planking to still be bright yellow and smell of Ronseal. They were windowless and had gabled roofs surfaced with black felt.

"Did you hear that?" asked Lesley.

"What?"

"Dogs," she said. "Barking."

I listened, but all I could hear was the wind and something making a belching squawk that I assumed was a bird.

"Nope," I said.

We followed the track down the rise until we reached the first shed. Now, the closest I've ever got to DIY is arresting shoplifters in B&Q but even I know green wood when I'm right up close and can see where it is warping out of shape. Some of the planks in the walls here had peeled off the frame. I looked closer and found that there were no nails. The planks had been held in place with wooden plugs. When I checked the door, I saw that the hinges were wooden and that there were no locks, only a crude wooden latch.

Lesley reached out to open the door.

"Wait," I told her, and she hesitated. "Dogs," I said.

"Dogs?" asked Lesley.

I did a three-sixty and found what I was looking for behind me on the opposite side of the tracks—a bare slender tree with thin branches within arm's reach. I crossed over and tried to break the smallest I could get—a branch the thickness and length of a pool cue. It didn't come easy, and the cold bark scraped my hands as I yanked it off the tree, peeling a strip of bark away from the main trunk along with it.

Nightingale had said that the younger and greener the stick the better. I brandished it at Lesley.

"Dogs," I said.

I walked back to the first shed and used the far end of my stick to lift the latch and a convenient fork of twigs near the top to hook the handle and pull it open.

"Oh," said Lesley. "Dogs."

She let me enter the shed first. Without windows it should have been pitch black, but the warped planks had opened long thin gaps of daylight in the walls. Equipment racks lined the shelves, all constructed of the same green wood and arranged like bunk beds in a barracks. The shelves were empty, but judging by their depth they'd been built to store something less than half a meter deep and from their vertical spacing not more than the same in height. The units were sturdy and massively over-engineered, so whatever they had been storing, it had been heavy,

Lesley joined me and used her penlight to indicate the floor, which I saw was also composed of thick planks of green wood. The air was heavy with the smell of pine edged with damp—it was worse than an Ikea warehouse.

"Swedish dogs," I said.

"Nightingale did say the Vikings invented it," said Lesley. "If you're thinking what I think you're thinking."

"I might be wrong," I said, and fell silent. Because just then I'd found the one shelf that wasn't empty.

"Oh fuck it," said Lesley. "I hate it when you're right."

A demon trap is a sort of magical landmine developed, so says Nightingale, by the Vikings to defend their long-houses from supernatural threats during the long winters. When I'd asked what kind of threats, he'd shrugged. "Other Vikings," he'd said. "Dire wolves, trolls."

"Moomins," Lesley had added, and then had to explain what those were to both me and Nightingale.

The demon trap we'd watched Nightingale deactivating at Christmas had been a round sheet of stainless steel the size and shape of a dustbin lid, but what we'd found in the shed was different. It was composed of two stainless steel plates for a start, and they were square, sixty centimeters to a side and half a centimeter thick. The plates were held seven or eight centimeters apart by wooden columns fixed at each corner through holes cut in the sheets. The wood was green, and crudely shaped bark was still clinging to sections. They were twice as thick in the middle and put me in mind of the ceramic insulators you see on telephone wires and high tension electricity lines.

The demon trap Nightingale had disarmed had had two circles incised near the center—that being where the "payload" was stored. Traditionally, this had been the ghost of a human being tortured slowly to death and their essence trapped at the moment of expiration. We'd found that the Faceless Man had learnt to substitute dogs instead—the effect was the same. Or rather, *effects*. Because the tortured ghost, the demon in the trap, could be used to power a range of results, ranging from knocking down whichever poor sod triggered it, to turning him and his mates inside out. So you can see why me and Lesley approached with a certain amount of caution.

Then I recognized what it was we were looking at.

"Remember the metal plates in the garage?" I said.

"Oh yeah," said Lesley. "This is the same thing. Do you think they were stored here?"

"Maybe they were made here," I said and that's when the Asbo's car alarm went off. The Asbo had a good one too, a really annoying woo-woo-woo followed by the sound of a donkey being castrated with a rusty saw and then back to the woo-woo-woo. It cut off midway through the third cycle.

"Somebody knows how to steal a car," said Lesley.

I pulled out my mobile and saw that we were living in the land of no bars.

"Shit," I said. "Do we wait here or what?"

Lesley laughed.

"I say let's stroll up the yard and give them a hard time for breaking into our car," she said.

"And if they're the guys that killed the trees?"

"Then we arrest them and Bromley will be that much less pissed off with us."

Policing, whatever else you've heard, is by consent. Even hardened professional villains consent to be policed. This is clear from the way they complain that nonces, rapists and bankers get shorter sentences than decent ordinary criminals. It's the same with all the other criminals, the weekend shoplifters, the drunk drivers, the overexcited protestors and executives who pop into the loo for a quick snort. When it's their stuff that goes walkies, or their car that's damaged, when their kids go missing and their briefcases get snatched, they all seem to be pretty consensual about the police. Everyone consents to the police. It's just the operational priorities they argue about.

That's why ninety-nine percent of the time a pair of police can expect to approach a bunch of thugs with perfect safety, protected only by the majesty of the law, the social contract and the strong implication that anyone messing with you will face unprecedented levels of grief in the very near future.

It's the other one percent that buggers you every time.

It started quite well, though, with me and Lesley nonchalantly strolling into the farmyard smiling brightly.

"Hello," said Lesley in a cheery voice. "We're the police—can anyone help us?"

There were two of them in the yard, both white, in their late twenties, both dressed in army surplus combat trousers and khaki jackets. One of them had squinty eyes and wore a bush hat, the other had a round pink face and floppy blond hair.

Squinty Eyes was climbing out of the Asbo, which he'd obviously just hotwired and driven into the farmyard. Pink Face was holding the gate open for an incredibly muddy Range Rover—I thought there might be more than one person inside, but the details were obscured by the glare off the windscreen.

"What do you want?" asked Pink Face.

"Do any of you own a white Transit van?" asked Lesley and ran off the license plate from memory.

Pink Face looked at Squinty Eyes who looked at whoever was in the Range Rover and then past me at something behind me. It was all the warning I needed. Emerging from the back door of the bungalow was yet another white guy in combat trousers and jacket, only this one also had a double-barreled shotgun and as he walked toward us, he raised it to his shoulder.

From an ordinary policing point of view the best way to deal with firearms is to be outside the operational perimeter while SCO19, the armed wing of the Metropolitan Police, shoot the person with a gun. The second best way is to deal with the weapon *before* it gets pointed at you.

I cast a simple *impello* on the shotgun and yanked the twin barrels straight up before he had a chance to take aim. There was a double boom as he involuntarily squeezed both triggers and then I dropped the butt on his face. The man squealed, let go of the stock and staggered back clutching his nose.

I glanced around to see how Lesley was doing, and caught sight of a slim figure in a charcoal-gray trouser suit climb out of the Range Rover. Nightingale has been training us to cast certain spells practically by reflex, and as soon as I recognized her I had my shield up. It saved my life, because the next instant I was struck by a freight train full of icicles.

The impact cartwheeled me off my feet and I saw sky blue and frost white whirl around my head and then I hit the ground on my back hard enough to make my vision dim. I tried to get up, but what was unmistakably a boot crashed down on my chest and drove me back onto the ground.

Above me loomed the man with the shotgun, his nose was crooked and beginning to swell and blood was seeping from one of his nostrils. He'd retrieved his shotgun and had the business end pointing at my head. It was possible he hadn't had a chance to reload, but strangely I didn't feel at all tempted to find out.

Varvara Sidorovna's face appeared above and looked down at me. When she saw me, she sighed and muttered something under her breath in Russian. Then she walked out of my view, her muttering getting louder until she was swearing noisily.

I was struck by what a good language Russian was for swearing in—very expressive.

17

Prisoners of War

DOG FIGHTERS DON'T see themselves as criminals at all. They see themselves as upholders of a fine rural tradition that dates back centuries and has been unfairly penalized by sanctimonious urbanites. They don't fight their dogs for the money—although the betting can be brisk and the stud fees lucrative—they fight them for honor, for ego and for the sheer thrill of the combat. The rules of a proper dog fight were codified in the 1830s. The ring is always a square with sides twelve feet long and two feet six inches high, and there's normally an old carpet laid in the bottom to soak up the blood. It's really very distinctive and makes them easy to recognize, especially when you're kneeling in the middle of one with your hands on your head.

The ring was in the old barn, which was much better maintained than the new concrete one and had racks of empty dog cages along each wall. That explained why it had been so securely locked.

They had me and Lesley facing the barn door while behind us stood at least two of the combat trouser brigade—both armed with shotguns. Varvara Sidorovna knew our capabilities and wasn't taking any chances. We'd been there long enough for my knees to start seizing up and for our guards to forget we were listening.

"This is fucking stupid," said Max, who had repeated this statement at regular intervals since we'd arrived here. By a process of elimination I'd decided this was the round pink-faced guy, and we knew his name was Max because his partner had used it the last time he'd told him to shut the fuck up. I was pretty certain his partner was the squinty-eyed guy and I knew *his* name was Barry because Max had used it when he told him to fuck off.

"Shut up," said Barry.

"Well, it is fucking stupid," said Max. "We should be well out of here by now."

"Not until the Comrade Major says it's time to go."

"Fuck the fucking Comrade Major," mumbled Max.

"I wouldn't try if I was you," said Barry. "She'll freeze your balls off."

"Oh yeah," said Max. "Seriously frigid."

"Look," said Lesley. "It's bad enough that you're holding us prisoner, but can we at least dispense with the fucking sexism?"

"You're a mouthy cunt, aren't you?" said Barry.

"What I am is a police officer," said Lesley. "And if anything happens to me or my partner here I personally guarantee that you won't survive the subsequent arrest."

"What?" asked Barry.

"Damage us," I said, "and our colleagues will fuck you up big time."

"Shut up," said Max.

"Yeah," said Barry. "Shut the fuck up."

"Not them, you dickhead," said Max. "You shut the fuck up as well."

My stomach was churning. I didn't want to die in a dog fighting ring. In Essex, for god's sake, what would my dad say? And my mum would be so pissed off with me. Better all-round if I avoided the whole dying thing altogether.

"You know, after today you two are going to be disposable," said Lesley.

"She's right," I said. "We tracked you here through the van and we reported in before we came here."

"She gets you to top us," said Lesley. "And then she leaves you hanging out for the police."

My throat was dry and I had to cough before I could say, "That's a bit too risky. More likely she zaps them and then burns down this place with them in it."

"People are always setting themselves on fire when they do arson," said Lesley. "They'll think you murdered us and then did yourselves in by accident. Case closed, and the Comrade Major gets away scot free."

There was a long pause and then Max said, "We're not listening to you, you know."

But I thought they might be.

I think we might have been there for another hour after that. Barry was complaining that he wanted a slash, my knees were killing me and I had shooting pains in my shoulders from keeping my hands on my head. I did wonder, given how long Max and Barry had been standing there, whether they might be equally stiff and unresponsive.

There was nothing in my forward field of view that I could grab with *impello* and the bloody Comrade Major Varvara Sidorovna had instructed Max and Barry to randomly move around behind my back and stay separated so that I couldn't just blindly smack them down. Nothing I could do was going to be faster than their trigger fingers—however stiff they got.

Still, when the barn doors opened in front of me I did my best to clear my mind and be ready for any opportunity.

It was Varvara Sidorovna carrying, I couldn't help noticing, two plastic jerry cans. Judging from the way they weighed on her shoulders they must have been nearly full and I didn't think it was with water. By the time I'd registered that, she'd walked briskly out of our line of sight.

"Okay," she said from behind us. "In a couple of minutes I want you two to shoot these two in the head and douse everything with petrol." She spoke English with the deliberately regionless accent of a BBC Radio 4 presenter.

Being held at gunpoint is a police nightmare and you always tell yourself that should push come to shove and some vile scrote is about to actually shoot you, you'd at least make a play. Go for the gun, duck, attack the bastard with your bare hands. I mean after all, at that instant, what would you have to lose? But shove had arrived and I found I couldn't make myself move, not even a little bit. It was shameful. I had found the upper limit of my courage.

Fortunately for me, there is no known lower limit to human stupidity.

"They're police," said Barry, just as Varvara Sidorovna had crossed back into view and was heading for the barn doors. "I don't think this is a good idea."

Varvara Sidorovna turned and her face was a picture. I'm having a bad day, it said. And now there's you—thinking!

"Listen, Varvara," said Lesley. "You really want to talk to your boss before you do anything hasty."

I was still trying to make myself move and practically trembling with frustration. It's not like I've had trouble doing stupid things before, I thought. Why am I finding it so hard now?

"Varvara, call your boss," said Lesley, her voice tight.

"How do we know you won't get rid of us once we've done your dirty work?" asked Barry.

"I still need you to carry the gear when we get back to London," said Varvara Sidorovna.

"Yeah," said Max. "But—"

"Don't make me come back there and do it myself," she said.

"Okay," said Max. "But I don't think—"

Varvara Sidorovna threw up a hand to silence Max and cocked her head to one side—listening. Then I heard it too. A car engine drawing closer, tires crunching in the gravelly verge of the farmyard. The engine cut out and there was a creak as a handbrake was applied.

I felt Lesley tense beside me—no modern handbrake sounded like that.

There was the sound of a car door opening and then slamming shut.

Varvara Sidorovna gestured sharply to get Max and Barry's attention, pointed two fingers at her eyes, and then at me and Lesley. Then she took a couple of cat-quiet steps to the side of the barn doors and I saw her breathe slowly in and exhale smoothly. Her face became calm, still—expectant.

There was a long silence, I could hear Max and Barry breathing through their mouths and shifting from foot to foot and the tik tik tik of something small and clawed making its way down the line of cages—a mouse? Then suddenly there was a brutal crack like a giant stamping on a plate and daylight spewed through a sudden hole in the front wall of the barn—just above the double doors. Dust exploded into the air to hang in a roiling cloud—gleaming in the sunlight. Then the front of the barn literally unzipped—bricks fountaining up and away in two diverging streams and the doors abruptly ripped off their hinges and went spinning off through the air like something from a catastrophic decompression.

Suddenly I could see the farmyard outside, brightly lit by afternoon sunlight, bricks falling out of the clear blue sky like rain, dust puffing up as they landed, thudding, on the track.

And, having made sure everyone was paying attention to the front, Nightingale walked in through the back door.

The first we knew of it was when Max and Barry came flying headfirst into the dog-fighting ring, landing right beside us. I had a brief glimpse of their shotguns scything through the air at head height—aiming right for where Varvara Sidorovna would have been standing if she hadn't jumped and rolled to the left.

Max turned to look at me and there was a horrible tearing sensation in my shoulder as I swung my fist down to slam into his face. The pain actually made me scream, but it was totally worth it. He slammed back onto the filthy carpet and stayed ducked down there, as it suddenly got extremely dangerous above waist height. Across Max's quivering bulk I saw that Lesley had Barry in a headlock—his face red, his mouth open and gasping.

I'd expected ice again. But Varvara Sidorovna threw a brace of fireballs across the barn, which exploded among the ranked dog cages. There was a rattling thud as fragments smacked into the wooden side of the ring.

Lesley shouted my name and jerked her head at the gaping hole in the front of the barn. I only realized later that Nightingale had done that deliberately to make it easier for me and Lesley to clear the area.

I glared at Max.

"We're all going out the front," I hissed. "But if you give me any aggro I'll just leave you here. Understand?"

Max nodded, his eyes wide with fear. I was really tempted to smack him in the face again, but common sense prevailed.

"One," called Lesley. "Two . . ."

A ball of fire the size of my fist ripped through the air over my head and curved away to explode against a ceiling joint.

"Fuck it!" yelled Lesley. "Go, go, go."

So we went, went, went. I kept my eyes on the sunlit farmyard and, hauling Max behind me, I lurched to my feet and ran for it. Outside, the sunlight blinded me but I kept going until I bounced painfully off the Range Rover. I turned as Lesley, pushing Barry ahead of her, caught up with us.

The roof blew off the top of the barn. It didn't explode. It lifted, almost intact, ten meters into the air before crashing back down and breaking its back. Gray slate tiles cascaded off the slopes and crackled as they hit the ground.

We manhandled Max and Barry around the other side of the Range Rover and pushed them onto their faces in the mud. We didn't have our cuffs, so we made them put their hands on their heads and hoped they weren't stupid enough to move. Crouching, I took a careful peek over the bonnet just in time to see the roof of the barn collapse in on itself.

It went strangely quiet as a wave of brown brick dust rolled out across the farmyard, starting to flatten out as it reached the Range Rover. A solitary brick, falling from who knows how high up, thudded belatedly onto the ground.

I heard tentative birdsong beginning again, and the wind rustling in the tops of the hedgerow.

"Do you think we should . . ." I nodded in the direction of the barn.

"Peter," said Lesley. "From a purely operational point of view I believe that would be a really fucking bad idea."

I noticed then that Nightingale's Jag, which I swore I'd heard pull up in front of the barn, was nowhere to be seen.

I felt a tremor through the soles of my shoes.

A crack. And then the unmistakable sound of breaking sheet glass made me crane my neck to get a view of the bungalow. Left of the back door, where I judged the kitchen to be, a picture window had shattered. Chunks of glass fell outwards into the yard. Even as I watched, whorls of frost spread out from the empty frame, the surrounding pebble-dash cracking and flaking and popping off to expose the red brick underneath. Probably improving the value of the house, I thought.

A whimper caused me to check on our prisoners. I finally realized that we were missing one, the guy whose nose I'd broken with his own shotgun. I told Lesley.

"I know," she said.

"Do you think we should go look for him?"

There was a series of thuds from inside the bungalow, then a crash as an old-fashioned white-enamelled gas cooker exited via the window and cartwheeled jangling across the yard.

"Not just at the moment," said Lesley.

A blue 15kg Calor Gas bottle fell out of the sky, bounced once off the ground in front of the bungalow and came down again with a loud *boing* sound.

Me and Lesley hunched down and tried to make sure that every bit of our bodies had some Range Rover between them and the gas bottle.

I was just about to suggest that it might be empty, when it blew up—something that Frank Caffrey swears shouldn't happen spontaneously under any circumstances.

I managed to bang my head against the wheel arch in startlement, the Range Rover's windows cracked and a chunk of blue metal casing whirred over my head, over the fence, around the yard and off into the field beyond.

I heard a woman scream with rage and frustration and then grunt like a tennis player. The ground trembled again, and what was left of the Range Rover's windows blew out and showered us with crystal fragments—something I'd always thought couldn't happen with safety glass.

There was a rapid series of solid thuds like a boxer would make taking out his frustration on a punch bag.

Then silence and then Varvara Sidorovna said, "Enough, enough, I surrender."

I risked a look. She was squatting on her heels in the middle of the farmyard, her face cast down and her hands raised palms forward. Her natty suit had lost an arm and the pale pink blouse underneath was torn and bloodied.

We stood up for a better look, and saw that the bungalow had been cut in two as if someone had driven a freight train through it. Nightingale advanced on Varvara Sidorovna from its remains.

He was wearing, I noticed, a charcoal-gray lightweight worsted suit in a classic sixties cut which he must have acquired about the same time he bought the Jag. It was, I thought queasily, a suit my dad would have been glad to wear. It looked completely pristine and as he approached he shot his cuffs and checked the links—a completely unconscious gesture.

"Varvara Sidorovna Tamonina," he said. "I am arresting you for murder, attempted murder, conspiracy to murder, aiding and abetting before, during and after the fact and no doubt a great many other crimes." He hesitated and I realized he couldn't remember the modern caution.

"You do not have to say anything," shouted Lesley. "But it may harm your defense if you do not mention when questioned something which you later rely on in court. Anything you do say may be given in evidence."

I cautiously picked my way through the debris strewn across the yard. Nightingale pulled a set of modern handcuffs and tossed them to me. I helped Varvara Sidorovna to her feet and asked her to put her hands behind her back and slipped the cuffs on.

"For you, Major," I said, "the war is over."

Varvara gave me an exasperated look and then sighed. "If only that were true," she said.

At which point the Essex Police arrived with the fire brigade just behind them and tried to arrest us all, on the very sound policing principle of arrest everyone and sort out the guilty at the station. There was a certain amount of waving of warrant cards, calls to superiors and veiled threats that what had happened to the farm buildings could easily be repeated if someone didn't starting taking us seriously, thank you very much. They did take Max and Barry off our hands and a couple of hours later they found our third suspect, whose name turned out to be Danny Bates, five kilometers away, having run as soon as the fireballs started flying. Making him possibly the brightest there.

We all ended up at Chelmsford nick, because not only did it have a brand new custody suite but it was also a short walk from Essex Police Headquarters. Which allowed the Local Response Team to quickly shove their problems all the way up to ACPO rank and then scarper back to Epping.

Essex's ACPO contingent, awed perhaps by Nightingale's immaculate suit or, more likely, being equally desperate to punt the whole thing back to the Met, agreed to let us conduct our interviews on our own terms once the arrests had all been regularized. They gave us a windowless office to work in where me and Lesley promptly fell asleep. Nightingale woke us up with coffee, assorted fruit, cheese sandwiches and an interview strategy.

We were going to start with Varvara Sidorovna Tamonina before she could recover her poise. And me and Lesley would do it, so we could escalate up to Nightingale if necessary.

Nightingale eyed our less-than-enthusiastic faces.

"I'll ensure that more coffee is laid on," he said.

"Can I have a taser as well?" asked Lesley, but Nightingale said no.

Varvara Sidorovna sat on the other side of the interview desk dressed in the cheap white T-shirt and gray jogging bottoms that have become the uniform of shame now that we're no longer allowed to put our suspects in paper suits. There were no tapes in the double cassette recorder and while Essex Police might be taping the output of the CCTV camera mounted in a red perspex bubble above our heads, this was officially an unofficial interview. This had become our standard procedure, a chance for us and our interviewee to discuss issues that neither of us particularly wanted on the record.

"Can you state your full name please?" asked Lesley.

"Varvara Sidorovna Tamonina."

"And your date of birth?"

"November the twenty-first 1921," said Varvara Sidorovna. "In Kryukovo, Russia." Which I found, when I looked it up afterward, was now part of the sprawling Moscow suburb of Zelenograd and, incidentally, the closest the Germans got to the capital during the Second World War.

"Did you serve in the Soviet Army during the war?" I asked.

"365th Special Regiment. I was a lieutenant," she said, "not a major. Is the Nightingale going to show his face at some point?"

"He's about," said Lesley.

"I'd heard rumors about him, but I'd always thought they were exaggerations. Man, he's something." Varvara Sidorovna grinned and suddenly looked eighteen and fresh off the wheat fields. "I've never met anyone that fast with that much control before. No wonder the fascists put a price on his head."

It's important when interviewing a suspect to stay focused on what's broadly relevant to the investigation, but even so it took a great deal of self-control not to ask about that. I suspected that should we manage to bang her up in Holloway prison, Lieutenant Tamonina was going to have Professor Postmartin as a frequent visitor.

Who would no doubt also ask for more detail about her training, her wartime operations and her capture near Brynsk in January 1943.

"I didn't tell them who I was," she said. "The fascists had orders to shoot us on sight, so I pretended to be a medic." Even then she barely survived the initial abuse at the hands of her captors—we didn't ask for details and she didn't volunteer any. She didn't dare use magic to escape because by that point in the war the Germans had started to deploy their own practitioners to counter the Night Witches.

"They had these men they called werewolves," said Varvara Sidorovna. "Who were said to be able to sniff out anyone using the craft."

"Were they really werewolves," I asked. "Shape-shifters?"

"Who knows?" she said. "We had intelligence reports that their capabilities were real. But I never encountered one, so I don't know if they were truly men who became wolves or not."

She was drafted as slave labor as part of Organization Todt and found herself, much to her own surprise, in the Channel Islands. "They said we were on British soil," said Varvara Sidorovna. "For the first few days I thought Britain had been invaded, but one of the other prisoners explained that these were British islands that were closer to France than England." There were a couple of werewolves on the Island of Alderney, where the concentration camps were, but there were none on Guernsey where she was transferred in order to be worked to death building gun emplacements. But as soon as they were clear of the harbor, she knocked down one of the guards at the end of the marching column and escaped in the confusion.

"It's not like the Great Escape or Colditz," she said. "You couldn't hang around setting up escape committees or any of that nonsense. Any moment of the day some pig-faced guard might just shoot you in the head for the joy of it—you took your opportunities as soon as you could."

Varvara Sidorovna cheerfully admitted that she'd been totally prepared to off some locals to make good her escape, but fortunately for everyone concerned, except the Germans, she was spotted by an old lady and guided into the arms of the resistance.

"They called me Vivien," she said, after the actress, and provided her with false papers. "And taught me to speak English with my beautiful proper English accent."

After Liberation in 1945 she made her way to London with her new English name and identity and parlayed that into an official identity in the general post-war confusion. She said she got married in 1952 but refused to give any details about her husband.

"But in any case he died in 1963," she said.

They lived in a semi off the High Street in Wimbledon. There were no children.

"You're very well preserved for a woman in her midnineties," said Lesley.

"You noticed," said Varvara Sidorovna turning her head and striking a pose.

"Do you know why?" asked Lesley.

Varvara Sidorovna leaned forward. "I discovered the elixir of youth," she said. "In an Oxfam shop in Twickenham."

"Are you sure it wasn't Help the Aged?" I asked, about a millisecond before Lesley could—she booted me under the table in revenge.

Varvara Sidorovna waited patiently for us to behave ourselves.

"Was it something you did to yourself?" asked Lesley.

"God, no," she said. "One day I was getting older and the next day I wasn't."

So Nightingale wasn't the only one, I thought.

"Can you remember roughly what year it happened?" I asked.

"August Bank Holiday 1966," she said.

"That's a very precise date," said Lesley.

"I have a very clear memory of it happening," said Varvara Sidorovna. She'd still been living in the house in Wimbledon and she'd been hanging up washing in her back garden.

"It was as if someone had opened a door into summer," she said. "I felt suddenly filled up with"—she waved her hands around vaguely—"honey, sunlight, flowers. When I went to bed I dreamed in Russian for the first time in years. I wanted to go dancing and I wanted to get laid really, really badly. The next day there were thunderstorms."

"So you knew you were getting younger?" asked Lesley.

Varvara Sidorovna laughed. "No, dear," she said. "I thought I was having the menopause." When it became obvious she wasn't, she decided to take advantage.

"I went out dancing and got laid and very, very drunk," she said. And then she moved to Notting Hill, experimented with LSD and listened to far too much progressive rock than was good for her. "Take my advice and never try casting a spell while listening to Hawkwind," she said. "Or when you're on acid."

"How were you earning a living?" asked Lesley.

"You could drift in those days, there were squats and communes and groovy friends. People were always setting up co-operatives, bands and experimental theater groups. I worked at *Time Out* magazine although that might have been later on—there's a couple of years I've lost track of, 1975 in particular."

"When did you meet Albert Woodville-Gentle?" I asked—the original Faceless Man had dropped out of sight in the early 1970s so it was possible they might have met then.

"Much later," she said. "That was in 2003."

Varvara Sidorovna was already firmly back in the demi-monde by that time.

"You two must know what it's like by now," she said. "Once you know it exists it's always there in the corner of your eye. Plus I wanted to see if it was possible to go home, to Russia." She knew that most of her old wartime comrades would be dead, those that hadn't been killed by the Germans were most likely liquidated by Stalin. She was a little surprised to find that the *Nauchno-Issledovatelskiy Institut Neobychnyh Yavleniy*, the Scientific Research Institute for Unusual Phenomena had been revived and that they even had agents operating in the West.

Me and Lesley nodded sagely as if we knew all about this, while I imagined Nightingale adding the fact to his rather long list of things he should have known about but didn't.

But SRIUP being active in the Soviet Union could only mean that practitioners were still being tracked, and Varvara Sidorovna had no intention of coming under anyone's control ever again, not even the motherland's. So she spent the 1980s and 90s rediscovering her skills and picking up new ones. "Here and there," she said. "You'd be amazed."

"And how *did* you get involved with Woodville-Gentle?" I asked, because I was beginning to think that Varvara Sidorovna was messing us about.

"It was a job," she said. One not all that different from those she'd been doing since the late 1970s. "People like you and I straddle the mundane and the demi-monde. We make excellent middle men and go-betweens," she said, but refused to give details.

"Client confidentiality," she said. "You understand."

Obviously she didn't consider the Faceless Man, mark two, as a client any more because she was quite happy to explain how he'd started employing her for various jobs, most of them dull. "Finding people and things in the demi-monde," she said and we made a note to track back later and get a list. She was adamant that she'd never met the Faceless Man in person. Everything had been arranged over the phone.

"I was the one that found old Albert for him," she said proudly. "Took me six months—he'd been warehoused in a private care home outside Oxford." It had been the Faceless Man who arranged the flat in Shakespeare Tower. Varvara Sidorovna took advantage of its location to spend more time at the theater.

"And you did that for, what, nine years?" asked Lesley.

"Not full time," she said. "I had a couple of properly trained care nurses to look after the poor soul much of the time, and in the first couple of years he spent most of the day out."

"Out where?"

"I have no idea," said Varvara Sidorovna. "A very quiet young woman used to pick him up in the morning and return him in the afternoon."

"Do you know where she took him?" asked Lesley, and as she did I wrote *Pale Lady = no driver = FM near BARBICAN?* on my pad where she could see it.

"I was specifically being paid not to ask questions," said Varvara Sidorovna.

She hadn't known about the demon trap planted in the flat, but it didn't surprise her in the least. She'd moved Albert out of the place as soon our visit had finished and she suspected the device had been there as much to keep him under control as it was to catch someone like Nightingale or us.

We asked her about Robert Weil and his body-dumping activities, but she denied any knowledge. Did she know why the Faceless Man might want to shoot a woman in the face with a shotgun?

"If he wanted to delay identification," she said. "Or perhaps to cover up work he was doing on her face."

I felt Lesley stiffen beside me.

"What kind of work?" she asked.

"You've met some of his menagerie," said Varvara Sidorovna. "Perhaps he's looking to create new creatures."

Officially unofficial the interview might have been, but Varvara Sidorovna wasn't going to incriminate herself beyond what she thought we already knew. She claimed to know nothing of County Gard and laughed out loud at the idea she might have offed Richard Dewsbury, the drug dealer, by inducing a breakfast heart attack.

"Not my style, darling," she said.

Nor was she forthcoming about what exactly they'd been up to with their dogs at the Essex Farm. When we asked her what she'd been doing there, all she'd tell us was, "Tying up loose ends. Imagine my surprise when I found you two poking your noses in."

I glanced at Lesley and she shrugged. It was obvious to us that the tying up of loose ends, had we not intervened, probably would have proved fatal for Barry, Max and Danny. We questioned her about that, and she asked whether the world would really be worse off without them.

"Did you know about the wood nymph?" I asked.

"What wood nymph?"

"The one that lived at the base of Skygarden Tower," I said.

"I know a great many things," she said. "You'd be—"

"Did you know about Sky?"

I felt Lesley's hand on my arm, and I realized I'd half risen from my chair. A white Styrofoam coffee cup rolled around on the table between us—fortunately empty. Varvara Sidorovna had flinched back and was giving me a wary look.

"No," she said. "I don't know anything about it."

I took a breath and sat myself down.

"I'm going check on that," I said. "If you do know, then it would be better to tell me now."

Varvara Sidorovna looked to Lesley, who gazed impassively back.

"Somehow I doubt that," she said, and then held up her hand. "I swear I did not know. But it does explain what Max and Barry were burbling about when I picked them up this morning."

"You seem very relaxed," said Lesley. "Considering the severity of the charges against you."

"I have a longer perspective on life than you do," she said. "I was held prisoner by the SS—do you really think the Met frightens me? Or even the Isaacs? I love that nickname, by the way. 'The Isaacs.' So very quaint. You must know that no conventional prison could hold me if I chose to escape. You're not about to summarily execute me. And it would be an enormous waste of your time to guard me. No, sooner or later, we shall come to an arrangement. And in any case, I may yet prove useful."

"But you were going to kill us," said Lesley. "Remember?"

"If you're afraid of wolves," said Varvara Sidorovna, "don't go to the woods."

18

Space Left Over After Planning

IT HADN'T REALLY sunk in at the time, but my beloved Ford Focus ST was kaput. If the half a ton of bricks falling on it hadn't written it off, the fact that an elephant had gone for a kip on the bonnet would have. Nightingale never could figure out whether that was something he or Varvara Sidorovna had done, and she just laughed in my face.

Nightingale's Jag had been safely parked a hundred meters further down the farm access road. He said he'd conjured the sound of his arrival to distract whoever was holding us in the barn while he sneaked around the back.

We spent the night in the Chelmsford Travelodge. I had a room with a charming view of the nearby flyover, but at least the bed was soft and the shower worked. In the morning me and Lesley had a competition to see who could pile the most food on their plate at the continental style all-you-could-eat breakfast. There were no sausages, bacon or fried slice—neither Toby nor Molly would have approved.

DCI Duffy arrived midmorning with a car full of officers from Bromley and took over interviews with Max and Barry—criminal damage—while throwing Danny back to the Essex mob—illegal possession of a firearm, threatening behavior and bringing rural England into disrepute.

We had to give our own statements which took most of the day, because we had to keep stopping and reworking sections that DCI Duffy and the Assistant Chief Constable overseeing the case found to be "problematic"—which was pretty much everything. In the end we blamed most of the property damage on an accidental fire and Calor Gas cylinder explosions, plural.

Nightingale had to stay in close proximity to Varvara Sidorovna, so we went out to a seafood bar by the River Chelmer to fetch some fancy fish and chips. Before we hauled them back to the nick we spent a couple of minutes on a walkway by the river feeding chips to the ducks and seeing if anyone was at home. No joy.

"Maybe not every river's got a personality," said Lesley.

We spent the rest of the evening completing our notebooks and typing our reports for not one but two major inquiries, and then back to the Travelodge. We set our alarms early so we could stuff our faces at the breakfast before we had to leave.

Essex Police provided us a car and driver, the better to speed us out of their force area. We headed back to London in the backseat with our pockets stuffed full of Babybel cheese miniatures and our hearts full of doubts.

Without my beloved Asbo, the first order of business was getting some wheels. We tossed a coin, I lost, and so it was me that got dropped off at Skygarden to check on Toby while Lesley headed off to look up a friendly civilian auto worker she knew who handled fleet re-sales. My bet was that it would be a silver Astra, but you never know.

From the walkway, the garden around the tower didn't look different. Still green in the patchy sunlight. According to the specialist Bromley had called in, it would take years for the big trees to die. So why had Sky died that night—almost instantly? And why had the Faceless Man had the trees destroyed? And so clumsily, using such incompetent cut-outs as Barry, Max, Danny and their late lamented and drowned mate—now identified as Martin Brown of Long Riding, Basildon. All of them in that category of low-level chancers whose ambitions to become professional criminals were frustrated by their inability to pass the entrance exam.

I wanted to go down to the garden, but there were still officers from Bromley MIT among the trees doing a last sweep before they packed away. I didn't want to be identified while there was still mileage to be had by staying undercover.

Why had the Faceless Man wanted the trees dead? Jake Phillips had said that the trees were what kept Skygarden as a listed building. Had they been destroyed so that the tower could be delisted and the demolition begun? There was a vast amount of money involved in the redevelopment project. Was it possible that the Faceless Man's motive was that mundane?

I glanced down at the garages, at the ones with the County Gard seals and the line of curing concrete that stretched from four of them into the base of the tower. No, this was not a real-estate scam—in the first place those kinds of scams were effectively legal, and in the second place they hardly needed magical assistance.

Had he known about Sky when he'd arranged to have the trees killed? Probably not, given the people he'd tasked with the job. But why not just get Varvara Sidorovna to do it? I was certain she could have blighted the whole garden with a killer frost had she wanted to. If she'd timed it right it could have been put down to freak weather.

But not by us, not by the Isaacs, because we would know better.

Which meant the Faceless Man either knew we were here, or at the very least was keeping a close eye on the place.

But why take the risk—even with the expendable Essex boys?

Unless he was on a time table and he couldn't postpone regardless of our presence.

From the walkway I spotted that the doors to the lower ground floor had been wedged open, which was a sure-fire sign either that the council had workmen in, that someone was moving out, or burglars were looting a flat. I checked the car park for clues and saw only a white Citroen van with the Southwark Council logo stencilled on its side. But, because it's good practice, I made a note of its index.

It was dark and cool inside the ground floor foyer. I hit the button for the lift and while I waited I gazed at the not-really-a-tuned-mass-damper that hung down the center of the tower. Stromberg had designed Skygarden to soak up *vestigia* from its environment, and if it had done its job then that power had to have gone somewhere. We'd assumed that the whole grandiose scheme had failed because it hadn't been channelled up and out of the *Stadtkrone* on the roof. But what if the power had accumulated, but hadn't been released?

What if it was still stored in the thirty-story length of plastic hanging over there? I ignored the lift doors as they opened behind me.

Power that could be drained off into the metal plates stacked neatly in the garages that surrounded the tower. The Faceless Man didn't need the staff technology Nightingale was teaching us—he'd adapted the demon trap technique to create vessels for storing the power—dog batteries.

This was not a real-estate scam, I realized. It was a heist.

I turned to rush up to the flat, but the lift doors had closed now and I had to wait for it to come back down again.

When I let myself into the flat I found that the living room was full of bodies.

The curtains were drawn and the lights were off. In the gloom I could make out at least three people lying on the sofa-bed and another five or so on the floor. They all seemed to be men and, judging from the smell of spilled beer and the layer of crisp packets and takeaway cartons, they were sleeping off a serious night in. I noted the donkey jackets with the high-viz strips and made an educated guess as to who they were.

I slowly pushed open the bedroom door and peered inside. Stromberg had carefully designed the master bedroom to be too narrow for a king-size bed placed across it and, when placed lengthways, to provide a mere fifteen centimeters of clearance between bed and wall. The width of the end wall was taken up with a sliding patio door and the length precisely calculated so that you could have a wardrobe, but only if it blocked access to either the patio or the rest of the flat. It was for such attention to details that Erik Stromberg was once described by the *Guardian* architectural correspondent as *emblematic of modern British architecture at its most iconoclastic.*

Zach lay face down on the bed naked except for his bright red underpants and, despite his eating habits, I couldn't help noticing that he was skinny enough for me to count every vertebra on his back.

Carefully, I crouched down until I could put my lips a couple of centimeters from his ear and shout, "Police!"

The results were instructive. Not only did he leap at least a meter upward, but he was already twisting like a cat so that he came down on all fours with the bed between us.

"Shit," he shouted, and then slapped his hand over his mouth.

"Why have you filled my living room with Quiet People?" I whispered.

"Community outreach," whispered Zach. "I'm trying to get them used to interacting with the surface world."

"You took them on a pub crawl, didn't you?"

And Zach claimed it had worked, too.

"One of them ordered a souvlaki up Green Lanes," said Zach. We'd retired to the kitchen for coffee and conversation in something close to a normal voice. "Brought a tear to my eye, I was that proud."

"Why did you bring them here?"

"It was late. This was the closest."

"You got any tea?" asked a figure in the doorway. He was short and wiry with that bantamweight boxer aura of density and strength. His face was long and pale, his eyes were huge, gray and beautiful. His voice, when he spoke, was deep and resonant but barely louder than a murmur. He looked me up and down and stuck out a hand.

"Stephen," he said. His hand was strong, the skin as rough as sandpaper.

"Peter," I said. "We've already met—you buried me under a platform at Oxford Circus."

Stephen shrugged. "You needed the rest," he said.

"How was the pub crawl?" I asked.

"Mildly successful," he said. "Better if we could have slept in, but the drilling keeps waking me up."

Me and Zach listened, but we couldn't hear anything beyond distant traffic and the kettle coming to a boil.

"What drilling?" I asked—thinking about the council contractors downstairs.

Stephen put his hand against the outside wall of the kitchen and closed his eyes. "Downstairs, about thirty feet. Half-inch masonry drill bit going six inches into concrete. The good quality stuff," said Stephen and rapped the wall with his knuckle. "Not this crap."

Zach handed him a mug of tea.

My tea, I thought, that I bought from all the way down the road. But, given we'd left Zach in the flat for two days, I was probably lucky there was anything left at all. Which reminded me.

"Where's Toby?"

Toby was down in the deconstructed children's playground frolicking among the fallen cherry blossoms which lay everywhere like old snow. There was nobody in sight, so I floated a couple of water balls around for him to chase and thought about how it really was past time that the Faceless Man went away. Up the steps or down the mortuary, I really didn't care which.

"He's just another criminal," Nightingale had said. "He doesn't have a plan for every contingency."

He didn't reckon on us finding the book, I thought, or connecting it with Skygarden. Or turning up just as his plans, whatever they were, were getting under way. He panicked—hence the attack on the garden and then getting Varvara Sidorovna to clean up the evidence. If we push him again, we can keep him off balance. But where to push?

He wears a mask and he moves in the shadows, but he still has to act in the mundane world. Somebody had to load those garages with dog batteries, a somebody who then sealed them up behind shiny steel doors with a neat logo stencilled on the front—everyone's favourite full service lackey of capitalism—County Gard.

I could have contacted Bromley MIT and seen whether they'd done an Integrated Intelligence Platform check on the company yet. But I really didn't want to aggravate them any more than I already had, so I went to the next best thing.

"Why do you want to know?" asked Jake Phillips as he warily eyed Toby sniffing the base of his palm tree.

"I thought I'd pay County Gard a visit," I said.

"In what capacity?" he asked and for a moment I thought he'd twigged I was police.

"As a committed blogtavist," I said. "Ready to harness the might of social media in the service of a brave new world. I want to save this place."

"You've only been here a week," he said.

"But what," I said and waved my hand at his garden in the sky, "if all the balconies were fixed like this, this place would be like the hanging gardens of Babylon—this could be a wonder of the world."

A lifetime of disappointment had made him cynical, but you don't stay an activist without a core of stubborn belief that things can get better—it's a bit like being a Spurs supporter really.

"You think so?" he asked.

"I think it's worth fighting for," I said and realized even as I said it that I was telling the truth.

So, humming the *Internationale* under his breath, Jake led me to his spare room stroke office where he had genuine gray metal filing cabinets—saved from a skip in 1996 he said. He pulled a fat manila folder from a middle drawer and found the information. Just in time I remembered to ask him for scrap paper rather than pulling my notebook out, and wrote down the details.

I trotted down the four flights to our floor and entered the flat to find Lesley arguing with Zach. It was one of those low-key arguments where one party hasn't twigged that the other party's mind is completely made up.

"You can't stay here," said Lesley. Then she saw me and cruelly dragged me into it. "Can he, Peter?"

"If it's about all the food, I can totally go shopping," he said.

In the living room Stephen and the rest of the Quiet People were standing around with the embarrassed air of people who were more than ready to move on before the crockery started flying.

"We're running an operation here," said Lesley. "This is work and you're a distraction—sorry."

Zach looked at me for confirmation and I nodded— because you always back your partner up. He sighed and, after a bit of furtive kissing, which I went into the bathroom to avoid, Zach and his cohort of underground denizens left.

"One less set of people to worry about," she said quietly and then, louder, to me, "Are we going to stay here or pack it in?"

"Neither," I said. "I thought we'd go and cause a bit of trouble."

County Gard and its sister companies County Watch, County Finance Management ("You Can Count On Us") and County System Co. were all located in a place off Scrutton Street in Shoreditch. They resided in rented offices in a converted nineteenth-century warehouse with blue plaster rustication around its main gate. It was the sort of place you'd expect to find a software start-up or TV production company that had fallen out of favor— not a full service property management company. Especially one that had a fleet of liveried vehicles. There was definitely no parking around Scrutton Street, as we found when we looked for somewhere to put our brand new wheels—well, not brand new, but at least not a silver Astra. Another Ford Asbo with 2010 plates and a painfully high number on the clock, but obviously loved by someone because it was still sweet to drive. Sadly, it wasn't orange but a rather serviceable dark blue, which at least meant it wouldn't stand out so much on an obbo.

In the end we wedged totally illegally onto the pavement and hoped we wouldn't be there long enough to get a ticket.

We showed our warrant cards at the building reception desk and asked for directions. After one flight of steps and a slight mistake where we went left instead of right, we found ourselves outside a plain gray reinforced metal door with the County Gard logo printed on a piece of A4 paper which was attached to the door with Sellotape. I tried the handle—it was locked. I knocked on the door, we waited, but there was no answer.

I checked my watch. It was three o'clock in the afternoon—no office closes that early. I put my ear to the door and listened.

"There's nobody in there," I said, but even as I said it I heard a hoover starting up. I banged the door hard with the flat of my hand and yelled "Police—open up." I listened again and heard the hoover turn off. It seemed to take a long time for the door to open.

When it did, we found ourselves face to face with the tallest Somali woman I've ever met. Mid thirties, I thought, and a good ten centimeters taller than I was, with a grave calm face and sad brown eyes. She wore a blue polyester cleaner's coat which fit her like a waistcoat and her hijab was of expensive purple silk.

"Yes," she said. "Can I help you?" Her accent was Somali but her English was smooth enough that I figured she'd learnt it as part of an expensive education back in Africa.

I showed my warrant card and explained that we were investigating County Gard.

"That has nothing to do with me," she said. "I'm employed by Fontaine Office Services."

Lesley slipped past us to check the office.

"How long have you been here?" I asked.

"About eleven years," she said. "I have a passport."

"No," I said. "How long have you been in this particular office today?"

"Oh," she brightened. "I just got in."

"Do you know where all the people are?"

"I thought it might be a company holiday."

"Peter," called Lesley urgently. "Come and have a look at this."

It was your standard open-plan office laid out with cubicles for the ants and glass box meeting-rooms for the grasshoppers. It looked like every working office I've ever seen, including the outside inquiry office of a Major Investigation Team—papers, coffee mugs, post-it notes, telephones, lamps, occasional human touches—photographs and the like.

"What am I looking at?" I asked.

"What's missing?" asked Lesley.

Then I saw it. Every cubicle desk had its bog standard flat screen monitor and cheap keyboard, but the main columns were missing. Paperwork was still piled up in in-trays, desk calendars were still pinned to the beige fabric-covered partition walls and one worker seemed to be deliberately trying to create the Olympic symbol using coffee rings, but there wasn't a single operating hard-drive in the office.

I walked back to the cleaning lady and asked whether

she'd been in the day before and whether the office had been staffed.

"Oh yes," she said. "It was very busy yesterday. It was hard to get my work done."

I reassured her a bit, took her name, Awa Shambir, and her details and told her that she might as well move onto her next job since I didn't think this particular office was going to re-open.

"Friend of your mum's?" asked Lesley as we watched the lady neatly stow her cleaning gear and collect her personal things.

"Don't think so," I said. My mum doesn't know every cleaner in London, just the Sierra Leoneans, most of the Nigerians and that Bulgarian contingent she's been working with in King's Cross. "Remind me to run her name when we get a moment."

"If you're suspicious, we should stop her now," said Lesley.

She'd handled her gear like a professional, but I don't know any cleaners who'd go to work in an expensive hijab like she'd been wearing.

"No," I said. "We need to get back to the tower. This is his legitimate front organization. If he's shut it down it means he either doesn't need it any more or after today it might be a security risk."

"Hence all the missing computers," said Lesley.

"Whatever he's planning, I think he's doing it today or tonight."

I felt weirdly panicky all the way back across the river, and through the vile traffic around Elephant and Castle. But I couldn't work out why.

"Somebody tried to kill us a couple of days ago," said Lesley when I mentioned it. "I'm amazed we're not on psychiatric medical leave."

"That which does not kill us," I said, "has to get up extra early in the morning if it wants to get us next time."

Lesley said she was glad to hear it but she was putting more reliance on the fact that we'd been authorized to deploy with tasers in any Falcon operation. She'd picked them up from the Folly on her way back.

Lesley had also called Nightingale, who was still stuck in Essex guarding Varvara Sidorovna, and he said he'd talk to DCI Duffy. Bromley MIT could follow up on the office.

The council work vans were still in the car park when we got back.

"You keep an eye on them while I get the go bag," I said.

"Are you expecting trouble?" asked Lesley.

"Just want to be on the safe side," I said. I wanted my Metvest, if only for the psychological comfort. See, I thought as I waited for the lift, someone tries to kill you and suddenly you're all cautious.

Emma Wall, looking very cheerful for once, stepped out of the lift when the doors opened—she practically jumped when she saw me.

"Hello, Peter," she said. "I'm just going out to the shops. Do you want anything? I can pick you something up. Where's Lesley?"

"Outside," I said.

"Okay," said Emma. "See you." And half ran out of the door, without waiting for a reply to her shopping offer.

Definitely drugs, I thought as I rode up in the lift. That's what brung our fallen princess low—definitely drugs.

Toby started barking as soon as he heard the key in the lock and stayed barking as I suddenly paused before unlocking. Emma's flat had been sealed with one of County Gard's shiny steel doors. Could she have left or been evicted? But she'd said that she was just going out to the shops. And that was fast work for a company whose office was currently empty.

I finished opening the door and ignored Toby as he bounced eagerly around my legs. I grabbed the go bag and took it back out onto the landing where Toby did his best to climb inside. I pulled out my mobile and speed-dialed Lesley.

"Is Emma with you?" I asked.

"No," she said. "She's gone to the shops."

"If you see her, grab her and don't let those vans leave before I get down there."

Lesley said she thought I was becoming unhinged, but she agreed to park the new Asbo across the culvert so they couldn't escape.

Your Metvest comes in two bits, the knife- and bullet-resistant panels and a tough fabric sheath—the vest bit. The plain sheath was for plain clothes, but this time I wanted my multi-pocketed and comforting blue uniform vest with POLICE on the back in fluorescent letters. Once I'd distributed my kit about my person, I walked over to the newly installed County Gard security door and, pausing only to turn my phone off, blew the lock out with a fireball.

Then I had to wait about two minutes for the metal to cool off, which made me wonder whether I could get Varvara Sidorovna to teach me the *formae* for that freeze-ray she kept flinging at me.

Finally I used the end of my baton to prize the door open and, keeping the baton extended and ready, I stepped inside the flat. If she'd really moved out or been evicted then she certainly believed in traveling light. The flat was dirty in the way I remembered from the last time

I lived with a bunch of male coppers, not squalid but un-kempt with dirt accumulating in the corners. My mum wouldn't have tolerated it. In the bedroom, underwear hung halfway out of drawers, the duvet was rumpled and the pillows had fallen on the floor. The living room was nasty with a filled ashtray acting as a centerpiece for a stained coffee table—no obvious signs of paraphernalia, I noticed.

Out in the hallway of the flat Toby sneezed, raising a little cloud of tan-colored dust. I hadn't noticed him follow me in.

Dust covered half the hallway and was concentrated in front of the door of a storage cupboard to the left of the front door. I could see where heavy boots had ground the dust into the imitation wood flooring.

"Many men have passed this way, Toby," I said and remembered Stephen's complaint about the drilling. "Carrying heavy DIY equipment."

Stromberg had designed Skygarden to be supported by nine big pillars that ran up the height of the tower. He'd tried to keep them from intruding into his nice rectilinear flats, but four of the flats on every level ended up with the rounded circumference in what was supposed to be their bathroom. Stromberg's solution was to pretend that he'd always intended the bathrooms to be the size of a telephone box and build a "cupboard space" around the curved side of the pillar.

I think I must have subconsciously known what I was going to find, because I found myself opening the cupboard door very carefully. When I saw what was inside I stopped breathing.

A grid of holes had been drilled into the concrete of the support pillar and then stuffed with a material that looked exactly like gray Plasticine. From their squidgy ends protruded gray cylinders which sprouted wires which were neatly gathered and fed down into a gray container the size and shape of a cashbox that had been securely duct-taped to the pillar.

I wondered what would happen if I just yanked all the detonators out at once. Then I noticed a yellow post-it note that had fallen to the floor below the box. I picked it up and read, *This device has been fitted with counter measures. Please do not tamper, as being blown up often offends.*

19

A Momentary Dismissal of Irrelevancies

IT WAS THE utter brazenness that frightened me. Whoever had planted the explosives hadn't been worried about anyone seeing them. Which meant what? That they assumed nobody would break the County Gard seals? Or, worse, because they'd detonate too soon for anyone to find them?

I couldn't remember a single step of any procedure relating to the discovery of a bomb, but I was pretty certain that step one wasn't hyperventilating.

No, step one was to scream for help, but in a measured and sensible fashion. And don't use your mobile or airwave, in case the RF set off the detonator. Since Emma had walked out of her flat with just the clothes she was wearing, the first thing I did was check her landline—not a wireless handset thank god—and found it had a dialing tone. I punched 999 and identified myself to CCC who asked me to confirm where I was exactly and that a bomb was on the premises.

I remembered Stephen complaining about the noise of the drilling, but he'd said that it was downstairs from the flat and I didn't doubt his hearing—not when it came to rock and concrete. If there was more than one drill site, then the chances were that more bombs had been drilled into the support pillars. My friendly neighborhood Faceless Man was going to pancake the building in a controlled explosion.

"Not just one bomb, they've drilled into the primary supporting structure," I said. "I have reason to believe that they plan to bring down the whole building, for which they would need multiple IEDs at multiple locations. They also left a note saying that the IED was booby trapped."

The Met has a tin ear for operational mnemonics, and the one for being the first officer on the scene at a major incident is SADCHALETS. *Survey;* oh god there's a bomb. *Assess;* oh god there's more than one bomb and everyone in the tower will die. *Disseminate;* oh god there's a bomb, we're going to die, send help. For the life of me I couldn't remember the CHALETS bit—*Casualties, Hazards,* something, something and I remembered that the last S stood for *Start a Log* because it was such an obvious cheat.

The operator asked me whether the device was Falcon.

I told her that this was a Falcon-involved operation, but that the device appeared to be ordinary. There was another couple of seconds while this was digested. They told me to leave the vicinity of the device right away, but before I hung up I told them that Lesley was downstairs and gave them her mobile number.

Then I hung up.

I crept back into the corridor and looked at the bomb. It really did look like Plasticine and there was a screaming bit of my brain that was persistently trying to convince the rest that that's all it was.

The Major Incident Procedure Manual has a long list of things the first officer on the scene is supposed to do and at the end, with its own section number, are the words,

The first officer on scene must not get personally involved in rescue work in order to fulfill the functions listed above.

The first response vehicle would be less than two minutes away, the London Fire Brigade no more than five. The first priority would be to evacuate, and they'd start at the bottom and work their way up. I was already on the twenty-first floor — there were five balcony floors between me and the roof, each consisting of two-story flats. If I worked my way from where I was, then I might get them clear before the building went.

And this is where the Job kills you, because there was no way I could run downstairs and leave them to their fate. No matter what the Major Incident Procedural Manual says.

How long, how long? I checked my watch and glared at the bomb.

"If this was a film you'd have a countdown on the front," I said. "In large glow-in-the-dark LEDs."

Then at least I'd know how long I had.

I walked briskly, there was no point in running I had to pace myself, back out onto the walkway. With Emma gone there were only two occupied flats on the twenty-first floor. I headed for the first with Toby yapping at my heels. Either he'd picked up on my panic or he still thought it was time for walkies.

I rang the doorbell.

You don't bang on the door and shout police first time, especially not in a place like Skygarden. It's hard to believe, but in some sections of society the police are not looked upon as the dependable guardians of law and order. Yelling police loudly can often cause residents to pause before answering the door, some because they've had bad experiences either here or abroad, some because they don't want to get involved, and some because they need to flush whatever it is they need to flush down the toilet before they let you in.

A small brown boy opened the door and looked up at me with wide-eyed surprise. I asked if his parents were at home and he fetched his father to whom I showed my warrant card.

"I'm sorry, sir," I told him before he could speak. "I need you and your family to leave your flat immediately and make your way downstairs."

"What have we done?" asked the father.

"Nothing, sir," I said. "We're evacuating the whole building. Please, sir, you have to leave immediately."

He nodded and walked back into the flat talking quickly in what I thought was probably Tamil. Raised female voice—the mother? She wasn't buying.

Come on, come on.

I strode into the hallway and did my best to loom authoritatively in the kitchen doorway. The woman jumped when she saw me and shut up. I gave her a polite but firm nod.

"Ma'am, you have to leave the building now," I said. "Your lives are at risk."

She turned to her husband and barked orders. I retreated back the way I'd come as the young boy and what I took to be his two sisters were shoed, jacketed and ushered out the front door in less than a minute. I guided them to the emergency stairs and as the father went past me I scooped up Toby and thrust him into the startled man's arms.

At the next flat along there was no response to the ring, the loud knock and the shouting. I looked through the letter box and it seemed empty.

Time was passing.

How long, how long had I got?

I left what I hoped was the empty flat and jogged up two flights of stairs to the twenty-third floor. They say that in this situation the vital thing is that you have to avoid panic, which is why you don't shout, "There's a fucking great bomb, run now or die." But avoiding panic isn't easy when the mental state you are aiming for is the sense of fear and urgency that lies just below full blown panic.

Three occupied flats on this floor, two seemed empty and the third was inhabited by a Polish couple who, gratifyingly, were out of their flat practically before I'd finished my first sentence.

How long?

By my watch I'd called it in ten minutes earlier. The LFB would be handling the inner cordon, the arriving police would be pushing back the outer cordon.

How long is a piece of string?

Another two flights of stairs to the twenty-fifth floor, where not one flat had a County Gard steel door, so I went straight to Betsy's flat. By this time the palm and side of my right hand were bruised from banging on doors, so I used the handle of my baton to knock.

I heard Betsy yelling, "Hold your horses I'm coming."

She was genuinely shocked when she saw me.

"Peter," she said reproachfully. "You're the filth."

"Betsy, listen to me," I said quietly. "Someone has planted bombs all over the tower. You, Sasha and Kevin have to get out right now."

Betsy's mouth opened, then shut. "On your mother's life," she said.

"On my mother's life," I said. "You have to get out now."

She looked over my shoulder and then back at me.

"Are you the only cop on the spot?" she asked.

"Lesley's downstairs," I said. "I'm the only one this far up. More on their way."

"You done this floor yet?"

"No, I came here first," I said.

"Good boy," said Betsy. "Tell you what, me and Kevin will clear this floor for you."

"All right," I said. "But don't hang about, and don't use the lift."

"After," she said, "you and I are going to have a little chat about lying to your neighbors."

"Sounds good to me," I said.

"Well, get on with it then," she said.

God bless busybody community matriarchs, and all that sail in them.

I found myself at the top of the next two flights without any clear memory of having run up them. Four occupied flats on this floor, one of which was Jake Phillips'. I left him to last—I reckoned he was going to be trouble.

I rang the first doorbell and the next door neighbor, a white man in his mid-forties emerged.

"Are we evacuating?" he asked. "Only it's on the news."

"Yes sir," I said. "If you'd like to make your way down the stairs as quickly as possible." Or you could go back inside your flat and watch yourself explode on TV.

The next door in front of me opened to reveal a ridiculously good-looking West Indian woman in her early thirties who gave me such an open and friendly smile that I was temporarily taken aback.

"Can I help you, Officer?"

"We're being evacuated," said her neighbor.

"Are we?" she asked, and I explained quickly that for their convenience and continued existence they might want to think about leaving the tower just about as fast as their legs could carry them. If it was not too much trouble.

"What about my boys?" she asked.

"Are they in the flat with you?" I asked.

"No they're at school," she said.

"So are mine," said her neighbor. "They go to the same school."

"Would you like to see them again?" I asked. "Then please make your way downstairs as fast as possible."

It still took me another two minutes to get the pair of them to the emergency stairs.

How long?

More than twenty minutes. The LFB would be in the tower, clearing it floor by floor. Everybody Walworth Road nick had handy would be securing an outer cordon and setting up the Scene Access Control. And tucked away in a non-obvious place, to avoid secondary devices, would be the Rendezvous Point with one of the specialist control vehicles with a CCTV camera on a pole. It would be filling up with mid-ranking officers who were nervously contemplating the fact that for the time being the buck was stopping with them.

Third flat, no response and when I looked through the letter box I found it was fitted with a protective box on the inside that blocked the view. I couldn't tell if there was someone in the flat, so I blew the lock out and barged my way inside. My sleep's troubled enough without them pulling a body out of the rubble and comforting me with the words "Well, you weren't to know."

There was nobody in the flat, but at least now I knew.

They also had a couple of a cans of Coke in the fridge, one of which I nicked.

"Go away," shouted Jake as soon as I rang the doorbell. It sounded like he was in the hallway, and I think he'd been waiting there just so he could tell me to go away.

"Jake," I said. "The building's going to blow up."

He opened his door with the chain on and glared at me through the gap.

"I might have guessed," he spat. "Blogtavist—hah. What are you, Special Branch?"

"I'm with the Serious Fraud Office," I said because *I'm with the small department that deals with magic* often raises more questions than I had time to answer. "We've been investigating the developers."

"Are they the ones behind this bomb scare?"

"It's not a bomb scare," I said. "I've seen the bombs and they're real and unless you leave now there's a good chance you will die."

"I can't leave my garden," he said slowly.

"Jake," I said, "we need you . . . as a witness against County Gard, among others, and if you die then they're going to win. And then what the fuck was all your work for?"

How long?

Twenty seconds to make up his mind, thirty seconds to unchain his door and emerge onto the walkway. Another sixty to get him to the emergency stairs.

How long?

Last two flights of stairs to the twenty-ninth where I found that every single flat had a County Gard seal on it—there was no one up there to evacuate. I was just turning to start a dignified but hopefully swift descent, when I noticed that the security doors that blocked the stairs up to the roof were hanging open.

How long?

Long enough for there now to be the whole glorious multihued panoply of a Major Incident response down below. With Gold and Silver commanders and Bronze commanders spawning like frogs in concentric circles around Skygarden.

I went up the last flights of steps, because I had to be sure.

The Faceless Man was waiting for me up there—the bastard.

Another good suit in navy blue, matching scarlet cravat and pocket handkerchief. I don't think he even bothered with the concealment glamour and his tan featureless mask reminded me disturbingly of Lesley's.

He was standing leaning against the railings with the same studied nonchalance he'd shown the last time I'd met him. Good, I thought. He's not going to blow up the building with him on top of it.

Hopefully.

I sauntered toward him, but veered slightly to the left so that I drew closer to the concrete cylinder that hid the *Stadtkrone*. I thought it might serve as useful cover in an emergency.

I was within six meters when he languidly held up his hand to indicate I should stop—I took a couple of extra steps just on the general principle of the thing. Plus it put me closer to the cylinder.

"I've got to ask," I said. "What's with the mask—who were you expecting to meet up here?"

"Your master," said the Faceless Man. "Or do you call him your guv-nor?"

"Fair enough," I said sauntering a couple of steps closer to the cover. "Have you considered a cape? You'd look good in a cape. You could throw in an opera hat."

"Very funny," he said. "But I'm not the walking anachronism around here."

"He'll be here soon," I said. "You know he took out your Russian witch?"

"I heard," he said. "Very impressive."

"She was all like, 'Oh no you don't' and he was like — splat! And that's all she wrote."

"Do you have a radio?"

"What?"

"A radio," said the Faceless Man. "A means to contact your superiors."

I showed him my airwave.

"Are you planning to surrender?" I asked.

"Hardly," he said. "I want to know if the building has been evacuated." He patted his jacket pocket. "Before I set off the fireworks."

I keyed the airwave and asked for MS 1, the Walworth duty Inspector.

There was a couple of seconds' silence and then a response; "MS 1 receiving." Then another voice; "Go ahead." An older woman with an old-fashioned estuary accent and lots of attitude — I bloody loved the sound of that voice.

"I'm on the roof facing and talking to an unidentified Falcon-capable suspect who claims to have a detonator for multiple IEDs in the building. He wants to know if the building has been evacuated."

"The building has been investigated, EOD is with the device on the twenty-first floor."

Meaning, yes of course the bloody building's been evacuated and can you please get more information for the bomb squad.

I told the Faceless Man that the building was cleared except for the disposal team.

"Tell them that I will detonate the device in five minutes, so they'd better pull everyone out now. If I so much as hear a helicopter in the distance I'll detonate there and then," he said. "Make sure they understand I'm serious."

"He says you have five minutes to evacuate any personnel before he detonates the IEDs; if he sees or hears India 99 or a helicopter he will detonate immediately."

"Are you free to speak?" asked MS 1.

I said no.

"Is there anything you can do?" she asked.

"No," I said. "I'm totally buggered."

"Understood," she said and then my airwave went dead. They'd cut me off and from that moment on I was a hostage not an asset.

Five minutes.

The Strata building overlooked Skygarden and might be close enough for a sniper, but I rather suspected the Faceless Man had positioned himself carefully so that the central cylinder blocked the line of sight.

"What's all this in aid of, anyway?" I asked.

"Can't you guess?"

"I know that Stromberg built this tower in order to harvest magic, but I don't know why," I said. "I know you're planning to steal it, but I don't know how."

"Peter," said the Faceless Man, "you're an exceptionally bright boy and I know you've been to the farm, so why don't you stop pretending and tell me what you really know."

"I know that you used demon trap tech to engineer a sort of dog battery for storing magic. And I know you've got them connected to the plastic core that runs down the center of the tower," I said. "What I don't know is why. Since you're obviously plugged in, why haven't you siphoned off the power already?"

"Dog batteries," said the Faceless Man. "Good one. Although they act much more like capacitors than batteries."

"Canine capacitors, then?"

"Oh very sharp, yes, canine capacitors," he said. "Magic is not like electricity, it's slippery stuff and much harder to manipulate. This tower is much like a cafetière, one of those coffee plunger things, the coffee grounds are held in suspension within the hot water and, in order to concentrate them, one must use the plunger."

"Have you actually ever made coffee using a cafetière?" I asked.

"I admit that I should have spent a bit more time on that simile, but you get the basic idea," he said.

"You're going to collapse the building, and that should drive the magic into the dog batteries," I said. "Then I presume you have a company that specializes in clearing demolition sites all set up and waiting to swoop in with a low bid—then they just load up the dog batteries and off you go."

He has no idea about the *Stadtkrone*, I suddenly realized, that's why he had to blow up the building. But how can he not know?

"What do you want all that magic for?" I asked.

"Oh, I have done some extraordinary things with just the power of my body," he said. "Imagine what I might do with the forty years' accumulated potential here." He looked at his watch. "I think they've had enough time to evacuate, don't you?"

"What about me?" I asked.

"I'm afraid you've got to stay here," he said. "I may wish to avoid mass murder, but let's be honest . . . I'd be extremely stupid to let you live."

"Why not just kill me now?"

Well done, Peter, I thought, let's put that idea into his head.

"Why should I?" he asked. "Besides—"

I caught him mid-sentence. It was a beauty, *impello* with no modification, just the biggest impact I knew how to do focused down to a single point. He still managed to a get a shield up before I could strike. There was a crack like concrete breaking and he flinched—which made me feel better.

He straightened and made a show of dusting himself down.

"Really, Peter," he said. "I thought you'd progressed a bit further than that."

I let him think that I'd missed but before I could say something witty in reply, he drew out a wireless detonator and blew up the building.

I heard the charges go off below me, weirdly distant like something in a nightmare. I felt them as a thudding sensation through the soles of my shoes. I staggered toward the Faceless Man, expecting any moment for the roof to literally drop out from beneath my feet.

I felt it then, a great solidity, like the wave of power I'd felt come off the Thames at the Spring Court. Or the air that had so nearly floated me aloft when I was dancing with Sky. The building was holding itself up, trying to retain its shape.

I took the opportunity to close the range to the Faceless Man, until I'd got within three meters of him. But he didn't seem afraid.

"I wouldn't get your hopes up," he shouted. "It's not going to stay standing long."

I heard people screaming far away and hoped that it was startled onlookers on the ground.

The trembling had become shaking—the wavelength of the oscillations lengthening. Once they reached a certain length, the tower would pull itself apart.

Come on, Erik, I thought, if you'd wanted it to be a piston, why would you have put the bloody glass pimple at the top?

Then I heard a crack from behind me as, finally, the *Stadtkrone* exerted enough pressure to open the fissure I'd smashed in the top of the cylinder.

"Surprise," I shouted, and the blast knocked me off my feet.

And the *Stadtkrone* fell open in segments exactly like a practitioner opening his hand. Or more like a chocolate orange because, like every chocolate orange I'd ever opened, some of the bits stuck together.

I don't know what Stromberg had been expecting to see from his roof garden in Highgate. Something *Lord of the Rings*, I expect—streamers of light pouring upward into a rapidly opening circle of clouds. Instead it was a barely visible shimmer, like a column of heat haze. But I felt it. A wave of cooking smells and tastes, grease and peppers, green curry and macaroni cheese, spirit gum, the feel of wet papier-mâché and children crying. People ironing, shaving, singing, dancing, grunting and fucking.

"Here's Bruno!" I shouted. But the Faceless Man wasn't listening to me. He was staring at the *Stadtkrone* and, even with his mask on, surprise and anger were written along the length of his body. The roof lurched underfoot, dropped a centimeter, stopped, dropped again—Skygarden was not about to defy gravity for much longer.

The Faceless Man turned, took three steps and threw himself over the railing.

I ran after him and followed him over.

What else could I do—it's not like I could stay on the roof, was it?

Besides, the Faceless Man didn't strike me as the suicidal type. And if he had some plan to survive the fall, then I didn't think he should be allowed to keep it to himself.

Otherwise, I was going to have to think of something on the way down.

I didn't fall far before landing on his back. Then I threw my arms around his neck and hung on. He was definitely doing some sort of magic, a spell involving *aer* I thought, that caught hold of the air like a parachute. Or more like a para-wing, because we were gliding rather than falling.

"You just keeping going, my son," I whispered in his ear. "Because I've got nothing to lose."

He must have carefully calculated it against his own weight, but with mine added he fell dangerously fast. I made sure that I was the one riding him down—thinking heavy thoughts. We must have been falling at the same speed as the tower, because I could hear rending and crashing of concrete behind us and see billowing, dense gray and brown clouds reaching out around us.

We were roughly heading for the gap in the blocks where Heygate Street met Rodney Place. There, I presumed, he'd have a getaway vehicle standing by. But he wasn't going to make it with yours truly on his back. And he couldn't even squirm without breaking his concentration.

Serves you right for being an arrogant dickhead—if it had been me, I'd have tripped the explosive from the viewing gallery in the Shard.

I looked down and saw the big wide world rushing up to meet me fast. I really hoped it was going to be friendly.

We came down in the garden just short of the far edge. He hit first and tried to roll, but I made a point of breaking his center of gravity so that he went down hard. Unfortunately, so did I. Then the dust cloud rolled over us and we were fighting blind, only he was in a suit and I was wearing Doctor Martens. Before he could get up I got one good kick to his head, and down he went. I put him face down, and got hands behind his back in the approved fashion and cuffed him.

"You're nicked, you bastard," I said.

I heard Lesley calling my name.

"I'm over here," I shouted, but you couldn't see more than half a meter because of the thick, rolling clouds of dust.

I choked on it, so did he. I hauled him up until he was sitting upright. I didn't want to risk positional asphyxiation.

Lesley called again and I shouted back—the dust seemed to be settling.

"I am genuinely impressed," he said.

"I'm so pleased," I said.

"I believe this is the moment of decision," said the Faceless Man.

"I already made up my mind," I said and reached for his mask.

"Sorry," said the Faceless Man. "But I wasn't talking to you."

Lesley tasered me in the back of my neck.

I know it was her, because she dropped the taser half a meter from where I was lying. It matched the serial number of the one she'd been issued. However, she didn't drop it before tasering me again when I tried to get up.

It's painful and it's humiliating, because your body just locks up and there's nothing you can do.

The Faceless Man's shoes appeared in front of my face. I noticed they'd got quite badly scuffed during the fall.

"No," said a muffled voice that I later decided had been Lesley's. "That wasn't part of the deal."

And then they walked away and left me.

20

Working For A Stranger London

SOMETIMES, WHEN YOU turn up on their doorstep, people are already expecting bad news. Parents of missing kids, partners that have heard about the air crash on the news—you can see it in their faces—they've braced themselves. And there's a strange kind of relief, too. The waiting is over, the worst has happened and they know that they will ride it out. Some don't, of course. Some go mad or fall into depression or just fall apart. But most soldier through.

But sometimes they haven't got a clue and you arrive on their doorstep like god's own sledgehammer and smash their life to pieces. You try not to think about it, but you can't help wondering what it must be like.

Now I knew.

I got up off the ground and went after them. Because otherwise what good am I?

I was covered in dust and I must have looked pissed off, because random strangers would rush forward with offers of help only to back off quickly when they got close enough to see my face. I grabbed one that had foolishly got within arm's reach.

"Did you see a woman in a mask," I shouted. "She had a man with her—did you see where they went?"

"I haven't seen anyone, mate," he said and broke away to leg it.

I reached the outer cordon where a uniformed skipper took one look at me and ordered me to the ambulance assembly point. He sent a probationary constable to guide me and, although she looked about twelve years old, she already had the command voice down pat.

I should have told them who I was, not least because all the gold, silver and bronze commanders thought I'd been on the roof when it came down. But certain things have to be kept in the family.

There were at least a dozen ambulances in the casualty marshalling area on Elephant Road, but even as I was being bundled into the back of one I saw a couple peel off and head back into general circulation. The London Ambulance Service is one of the largest and busiest in the world, and can't afford to hang about waiting for people to get injured. Not even at a major incident.

A paramedic checked me over and I asked him if there were any casualties.

"There were two people on the roof when it went down," said the paramedic. "But they haven't been found yet."

And that's when I should have told them I wasn't dead. But as I explained to the subsequent investigation by the Department of Professional Standards, I'd just survived having a tower block collapse on me so they should cut me some slack. The real reason was that they would have asked too many questions that I couldn't answer until I'd talked to Nightingale.

I told the paramedic I wanted to call my dad and could he lend me his mobile. He handed it over but only after assurances that my dad wasn't living in Rio or Somalia or somewhere exorbitant like that. I called Nightingale and I could tell he'd been worried by the tone of his voice.

"What the hell happened?"

"I had him sir, I had the Faceless Man. Had him bang to rights and Lesley tasered me."

There was a shocked pause.

"Lesley tasered you?"

"Yes, sir."

"To facilitate the suspect's escape?"

I believe this is the moment of decision.

"Yes, sir."

"Are you in any doubt about Lesley's participation?"

That wasn't part of the deal.

"No, sir."

"Peter," said Nightingale, "as your first priority you must secure the Folly and inform Molly that Lesley is off the guest list. You must do this *now* regardless of instructions from any other senior officer. Once you are there contact me again — was that clear?"

"Yes, sir."

"Good lad," he said. "Get a move on."

I can have trouble getting taxis as the best of times, but nobody was going to stop for me when I was white with dust. To avoid disappointment I merely stepped in front of the first black cab I saw and used the combination of my warrant card, a twenty-pound note and hints that I was part of a vital anti-terrorist operation to get my ride. He got me back fast enough — he was in such a hurry to get rid of me he didn't wait for a tip.

I went in through the double doors at the front on the basis that I almost never used them and if somebody, if Lesley, was laying an ambush she'd do it at the back door. I paused at the guard booth in the lobby to listen and, hearing nothing, I slipped past the statue of Isaac Newton and into the atrium.

Molly was waiting for me. She took the instructions from Nightingale with the same grave expression with which she accepted menu requests. Then she went silently gliding up the stairs—hopefully to check that the upper floors were clear.

The telephone in the Folly atrium has its own desk complete with blotting pad, notepaper and bendy lamp. I picked up the Bakelite handset and dialed, literally dialed, Nightingale's mobile. He answered almost immediately.

He gave me a series of instructions and told me to call him back once I'd followed them.

I went down the back stairs, turned left, went past the door to the firing range and paused in front of the armory. Inside, we had some 9mm Browning Hi-Power automatic pistols that Nightingale had planned to teach us to shoot with. I was tempted to fetch one, but Frank Caffrey had once told me that you should never carry a weapon you don't know how to use. Besides, I wasn't even sure if push came to shove I could shoot Lesley. And that was Caffrey's other maxim—don't point a gun at someone unless you're prepared to shoot them with it. I checked to see that the door was still firmly locked and moved on. Then right down a rectangular, brick-lined corridor that, being unlit and damp smelling, I'd never bothered to walk down. And, judging by the dust and cobwebs, neither had Molly or anyone else in the last couple of decades. At the far end was a crude wooden door, the sort you might find on a garden shed. I opened it to reveal another short corridor and a much more formidable gray door of what, I learned later, was face-hardened battleship steel. There were no handles or visible locks, instead a series of overlapping circles were incised into the metal. They looked disturbingly like the payload zones of a demon trap and even more disturbingly like modern Gallifreyan.

None of the circles appeared damaged or disturbed in any way and I for one had no intention of touching them.

I went back up to the atrium and called Nightingale.

"Thank god," he said. "That was my worst fear."

"You never told us about that door," I said.

"And that has proved to be a wise precaution, has it not?" said Nightingale.

I knew better than to ask what was behind it over the telephone, but the question definitely went to the top of my to-do list.

It took eight hours for Nightingale to arrive back at the Folly. As Lesley's senior officer and line manager it was down to him to meet with the Department of Professional Standards. Because he didn't dare leave Varvara Sidorovna unsupervised, she had to be towed around behind him like an unwanted younger sister. While he was spending quality time with the DPS at their offices in the Empress State Building in Brompton, I was stuck guarding the Folly. Not that I had to do that alone, because Frank Caffrey turned up with a number of his mates, all mature but suspiciously fit men with short haircuts and camera cases full of things that weren't actually cameras.

Nine hours after the Skygarden tower collapsed, Toby turned up at the back door, barked to get Molly's attention and then settled into his basket with a sigh and a couple of sausages. He must have walked home from Elephant and Castle on his own. A distance of about four kilometers, I pointed out, less than an hour's walk but who knows? Maybe he stopped off to take in a show at the Lyceum. I'd have berated him a bit more, but Molly shooed me out of the kitchen.

Nightingale arrived back at the Folly at three in the morning, looking as rumpled and as pissed off as I've ever seen him. He still had Varvara Sidorovna in tow and informed Molly that she would be our "guest" until further notice. I could hear the quotes around the word "guest" and so could Molly, who took up watching the woman from the shadows as a sort of hobby.

"What is she?" Varvara Sidorovna asked me one day when Molly was safely out of earshot.

"You don't want to know," I told her.

Nobody was happy with us that month except maybe Sussex Police because at least Operation Sallic showed a result when Robert Weil finally pleaded guilty. He claimed to have attacked and killed a complete stranger, shot her in the face and buried her in the woods all on the same night. The fact that Sussex MCT couldn't find the shotgun, hadn't identified the body and plainly just didn't believe the motive for one moment was irrelevant. They had a confession and enough supporting forensic evidence to take to court, so up the steps Robert Weil did go.

Operation Tinker, Bromley MIT's investigation into Patrick Mulkern's horrible human kebab impression, essentially stalled on all fronts. Sky remained an unidentified adult female found dead in suspicious circumstances, but since there were no signs of violence and Dr. Walid could find no discernible cause of death that was probably going to end up as death by misadventure. All they had to show for a homicide investigation was a criminal damage case against Max and Barry.

No doubt both cases would have garnered more interest in the media had not a tower block been blown up right on top of them. That case went straight to Counter Terrorism Command and became Operation Wentworth before mutating into a joint case with the Serious Fraud

Office when the apparent motive was revealed to be removing Skygarden Tower, a Grade II listed building, as a barrier to the massively lucrative redevelopment of Elephant and Castle. It's a case that could take years to come to court and I expected the Faceless Man had a couple of expendable colleagues to throw, as Varvara Sidorovna put it, out of the troika to keep the wolves busy.

I went to see Mr. Nolfi, our impromptu children's entertainer, now released from hospital, at his home in Wimbledon. I took Abigail along, to teach her how to interview a witness without getting bored and fidgeting.

"Good Lord," he said. "Is it bring your daughter to work day?"

"My cousin," I explained.

"I'm doing a project for school," said Abigail.

"How enterprising," said Mr. Nolfi.

We asked him if he'd managed to replicate his magic trick since he'd been released home and he conjured a werelight right in front of us.

"Beautiful, isn't it?" he asked, despite my horrified expression. "I tried doing them for weeks after I got out and then just two weeks ago it was like somebody had turned on the electricity."

"You mustn't tell anyone about this," I said.

"Why ever not?

That was a good question.

"Because it's like the magicians' circle," said Abigail. "A magician must never reveal his secrets."

Mr. Nolfi nodded sagely. "Mum's the word eh?" he said.

"Believe it," said Abigail.

I found Zach behind a bar in a pub situated ten meters below Oxford Street and accessible only via a Crossrail service tunnel. It had a vaulted ceiling and walls that were covered in something that looked like faded wood paneling until you ran your finger across it. The clientele were all men and dressed universally in moleskin trousers, leather waistcoats and high visibility jackets. They sat around the tables, hunched over their beers, heads almost touching and talking in whispers. A Zodiac jukebox stood by the bar and played Dire Straits very, very quietly.

I leaned over the bar and whispered, "You've been avoiding me."

"Do you blame me?" asked Zach.

"Did you know?"

"Did I know what?"

I held up my hand to stop him.

"No," he whispered.

We drank in silence for a bit.

"Have you talked to Beverley?" he asked.

"Why do you ask?"

"Because she came here to talk to me about you," he whispered.

"Why?"

He shrugged. "I don't know. Suddenly everyone seems to think I'm the Peter Grant expert."

"Really? Who else?"

"Your boss, for one," whispered Zach. "Then Lady Ty snuck up on me while I wasn't looking and nearly scared me to death. And Oberon wanted to know on behalf of Effra who probably was asking on behalf of Beverley."

"How's Nicky?"

"Not a happy camper, but she's young and immortal," he whispered. "She'll get over it eventually."

With a worryingly creaky mechanical sound the jukebox flipped records and started playing *Sultans of Swing*.

"Why Dire Straits?"

Zach waved his hand at his whispering clientele.

"They're working their way through the last hundred years of popular culture. It was the early 70s last month."

"But Dire Straits?"

"They were getting a little bit too fond of Marc Bolan," he whispered. "I did consider introducing them to the lo-fi percussion and funky R&B goodness that was the Washington Go Go sound, but in the end I reckoned that might be just a bit too much for their tiny little minds to cope with."

"You could try Public Enemy," I whispered.

"I hear you're living with the Night Witch," whispered Zach. "What's that like?"

"Creepy in a sort of charming Bond villain way," I whispered. "We're all very polite and careful around each other. We're getting rid of her soon." Nightingale was forging a bracelet that he planned to seal around her wrist using his magic metal-fusing powers so she couldn't get it off without more magic or some serious bolt cutters. To prevent the former it was fitted with the guts of an electronic tag that reported her location every sixty seconds—if Varvara Sidorovna used magic it would blow the chip and sound the alarm.

"Nightingale's told her that if he has to track her down again he'll deport her back to Russia," I whispered.

"Won't they just give her a medal?" asked Zach. "Heroine of the Great Patriotic War and all that." He caught me staring at him. "I did a history GCSE you know. I liked the Russians—I could relate."

"Shoot her or recruit her," I whispered. "The point is she becomes their problem not ours."

The jukebox flipped to *Who Wants To Live Forever* by Queen.

"You're kidding me?" I said too loudly and got glared at.

"We have karaoke nights," whispered Zach. "This is the favourite followed by *I Want To Break Free*."

I finished my pint and made to leave.

"Have you considered the idea," asked Zach, "that Lesley might be doing this as a way of worming her way into the Faceless Man's organization—under cover double agent style of thing?" He trailed off.

"He's promised her her face back," I said.

"You can't know that," hissed Zach.

No, but I knew that Dr. Walid had found chimeric cells on a woman who'd had her face erased by a shotgun blast. Covering evidence of experiments by the Faceless Man aimed at restoring Lesley's face. A bait he must have reckoned she couldn't resist—how could anyone? He'd probably planned to keep her in the Folly and get her to spy on us. Nightingale had said that the Faceless Man wasn't Moriarty, but from my perspective he was doing a really good impression of the man.

"That's the only motive that makes sense," I hissed back.

"It might be both," whispered Zach. "You've got to at least consider that possibility."

I shook my head.

"If she gets in touch with you, will you let me know?" I asked.

"What do you think?"

I thought that there was not a chance in hell he would.

"Fair enough," I said and went home.

Architectural and Historical Notes

As far as I know there was never an expatriate German architect named Erik Stromberg and none of the buildings I have attributed to him actually exist. The infamous Skygarden Estate has been placed at the location of the equally infamous but undeniably real Heygate Estate near Elephant and Castle and his modernist shrine to dysfunctional functionalism sandwiched into a non-existent gap between two real buildings in Highgate. Bruno Taut was real as were his ideas about *Stadtkrone* (city crowns). Taut is also famous for actually using colors other than white, brown and beige in his designs and for the Glass Pavilion at the Cologne Deutscher Werkbund Exhibition. If you want to know where the inspiration for the Gherkin came from, look no further.

I have described Varvara Sidorovna as *Nochnye Koldunyi* (Ночные Колдуньи) to differentiate her from the heroic women of the 588th Night Bomber Regiment (later the 46th 'Taman' Guards Night Bomber Aviation Regiment) who, flying planes made of canvas and string, so terrified the Germans that they named them *Nachthexen* (Nightwitches), or in Russian, Ночные ведьмы.

Acknowledgments

I'd like to thank John Tygier RIBA, Mike Butcher of the RSPCA and Bob Hunter and Stephen Dutton of the MPS for all their help and putting up with some very stupid questions. My mates Mandy and Christine Blum for frequent German, Chris Kendall and Cynthia Camp for remedial Latin and Elena for emergency Russian. Andrew Cartmel provided big help with spooling an' grammar an' stuff! As always all mistakes are mine, mine I tell you—you can't have them . . .